CONSEQUENCES

by

Lurma Swinney, PhD

A Story of Friendship

Consequences

A novel published by SD Publishing House

ISBN 978-0-9674091-0-8

For permission please contact SD Publishing House Post Office Box 7676 Florence, SC 29502 U.S.A.

www.sdpublishinghouse.com

Printed in U.S.A.

Cover Designed by Jay Swinney

To the memory of my beloved Sister, Linda Swinney-Pigatt, who was my first audience.

Acknowledgements:

I would like to thank God for making this all possible for me. I want to thank my sister, Audrey Davis, who always support me in all my endeavors; my friend, Felix Alexander, who is always there to lend me a helping hand; my friend, Mallory Kershaw, who has always been like a brother to my sisters and me; my aunt, Brenda Robinson, who took me in her home when I was in a strange city; my uncle, Haywood McCall, who always make me laugh; my uncle, Claywood McCall, who helps my family in its business; my Godchildren, Quadrick McDonald, Travis Canty, and Jihad Burns, who brought special love into my heart; and a very special thanks to my son, Jay, who was always patient while I worked. I love you all.

Part One

February

Chapter 1

The luxurious hotel suite was illuminated by the flaming, multicolored, brick fireplace. The plush, thick, navy-blue carpet emphasized the modern living room area with the blue, soft, leather sofa and matching love seat. In the middle of this breathtaking, dimly lit scene, she stared blankly at her blood-soaked hands, as she released a blood-dripping knife to the blood-stained carpet, where a crumpled body lay bathing in its own blood. "Oh, my God!" the beautiful, bronze, biracial lady breathed out of trembling lips, as she covered her mouth in a deep trance, while her beautiful, long, black hair glimmered by the light from the flaming fireplace. Suddenly an outside noise sobered her to realization, and she noticed her bloodstained hands for the first time. She rushed to the telephone and grabbed up the receiver. She dialed a few numbers, then froze abruptly, and slammed the receiver back in its cradle. Acting quickly, she pulled a Jennifer Roper scarf from around her neck, wiped the telephone clean, then her hands. Her trembling, sweaty handpicked the knife up slowly and wiped it clean also, and then she dropped the knife in her Lori Fenzo purse. Her nerves wouldn't allow her the luxury of thinking. She grabbed the knife from her purse and started for the fireplace, but she heard another noise from outside again and dropped the knife in her purse once more. However, she did manage to throw the scarf into the open flames. She took a deep breath then rushed to the closet. She took out a Jennifer Roper hat and placed it on her head. She buttoned on an Eliza DuHaire trench coat then took one final glance around the room before exiting it quickly. After she had gone, a man in a dark blue suit entered the room, where the bloody figure lay crumpled on the floor, from another room in the same suite with a very expensive camera hanging from around his neck.

****

The woman walked down the decorated halls of the hotel to the glass elevators. She stepped inside and sighed deeply. She looked down at her trembling hands then stuffed them into her pockets. When the elevator stopped, she walked out briskly, in the bright, midday sunshine and handed the valet her ticket. As she stood waiting for her car, an image of the bloody body falling to the floor, flashed before her eyes, and she jumped with fright. She closed her beautiful emerald eyes momentarily, to calm her nerves. A tan Mercedes Benz pulled up. The valet exited it, and she handed him a twenty-dollar bill, jumped in, and drove away so quickly she didn't even hear his excited, "Thank-you."

****

The tan Mercedes glided in the parking lot of a tall medical building. The estranged woman parked and ran into the building through a back door. She walked into an office, and a very flashy, big hair, need-a-tan blonde looked up from behind her computer, flashed all thirty-twos and said, "Hi, Cecily."

"Hi, Cindy. I'm sorry I'm late. I know you've been catching it!" the lady replied rushing into another office labeled, DR. CECILY WADE, PEDIATRIC SURGEON. She hung up her coat and hat then proceeded to wash her face and hands when the door opened, causing her to jump.

"Cecily," a fiftyish, chocolate tanned lady, in a nurse's uniform, spoke. "Is everything all right?"

Drying her face and hands the beautiful doctor murmured, "Everything's fine. Why?"

Looking at her watch, the nurse answered, "Because you're never *this* late getting back from lunch." She noticed the trembling doctor pulling on her white smock. "What's wrong, Cecily?"

"I'm fine, Ruth!" insisted the doctor securing her long, black, wavy hair up in a ponytail. "Let's get started. I know it's backed up." Cecily forced a smile then pushed the intercom button on her desk.

"Yes, Cecily."

"Cindy, call my husband, please, and tell him I'll be very late tonight."

"Okeydokey, Cecily."

Looking at the worried glare on Ruth's face, Cecily blew hard then forced another smile. "Lead me to the troops!" she joked trying to cheer the nurse up.

****

Ruth handed the doctor a chart as they entered an examining room. "Hi, Maria," Cecily smiled.

"Hi, Dr. Wade," the nervous teenager squeezed out of trembling lips.

Looking at the girl's chart, Cecily said, "Wow! It's been almost ten years since I removed your tonsils. Time flies."

"Yes, Ma'am," the nervous girl replied.

"I see that your doctor referred you this time for me to check to see if your appendix need to be removed," Cecily continued, still looking at the child's chart. "What problems are you having, Maria?"

"I've been having blackouts," the girl replied softly, wringing her hands together.

"Complete blackouts or just fainting?"

"Ag...fainting."

"She has a fever, Cecily," added Ruth. "And, her BP is 140 over 90."

"Gee! That's pretty high for a girl your age, Maria," replied Cecily. "When was your last period, Honey?"

"A little over a month ago."

"Lie back, Maria," Cecily spoke, and the girl immediately obeyed, so the doctor pressed the girl in the abdominal area. "Do you think you're pregnant, Maria?"

Wiping a tear from her cheek, the girl said very weakly, "I don't think so. Ricky said he knew what he was doing. He said I could trust him."

"Many babies have been born on *trust me*, Maria," Cecily made known, handing the girl a tissue. "I'll run some tests. If they come back positive, you'll have to see an obstetrician right away." Cecily squeezed the weeping girl on her shoulder lovingly, trying to make her feel better, as she handed her another tissue. "Don't worry, Maria. Everything will be fine."

"If I'm pregnant, my mother will *kill* me."

"I doubt it," Cecily smiled then looked at her nurse. "Take a specimen, please, Ruth."

****

Cecily walked into her office with a patient chart, and a couple was waiting for her. "Hello, Mr. and Mrs. Carlton," greeted Cecily, shaking their hands.

"Hi, Dr. Wade," the lady replied.

"Dr. Wade, I can't for the life of me, remember where I know you from," added the man.

"Henry, don't start *that* again," his wife chuckled. "Both times you've seen Dr. Wade, you've said that."

"I never forget a face, Betty," he insisted.

"They say everybody has a double," Cecily smiled, taking the seat behind her desk.

"I suppose so," he concurred still staring at her.

"Dr. Wade, what's wrong with Jimmy?" the worried mother asked.

"It's his tonsils. I'm afraid they'll have to come out."

"My God. I was afraid of something like that!" blurted Mrs. Carlton.

"Are you sure?" was the father's question.

"Yes, I am."

Mrs. Carlton sighed deeply and asked, "What do we do now, Doctor!"

"We operate. Those tonsils need to come out as soon as possible."

"When can you schedule it?" Mrs. Carlton asked.

"As soon as you like. All it takes is filling out a few papers."

"I want to do the paperwork *now*," Mrs. Carlton replied.

Jumping to his feet, Mr. Carlton exploded, "Now wait just a dog blasted minute, Betty! My son ain't going under no knife until I get a second opinion!"

"I understand, Mr. Carlton. I can recommend someone!" suggested Cecily.

"We'll find our own doctor, Lady!" he fumed on.

Jumping to her feet now, Mrs. Carlton retaliated, "What are you talking about, Henry?!"

"I'm talking about I don't want some *lady* telling me she's going to cut on my boy! I hate I even let you talk me into bringing Jimmy to her!"

"Dr. Wade was highly recommended by Jimmy's doctor in New York, who happens to be a *man*!" Mrs. Carlton blew hard. "Do you think I would have brought Jimmy to just *any* doctor, when we moved here a few weeks ago?!"

Pointing a finger at his wife, Mr. Carlton insisted, "Say what you want, Betty, but I don't intend to let no....ag.... *beauty queen* cut on my son!"

"That's crazy! We're talking about Jimmy's health, and you're worried about how the doctor *looks*! She can't help being beautiful any more than you can help being bald!"

"Well, I sure can help letting her cut on my son!"

Clearing her throat, Cecily interrupted, "Perhaps you would like to discuss this at home."

"You have no say-so, Betty!" Mr. Carlton continued as if he didn't even hear Cecily. "I hold the insurance policies! I am not letting a woman, who looks like a...a... *playboy bunny* cut...!" He froze in his tracks as his eyes locked with Cecily's. An image of the beautiful doctor in a red wig, gently caressing his body with soft, tender, seductive kisses, popped in his mind. Cecily turned abruptly from his stare. He shook his head slowly, found his voice, and added in a low, deep, throaty whisper, "No Way!" He was out the door before his wife could protest any further.

"I'm sorry, Dr. Wade," apologized Mrs. Carlton. "I'll speak to him and get back with you." The woman ran out quickly, and Cecily dropped in her chair.

Cecily dropped her head backward, closed her eyes, and drifted into the past:

Cecily, years younger, in a short-cut, curly, red wig, black bikini-styled negligee, heavily applied make-up, three-inch black heels, and a big smile; popped out of a cake, among a drunken bunch of loud, hollowing, yelling, obnoxious, over-weight, sex-starved, lustful animals, we call men. "She's all yours, Henry ole boy," *one man said smiling to Henry Carlton.*

"Fellows, I didn't want this," *a red-faced Henry replied feeling very embarrassed.*

"Man, you just came from sea. This is <u>your</u> night," another man said; then indicating Cecily, he added, "Of course you want <u>that</u>. She's gorgeous!"

"And when you're finished with her, I'll take her, ole buddy," a third man interjected. "Spencer said she's hot!"

"Fellows, I appreciate what you're trying to do, but I'm a married man," added Henry. "All I want to do is get home to Betty, the greatest woman in the world. I don't want to get something from this woman and take it back to my wife!"

"Henry, Spencer's girls are clean," another man blurted out.

"Now, get in there and give that little lady what she wants," chuckled the first man.

Laughing also, the second man added, "And have a real welcome home."

****

Henry walked into a dimly lit room and focused on Cecily's nude body exposed across the huge bed. She slid seductively to him and began undressing him as she bathed his body with kisses. She slid her hand across his head, and his added hair fell in her hand. "Oh, you're bald in the top. I like bald men. You are so sexy," she cooed, guiding him to the bed. "Have you ever had a tongue bath, Henry?" He shook his head, because he couldn't find his voice, as she straddled her warm, soft frame across his portly, hairy body and proceeded to massage his neck and face with her tongue. "Well, you're about to experience something real special. Relax, baby, and enjoy."

Ah, this beautiful woman was driving him crazy, and she knew it. Looking at her body was enough to send him soaring into an explosive climatic high, but he knew he couldn't go through with it, no matter how gorgeous this woman was. "Please stop," he protested, pushing her away gently.

"What's wrong, Baby?"

"This is wrong," he replied. "I know the men meant well, but this isn't me. I have a very lovely wife at home, whom I love very much."

"I don't wanna marry you, Henry," she chuckled. "I'm just paid to entertain you."

"I don't want to hurt you. You're a very beautiful woman, but I love my wife. I don't want _you_ or anyone else," he explained, beginning to put his clothes back on. "Most importantly, I'm a God fearing, Christian man."

"I hope your wife knows how lucky she is, Henry."

"No. I'm the lucky one, to have her."

"So, what'd we do?"

"Well, you can start by putting your clothes back on, if-you-know-what-I-mean," he laughed.

Laughing also, Cecily said, "I understand." She pulled on a red bathrobe, trimmed in white lace.

"Do you mind if I ask you a personal question?" he asked growing serious.

"What's a nice girl like me doing in a place like this?" Cecily sarcastically finished for him.

"I mean, you are so beautiful, ahhh..."

"Sissy."

"Sissy, you are about the most beautiful woman I've ever seen in my life. Surely you can find something more meaningful to do with your life. I mean, a playboy bunny is better than this."

"Henry, sometimes we don't have a choice. I mean, we have to do what we have to do."

"Sissy, I think we always have choices," he said, and she just chuckled. Then he reached in his wallet and handed her a business card and added, "Call me if you ever want help. Now you do have a choice."

*"Thank you," she said sadly, fighting to hold the tears back. "You're very kind." *

"Cecily," Ruth called, bringing the daydreaming doctor back to the present. "Your last appointment has been canceled. You can go home now and get some rest."

"That's great!" Cecily said standing. "I'm beat." She removed her white smock and replaced it with her trench coat. "See you tomorrow."

"I'm out of here, too," Ruth said exiting the office.

****

As Cecily drove home listening to Gladys Knight and the Pips' *Midnight Train to Georgia*, an image of the bloody body suddenly appeared in her mind, and she shook her head to rid her thoughts of it. Then she focused on her blood-drenched hands. It startled her so much; she lost control of the car and ran off the road. Cecily expertly maneuvered the car to an abrupt stop just before it plunged into a tall palm tree. "Oh, God. What am I going to do?" She burst into tears as she dropped her head on the steering wheel. "What am I going to do?" She surrendered to her emotions and cried hysterically, as she realized her imagination was playing an incredible trick on her.

****

Cecily took control of her emotions, dried her face, and headed home. She entered a community with big, beautiful, *Beverly Hills* style mansions, equipped with indoor and outdoor swimming pools, tennis courts, large professional landscaped lawns, and initial-carved golden gates at each entrance. She drove to one of the beautiful mansions, pushed her remote control, and the *W* on the gate divided in half as the gate opened slowly. Cecily wheeled around the circular driveway, until she was inside the garage. Then she stepped out of the Mercedes Benz and dashed into the house.

When she opened the door, it was like opening the doorway of a dream. The beautifully decorated mansion glistened with brass chandeliers, an elegant array of beige and brown furnishings in the living room, touched by a mellow accent of brass lamps and tables. Cecily ran up the brass spiral staircase.

Cecily tiptoed quietly into a dark bedroom, where a silhouette of a man lay on a king-sized marble bed. She put her coat and hat in the closet and pulled the knife out of the coat pocket.   She then proceeded to tiptoe towards the door when, suddenly she jumped against the marble chest at the sound of her name. "Did I frighten you, Darling?" the man asked sitting up in bed, as she slowly pulled the knife behind her back and dropped it in the chest, while he turned on the bedside marble lamp, exposing his extremely captivating boyish good looks, with his dreamy, soft, blue eyes and short, wavy, dusty-blonde hair.

Finding her voice, Cecily squeezed out of trembling lips, "I thought you were asleep." She took a deep breath. "I'm sorry I woke you, Darling."

"It's okay," he yawned. "I can't sleep too soundly when you aren't here anyway."

"I finished early today, but I had to stop by the hospital. I have a few patients there. Go back to sleep, Isaac. I'll be quiet."

"Don't I get a kiss?" he smiled, exposing pearly white teeth.

Walking to the bed, Cecily smiled, "Sure." She sat on the edge of the bed, and he pulled her in his strong, masculine arms, and their lips met softly.

"Ummmmm," he cooed. "Are you coming to bed?"

"In a minute."

"What time is it?"

Looking at the bedside marbled clock, she replied, "Nine thirty."

"Wow! Aren't you working rather late, Doctor?"

"That's an understatement," she chuckled.

"Come on to bed, Baby," he cooed again, nibbling on her ear.

"Can you wait until I shower?" she chuckled again.

"No!" he exploded, moaning like a monster. He playfully threw her on the bed, fondling her soft, silky body. She laughed uncontrollably as he groaned like a wild animal devouring his prey.

"Honey!" Cecily protested in laughter at no response from her husband. He was on top of her now, massaging her stomach with his tongue, working his way down her body. Cecily knew there was no use protesting, so she dropped her head back to enjoy the treatment her husband was giving to her. As she massaged his soft hair with her fingers, she held up a little, basking in the pleasure of her husband's wild excitement. Hypnotized by the sensation, Cecily focused on her hands and, suddenly they were covered with blood. She jumped so hard Isaac tumbled on the floor, and Cecily was on her feet.

"What the ..."

"I need a shower," she blurted out.

"A *shower*?!" an excited Isaac repeated, almost shouting. "*Now*?!"

"Yes. *Now*!" she insisted, turning her back to him.

"Fine. I'll take one with you."

"No," she replied as she ran into the bathroom and slammed the door.

Isaac rushed to the bathroom door, calling, "Cecily!" He found that the door was locked. "Cecily!" He heard the water running in the shower, so he took a deep breath, walked back to the bed and lay down.

Cecily was not in the running shower at all. She was sitting on the bathroom floor, behind the door, silently crying hysterically. She realized that her hands were not covered with blood after all, but her imagination was still playing tricks on her.

****

When Cecily finally stepped out of the bathroom in a short, pink teddy, Isaac was sitting in bed staring in her direction. "Why did you lock the door?" he asked in a very weak voice.

"Isaac, I'm not a machine!" insisted the distraught woman. "I had a very hard day at work! I'm very tired! I just don't feel like making love tonight!"

"What's going on, Cecily?!" he demanded. "Tired is one thing, but you're acting...I don't know...ugh...*weird*! What is wrong with you?!"

"Nothing is wrong with me," she retorted, getting into bed beside him.

He turned her head towards him with his finger, "Hey, this is me you're talking to. Your husband. Remember? I know when something isn't right with you. Now, tell me what it is."

Cecily took a deep breath, and then she said very softly as a tear trickled down her cheek, "I'm just very tired, Baby. Can't you understand that?"

"Sure, I can understand that, if that's *all* to it, but I know it isn't," he empathized then planted a kiss on her forehead. "I love you, pretty lady."

"And I love you."

Pulling her gently into his strong arms he said, "Let's get some sleep." They eased down in the bed, and Cecily turned her back, so Isaac hugged her from the rear. He snuggled up close to her as she stared at the marble chest where she had dropped the knife.

****

A dry cough awakened Cecily, and she rolled out of her husband's arms and out of the bed. "Are you all right, Baby?"

"Yeah," she said. "Go back to sleep, Darling. I'm going to get some water." He turned over and went back to sleep. Cecily walked over to the marble chest and began looking for a robe. She felt a hard-pointed object and remembered that it was the knife. She pulled on her robe, looked towards the bed at her husband, and then slid the knife in her pocket. Cecily then tipped out of the room.

Cecily went downstairs and into the huge den with a flaming fireplace. She opened the decorated glass on the fireplace and threw the knife in the flames. She strolled into the luxurious black and white kitchen and poured herself a glass of milk. Next, she walked back into the den, curled up on the deep burgundy, soft leather couch, and focused on the flames as she drifted into the past:

*   *"Rocky! Rocky! Rocky!" an audience of young, enthusiastic, rambunctious teenagers yelled at the top of their vocal strength, as a bunch of tight pant, big natural hair, sweat soaked, young men hopped around on a big, glittering stage, screaming lyrics, which they called singing, to the top of their vocal capacity, in their sequined, gleaming attire.*

Fifteen-year-old Cecily sat screaming in the audience, as she sat with two other African American girls, who didn't seem to be as impressed by the group as the rest of the over-excited, over-active, over-hormonal, young teenage girls. "Rocky's so fabulous!" Cecily yelled to her friends, who shared anoint smirks at each other. Cecily's natural beauty, though slightly immature, glowed with her gleaming smile. The only make-up she wore was a light application of cherry lipstick. At five feet seven inches, her small frame was rather shapely in her blue jeans.

"I don't know what you see in that black nigger, Cis," snarled Lillian Martin, the shortest, at five feet, six inches, and the darkest, with a pecan tan color, of the trio. Her thick, curly black hair hung a little below her shoulders with a hair band encircling it. Her natural beauty shone with no makeup on at all.

"And he's old as hell!" Trudy Miles added, so Cecily punched her arm. Trudy, the tallest of the trio, at five feet, eight inches, tried unsuccessfully to hide the freckles on her face with a mask of make-up. Her short, fire-red hair was in an array of curls around her almond colored skin. She was on the chubby side, compared to her two thin friends. Although Trudy would attract attention from the opposite sex, with her very short, black, leather,

mini skirt, she was not, in any stretch of the imagination, a pretty girl.

When Rocky, the leader of the group, sang a slow, love song, Cecily felt as if he was singing it directly to her. "Ahh, I'm in love," Cecily cooed, and the other two girls burst into laughter.

****

After the concert was over, Cecily, Lillian, and Trudy stood in front of the concert stadium drinking sodas. "I'm going to meet Rocky," Cecily announced.

"What?!" exploded Trudy.

"I'm going to meet Rocky."

"How?" Lillian asked.

"Danny, the bellboy at the hotel where Rocky's staying, said he would help me. Rocky has room service every night at one o'clock after the concert. Danny's gonna help me sneak in," Cecily explained with gleam in her eyes.

"You're crazy!" exploded Trudy. "You couldn't possibly get in to see Rocky."

"Cecily, I don't think this is a good idea," added Lillian. "He might have you arrested."

"I have to try, Lil. I'm in love with Rocky," Cecily replied in a dreamlike state. "I know Rocky is a nice person. I just know it. He's so handsome and so sexy."

"He'll sex you!" protested Trudy again.

"Cecily, if you had any sense, you'd come and go home with us," Lillian demanded.

"Lillian, I told my grandma I was staying with you, so leave the window open for me," Cecily said, ignoring her friends' warnings.

Lillian took a deep breath then insisted, "Cecily, this is dumb! You don't even know this man!"

"Lillian, I might not have another chance to meet him," Cecily whined with tears in her eyes, and the girls knew it was no use talking to their friend. They knew she was going to try to see Rocky, even if it killed her.

"Let's go, Tru," Lillian suggested. "Cecily, please come with us."

"I won't stay long, Lil," insisted Cecily. "I'll be at your house soon. I just want to meet Rocky and get his autograph." Lillian shook her head, and she and Trudy started walking, while Cecily walked in the opposite direction.

****

When Cecily arrived at the hotel, she and Danny talked. Then he took her up to Rocky's floor just as a lady was wheeling a room service cart down the hall. When Danny called the lady, Cecily knew that was her cue. When the lady walked away from the cart and went to Danny, Cecily seized the cart and rushed it down to Rocky's room. With trembling hands, she pounded on the door. "Who's there?!" a gruff voice called.

"Room service," Cecily called back. Suddenly the door flew open, and a two-hundred-fifty pound, six feet, ten inches, bearded, charcoal black man

towered over Cecily.

Stepping aside, he said, "Push it there." Then he called, "Rocky, your food is here!" The man focused back on Cecily and barked, "Beat it, Kid!"

"I want to see Rocky, please," she squeezed out.

"Yeah, Kid. You and ten million other brads!" the hulking man snarled again. "Beat it!" He yanked the door open just as the lady stood there about to knock.

"Did Mr. Simpson get his tray?" she asked.

"Yeah."

"Good," she said exhaling a sigh of relief. "I'll be back in a couple of hours to get it." She turned and left quickly.

"I said beat it, Kid!" the man demanded to Cecily, as Rocky entered from the bedroom wrapped in a towel.

"Rocky," Cecily squeezed out. His dark brown eyes focused on her, and she felt as if she would die. Without all the stage makeup and costumes, Rocky was even more handsome than Cecily had ever realized.

"Are you going to beat it, Kid, or do I have to throw you out?" the man insisted again.

"Take it easy, Clarence," Rocky spoke in his soft, sexy, masculine voice. "Have a seat, young lady."

"Me?" Cecily asked, not believing that Rocky had just spoken to her.

"Yeah, you," he smiled exposing gorgeous white teeth.

Heading for the bedroom, Clarence demanded to Rocky, "I want to see you."

Winking an eye at Cecily, Rocky said, "Be right back, Beautiful." He exited behind Clarence and closed the door, but Cecily could still hear their conversation.

"Rocky, what in the hell are you doing?!" demanded Clarence. "That girl can't be more than sixteen!"

"I haven't done <u>anything</u>, Clarence," Rocky chuckled. "Why are you getting so crazy?"

"I'm sick and tired of getting you out of trouble with these hot ass young girls!" Clarence fumed. "Let the girl go home!"

"Clarence, you're overreacting," Rocky chuckled again. "Maybe you're working too hard. Go and find you a woman and get some, Man."

"Rocky..."

"I won't touch her," Rocky insisted. "I promise." Clarence blew hard and Rocky repeated, "I promise. Now, run on and get my stuff." Clarence just stared at the singer, and he repeated holding up his hand like a boy scout. "I promise."

"Well, your promises don't mean shit, Rocky. When your dick gets hard, your promises get soft!" Clarence insisted, and Rocky burst into laughter, as Clarence opened the door and walked back into the room with a fidgeting Cecily. "Go home, Kid," he pleaded to her again.

"Rocky said I could stay," she retreated.

"And, you can, too," replied Rocky.

"Rock..." Clarence started.

Cutting him off, Rocky finalized, "See you later, Man." Clarence took one final look at Cecily, and then he stormed out, slamming the door.

Turning his attention to Cecily, Rocky asked, "Would you like something to eat, pretty lady?"

"No, thank-you," she smiled. "You go ahead." He transferred the food from the cart to the table then sat to eat. "I can't believe I'm sitting here with the Rocky Simpson!"

"Do you have a name, pretty lady?"

Giggling hysterically, she said, "Oh, yeah. Cecily Allen."

"A pretty name for a pretty girl," he smiled with her, as she sat at the table with him.

"Wait until I tell my friends that I actually met Rocky Simpson! That I sat right at his dinner table. They'll never believe it!" the young girl glowed, as he ate slowly focusing on her low-cut blouse.

"How did you get so beautiful, Cecily? Your mother must be a knockout."

"My mother was a very pretty lady."

"Was?"

"She died when I was a baby," Cecily replied sadly. "My grandparents are raising me."

"Where is your father?"

"I don't know. I never knew him, either."

"Why?"

"My mother and father had a forbidden love. She was white and he was black. So, he had to leave, to save his life, when my mother became pregnant. She was only fifteen and he was thirty,"

"I'm sorry."

"It's okay."

"So, are your father's parents raising you or your mother's?"

"My mother's."

"So, you are being raised as a white girl?"

"No, not really," she giggled again. "Anyone who looks at me knows I'm not white, and all my friends are black. Black people accept me better than white people."

"Well that's hard to believe. You're so charming, any race of people should be more than happy to accept you," he said then planted a soft kiss on the back of her hand.

"Wow," she glowed.

"Rising, he said, "Let's sit on the couch." She eagerly followed him.

Just as he was about to sit beside her, his towel dropped to the floor, exposing his nude, ebony, well-built body, among other things. "OOPS," he cooed as if he was surprised. Cecily swallowed a lump in her throat hard then picked the towel up and handed it to him. He flung it aside as he rubbed his fingers in her hair. "We don't need it," he said softly, and Cecily swallowed another lump in her throat. "Are you a virgin, Cecily?" She nodded slowly.

Rising slowly, Cecily announced softly, "I better go." She licked her dry lips.

"But the fun's just beginning," he said placing his arms around her tiny waist. He began to nibble at her ear, and the sensation was unbearable to

her. She had never experienced this feeling before. He expertly zipped her jeans down and began pulling them to her feet.

"No," Cecily protested softly. "I'm scared. I've never done this before."

"I won't hurt you, Baby. I promise," he breathlessly replied. "Trust me, Cecily."

"I don't know. I..."

"I thought you liked me, Cecily," he insisted growing a little frustrated.

"I do like you. I think I even love you, but..."

"But what? I like you, too. Come on, don't be a baby. You didn't come here for nothing, did you?"

"I just wanted to meet you."

"And, you have," he said sweeping her up in his arms. "But you're going to get a whole lot more, and you will enjoy it. I promise." He carried her into the bedroom and lay her on the big, luxurious, red, satin, sheets, smothering her with soft, wet kisses, as he expertly relieved her of her clothing. She loved him too much to protest any further, and she wanted him to love her. She thought how great it was going to be, having Rocky Simpson as her boyfriend. All the girls would envy her. Rocky and she would get married when she finished high school. This is going to be great. She now wanted him. Oh, how she wanted him! She wanted him to take her. To possess her. To make undying love to her, like they do in the movies, and she knew he would be hers forever.

****

When his deed was done, Rocky collapsed on Cecily, just as the bedroom door flew open, and Clarence was standing there steaming, breathing deeply, and looking in Cecily's star-struck, naive, little eyes.

"I thought I told you to go home, Kid," he snapped.

Rolling off her and pulling her in his arms, Rocky squeezed out breathlessly, "She's my guest. Leave her be." He planted a kiss on her forehead. "That was great, Baby." He sat up and focused on Clarence. "You got my stuff?"

"Yeah, I got it, but the kid goes."

"She stays," Rocky insisted then kissed her lips. "I found myself a little virgin." He dropped back on the bed. "Now can we have some privacy, Man?" Clarence gave Cecily one final leer, and then he walked out slowly.

*

"Cecily!" Isaac called, bringing her back to the present. "What's wrong, Sweetheart?"

Wiping a tear from her eyes, she said, "Nothing, Darling."

"Cecily, please, don't shut me out of your life."

"I'm not shutting you out, Baby. I just have a lot on my mind."

"Anything concerning me?"

Standing and walking to her husband, she said, "Of course not, Darling. You're the *one* sane thing in my life."

"Share the other *crazy* things with me."

"Not tonight, Honey. I'm too tired," she yawned. "Let's go to bed." Cecily took Isaac's hand, and they started out the door. She stopped suddenly and picked up a picture of a milk chocolate tan lady with heavily applied make-up on. She rubbed her fingers across the picture lovingly. "At times like this I wish you were here, Cotton."

"You loved her very much, didn't you?"

"She was the only adult I felt really loved me when I was growing up. I wish you could've met her. You two would've loved each other."

"I've heard you talk so much about her; I feel as if I did know her," he planted a kiss on her forehead. "Let's go to bed. You need your rest if you're going to help Lillian move in tomorrow."

"I still can't believe Lil's moving right next door to us. It's going to be great!" Cecily exploded, bubbling in enthusiasm. "It's been so long since I've seen her. I've never even met her husband."

"You haven't met your best friend's husband?! Why?"

"Well, I was all set to be Lil's Maid of Honor, but I had a nervous breakdown and was hospitalized. I missed the wedding. I visited her a couple of times, but he was out of town. He used to travel a lot on business. And Lil, Tru, and I just didn't stay in touch like we should have. But we're going to change that."

"What about Trudy? Where is she?"

"She's living in New York now. She's a very successful fashion model."

"I bet you girls were *quite* a trio."

"We were," Cecily said bursting into laughter. "We *were*!"

Chapter 2

Cecily sat at her huge oak desk as Cindy buzzed. "Dr. Wade, Mrs. Carter is here to see you."

Smiling big she said, "Send her in, Cindy." Cecily jumped up and rushed to the door, just as it came crashing open, and a little pecan tanned girl with shoulder length ponytails, hanging on each side of her ears, exploded in the doctor's arms.

"Hi, Aunt Cecily," the child yelled in laughter, as Cecily scooped her up and spun her around.

"Hello, my precious little angel," Cecily replied joining in on the child's enthusiasm, as a one hundred ten pound, pecan tanned lady strolled in slowly, caressed in a full length light gray, female mink coat, with a matching hat pulled down over her luxurious, light brown, shoulder-length curly hair. When Cecily saw the beautiful woman, she released the child, then she and her long-time friend, Lillian, simultaneously fled into each other's arms in joyful tears.

"It's been a long time, Doctor," Lillian said in her deep, sexy, feminine voice, wiping her tears with tissue she had taken out a dispenser on Cecily's desk.

"Yes, it has been," Cecily said wiping her own tears. "You're still as beautiful and suave as I remember, Lil."

"And, so are you, my friend. So are you," Lillian said, laying her little girl's white fur coat across a chair. "Wanda just couldn't wait for me. She wanted to see her Aunt Cecily."

"She's so beautiful," Cecily smiled taking the child's hand.

"Thank you," smiled the proud mother.

"Have a seat, Lil."

Looking around Lillian joked, "Cecily Allen, you've come a long way, Baby."

"We *all* have!"

"Ever since you were a little girl, you've always wanted to be a doctor. Is it everything you expected?"

"And *more*!" The women sat in front of Cecily's desk, as little Wanda played with a puzzle behind the desk. "Did you see Trudy's picture on the cover of *Fashion and Glamour Magazine*?"

"Yes, I did. Who would've thought that that plump-little-freckled-face-insecure girl would've grown up to be a beautiful fashion model, envied by millions of women?"

"Go figure," Cecily laughed, and Lillian laughed with her. "We did it, Girl! We all did it!"

Growing serious Lillian said, "Well, maybe you and Trudy did it, but not *me*."

"What's up with you, Girl? What the hell are you talking about?"

"You know what I'm talking about.   You are a doctor, and Trudy is a fashion model, and what am I?"

"You're a wonderful wife and mother!"

"But I don't have a *career* like you guys."

"Oh, I think running a household and taking care of a family is a full-time career."

"Don't get me wrong. I love my life, but it seems pretty dull next to yours and Trudy's."

"But it was *your* choice, Lil. You are a college graduate. You could've chosen any career you wanted, but you chose to be a housewife. And, I think that's great, if you're happy with it.   And, if you're not, there's still plenty of time to have a career." Cecily said. "Do you still draw?"

"Sometimes, but not much."

"You used to be so talented."

"Well, that was a long time ago."

"What about singing? Do you still sing?"

"Only in *church*," Lillian chuckled.

"At least you're still using that beautiful voice."

"You're good for my ego, Girl," Lillian laughed, and Cecily laughed with her. "But, seriously, at one time, when Alton was traveling a lot, I felt that I had made a mistake for getting married instead of pursuing a career, but now that his work is more stable, and he's home all the time, my life is okay."

"Just *okay*?"

"All right, it's *great*!" she exploded, and they burst into laughter. "Let me get out your hair so you can get some work done."

"I'm planning to leave early today anyway, to help you move in."

"Oh, that's all taken care of."

"What'd you mean? It's all taken care of?"

"A decorator is handling all of that, and Gracie, our maid is there to help out."

"A *maid*!" Cecily repeated sarcastically. "I'm impressed."

"Doesn't *everyone* have one," Lillian joked in a British accent.

"No!" Cecily said again with sarcasm. "*I* don't for one."

"Well, I know it's not because you can't afford one," Lillian replied. "You know what your trouble is, Cecily Allen Wade? You just don't like to be waited on. I can remember when we were growing up, you were the only rich kid I knew who called her maid *Mrs.*"

"We were *not* rich. My grandfather was *just* a judge."

"Well, you were the richest kid *I* knew," Lillian stressed, standing, then focusing on her daughter. "Ready, Sweetheart?" Wanda jumped up and ran to her mother.

"She's growing up so fast," Cecily remarked. "She'll be six soon."

"Yes. Soon she won't be Mommy's little baby anymore."

"Yes, but I bet she'll *always* be Daddy's little girl," Cecily said helping Wanda put on her coat.

"You got that right," added Lillian. "Cecily, you've never met Alton, have you?"

"No, I've never met *Mr. Wonderful.* I'm looking forward to finally meeting him."

Laughing, Lillian said, "What about tonight?"

"Tonight?! You've just moved in!"

"So? Gracie has to cook for us. Adding two more ain't no big deal."

"Are you sure?"

"Of course, I'm sure."

"Okay. I'll check with Isaac and get back with you."

"Fine," Lillian said looking in her Louie Fenton purse. "Let me jot down my landline number." She handed the paper to Cecily.

"I'll call you as soon as I speak to Isaac."

"Cool," replied Lillian. They hugged one more time. Then Cecily hugged Wanda, and they left.

Cecily closed the door behind them, then she buzzed her secretary. "Yes, Cecily," the high-pitched voice answered.

"Cindy, will you get my husband on the phone, please?"

"Sure," Cindy said then picked up the telephone and dialed with her long, perfectly rounded, red fingernails.

"Wade Architectural Firm," a buckteeth lady with horned-rim eyeglasses answered.

"Dr. Wade for Mr. Wade, please."

"Hold, please."

Isaac was standing at the filing cabinet when he heard the buzz. He pushed the drawer shut, went to his desk, and pushed the button. "Yes, Judy."

"Mr. Wade, your wife's on line two."

"Thanks, Judy," he said sitting behind the big pinewood desk in the huge office, equipped with plush blue carpet, soft blue couch with matching blue drapes covering stained-glass windows, and a well-stocked pine-wood bar. "Hi, Darling."

"Hi, Sweetheart," Cindy said smiling.

"Oh, hi, Cindy," he said with a melting smile. "I thought you were Cecily."

"How are ya, Isaac?"

"Fine, Cindy. How are you?"

"I'm okay," she said growing serious. "Angela misses you."

"I've been busy. I'll stop by soon," he replied, then blew hard. "Tell Angela I love her."

"She'd rather hear it from *you*."

"I'll see her soon," he insisted.

"Not many men would neglect their *only* child, Isaac."

"I'm not neglecting her! A thousand dollars a month is hardly neglect. I hope you're not filling her head up with lies about me!"

"You know I wouldn't do that!" she retaliated. "When are you going to tell Cecily about us?"

"There's *nothing* to tell about *us*! It's over! It has been for a long time!"

"Yes, but we still have Angela. When are you going to tell your wife about our daughter? Then maybe you can finally be a Daddy to Angela!"

"I don't know, Cindy. Please, don't pressure me," he sighed deeply. "You realize if Cecily finds out, you might not have a job anymore?"

"For the sake of my child, I'll risk it."

"Why, Cindy?"

"Why what? I told you! For my child!"

"Is it really Angela or *you*?"

"Isaac, I can't deny my feelings for you, but I wouldn't want to do anything to hurt Cecily. She's the best boss I've ever had. But Angela needs you."

"I'll see what I can do. Put Cecily on, please. I'm very busy."

Growing angry, Cindy snapped, "Hold on, Mr. Wade!" She pushed the button. "Cecily, Mr. Wade is on line one."

"Thank-you, Cindy," Cecily said dropping in the chair behind her desk. "Hi, Darling."

"Hi, Beautiful," he smiled also. "What's up?"

"Lil wants us to have dinner with them tonight."

"So soon?"

"Yeah. She said it's cool."

"If that's what you want, Baby, it's fine with me."

"Great! I'll call Lil. See you later."

"I love you."

"I love you, too," she said as Ruth entered. "Bye." She hung up.

"Cecily, what about Jimmy Carlton? You haven't scheduled his surgery yet."

"I can't right now, Ruth. His father wants a second opinion," Cecily said standing as she took a deep breath. "He has some hang-ups about women doctors, especially *me*."

"The man's a fool!"   exploded Ruth. "Doesn't he know your reputation?"

"That doesn't matter to him," Cecily replied as the buzzer sounded. She walked to it and pushed the button. "Yes, Cindy."

"Cecily, Mr. Carlton is here to see you."

With a shrug of her shoulders, looking at Ruth, Cecily replied, "Send him in, Cindy." She focused back on Ruth and added, "Speak of the devil."

"Good luck," the nurse said with a smile as she opened the door and focused on Mr. Carlton.

"Come in, Mr. Carlton," Cecily spoke. Ruth closed the door as she exited. "Have a seat, please." She sat behind her desk as he sat in front of it. "What can I do for you, Mr. Carlton?"

"Dr. Wade, I'm having a difficult time explaining to my wife why I don't want you to operate on my son. I need your help. I mean, I..." he paused. "I don't want to expose your little secret. I'm sure you've fought very hard to hide it."

"I can't help you, Mr. Carlton," she announced nonchalantly.

Jumping to his feet, the short, bald man yelled, "The hell you can't, lady! And I use the term *loosely*!"

"I happen to believe your son needs me, Mr. Carlton. I won't abandon him because of *your* stupidity," Cecily retaliated, standing her ground.

Mr. Carlton's face turned a bright red, as he shouted, "I be damned if I'd allow some call girl to cut on my boy! No way! No damn way!"

"I am *not* a call girl!" defended Cecily. "And, please keep your voice down." She was on her feet now.

"What the hell do you call it?! A whore! A hooker! A bitch! All the same!"

"That was a long time ago!"

"Not *that* long! And, I don't want you transmitting any diseases to my son!"

"That's absurd! Even if I had a disease, I couldn't pass it to your son! And, furthermore, how in the hell do you know a *man* doctor wouldn't have some disease?!"

"I'll rather take my chances with someone that I don't *know* to be a whore," he sighed deeply. "The bottom line is I don't want *you* operating on my son! Now, if I have to, I'll tell my wife, and she'll feel the same way I do!"

"I don't think so."

"Listen lady, *I* know my wife better than *you*."

"Your wife doesn't strike me as being a fool, Mr. Carlton."

"Call it what you like, Dr. Wade, but it will be over my dead body that you cut on my boy!"

Dropping in her seat, Cecily said very softly, "A long time ago, Mr. Carlton, you offered a perfect stranger help if she ever needed it. Now, I'm asking for that help. Please, forget the past. I wouldn't be where I am today if it were not for my past. Please, forget it, and let *me* forget it," she took a deep breath. "I once told you that your wife was a lucky woman. Don't disappoint me."

With extreme sincerity, he replied, "I wish you a lot of luck, Dr. Wade.

You have a lot of spunk. I'm an old-fashioned man. I can't help that. I admire you, but I just can't let you operate on my son." He walked out slowly, and Cecily dropped her head on the desk.

Cecily's thoughts took her in the past:

*   *Teen-aged Cecily, Lillian, and Trudy sat around a huge table with scattered books, paper, and pencils. "Cecily, do you have the answer to number five?" Trudy asked.*

"No."

"Cis, I don't believe you don't have that answer, yet, " Lillian replied. "I have that one." She grabbed Cecily's paper and looked at it. "You haven't even started yet."

"What's with you, Cis?" Trudy asked, popping her bubble gum.

"Nothing," announced Cecily, nonchalantly, brushing her long, wavy, black hair out of her face.

"It's us, Cis," replied Lillian. "What's up, girl?"

With tears rolling down her face, Cecily squeezed out, "I'm pregnant, and I can't get in touch with Rocky, to tell him."

"Oh, my God," Lillian squeezed out, pulling the weeping girl in her arms. "Are you sure?"

"Of course, she is!" added Trudy, growing angry. "And, you can forget about getting in touch with that black son-of-a-bitch! Do you honestly think he cares?! To be so smart, Cis, you sure did do a dumb thing by letting that low-life bastard fool you into the sack!"

"He didn't fool me!" Cecily insisted, jerking her head off Lillian. "I'm special to Rocky! I know it!"

"Yeah, you and ten million other girls he can take the advantage of," Trudy sarcastically added.

"Shut up, Trudy!" Lillian yelled. "Getting upset won't solve anything! We have to help Cecily now, then try to find Rocky."

"Lil, you're just as naive as Cis. Rocky doesn't care about her, or anyone else he happens to knock up! He might even deny ever being with her!"

"No, he wouldn't!" Cecily yelled. "He loves me!"

"It's been almost three months since he fucked you, Cis!" Trudy insisted. "How many times has the sorry bastard picked up the damn phone and called your stupid ass?!" Cecily dropped her head. "Yeah, he loves ya, all right." Just then the door flew open and a huge black lady in a maid's uniform stood there.

"Cecily, what's going on?" she demanded. "I can hear you kids all the way down the hall!"

"I'm sorry, Mrs. Clarke," Cecily said, turning around so that the woman wouldn't see her tears, as she tried to wipe them discreetly.

"You girls keep it down. Judge Allen is sleeping."

"Granddaddy's home?" Cecily asked, now facing the lady.

"Yes. He came home early, so he could rest. So, keep it down."

"Yes, Ma'am," replied Cecily, as the lady exited.

"We have to work quickly," Lillian took control.

"You're keeping the baby?" asked Trudy.

"Of course, I am," Cecily snapped.

"Cis, that's crazy," exploded Trudy. "Just go down to the clinic and get rid of it."

"No!" Cecily insisted. "I want my baby!"

"If your grandparents find out, they'll make you get an abortion," Trudy added.

"That's why they can't know, until it's too late to make me do anything like that."

"The most important thing right now is to find Rocky," added Lillian. "He can help you."

"I know," agreed Cecily. "But, how can we find him?"

"Don't worry, we'll figure something out," Lillian said with a loving smile.

"Cis, think, " Trudy insisted. "You wanna be a doctor someday. How can you take care of a baby and go to medical school? Hell, you have to finish high school first. How are you going to do that?"

"Rocky will help me. Maybe we can get married, and he can hire someone to take care of the baby while I finish school." Lillian's eyes locked with Trudy's, and Trudy shook her head slowly.

*"We got work to do," Lillian spoke up. "Let's go." *

"Cecily," Ruth called, bringing the doctor back to the present. "Aren't you leaving early?"

"Yes. Are we finished?"

"Yes," Ruth said. "Maria's test results are back."

"Positive?" Cecily asked, and Ruth nodded. "I was afraid of that, but I was hoping, for her sake, she had good news."

"Hey, you play games, you win prizes," Ruth sarcastically replied.

"She was playing the most dangerous game of all. It's called trust."

"There's no such game."

"Tell that to the millions of girls who play it every single day."

"When will they learn?"

"When it's too late," added Cecily. "Tell Cindy to call and schedule an appointment with Maria and her mother. She's still a minor."

"For when?"

"Tomorrow, if possible. She needs to know as soon as possible, so she can get the proper prenatal care," Cecily explained, putting on her coat. "I think I'll pick Lillian up for lunch. See you tomorrow, Ruth."

****

Lillian and Cecily walked into a beautiful restaurant. Lillian and Cecily both removed their coats and checked them in. The Maître d' showed them to their table, and they sat. "Lil, I'm so glad you were free. Since I was supposed to get off early to help you settle in, I realized we could still have lunch."

"I'm glad you called. After I enrolled Wanda in school, I didn't have anything else to do."

"Would you ladies like to have something from the bar?" the waiter asked.

"Yes, I'll have a glass of Chablis, "Cecily spoke.

"White wine," added Lillian.

"I'll be right back with your cocktails and to take your orders," he said then exited.

"The duck here is very good, Lil."

"Oh, duck," Lillian exploded excitedly. "I haven't had duck in a long time. I'll try it."

"Lillian, it's so good to have you here," Cecily said with a big smile. "Now I'll have someone to talk to." She sighed deeply.

"What is it, Cis?"

Taking a deep breath, Cecily replied, "Isaac is good, but he doesn't know about my past, so I can't really talk to him about some things."

"Why haven't you told him?"

"He said the past is the past. He said whatever is in our past can stay."

"That's very admirable of him," Lillian replied as the waiter returned with their drinks.

"Are you ladies ready to order?"

"Yes, " answered Cecily. "We'll both have the duck."

"Very well," he said collecting their menus. "I shall return." He left.

"Cis, I think you should've still told Isaac about your past. It might come back to haunt you."

"I know, but I can't bring myself to tell him."

"Cis, what is it?"

"Lil, there's so much I need to talk to you about."

"I'm all ears."

"Isaac and I have been having problems."

"What kind of problems?"

"I don't feel anything for him physically."

With a Smirk on her face, Lillian whispered, "Oh, it's true what they say about white boys?"

Bursting into laughter, Cecily said, "Oh, Girl, stop! I'm serious."

Trying to regain composure, Lillian said, "So, how is it, Cis? I mean, *really*?"

"Believe me, Girl. Isaac dispels all...I do mean *all* those myths about white boys' sexuality."

"I hear ya, Girl," Lillian laughed. "Then, what's the problem?"

"I don't know. I mean, I just don't feel sexually attracted to him anymore."

"That happens sometimes, Cis. I mean, I don't know why it happens, but it does, and Lord knows, the man is *fine*."

"Yes, he is. And, he is just as sweet and understanding as he is fine. I don't understand it. When he comes near me, I turn to ice. Could I still be in the past and not know it?"

"What're you talking about?"

"I'm talking about all those men. Is it possible that *one* man can't satisfy me anymore?"

"Cis, that's absurd," Lillian chuckled.

"I'm serious, Lil."

"You once had a man in your life who satisfied you a great deal. Don't you remember?"

"Yes," Cecily said thinking of him. "David," she took a deep breath. "Oh, David. He was so special. That man touched buttons in me I didn't know I had."

"Maybe you should look him up."

"I wouldn't know where to start," she replied. "Besides, he's married."

"How do you know he's still married?"

"Lil, when I met David, I was a hooker. He was one of my clients. He wouldn't want me."

"You said he loved you."

"Maybe I just *thought* he did, because I loved him so much."

"You've never gotten over him, have you, Cis?"

"No," she sighed deeply. "You don't get over a man like David too easily. I still love him as much as ever, and it's been years since I've seen him. I can still remember his perfect smile. I can still remember his cologne, his beautiful eyes, his touch." she closed her eyes momentarily. "Oh, how I loved that man."

"Then you should look him up," Lillian insisted. "Look at you. You're getting goose bumps just thinking about him. Girl, your love for that man is as strong as ever."

"Lillian, I poured my heart out to him the last time I saw him, and all he could say was he loved his wife," Cecily explained, feeling the pain all over again, as she wiped her tears. "When he went to sleep that night, I ripped up all his important papers and left. I felt as if someone had just stuck a knife in my back. I really wanted to die. I know that if I weren't a hooker, he would've left his wife for me. I know he loved me, Lil. I *know* it."

"Then look for him," Lillian insisted as the waiter brought their food.

"Here we are, ladies," the waiter said. "Would you care for anything else?"

"No, thank you," Lillian said as Cecily shook her head, too choked to speak, wiping her sad tears. He exited.

"I mean it, Cis. Get a private detective."

"And, what do I do if I find him? What if he's still married? What if he doesn't want to see me? I know I cost him a lot of money and time, that night when I ripped up those papers. He told me how important those papers were. And last, but not least, what in the hell do I do with Isaac?!"

"I don't have all the answers, Cis. All I know is that if you love this man as much as you say, then you owe it to yourself to at least see him again," Lillian suggested. "You know how much I care for Isaac. He's a wonderful man, but you have to think about your happiness, too." She paused. "And, you certainly can't be helping Isaac by living with him and loving another man."

"I really do love Isaac in my own way, but not like a woman should love her husband," she said. "Recently, something happened in my life that's making me think of the past a great deal now. But, that's another story. I'll tell you about it someday."

****

Later, when Cecily and Lillian walked out of the restaurant, a man stood, folded a newspaper, and walked out behind them, still with a camera around his neck.

****

Cecily took Lillian home, then she went home. She walked into the bedroom and lay across the bed. She drifted into the past:

**   Cecily strolled into a dimly lit bedroom, in a see-through black negligée, leaving <u>nothing</u> to the imagination. Her beautiful, long, black hair outlined her beautiful, bronzed face, combining with her black skimpy attire. She strolled over to the bed, where a milk chocolate tanned man lay with out-stretched eyes, soaking up her beauty. To say he was handsome would be a drastic understatement. His well-groomed, low hair cut set off his soft brown eyes, his strong cheek bones, and his artistic lips, to make up one gorgeous, devastating, sophisticated, breathtaking man, with no facial hair at all. His smile could melt the entire ice age, with his perfectly even, white teeth. "Wow!" he smiled,* sitting up, focusing on Cecily. "What do I owe for this unexpected pleasure?" His voice was smooth, even tone, well bred, trained, educated, and soooo sexy.

"I love you, David. I love you very, very much."

"Sissy, I ..."

"Let me finish, Darling," she said putting her finger to his lips, silencing his words. "I'm getting out of this business. But life wouldn't be worth living without you. Please, say you'll be mine. I've never loved anyone like I do you." She wiped a tear from her face. "I can make you happy. I know I can. Please, be mine."

"Sissy, I....I don't know what to say. You know I'm married, and....I...I love my wife. I care a great deal for you, but it's my wife that I love."

"You never loved me?"

"I care for you more than I should, and I'm glad you're changing your life. I wish you well, but I can't leave my wife...for _anyone_."

"You mean, for a _hooker_?"

"No, I don't. I mean for _anyone_," he said. "We have good times together. Let's keep it that way."

"Sure, David," she tried to smile. "I could never leave this business anyway."

"But you said."

"Forget what I said. I think it was the wine we had at dinner. I'm terrible with alcohol," she said getting off the bed.

"Where're you going?"

*"I'll be right back," she said then blew him a kiss. "Don't you go away."
Cecily went into the bathroom, closed the door, and melted to the floor
in tears.* *

"Cecily," Isaac called, bringing her back to the present.

"Darling, you're home," she said wiping her tears before he noticed
them. Then she strolled into his arms. "How did you get away so early?"

Planting a kiss on her lips, he said, "I wanted to spend some time with
my beautiful wife before taking her in the company of others."

"Oh, you're so sweet," she smiled as their lips met again. He guided
her to the bed and laid her down. "Honey," Cecily tried to protest, but he
wasn't listening. He showered her neck with kisses, as he maneuvered her
blouse open. Suddenly Cecily jumped up, knocking him aside, and stood
on her feet.

"What the hell..." Isaac started.

"I'm sorry, Darling, but I don't feel like it right now."

"When *will* you feel like it, Cecily?!" he insisted strongly, rising also.

"Please don't bully me, Isaac."

"*Bully* you?!" he chuckled. "I don't believe this. We haven't made love
in months, and *I'm* bullying *you*!" He swirled her around by her shoulders
to face him. "What is going on, Cecily? What in the hell is going on with
you?!"

"I don't know what you're talking about," she nonchalantly replied,
about to turn her back again, but her persistent husband wouldn't let her.

"Tell me the truth, Cecily! Why won't you let me touch you anymore? Is there someone else?"

Chuckling, she replied, "Don't be absurd."

"Is it, Cecily?"

"Yes! It *is*! There's nothing wrong. I've just been tired lately. Now, let's get ready. I don't want to keep Lillian and her family waiting."

"Tomorrow, we've got to have a long talk, Cecily."

"Okay," Cecily agreed as she exited into the bathroom.

****

As Cecily stepped out of the bathroom, still towel-drying her hair, she could hear Isaac in his bathroom, taking a shower. She sat in the brass and velvet vanity chair and stared into the mirror. Soon she was in the past:

*   Nineteen-year-old Cecily sat on a stool with the ebony lady, whose picture is in her den, as the lady applied make-up on her face, while looking in a mirror. "Cotton, why do you put on all that make-up? You're pretty without it." Cecily asked.*

"Oh, Sissy, you my bigges' fan," the lady chuckled, with her slightly protruding overbite and a trace of a still fading southern accent. "I'm far from bein' pretty. In this business, you gotta attrac' men. This is how I do it." She stood and placed a fluffy, curly, auburn, natural wig on her head. She smoothed down her black mini skirt and stepped into some

ankle-length black boots. "Well, how do I look, Kid?"

"You look beautiful," Cecily smiled big. Cotton picked up a beaded, black shoulder-strapped purse, and threw a cheap, white, fake fur wrap around her shoulders, then headed for the door.

"Sissy, lock this here doe, and don't you dare open it for nobody," she insisted.

"Cotton, I told Barry he could come over."

"Now, I don't have time to argue, Missy. You tell that big, over-grown, cock-sucking jock to stay the hell home tonight. Don't you have a test tomorrow?"

Bursting into laughter, Cecily said, "He's going to help me study."

"Yeah, I bet," she said sarcastically, laughing also. "Call him. I don't wanna see tha' horny mutherfucker here when I git back!"

"Cot..."

"Sissy!"

"Okay, Okay," she pouted.

"Good-night," Cotton said, then planted a kiss on her forehead.

*Cecily couldn't help but smile, "Good-night." She had never gotten kisses from adults until Cotton. Cotton's kisses always gave her such a warm feeling inside, and she liked it.   ***

"Aren't you ready yet?" Isaac asked, bringing Cecily back to the present.

Cecily looked up in a handsome Isaac's face, as he stood there in his dark blue Wilco Jenx three-piece suit. "Wow!" she smiled. "You look great."

"You better get a move on, pretty lady," he smiled. "And, I'm glad you approve." He started for the door.

"I do. I do," she smiled. "Where're you going?"

"To bring the car around," he said exiting. "Hurry up." He blew a kiss at her on his way out, and she smiled lovingly.

****

"I'm ready," Cecily announced stepping into the living room where Isaac sat waiting patiently. He stood and whistled, admiring his beautiful wife. Her hair was in an upsweep on top of her head, with loose curly locks of hair encircling her face. Her sequined, V-neck, baby-blue, lace, calf-length, Gloria DuSant dress caressed her perfectly rounded curves, until it reached her lower thigh, then it ballooned out in an array of lace. Her flesh-toned Maggie Sinclair pantyhose accented her long, beautiful, shapely legs, with a streak of blue lace running down the side of each leg, right down to her baby blue, two-inch lace heels. A pearl necklace with matching earrings massaged her skin as if they were made just for her.

"Wow!" Isaac exploded.

"You like?" she smiled big, bending in a small curtsy.

"I like," he said smiling also as he walked to her and planted a kiss on her cheek. "I don't know if I want another man looking at my beautiful wife."

"You don't have to worry about that. Lil is very happily married."

"Yeah, but is *he*?" Isaac laughed.

Cecily shoved him slightly, laughing also, as she said, "Let's go, you idiot."

****

When Cecily and Isaac arrived at Lillian's house, the maid opened the door and took their coats. She showed them into the huge den, as Lillian and Wanda entered. "Hi, Cecily," Lillian smiled as they touched cheeks.

"Hi, Lil. You look great."

"So, do you," Lillian said moving to Isaac, while Cecily and Wanda began their hugs and kisses.

"Hello, Lillian. You look beautiful," Isaac said, and they embraced.

"Thank-you. And, you're still as handsome as I remember."

"Thank-you," Isaac smiled, admiring this beautiful lady standing before him. Her hair was also in an upsweep on top of her head, with no locks hanging. Her yellow Carl Trousseau dress was accented by a rounded neckline with white lace attached to it that reached up to her chin, and ballooned from the waist, down to her calves. Her two-inch yellow pumps caressed her feet tenderly. Her earrings were made like yellow swans, eloquently matching her bracelet.

"Isaac, this is Wanda," Lillian introduced, catching the child by the hand. "Wanda, this is your Uncle Isaac."

"Hello, Wanda," Isaac said as he bent down to her.

"Hi, Uncle Isaac," she smiled, speaking softly.

"I can certainly see where her beauty comes from," Isaac said standing again. Wanda smiled big, in her little lace pink dress with pink shiny shoes. A pink, lace ribbon tied on the side of her head in her mass of soft, flowing curls, accented her face.

"Thank you," Lillian smiled. "Have a seat." Isaac and Cecily sat on the couch, Lillian sat in a matching white leather chair, and Wanda sat on the matching ottoman.

"Would you like drinks now, Mrs. Carter," the maid asked as she entered.

"Oh, yes, Gracie," Lillian glowed. "Cecily, Isaac, this is Gracie, my *right* hand. Gracie, this is Mr. Isaac and Dr. Cecily Wade. They're our next-door neighbors."

"Yes, I know," Gracie said, and they extended greetings.

"State your poison," Lillian smiled big.

"White wine," Cecily said.

"Gin and tonic," added Isaac.

"I'll take my usual, Gracie," Lillian said. "Oh, and bring Alton his, too."

"Very well," the lady replied, then proceeded to walk across the room on the thick, plush, white carpet to the multi-colored, lighted bar.

Standing, Isaac said, "Gracie, I'll get the drinks. I know you have plenty to do."

"Thank-you, Mr. Wade," she smiled sweetly then exited.

"Lillian, what's the usual?" asked Isaac.

"Whiskey sour for me and a vodka martini for Alton. Thank-you, Isaac." Lillian said then looked at Wanda. "Honey, run upstairs and see what's keeping Daddy. If I know that man, he is on the phone conducting business. He's a workaholic." Wanda jumped up and skipped out, as Isaac brought their drinks.

"Thanks, Isaac," Lillian said, receiving her drink. "Just put Alton's on the table." He did so, then walked to the couch and handed Cecily her drink.

"Thanks, Darling," she said.

"It's a pleasure serving such beautiful ladies," Isaac said smiling then sat beside his wife.

At the sound of Wanda's giggles, coming from the direction of the stairs, Lillian said, "It's about time." She saw her husband first, and they shared a smile.

"I'm sorry. I couldn't get this tie on," his cool sexy voice explained.

Just as the tall handsome figure stepped into focus, his eyes locked with Cecily's, and she choked on her drink, resulting in a violent cough. "Are you all right, Honey," Isaac asked, placing their drinks on the table. As she fought to regain her breath, a million things ran through her mind. It just couldn't be. It *just* couldn't be!! She couldn't believe her eyes. It was *David*. Lillian's husband was the man that stole her heart so many years ago and returned it in pieces. *Alton is David.*

"I'm fine," she finally said to Isaac when she found her voice.

"Alton, this is Mr. Isaac and Dr. Cecily Wade,"   Lillian introduced proudly, taking his arm and moving him forward to them. "Isaac and Cecily, this is Alton."

"Pleasure, Man." Isaac spoke extending a hand.

"Likewise, Man?" Alton agreed shaking his hand. Then he extended a hand to Cecily. "Dr. Wade, how are you? I've heard so much about you."

"How do you do?" she replied, trying to avoid his beautiful brown eyes, as she took his hand slowly. She was actually trembling and sweating as she shook his hand, as she thought, *Oh God, he's even more gorgeous than I remember.*

"I never expected such beauty, from such a brilliant mind," Alton added, but thinking, *My God, it's <u>Sissy</u>! It's really <u>her</u>! Lillian's best friend is <u>Sissy</u>. Lordy, she is still a <u>very</u> beautiful woman.*

"Thank-you" Cecily replied, pulling her hand away, wondering why he was toying with her. Is it possible that he doesn't even remember her?

"Mrs. Carter, dinner is ready," Gracie announced, then exited again.

"Honey, your drink is on the table," Lillian said to her husband.

"Oh, thank you, Baby."

****

All during dinner, Isaac noticed a peculiar expression on his wife's face whenever Alton said or did *anything*. He also noticed that when Alton passed the saltshaker to Cecily, their hands touched a little bit longer than necessary. He noticed that his wife seemed to be absolutely uncomfortable around this man who was supposed to be a stranger to her.

Alton couldn't keep his eyes off Cecily. He could not believe it was *really* her as he drifted in the past:

*   *Alton opened his hotel room door, and Cecily was standing there in a blonde wig that hang to her shoulders, knee-length, black boots, red miniskirt, white blouse, and a fake fur wrap. His heart melted because he felt she was the most beautiful woman he had ever seen in his life. "David?" she asked.*

"Yes. You must be Sissy."

"Yes."

"Come in," he said stepping aside to let her in. As she passed him, his nature immediately began to rise. Closing the door, he said, "You are a very, <u>very</u> beautiful woman, Sissy."

"Thank-you," she said removing her fur wrap, and closing in on him, by putting her arms around his neck.

"Wait a minute, Sissy," he said taking her hands off him. "Can we talk?"

"<u>Talk</u>?" she exploded.

"Yes, talk," he laughed. "I want to get to know you."

"<u>Know</u> me?" she exploded again. "Well, this is a first."

"Excuse me."

"This is your first time?"

"It shows, huh?"

"Yeah, a little," she chuckled. "David, you're handsome and all that, but if I don't bring Spencer at least five hundred dollars back, he'll go into fits, so I can't stay here all night talking."

He reached into his pocket, opened her hand, and placed a wad of bills in it, and said, "Is that enough?"

She counted slowly, then said, "This is a <u>thousand</u> dollars."

"Is it enough to keep you off the streets tonight?"

"What'd you want to talk about?" she asked smiling big.

"You can start by taking off that wig."

"You don't like my wig?" she laughed.

"No," he laughed with her.

"I'll be right back," she said then exited into the bathroom. When she returned Alton couldn't believe how beautiful she was without all the makeup and wig. Her beautiful black hair was stunning.

"You are <u>so</u> beautiful," he said softly.   *

"Honey!" Lillian called bringing Alton back to the present.

"Yes, baby."

"Where is your mind?" she laughed. "I bet it's on business!"

"No. Nothing in particular," he smiled, feeling a little embarrassed as his eyes locked with Cecily's, and *she* had a feeling she knew what he was thinking. So, he *did* remember her.

****

After dinner, they went into the den again, to have their coffee. Soon Gracie entered and said, "Mrs. Carter, Wanda' s bath is ready."

"Mommy, can I stay up a little longer, since we have company?" Wanda begged.

"Honey, you have school tomorrow," smiled Lillian. "We're here to stay. You'll see a lot more of Aunt Cecily and Uncle Isaac. Now say good-night."

The child pouted as she went to Cecily and received a hug. Then she went to Isaac and received a hug. Next, she shuffled over to Alton and received a double hug, a kiss, and some tickles. Lastly, little Wanda was in a good enough mood to give her mother a hug. Then she skipped out with Gracie.

"Isaac, Lillian tells me you're an architect," Alton said.

"Yes, I have a small company," Isaac replied modestly.

"I've heard of your company," Alton added. "Your reputation has preceded you. You're very modest."

"Thank you," chuckled Isaac. "I hope."

"It has been all good, I assure you," Alton chuckled slightly. "I admire a man who can build a business on his own. My company was handed to me by my father just before he died. But he built it, all by himself."

"What business is that?" Isaac wanted to know.

"Carter Construction Company."

"Now, your reputation has preceded you," Isaac said. "A very reputable company."

"Thank-you," replied Alton. "I must admit I was a little leery about moving here because the town is so small." Chuckling, he added, "Who in the hell ever heard of Poka, California?"

"That's true," Isaac laughed also. "But, since it's so close to LA, it does quite well."

"All right, Fellows, enough shop talk," Lillian interrupted. "Alton, why don't you show Cecily around, to get better acquainted? And Isaac and I can get to know each other. We *are* going to be neighbors."

Cecily's eyes stretched wide, as Alton agreed, "That's a splendid idea."

"It's getting rather late," Cecily spoke quickly as her heart pounded so hard, she thought everyone could hear it. "Maybe we should be on our way. We have to work tomorrow."

"Nonsense. It's early." Lillian insisted. "Run along. Alton doesn't bite."

"Shall we?" Alton stood, extending a hand to Cecily. She knew she was trapped, so she reluctantly stood slowly without taking this hand, and he led her out.

****

Alton and Cecily walked in his huge, paneled home office, and he closed the door. They just stood, staring at each other for a while. Then, he finally took a deep breath and said very softly, "Sissy, I...I don't know what to say. I thought I would never see you again."

"Likewise," she squeezed out, almost to choked up with emotional tears to speak.

"Can I get a hug?" he asked very weakly, extending his arms, and she surrendered, so they held each other so tight, she could feel the blood rushing through her body, and her tears flowed softly down her face.

****

"So, Isaac, why don't you and Cecily have children?" Lillian asked. "I know Cecily loves children, and you seem to also."

"Well, actually, Lillian, we have been trying for some time now, but we just haven't conceived yet."

"Oh, I see. Well, as long as you're trying," she laughed.

"We are," Isaac said laughing with her. "We are."

****

Pulling away gently, Cecily wiped her tears with the handkerchief he gave to her and asked, "Why didn't you tell me your *real* name?"

"Why didn't you tell me *yours*?" he replied, and they both smiled. "Well, you know as well as I do in that line of business, nobody uses his or her *real* name."

"I had no idea you were Lillian's husband."

"And I had no idea you were the famous Dr. Cecily Wade," he said, then walked to her and lifted her head with his fingers. "Why didn't you tell me?"

"Would it have made a difference?"

"I guess not," he sighed deeply. "Gosh, you're beautiful. You've always been beautiful."

Changing the subject, she asked, "How've you been, Dav.... ag...Alton?"

"I've been fine, and you? How are you?"

"I'm okay."

"You know, I should be mad at you, young lady. The last time I saw you, you cost my father a lot of money, and *me* a lot of time, but I forgive you, pretty lady."

"I'm sorry about that, Alton. That was stupid of me. I was just so hurt. I was sure you felt about me like I felt about you. If I had known who your wife was, I would've known I couldn't compete."

"It had nothing to do with competition, but *commitment*, and I was very committed to my wife."

"Then why did you ever come to Spencer in the first place?"

"I used to travel a lot. What can I say? I got lonesome. I used to hear guys talk about Spencer's girls, so I tried it, met you, and got stuck."

"Who does Spencer have you fixed up with now when you're in New York?"

"Cecily, you might not believe this, but I haven't used Spencer's services since you left. The reason I used Spencer's services in the first place is so I wouldn't get involved, but I did. After you left, I realized how much I cared for you. I tried to find you, but Spencer said he didn't know where you were. And, the way he talked, if he ever finds you, you've better watch out."

"I'm not afraid of Spencer anymore," Cecily frowned. "But, thanks anyway."

"You're so beautiful."

"You said you tried to find me?" Cecily asked, avoiding his eyes.

"Yes, I did."

"Why?"

He lifted her head again with his fingers and said very softly, "Because I cared about you. And I knew I hurt you. I wanted to make sure you were all right." He paused then continued, "I wanted you to be mine. I wanted to know if you would have me, without my having to leave my wife. I wanted to take care of you, so you could get away from Spencer."

"You did?" Cecily asked carefully, and he nodded. "I loved you so much."

"And now?" he asked, and her eyes widened. "How do you feel about me now, pretty lady?"

* * * * * * * * *

Isaac stood and started for the bar. "Whiskey sour, Lillian?" he asked.

"That's right," she nodded. "It must've been miserable growing up without parents."

"It was, but I survived," he said, as he focused on Cecily and Alton walking in the beautiful, green, landscaped garden from the window. As Lillian talked, Isaac's attention had focused totally out the window as he saw another man take his wife in his arms and kiss her very passionately.

****

Breaking away gently from him, Cecily said, "No, Alton. Lillian is my best friend." She turned her back to him.

"That's unfortunate because we care for each other," he said swirling her around by her shoulders to face him. "Don't we?"

Wiping a tear from her face, Cecily squeezed out, "I will always love you, but I don't want to be hurt again."

"I will never hurt you."

"And you can never offer me anything, but a hotel room, when you can get away," she insisted. "Is it fair for us to play with other peoples' lives? We're both married to wonderful people. How can we even <u>think</u> about hurting them?"

He dropped his head slowly and took a few steps away from her. He blew hard, then turned again to face her and said softly, "You're right. I'm so sorry. I've missed you so. I guess I just got caught up in finally seeing you again and not wanting to lose you this time. I'm sorry. I was just selfish. Can you forgive me?" She nodded slowly, then he sighed deeply. "Let's go back inside. The temperature is dropping, and it's getting late."

"I'm glad we had this talk."

Nodding, he said, "Me, too."

Chapter 3

"Maria, you're pregnant," Cecily said to the teenager that sat in front of her desk.

With falling tears, the girl squeezed out, "My mother will kill me."

"I doubt it," Cecily chuckled. "Where is your mother? I wanted her to be here."

"I'm sorry, Dr. Wade, but I didn't tell her. I knew I was going to get bad news today."

"You do need to tell the father of this baby as soon as possible. Maybe he can help you."

"He's in the army. He's stationed in Germany," she wept. "It was my *first* time."

"Do you think he'll want the baby?"

"Oh, yes! Very much, but I know my parents won't let me have it. They will make me get an abortion or give it up for adoption."

Cecily walked to the girl, bent down to her, and pushed Maria's hair out of her face. "If you want your baby, Maria, then keep it," the doctor spoke softly but firmly. "Don't let your parents make you do something that you don't want to do. Fight them to keep your baby. At one time it was *their* decision, but the laws have changed. You have rights over your own body!"

"But if I keep the baby without their consent, they won't help me with it. How will I take care of it? I'm still in high school."

"I didn't say it would be easy. But if you really *want* your baby, fight for it, or you'll spend the rest of your life regretting it."

"I want to keep my baby," the girl wept. "I was adopted, and I wouldn't want my baby to grow up like me, wondering every day who my parents are and why they gave me away."

"I'm sure they would've been very proud of you, Maria."

"Until *now*."

"Everyone makes mistakes, Honey. The important thing is not to let your mistakes ruin your whole life," Cecily explained with a faraway look in her eyes, as she recalls the mistakes she made in the past. "Always remember, Maria, that everything you do in your life will always follow you. Never feel like you don't have a choice. Your past will always catch up with you, and if you have made bad choices, you have to pay the consequences. Try to never run up a debt so big that it will be difficult to pay."

"You're so understanding, Dr. Wade. I wish you were my mother," the sad girl replied. "I'll be only sixteen in July. I don't know what I can offer a baby."

Stroking the girl's hair gently Cecily said, "Think about it and follow your own heart."

****

Lillian walked in her house carrying an armful of groceries, shouting, "Gracie!"

"Right here, Mrs. Carter," Gracie called back running to help her.

"Chuckling, Lillian said, "I guess I got too much."

"I thought you were only getting a *couple* of things," Gracie laughed as they walked in the kitchen.

Laughing also Lillian said, "I did, too." She dropped a few grapes in her mouth, as Gracie began putting the groceries away. "Gracie, I passed a little church about ten blocks away. Do you know anything about it?"

"That's Pastor Graham's church. He's a very good person. I've only been there once, so I can't tell you much about it."

"It reminds me of my hometown church when I was a child. I think I'll ask Alton to go with me Sunday morning."

"From what I've heard, I think you'll like it."

****

Cecily sat at her desk, looking at some charts when Ruth entered. "Cecily, how did Maria take it?"

"Not too good," she said as a picture dropped on the floor. "That poor girl. She's so afraid."

Looking at the picture that she retrieved from the floor, Ruth asked, "Who is this in the picture with Maria?"

Receiving the picture Cecily laughed, "Are you crazy? Or just blind? That's *me* and the woman who raised me. Her name was Cotton."

"Cotton? That's an unusual name."

"Well, that wasn't her real name. Her real name was Christina, but very few people knew it."

"Cecily, I swear, if Maria was a little bit lighter, and her hair a little bit longer and straighter, she would be the splitting image of you at that age," Ruth added walking to the door. "I'll get Timmy Moore ready." She exited.

Cecily picked up the picture again and stared blankly at it, as she leaned back and drifted into the past:

*   *"I want to keep my baby!" young Cecily yelled to a distinguished looking, elderly, white couple.*

"Shut up!" the lady shouted as her hand flew back and landed on young Cecily's face. "We said you will give that baby up for adoption, and that's what you will do! I will not have you disgracing this family like your mother did! But, more importantly, I will not have you dropping out of school to take care of a baby! And I sure as hell will not take care of it for you!"

Crawling to the man, who sat silently in a chair smoking a pipe, Cecily pleaded hysterically, "Grandfather, please, don't let her give my baby away. If you love me at all, Grandfather, please, don't do this to me."

Looking down at his hysterical Granddaughter, he said softly, "Cecily, you have hurt your Grandmother and me very much. We can't let you destroy your future because of a mistake. We owe you that much. One day you will understand."

"I'm sorry I hurt you, Grandfather," she wept uncontrollably. "I made a mistake. Please don't punish my baby for it. I want this baby. I love it."

"And we love <u>you</u>. This is why we can't let you destroy your life."

Jumping up, Cecily screamed, "You just don't want me to disgrace the family! <u>She</u> said it!"

"Watch your tone of voice, young lady!" her Grandmother warned.

"I swear to God, if you give away my baby, I'll never speak to either of you again for as long as I live!" Cecily retaliated. "I'll run away, and you'll never see me again!" she jerked around and stormed out the room.

****

Cecily, Lillian, and Trudy walked into a huge elegant hotel. "Are you sure Rocky's staying here, Cis?" Trudy asked.

"Yes. My uncle's wife runs this hotel. I heard her telling my folks that Rocky is staying here," explained Cecily.

"How do we get his room number?" Lillian wanted to know.

"Wait here," Cecily said as she strolled towards the counter.

"May I help you?" the lady asked, looking over small, oblong, wire-framed eyeglasses.

"My Aunt Janet said Rocky Simpson would give me his autograph," Cecily lied. "I was so excited when she told me I forgot to get the room number."

"Mrs. Allen is <u>your</u> aunt?" the lady asked raising an eyebrow.

"Yes."

"What's your name?"

"Cecily Allen," she said taking out her wallet. "I have identification."

"One moment," the lady said picking up the telephone receiver. "Mrs. Allen, I'm sorry to disturb you, but I have a young girl out here who says she's your niece." She paused. "Cecily Allen." Pause. "Yes, Ma'am." She hung up the phone, then looked at Cecily, with the biggest, friendliest smile she could muster, and said, "She'll be right out." Cecily went back to join her friends.

"Aunt Janet is coming out," she said nervously wringing her hands. "I don't know what to tell her."

"Just tell her that..." Trudy started but stopped when they saw an elegantly dressed young Caucasian woman walking towards them, in a two-piece, pin-striped, teal green Vay DeMills suit.

"Hi, Aunt Janet."

"Hello, Cecily," she spoke softly, sweeping a mass of reddish blonde curls out of her thin face then looked at the other girls. "Hello, girls." They greeted the woman shyly. "What's up, Cecily?"

"Aunt Janet, I need a big favor," Cecily said with a trembling voice. "I need to see Rocky Simpson."

Sighing deeply, she spoke with a sweet smile, "Sweetheart, you know I can't let you or any other teenager bother Mr. Simpson."

"Aunt Janet, it's very important," Cecily pleaded. "I'll leave your name out of it."

"What's this all about, Cecily?"

Cecily walked away a little, and the lady followed her. She turned Cecily around by her shoulders to look in her beautiful sad face. "I'm pregnant, and the father is Rocky Simpson. He doesn't know yet, and my Grandparents want me to put the baby up for adoption." Cecily blurted out with a tear rolling down her face.

"Oh, honey," the sympathetic lady said pulling Cecily in her caring arms. "When will you young girls learn what these celebrities are all about?"

Holding up and looking her aunt in the face, Cecily pleaded, "Will you help me, Aunt Janet?"

Aunt Janet took another deep breath then said softly, "He's in suite 8J, and you didn't hear that from me."

Smiling big Cecily nodded and said, "Thank you, Aunt Janet."

Janet rubbed Cecily's head lovingly and said, "Good luck, sweetheart."

"Thanks, Aunt Janet," Cecily said then gave the lady a big hug. As the girls walked away, the lady sympathetically shook her head slowly.

****

Cecily, Lillian, and Trudy stopped at the door of Rocky's suite. "How do I look? " Cecily asked.

"Oh, knock on the damn door!" scowled Trudy, as she pounded on the door herself. Suddenly the door flew open and Clarence was standing there towering over them.

"Hi, Clarence," Cecily smiled. "Remember me? I'm Cecily."

"Beat it, Kids!" he barked starting to close the door, but Cecily stopped him, by putting her foot in the doorway.

"Where is Rocky?" she demanded. "He'd want to see me."

"Listen, kid, if I don't know you, Rocky don't."

"He <u>does</u> know me!" Cecily demanded with tear-filled eyes. "I want to see Rocky!"

Suddenly Trudy kicked the man's shin, and Cecily flew pass him, into the suite, followed by the other two girls. "Rocky!" she called.

"Wait a minute, kid," the huge man protested, limping into the suite also, but Cecily was not to be reasoned with. She was determined to find Rocky, so she burst into the bedroom, followed by her friends. The girls froze abruptly in their tracks because the vision that focused in their eyes was more than they had ever expected to see.

Rocky sat in a chair, at a table, stark naked, with a naked Caucasian woman asleep in the bed. That didn't shock the girls as much as seeing what he was doing. A rubber tubing was tied around his arm, and he was carefully injecting a needle into his puffed-up vein. Various powders and other drug addicts' paraphernalia were spread about on the table. He was oblivious to the girls' entrance. After his deed was done, he dropped his head back slowly to gather the effect. Tears burned Cecily's eyes as Lillian tried to pull her out the room, but she would not bulge. After a moment Rocky focused on the girls for the first time. "What you doing here?" he blurted out. "Where the hell is Clarence?!"

"I thought you loved me," Cecily squeezed out weakly in tears, as Clarence entered, still limping.

"I called security," Clarence announced as the sleeping woman opened her eyes and focused on the group. She pulled the covers over her exposed body slowly, turning red with shame.

Walking to the singer, Cecily said softly, "Rocky, I'm pregnant. I was hoping you could help me. My Grandparents want to give our baby away."

"Do I know you?" he squeezed out, looking at her through squinting, glossy eyes.

"Yes," Cecily insisted. "You're the only man I've ever been with. I thought I was special to you."

Shaking his head slowly, he said weakly, "I'm sorry, I don't remember."

"Rocky's sterile," Clarence spoke. "He can't have any kiddies. And, if you try to go public with this, you'll be highly embarrassed."

Looking at the huge man, Cecily clenched her teeth and said, "Go to hell! I know Rocky is the father of my child! You can say whatever you want! Don't worry about your precious star. I won't go public! He's going to die soon enough anyway, if you continue to stand by and do nothing to save him, you blood-sucking, son of a bitch!" Three security guards burst into the room.

"What's the problem, Mr. Simpson?" one of them asked.

"Please see these girls out," Clarence insisted.

"We're going," Cecily said weakly, staring at the man she had loved with all her heart, and now she wondered why. As she slowly walked out, Lillian

and Trudy followed.

When the girls reached the steps of the hotel, Cecily's legs buckled under her, so Lillian and Trudy struggled to get her to a bench. She fell on Lillian's shoulder in hysterical sobs. The two girls could do nothing else but cry with their grief-stricken friend, for they felt her pain as well.

****

"Push, Cecily, push!"   A nurse yelled as sweat popped out of Cecily's forehead as she pushed for the final time, exposing her baby to the outside world.   "Good girl."

Cecily held her head up to see her baby, and the nurse was wrapping it up to take it out, and Cecily asked, "What is it?"

"We're not allowed to say," the nurse said then quickly took the baby out.

"No, please don't take my baby away!"

"Please stay calm, Cecily," the doctor said as he finished stitching her up.

"Please let me see my baby," Cecily cried hysterically.

Patting her on the shoulder, the doctor said, "It'll be all right."   Then he walked to the door. "I'll check on you later." He left.

Cecily melted to the bed crying hysterically, while a nurse came to her bed and began wiping her face. Cecily pushed the lady away. "Cecily," she whispered. "Shhh" Cecily looked at the caring lady. "It was a girl." she said focusing on Cecily's sad, tear-filled eyes. "Your baby was a girl."

"A little girl," Cecily squeezed out then burst into tears again. "A little girl." Cecily's attention fell on a wall calendar and the month of July was shown, with the number eighteen circled. ★

The picture dropping to the floor, out of Cecily's hand, brought her back to the present. She wiped her tears, opened Maria's file and searched for the birthday. July 18th hit her in the face like a ton of bricks. "No. It can't be," she whispered then dropped the file, in a daze. She covered her mouth and squeezed out, "Oh, my God! My baby." Wails of tears trickled down her face as she repeated, "My baby. My baby."

When Cecily regained her composure, she picked up the telephone and dialed a number. "Hello," Lillian said on the other end.

"Lil, the most incredible thing just happened."

"What is it?"

Taking a deep breath, Cecily said, "I just found my daughter." Lillian was speechless. "Lil, did you hear me?"

"Yes," she replied finding her voice. "When? Where?"

"She's a patient of mine."

"Are you sure, Cis?"

"Pretty sure, but how can I find out for *sure*?"

"Do you know the name of the adoption agency that handled the case?"

"Addison. I tried to find something out before about my daughter, but they wouldn't tell me anything."

"You just might be in luck, Cecily. Alton did some work for them, and I know some people there."

"Oh, Lil, that's terrific!"

"Hang tight. I'll call you right back."

"She was born..."

"Cis, I know when she was born. I'll never forget it. That was the day you ran away, and we thought we were never going to see you again," Lillian reminisced. "Talk to you later. Bye." The two women hung up, and Cecily leaned back in her chair and drifted into the past again:

*   *Young Cecily pulled on her clothes as fast as she could, tossing the hospital nightgown aside. The only clothes she had was what she had worn into the hospital: panties, bra, sneakers, blue jeans and a blouse. She didn't even have a hair bow, so she braided her long hair into one cornrow braid and let it hang to the center of her back. Then she found a rubber band on the floor to secure the end. She looked in her purse and counted only ninety-eight dollars and some small change. She peeked out the door and saw a nurse with her back turned, so she dashed out. She didn't know where she was going, because she couldn't get far on ninety-eight dollars, but she did know one thing for sure; that she never wanted to set eyes on her grandparents ever again for the rest of her life. <u>That,</u> she was certain of!*

****

Cecily went to the bus terminal and bought a ticket to New York City. She wanted to get as far away from Phoenix as she could.   She wanted to go even further than New York, but she didn't have much money.

****

After days of being cramped on that stuffy, smelly bus, Cecily finally arrived in New York City. When Cecily stepped off the bus, she trembled with nervous jitters.   A man dressed in a loud, burgundy suit and a matching hat approached her. "Hiya, Baby. Lost?" He said smiling big exposing a big gap between his two front teeth. Cecily shook her head slowly. "I'm Freddie. Come with me and I'll make all your dreams come true."

"Hey, Freddie, give the kid a break," a lady's strong voice yelled. Cecily looked into the face of a flashy, high stepping lady. Her skin was a dark chocolate color, with deep red rouge emphasizing her cheeks, and deep red lipstick caressing her big, full lips. She wasn't a pretty lady, but Cecily thought she was very attractive. A short, tight, brown, leather miniskirt emphasized every curve of her shapely body. The bright auburn natural wig bathed her head like a gleaming crown.

"What's happening, Cotton," Freddie chuckled exposing all thirty-twos.

"Give the kid a break. She just got offa the damn bus," Cotton insisted.

"Spencer won't get her, Cotton. I saw her first."

"Nobody going to <u>get</u> her," the woman defended the young girl.   "She

here visiting me." Cecily couldn't help but stare at the woman who was obviously trying to help her. But why? She didn't need anybody's help. Least of all a <u>prostitute</u>. What did the woman want from her? She had heard about the streets of New York. Nobody did anything for you for <u>nothing</u>. Everything had a price. What was this woman's?

"Ah, come on, Cotton," he chuckled with disbelief dripping from his tone.

"No shit, Freddie. She my brother kid."

"How can she be your niece?! She's white!"

"She ain't no damn white, you blind mutherfucker!" Cotton continued to lie, and then she focused on Cecily. "You a'righ', Honey?" Cecily nodded slowly, still wondering why this lady was trying to help her. "Cum on, Honey, let's git a bite to eat." She put her arm around Cecily's shoulder, and they walked away, leaving Freddie standing scratching his head.

****

Cecily and Cotton walked into a little cafe with rust and food stained concrete floors; curtains hanging off the windows from the holes, beer stains, and ground in dirt; and broken chairs leaning on tarnished tables. Cecily frowned as they sat in a booth that could barely hold their weights because of the worn-out seats. "Hiya, Cotton," the gum popping, buckteeth, and pop-eyed, anorexic looking waitress said, holding a pad.

"Hiya, Josie."

Gazing at Cecily the waitress said,   "Spencer sure is breaking them in younger and younger."

"She ain't none of Spencer damn girls," Cotton defended. "She my niece from outta town." She noticed the woman's raised eyebrows, and Cotton snapped,   "Her mammy is white! Damn! Y'all some goddamn nosy ass mutherfuckers!" She looked at Cecily. "Wha' cha have, Kid?" Cecily was speechless. "Cum on! I ain't got all nigh'!"

"Burger," Cecily spoke softly.

"Bring the kid some fries with that, too, Josie, and me a cup of yore ole nasty coffee. Oh, and a soda for the kid, too."

"Sure thing, Cotton," the waitress said walking away, still popping her gum.

Finally retrieving her voice, Cecily asked softly,   "Why are you doing this for me?"

"Um! Proper littl' thang, ain't cha?" Cotton replied sarcastically. "What yore story?"

"What?"

"Well, it don't matter. Everybody got a story," Cotton said then took a deep breath. "Listen, kid, and listen good. I can tell you from a good family. Go back home. Wha'ever happened, forgit it, and take yore littl', half-breed ass home! Ther' ain't nothin' in these streets but trouble."

"I'll be all right."

"Hav' ya ever bin to New York City b'for', Kid?"

"Yes."

"On the <u>streets</u> of New York City?! Not in the <u>Waldorf</u>! Hav' ya ever bin out here with the pimps and the pushers? The dope heads, the prostitutes? The muggers? The rapists? The whole goddamn ugly mess? That's wha' I'm talkin' 'bout!" Cotton insisted, and Cecily dropped her head, as Josie brought their food. "I didn't think so!" Josie left. "Yore ol' man raped you?" Cecily's eyes widen.

"No!"

"Anybody slap you 'round?" Cotton asked again, and Cecily shook her head. "Then, go back home! You ain't ready for these here streets, Gal. You littl' rich kids kill me. As soon as you can't git yore way, you bail out."

"It wasn't like that."

"But you are a run-a-way?" she asked, and Cecily dropped her head again. "Listen, Kid. Take my advice and go home! Nothin' worse than these streets. If the pimps don't git cha, the pushers will!"

"I'm smart. That won't..."

"That won't happen to me. Yeah! Yeah! Yeah! That's wha' happen to other people. Dumb people! Stupid people!" Cotton said sarcastically. "That's wha' we <u>all</u> say. But, let me tell you somethin', Missy. When yore littl' half-white ass git hungry, and you <u>will</u> git hungry, you will do anythang for that dollar. And I do mean <u>anythang</u>!" She took a deep breath. "Go home, Kid!"

"It's not that simple. Not after what they did. I can't go back."

"You <u>can</u> go back. Swallow yore pride and go home. If you don't, one day yore'll wish you had," she said, as a man entered and focused on

Cotton, so she waved to him.   "Gotta go t' work, Kid." She opened her purse and took out some money, and then she opened Cecily's hand and placed the money in her sweaty palm. "I was you fifteen years ago, and I wish someone done this for me. I got tire'of tha' sonofabitch beating me, so I left South Carolina with the intentions of makin' it <u>big</u>, just to show the bastard somethin', and my damn Mammy, too, who stood by and let him beat me and my sister, for no damn reason. But, hell, she couldn't do nothing. He beat her black ass, too." She stood and smoothed her skirt down. "Go home, Kid. That's the best advice I can give ya. <u>Go home!</u>"

****

Cecily, dirty, uncombed hair, and desperate, ravaged through a trashcan, searching frantically for food. It has been a month now that she has been living on the streets, and *she didn't have any more money. She was starving, but she still refused to go home, because she knew without a doubt that her grandparents didn't want her. They hadn't even bothered to look for her. They never loved her. She was just an obligation they thought they had because she was their daughter's child. Oh, how she hated them. She wanted to call Lillian or Trudy for money, but she knew their funds were very limited. She was searching for food so hard; she didn't hear two men walk up behind her. "Hey!" One man yelled, causing Cecily to jump so hard she bumped her head on the lid of the can. "Wha'cha doing in our can?" He spit a puddle of tobacco juice out of his mouth and wiped the drippings off his chin with the back of his hand, exposing a mouth full of decayed teeth and numerous empty tooth sockets.*

"I'm sorry," she tried to explain. "I didn't know it was yours. I'm very hungry."

"She a pretty littl' thing," the other man said behind a beard that was as unruly as his appearance.

"Hey littl' lady, we ain't had none in a while. Now, you be good to us, and we be good to you," the first man added as they walked to her slowly.

"Leave me alone," Cecily insisted backing away, as the men towered over her. She became very hysterical, as the men began ripping her clothes off, as she fought and screamed, while they giggled. When her breasts were fully exposed, one man savagely squeezed and fondled them, while the other man tore off her pants, forcing her to the dirty, urine-soaked, wet ground. One man pinned her down while the other man zipped his pants down when, suddenly, they froze in their tracks at the sound of a gunshot.

"You better put tha' wrinkled up dick back in yore stinking ass pants, you low-life, son-of-a-bitch, b'for' you be picking it up off tha' goddamn groun'," a lady's voice demanded, and Cecily looked up and saw Cotton behind her tears, standing there pointing a gun in their direction. She dropped her head back on the ground and continued to cry.

"Please don't shoot!" the first man begged, then the men took off so quickly; the last Cotton saw of them was the spot where they were standing. Cotton went to Cecily and helped her up.

"I though' I tole you to git yore littl' half-white ass home!"

"I couldn't," Cecily squeezed out in between tears.

"So, <u>this</u> is better than <u>home</u>?" Cotton added sarcastically, and all Cecily could do is cry. "You must have some hellava home life, kid." She took a deep breath. "I swear, yore jest as stubborn as I was fifteen years ago." She helped Cecily find her torn clothes and put them back on.

****

Cotton and Cecily walked into a dilapidated building, as people socialized everywhere on the outside. Some were drinking, some were snorting cocaine, some were dancing, and some were kissing, but everybody seemed to be in a world of his or her own. Cotton took Cecily into a small apartment, which was modestly decorated with cheap furnishings, but it was very clean and tidy. "It ain't much, kid, but it's home," Cotton spoke. "You can crash here until you decide to take yore ass home."

*Grabbing Cotton and squeezing her tight, Cecily exploded smiling big, "Oh, thank you, Cotton! Thank you! Thank you! Thank you!" **

The ringing of the buzzer brought Cecily back to the present. She pushed it and said, "Yes, Cindy."

"Mrs. Carter's on line two."

"Thanks, Cindy," she said then picked up the telephone. "Lil, what did you find out?"

"I went down there and talked to a friend," Lillian said then paused.

"And?"

"Are you sitting down?"

"You mean...?"

"Yes. That's exactly what I mean," Lillian said then took a deep breath. "You were right. Maria is definitely your daughter." Cecily was stunned to speechless. "Cis, did you hear me? Maria is the daughter that you were forced to give up fifteen years ago."

****

"Maria!" a lady called entering a pink bedroom with stuffed animals and doll babies on a canopy bed for decoration. The tall lady looked around the room, and then as she started out the door, she focused on a note taped to the mirror. She picked it up and read aloud, "Mom, I know you will be very disappointed in me. I'm pregnant and I must take care of it myself. I am at the clinic getting an abortion. I will see you tomorrow. I hope you can one day forgive me. I love you and Dad. Maria." She stood there with her mouth still open from shock, and then suddenly she ran out the room, shouting, "Sam!"

****

With uncontrollable tears rolling down her face, Cecily squeezed out,

"Lil, are you sure?"

"Yeah, Kiddo. I'm positive. Are you all right?"

"This is just so incredible. I have worried about my little girl ever since she's been in the world, and all the time she was right near me, and I didn't know," she cried hard now. "I didn't know, Lil. I didn't know."

Wiping her own tears Lillian asked, "What're you going to do, Cecily?"

"Taking a deep breath Cecily said, "I have to tell her, but I don't know how or when."

"Well, think about it and pray about it. I'm sure you'll do the right thing."

"I have to tell her soon. She's pregnant, Lil."

"Pregnant?!" Lillian exploded.

"Yeah, and she's so afraid. I want to be there for her."

"You're going to be a grandmother at thirty?!"

Laughing and crying simultaneously, Cecily said, "I guess I am. It's only fair since I was a mother at fifteen." They laughed together. "Thanks, Lil. I owe you," she added reaching for a Kleenex.

"No need to thank me. I'm glad I could help."

"I'll call you later," Cecily said, and they hung up. Cecily leaned back in her chair. "Oh, God, my baby. My precious little baby girl." She sat deep in thought for a while, then she held up and buzzed Cindy.

"Yes, Cecily."

"Cindy, call Maria and have her to come in tomorrow, please."

"Sure, Cecily," Cindy said. "And, Cecily, Mrs. Carlton's on line one."

"Thanks, Cindy," Cecily said picking up the receiver.   "Mrs. Carlton, hello."

"Dr. Wade, Jimmy's sick!" the hysterical mother blurted out in tears. "I brought him to Johnston Memorial!"

"Calm down, Mrs. Carlton. I'll on my way."

****

"We're looking for our daughter, Maria Carmichael. Is she here?" the lady exploded to the receptionist behind the desk.

"Calm down, Gloria," the tall two-hundred-pound man said putting his arm around his wife.

"We are not allowed to give out information on patients, Ma'am."

"I don't give a damn what you're not allowed to do!" the lady yelled. "If my daughter is here, you've better get *someone* who can help me, or I'll sue every damn person in this place!"

"One moment, please," the receptionist said, as she slowly picked up the telephone. "Dr. Kirkpatrick, I need your help out here, please."

"Honey, please, calm down."

"Sam, what made Maria do such a fool thing like this? An *abortion*! Is she crazy?" she said as the doctor walked to them, and the receptionist nodded her head to indicate the couple.

"Hello, I'm Dr. Kirkpatrick. What can I do for you?"

"I want to know if my daughter is here?" asked Mrs. Carmichael, wiping her tears.

"What makes you think your daughter is here?"

"Our daughter left a note telling us she was at the clinic getting an abortion," Mr. Carmichael said.

"She's fifteen," continued Mrs. Carmichael. "We want to stop her from doing a fool thing like that."

"There're dozens of clinics in LA," the doctor replied. "Why do you think she's here?"

"This was the closest to our house," answered Mr. Carmichael.

"I see," Dr. Kirkpatrick said then turned to the receptionist. "May I have the patient list for today, Miss Wallace." She obliged. "What is your daughter's name? "

"Maria Carmichael," the mother blurted out.

The doctor examined the list then said, "I'm sorry. She didn't come here."

"Oh, God, where is she?" Mrs. Carmichael cried.

****

Cecily exploded into the emergency room, where Jimmy lay, surrounded by doctors and nurses. "Is an OR ready?" she asked.

"Yes, Dr. Wade. Number three," an attending doctor replied.

"I've got to remove his tonsils right away," she said looking down the boy's throat. "Let's move!"

****

"Amy, I'm scared."

"Maria, there's nothing to be afraid of," a girl whispered back, as she and Maria sat in a basement with three other girls. "He did me a couple months ago."

"Is he a doctor?"

"Yes, but he lost his license, so he can't practice legally," Amy said. "It's still not too late to change your mind. But nobody else will do it since you're a minor."

"No. I'm not going to change my mind."

"Maria Carmichael," a nurse called. "The doctor is ready for you."

****

"Hi, Honey," Lillian said meeting Alton at the door with a kiss.

"That's what I call a *real* welcome home," he smiled, kissing her again, this time much longer. "Umm, where's Wanda?"

"Hi, Daddy," Wanda exploded in, separating them.

"Hold that thought," Alton said to Lillian smiling, as he picked Wanda up. "How's Daddy's girl?"

"Fine."

"Oh, Honey, I forgot to tell you. I visited that church I told you about.

The Pastor and his wife are very nice. I told them we'd visit Sunday. Is that okay with you?"

"That's fine, Baby. Anything you want," he said then attacked Wanda with tickles.

****

Cecily walked out of the operating room pulling off her surgical mask, and Mr. and Mrs. Carlton ran to her. "How is he, Doctor?" exploded Mrs. Carlton.

"He's fine," Cecily smiled. "He went through it like a champ."

"Oh, thank God!" Mrs. Carlton said falling in her husband's arms. "Thank God!" Then she looked at Cecily. "Thank you, Dr. Wade." She squeezed Cecily's hands lovingly.

"He's in recovery. You're may go to his room and wait for him there, so that the first face he sees when he wakes up is yours," Cecily added.

"Oh, great," Mrs. Carlton said bubbling with excitement. "Come on, Dear."

"You go ahead, Sweetheart. I want to talk to Dr. Wade," Mr. Carlton said, and his wife nodded, then she rushed out. "I don't know what to say, Doctor."

"You don't have to say anything, Mr. Carlton."

"Can you ever find it in your heart to forgive me?"

"There's nothing to forgive. I understand completely."

"Thank you, Doctor."

Nodding Cecily said, "Go ahead and be with your wife, Mr. Carlton."

"When I think how my stupidity could have killed my son, I..."

"But it didn't," Cecily stressed, then she smiled. "It didn't."

"You're one hellava woman, Dr. Wade."

"Thank you, Mr. Carlton," she said then squeezed his hand. "Good night."

"Good night."

****

Cecily walked in her house slowly, as Isaac entered the room from the kitchen drinking a glass of tea. "Hi, Sweetheart," he said.

"Hi, Darling," she replied entering in his open arms, allowing their lips to caressed softly. "Baby, I have some incredible news. Sit down."

"Want some tea?"

"Not right now," Cecily said pulling him down beside her on the couch.

"Wow, this must be something big."

"It's bigger than big!"

"Sharing her excitement, he exploded, "Then tell me! What is it?"

"Do you remember that I told you when I was a teenager, I gave birth to a baby girl, and my grandparents forced me to give her up for adoption?"

"Yeah, when you were about fifteen."

"I found her," she said fighting to hold back the enthusiasm.

"What?"

"I found my baby!" Cecily screamed, letting it all go now, by jumping up and grabbing Isaac's hands, forcing him to his feet also. "I found my baby, Isaac! I found her!"

"That's great, Sweetheart!" he said sharing her enthusiasm, pulling her in his arms. "How did you find her?"

Holding off him she said, "It's a long story. Lillian knew somebody who knew somebody, and so on. But, get this, the incredible thing is that she's my patient! Can you believe it?! She's my patient!"

"Do I know her, Sweetheart?'

"Maria."

"Maria. Oh, yes. I remember her. I think I said once that she looked like you?"

"Yes, come to think of it, you did. That day I introduced you to her and her folks at the mall," she said finally calming down. "Isn't it great, Isaac!"

"Yes, Baby. It sure is. I'm so happy for you," he said pulling her in his arms again.

Sighing hard she added, "Maria is pregnant."

"She is?"

"Ugh-huh, and I be damned if I'll make her do what my grandparents made me do. I'm going to be there for my baby, Isaac."

"I know you will be, Sweetheart."

"Oh, God," she laughed. "I'm going to be a granny!"

"Well, you're the best looking granny I've ever seen," Isaac said, and they burst into laughter.

****

The door of the ambulance flew open, and the EMS workers yanked the gurney out the vehicle and dashed through the hospital emergency doors. Amy jumped out her car and ran in also. "We have a young girl here. Internal hemorrhaging," the EMS worker blurted out to the lady behind the desk.

"What happened?"

"Botched up abortion. We called ahead and told you we were on the way."

"What's her name?"

"Maria Carmichael," Amy spoke up with tears in her eyes.

"Take her to OR five. It's ready. The doctors are waiting," she said then focused on Amy, as they hurried off. "I need to ask you a few questions."

"Is she going to be all right?"

"I don't know. The doctors will examine her," she said. "I need to call her own doctor. Do you know who that is?"

****

That night Cecily went to bed with a smile on her face. She dreamed of Cotton, and the fun they had, playing in the park, running, laughing, racing, and laughing some more. Without her working attire on, Cotton was a very plain looking lady with her full lips and short, black hair. The ringing of the telephone brought Cecily and Isaac out of dreamland. Cecily picked up the receiver and mumbled, "Hello?" She paused. "Yes." Pause. "Oh, my God! I'll be right there." As Cecily hung up the phone, she jumped out of the bed, searching frantically for clothes.

"What's wrong?"

"It's Maria! She's in the hospital!"

"Hospital?! What's wrong with her?"

Cecily answered, "A botched up abortion with complications! Oh, Isaac, what if...?"

"Cecily, calm down," Isaac jumped up and grabbed for his clothes. "I'll drive you, baby. Just try to stay calm. Don't go expecting the worse."

****

"What wrong, Baby?" Alton turned over in bed and asked a tossing and turning Lillian.

"I can't sleep."

"Anything on your mind?"

"I was just thinking about Cecily and how incredible it is for her to find her daughter after all those years."

"Yeah, that's something all right," he said pulling her in his arms. "But it's nothing to lose sleep over."

"I know but…"

"But what?"

"I pray that everything is well with Cecily. I sense something is wrong."

"My wife, the psychic."

"Not psychic, just saved, and when I can't sleep, God is telling me something."

"What do you think it is?"

"I don't know. Something about Cecily and her daughter," she said getting up.

"Where're you going?"

"I'm going to read a few scriptures in the Bible. I need to understand what God is telling me," she said walking out. "Go back to sleep, Baby."

"What time is it?" he asked, and she stopped at the door.

"10:10."

"Oh damn, I've got to meet Mr. Clytelle at the airport."

"*This* late?"

"His flight comes in at 11:00," he said getting up.

"He must be an important client. The boss *himself* is meeting him."

"*Very*!"

"So, I guess you'll be out all night."

"I'm hoping he'll be fine once I take him to the hotel," he said pulling on his clothes. "I hope his flight is on time."

"Mommy!" they heard Wanda scream, and they dashed out together.

****

Just as Cecily charged into the emergency room, she witnessed Maria's heart monitor blanking out then flat lining. "Noooo!" Cecily yelled as she seized the paddles from the attending doctor. "Clear!" An electric shock wave shot through the girl's body causing it to jump but with no reviving response. "Clear!" The girl's body jumped again with no response. Cecily dropped the paddles and began rhythmically pushing in the girl's chest. "Come on, Maria. You can do it. Come on, Baby." Cecily chanted to herself over and over, while the emergency room staff stared at her.

"Cecily, she's gone," a doctor finally said.

"Noooo!"

"There was nothing we could've done. She came too late," he explained.

"Noooo!" Cecily yelled again. "Noooo!" She burst into hysterical tears; simultaneously, her legs gave out on her and buckled under her body, as she hit the floor, witnessing only an unconscious darkness.

****

"Hello?"

"Cindy, Isaac."

"Oh, hi, Isaac. What's up?"

"Cindy, Cecily won't be in for a few days. Will you get Dr. Smiley to cover for her?"

"Sure, Isaac. What's wrong?"

"You had a patient named Maria."

"*Had?*"

"Maria just died."

"*What? Died?*"

"She had a botched-up abortion."

"Isaac, you're *kidding!*"

"I wish I were."

"Did they get the person who did it?"

"I don't know."

"Where's Cecily?"

"She's in the doctor's lounge."

"Oh, my God. Is there anything I can do?"

"Just get in touch with Dr. Smiley and call Ruth."

"Sure, Isaac."

"Thanks, Cindy," he said then hung up.

****

"Are you all right, Honey?" Cecily heard a voice ask, as she opened her eyes slowly and focused on her husband's worried face.

"Where am I?"

"You're in the doctors' lounge at the hospital," he explained. "You fainted."

With memories coming back to her, Cecily's eyes swelled with tears, and Isaac pulled her in his arms. "Isaac, she never knew. She never knew. My baby never knew I was her mother. She never knew how much I wanted her and how much I loved her. I hate them for killing her, Isaac. They never loved her because she wasn't their child. Maria said they would make her do something like this, and they did, and now my baby is gone. I *hate* them. They killed my baby." She cried hysterically on Isaac's shoulders.

"You don't mean that, Cecily. You're just upset."

Jerking away from her husband, with tears streaming down her sad face, she insisted, "I do! I hate them. They killed her!"

"You're upset, Baby. You're not thinking clearly."

"I know exactly what I'm saying!" she insisted again. "You don't have children. You couldn't possibly understand!"

"I *do* understand, Cecily."

"No! You don't!" she demanded, jumping to her feet. "How could you?!"

"Because..." he paused wondering if this could be the right time to tell Cecily about the child he fathered with Cindy, and he decided he just couldn't keep it from her any longer. "Because...I *do* have a child?"

"What?"

Standing and walking to his wife, Isaac said softly, "I have a daughter, and she's five years old."

"*Five*?" Cecily said breathless, not believing what she was hearing. "You had a child with another woman *during* our married?" He nodded slowly, as the door opened and Mrs. Carmichael exploded in, followed by her husband.

"Dr. Wade, where is my daughter?" she asked. "How is she?"

"You don't know?" she asked softly.

Taking a note from her pocket, she handed it to Cecily, and said "Maria left us this note, and we've been trying to find her all night to keep her from doing something *crazy*. Then we got a call from Amy telling us she was here. What is going on?"

"You really didn't know. I thought..." Cecily stopped because she realized she had been mistaken. These people loved her daughter. They were not responsible for this tragedy. She took the lady's hands and said very softly, "Mrs. Carmichael, Maria's abortion was not good." She took a deep breath as the tears ran down her face.

"What's wrong?" the lady asked cautiously. "What happened? Where is Maria?"

"Maria...Maria didn't make it," Cecily squeezed out still crying hard, but trying to keep as calm as she could.

"*What*?!" Mrs. Carmichael squeezed out.

"Maria is dead," added Mr. Carmichael.

"*Noooo!*" the lady screamed as her knees buckled under her, and her husband caught her before she hit the floor. "Oh, God, no!" she cried. "Not my baby! Not my child!" She and her husband cried together, as he helped her to the couch.

"Did they get the person who murdered our daughter?" Mr. Carmichael asked in his own torment.

"I don't know," Cecily said wiping her face. "Amy was with her. She is out in the waiting room area. Maybe she can tell you something."

"Amy was with Maria?!" Mrs. Carmichael said, and Cecily nodded, then Mrs. Carmichael jumped up and ran out followed by her husband.

Putting his hand on her shoulder, Isaac asked, "Are you all right, Honey?"

Jerking away she yelled, "What do you think, Isaac?! What do you think?!" Her tears were uncontrollable. "I just found my only child, that I was forced to give away fifteen years ago, and at the same time, I learn that my husband has not only been unfaithful to me, but he has a *child* as well! How in the hell do you *think* I feel!" She paused, dropping on the couch. "Why *now*? Why did you have to tell me *now*?"

"I just couldn't keep it from you any longer," he said reaching out to touch her, but she jerked away from him again. "I'm so sorry, Baby. "It was...." Isaac started, but Cecily jumped up and was out the door before he could finish. He dropped down in a chair and held his head in his hand as he took a deep breath. Then he regained his composure and ran after her. When Isaac reached the outside, he saw Cecily driving away. He called her name, but she did not stop. He didn't know if she had heard him or not. But it really didn't matter. All he knew was that she was hurting, and so was *he*.

****

Alton accompanied by two other men started out a bar and grill, when he looked up, and out of the corner of his eye, he spotted Cecily sitting at the bar. "It's nice doing business with you gentlemen," he said shaking the two men's hands. "We'll be in touch soon." When the men left, Alton walked over to Cecily and stood behind her. "Beautiful ladies shouldn't drink in bars alone."

"Get lost," she snapped in a drunken slur without looking at him.

"Is that any way to treat a neighbor?" he smiled, as she turned and looked in his face.

"David...I mean Alton!"

"In the flesh," he said taking a seat next to hers. "Are you alone?"

"*Quite* alone," she stressed. "Bartender, another one."

"Sissy, let me take you home."

"Home? Hah!"

"What's wrong?" he asked blocking her mouth from the glass with his hand, and then he took the glass from her and placed it on the counter. "Talk to me, Pretty Lady. What's going on?"

Looking in his deep brown eyes, Cecily said very softly, "I still love you, David."

"*Alton*," he corrected. "And, no, you don't. You're just drunk." He chuckled. "Let me take you home."

"No, I'm not drunk," she said leaning very close to him. "Take me to a hotel, David. I want it to be the way it used to be."

"No, Sissy."

"You said you looked for me, David. Here I am. Take me. I'm yours."

Cecily downed the rest of her drink with one final gulp then stumbled up. Alton caught her, and then she proceeded out the door. Alton dropped some money on the counter then had to walk briskly to catch up with her. A man from a nearby table, stood up, folded a newspaper, and followed them. A camera was strapped around his shoulder.

****

"Mommy, where is daddy?" Wanda asked as Lillian gave her a spoonful of Tylenol.

"Daddy had to go to a meeting, Honey," Lillian said. "Your fever went up slightly, but you'll feel better soon. Come here, Sweetie." She pulled the child in her arms, sat in the rocking chair, and began singing Jesus *Loves Me*.

****

When Alton opened the hotel room, Cecily wildly attacked him with kisses and caresses as she pulled to undress him. "Sissy, don't," he said trying to stop her. "I didn't bring you here for *this*. I know you don't want to go home right now, so I brought you here to sober up and to talk."

"I don't want to talk, David. I want you to make love to me, like we used to do," she purred, taking off his shirt.

"No, Sissy," he said trying to resist, but she was much too aggressive, and he allowed her to zip his pants down. He surrendered under pressure and kissed her back.

"I love you, David."

"*Alton*, Sissy," he said finally finding the strength to break her hold on him. "My name is *Alton*. Not *David*."

"I know, baby, and I'm *Cecily*. Big deal."

"That's right. I'm sorry. *Cecily* it is."

Cecily began taking off her clothes now. "I want you, Alton. I want you like I've never wanted anyone before. Please, Baby, make love to me," she said kissing him again. It was hard, but Alton managed to pull himself away from her. "What's wrong, Baby? Don't you like me anymore?" The only thing she wore now was a big smile.

With one quick movement, Alton zipped up his pants, grabbed his shirt and started out the door, saying, "I'll be back."

"Alton!" she called, but he was gone.

Alton pulled on his shirt as he got on the elevator. He took a deep breath and tried to put *things* back in perspective. When the elevator stopped, he walked to the lobby, sat on the couch, dropped his head back and said aloud, "What in heaven's name am I going to do now?" He knew he wanted her. Oh, God, how he wanted her! She was so damn beautiful. He hadn't been unfaithful to Lillian since *Cecily*. Never even *wanted* to. And now he was confronted with the same situation. But, only, a little bit different this time. Lillian and Cecily were good friends. *Best* friends. How would he be able to look Lillian *and* Cecily in the eyes if he made love to Cecily now. It's hard enough as it is. But he had his pride. Even if he had wanted to have an extramarital affair, his wife's friends would definitely be off limits. And besides that, Cecily was drunk. He would not take advantage of a drunk woman, no matter how gorgeous she was. He would have to let Cecily sleep it off, then get her up and take her ass home. Suddenly he jumped up. He's got to call Lillian.

****

Isaac looked at twelve o'clock AM as he sat up in bed trying to read a book, but it was no use because his mind was on his wife. How could he have been so stupid. Telling her about a child he fathered during their marriage when she had just lost her own child. The child she has grieved over all her life. If only he knew where she was, he could apologize and explain to her what happened between Cindy and him. No matter what he could tell her, the fact of the matter was that he had still been unfaithful to her, and that he would have to live with and deal with, if she could only forgive him. He took a deep breath then looked at the clock again. Only three minutes had past, but it felt like an eternity. "Where are you, Cecily?" he said aloud. "Where in the hell are you?"

****

"Hello?"

"Hi, Baby."

"Alton, where are you?"

"Listen, Sweetheart. I'm going to have to stay over here tonight to finish up some business."

"Where?"

"The Hilton. How is Wanda?"

"She's asleep right now. I just laid her down. If I need you, I'll call you."

"See you in the morning, Sweetie."

"Love you."

"Love you, too, Baby."

"Bye."

"Bye," Alton said then hung up. He got back on the elevator. "Cecily should be sleep by now, and I can get some work done. I wonder what happened to her. I've never seen Cecily like this. Maybe she'll want to talk about it when she wakes up."

Alton walked into the room, and he was right. Cecily was lying on the bed fast asleep. He pulled the covers over her bare body then went to the table to do some work.

****

Isaac looked at the clock again. It was three o'clock AM. "Where the hell are you, Cecily?" he said to himself. Cecily wasn't answering her cell phone. He picked up the telephone and dialed.

"Hello?"

"Lillian, I'm sorry to call you so late, but I'm worried about Cecily. Have you seen her tonight?"

"No, Isaac. I haven't," she said. "Is everything all right?"

"I hope so, Lillian. Would you see if Alton has seen her?"

"He isn't here, Isaac. He's at a business meeting."

"Until three in the morning?"

"It's not unusual," she chuckled, and then she heard Wanda call her. "Listen, Isaac, I'm sorry to cut you off, but Wanda's calling me. She's been sick all night."

"I understand."

"Don't worry about Cecily. She's probably with a patient. You know how she is about her work."

"Yeah. That's true," Isaac said. "I hope Wanda feels better."

"Thanks," she said, and they hung up.

Isaac stared into space for a long time with his mind drifting back to the time when he witnessed his wife in Alton's embrace, in his neighbor's garden. He felt a sick pain in the pit of his stomach as he said aloud, "Alton isn't home either." An image of Cecily and Alton kissing in his garden appeared to Isaac again. "Are you with him, Cecily?" Isaac took a deep and concentrated breath then exhaled slowly. "Are you with *him*?!"

****

Cecily tossed and turned as she restlessly slept on the big, king-sized bed, while Alton slumbered on the thick, soft couch. Suddenly, Cecily jumped up screaming, "Cotton!" Awakened by the anguished sound Alton jumped to his feet, turned on the light, and rushed to the bed. He sat on the bed, pulled her in his arms, and cradled her like a baby.

"It's all right, Sweetheart," he soothed her. "It's all right."

Gently pulling away from him, Cecily stared in his beautiful, caring, brown eyes.   She blinked as she vigorously shook her head from side to side. "What's wrong?" he asked.

"David?" Cecily asked slowly, because she just knew she *had* to be still dreaming.

"Yes, Cecily, it's me, *Alton*."

Looking around she asked, "Where are we?" She put her hands on her head.

"The Hilton," he said then smiled. "Headache?"

"What happened?"

"What do you remember?"

"The last thing I remember is sitting in a bar, then everything else is a blur," she said trying to put everything together in her baffled mind, when she focused on her nude body. "Did we...?"

Chuckling he said, "No, we didn't. That's not my style to take advantage of an intoxicated woman."

"You've always been good to me, David. Thanks."

"Don't mention it, Pretty Lady," he smiled sweetly. "And, Cecily, please remember, my name is *Alton*, not *David*."

"I'm sorry. I keep forgetting."

"It's okay," he said starting to get up. "I better take you to get your car, so you can go home. Isaac must be worried sick."

"I don't care."

"What happened, Cecily?"

"He cheated on me, Alton. Isaac has a daughter five years old and never told me."

"How did you find out?"

"Oh, let me tell you," she chuckled sarcastically. "Tonight, of *all* nights, he breaks the news to me when I was already as low as I could get. In other words, he added *salt* to my wounds."

"Isaac seems like a pretty level-headed guy to me. This doesn't sound like him. How did he say it happened?"

"Oh, come on, Alton. We *know* how people have babies."

"Yes, but what did he say the circumstances were?"

"I don't give a fuck what the circumstances were. He *cheated* on me!"

"Cecily, you owe him the opportunity to explain what happened."

"I don't owe him a damn thing!"

"Cecily, you need to talk to your husband. Come on. Get dressed and let me take you to get your car, so you can go home."

Taking his hand, Cecily quickly changed the subject and asked softly, "Did you really try to find me, Dav... ugh, sorry...Alton?"

"Yes, I did."

"I can't believe that after all those years..." she chuckled, then shook her head and added, "Never mind."

"What?" he said then held her head up with his finger. "What were you going to say?"

Staring deep into his eyes she said softly, "That I'm still in love with you."

"Cecily, I… " he started, but she silenced him with a kiss on his soft, brown lips, and he kissed back willingly.

"I love you, Alton."

"You're so beautiful," he breathed in between kisses, as she helped him undress. Their lovemaking was sweet, tender, and passionately, then when it was over, he rolled over beside her, and guilt set in, so they both stared at the ceiling, speechless.

"I love you so much, Alton," Cecily finally broke the silence. "I haven't felt so completely satisfied by *any* man since the last time that we were together."

"Cecily, I wish you wouldn't say things like that," he insisted. "We can't afford to be in love. Too many people will get hurt."

"I love Lil with all my heart. God knows I do, but I can't help the way I feel about you. I fell in love with you long before I knew you were Lil's husband. I will *always* love you."

Getting out of the bed, Alton insisted, "Cecily, this can't happen again."

"I know," she agreed sadly. "Oh, God, how I know." She took a deep breath. "I would rather die than to hurt Lillian. She can never know what happened here… or how we feel about each other."

Chapter 4

Isaac sat reading the newspaper when Cecily walked in, noon the next day. "Where have you been?" he asked softly.   "I've been worried about you."

"I'm fine," she nonchalantly replied.

 Jumping up, he yelled,   "Where in the hell have you been all night, Cecily?! And why weren't you answering your cell phone?!"

"I got drunk and went to a hotel!" she yelled back. "And my cell phone battery died!"

"Alone?"

"What?'

"You heard me. Were you alone or was *Alton* with you?"

"What're you talking about?"

"You love him, don't you?" he asked, and she didn't answer. "I asked you a question."   She still didn't answer. "The night we had dinner with Alton and Lillian I saw Alton kiss you in the garden."

"You're *spying* on me, Isaac?"

"Don't play games with me, Cecily."

"You are a fine one to speak of playing games!" she yelled throwing her hands in the air. "You! A man I trusted with my heart!"

"I made a mistake. You wouldn't let me touch you!" he defended. "What in the hell was I supposed to do?! I have needs, too, Cecily!" He sobered and grew calm. "I didn't want her. I never wanted any woman but you, since the first day I laid eyes on you. But I just couldn't take your rejections any longer."

"So, you're trying to say it's *my* fault that you cheated?!"

"No, I'm not. I take full responsibility for what I did. I know it was wrong." He took a deep breath. "Do you know what it's like to be so in love with someone and wanting that person so badly, and to top it off, sleeping in the *same* bed with that person, but not being able to touch her? I went through hell, Cecily! And I didn't deserve that *then*, and I don't deserve it *now*! And I see the same thing is happening all over again. We haven't made love in months, and you won't talk to me about what's bothering you."

"Then, I guess it's time to look for your little whore again!" Cecily sarcastically replied.

"She's not a whore."

"Oh, you're defending the little tramp!"

"No, I'm not defending *anyone*. I'm just telling you, she's not a whore. She fell in love with me, but I didn't love her. I've never wanted anyone but you, Cecily," he said then took a deep breath. "Are you saying you can't forgive me?" She didn't answer. "That woman means nothing to me, but what about *you*? How do you feel about Alton?"

"Alton's my best friend's husband. How am I supposed to feel about him?"

"You know what I mean," he said then took a deep breath. He didn't know if he wanted to hear the answer, but he had to ask anyway. "Are you in love with Alton?"

****

"Hi, Baby," Alton said planting a kiss on Lillian's forehead while she was sitting at the breakfast nook.

"*Long* meeting," she sarcastically said putting the newspaper down.

"And I'm beat," he yawned.

"Is it starting all over again, Alton?"

"What?"

"You know what. The long business meetings. The weekend rendezvous. Is it starting all over again?"

"No. This was just something I had to do. That's all."

"I'm not stupid, Alton. I closed my eyes all the other times because I knew how much Wanda needed you, but I won't do that again."

Chuckling he said, "What are you talking about?"

"I'm talking about the *women*!" she insisted.

"There are no women."

"I don't know what brought you home that last time, and frankly, I don't even care. All I'm saying is that I won't stand for it again. So, if you have a little bimbo on the side, you've better get rid of her, and I mean *fast*!"

"You've better get a hobby, Lillian. Your mind is playing tricks on you," he chuckled.

But his laughter subsided abruptly when she added, "Is that lipstick on your collar in my *mind* as well?"

****

Cecily was confronted with a question that she knew she couldn't answer truthfully, without hurting her husband dearly, and she truly didn't want to hurt him, nor did she intend to hurt Lillian. She and Alton had vowed never to see each other again, so there was no need to tell the truth now. She loved Alton with all her heart, but she knew her love would never, *could* never be returned, and she had to admit, she cared an awful lot for Isaac. No. She didn't just care for him; she actually loved him, just not in the same way as she loved Alton. She couldn't let her marriage be destroyed by fulfilling a one-night fantasy. Isaac was asking her the same question again, "Cecily, are you in love with Alton?"

And she replied weakly, "No. I'm not in love with Alton." She turned away from him, so he couldn't see the truth in her eyes.

"Were you with him last night?"

"No. I was alone," she lied.

"How long have you known Alton?"

"I met him a long time ago, but I didn't know he was Lillian's husband then."

"You had an affair?" he asked, and she nodded slowly.

"But that was before I met you, Isaac."

"I see," he said then walked to her. "Cecily, I know there's no excuse for what I did, but I want to know now, if you can ever forgive me. I swear to you, Baby, that *that* was the only time since I've known you that I was ever unfaithful to you. Are you willing to trust me again and give our marriage another try?" he asked, and she answered by walking in his arms. They embraced lovingly. "I love you so much." Their lips caressed gently.

Pulling away from him, Cecily asked, "Who is she, Isaac?"

Walking away Isaac said, "Darling, that really isn't important."

"It's *very* important. That child will be coming to our home sometimes, and I want to know who her mother is."

****

"Well, Alton, is that lipstick on your collar in my mind, too?"

"Lillian, I meet a lot of people in the course of a day. We hug. That's not unusual!" he defended, as Wanda ran into the room and jumped on Alton, so he picked her up.

"Daddy, you're home."

"Yes, I am," he smiled with her. "And what are you doing home? Don't you have school today?"

"I'm sick, Daddy."

"Sick?! You don't look sick to me," he said tickling her, and she laughed hysterically, as Lillian just stared at her husband.

****

Lights shining brightly, camera bulbs flashing repeatedly, and electric fans blowing simultaneously, as she stood forming one pose after another. Her shoulder-length auburn hair hang loose and straight in a mushroom around her petite, oval face, as the string bikini she wore caressed her beautiful, shapely 110-pound figure like a glove, emphasizing her silky, long, walnut-colored legs. "All right, Honey, make love to the camera," the photographer called out. "Yes, Baby. That's it. That's it." A six-feet tall Latino man entered in a dark blue Le Mouzon suit, stood at the door and watched. Although his body was lean, muscular, and hard like an athlete, and his skin was a beautiful naturally bronze color, encased with thick black, wavy hair, the acne he never outdrew kept him from being a handsome man; however, he made up for it in suaveness. "Beautiful, Baby. Beautiful!! Okay, Sweetheart, that's a rap!" She sighed deeply, and then she rolled her head from side to side, trying to relax. "I'm sorry it took so long, Trudy."

"It's okay, Max," Trudy smiled with her perfect white teeth and picture-perfect lips. A metamorphosis has taken place with Trudy, who was once the heaviest and ugliest of the trio, and now just as glamorous. The Latino man came over to her as the photographer left and handed her a bathrobe.

"That was lovely, Baby," he said in his deep Spanish accent.

"Thanks, Ramon," she said with no enthusiasm.

"What's wrong, Baby?"

"I guess I'm just tired."

"You've been tired before. It's more than that. What is it?"

"Nothing else, Ramon. I'm just tired."

"Aren't you going on vacation soon?"

"*No*. I'm taking a *leave* of absence."

"What'd you mean, a leave of absence?"

"Just what I said. I need it. I haven't had a vacation in years, and what's more, I haven't seen my two best friends in years. I need it, Baby. Please don't fight me on this."

"How long are you talking about?"

"I don't know. I haven't decided yet."

"Come on, Baby. I need you. What about the perfume layout coming up?"

"That's *months* away. I'll be back for that," she said, and he raised an eyebrow. "I promise," she insisted with a slight smile.

 Pulling her in his arms he said, "Now what am I supposed to do with all my time while you're away?"

"You'll think of something."

He kissed her lips, and she kissed back, then he added, "I could come with you."

"I'll think about it," she said smiling, and they kissed again.

"Um, are you finished for today," he cooed between kisses, and she nodded.

"Mr. Perez," a lady called, and Ramon turned around.

"Yes, Sasha."

"You have a telephone call in the office."

"Who is it?"

Looking at Trudy, she said, "A woman, Sir."

"What damn woman?!" he exploded.

Clearing her throat, the lady replied,   "I don't know, Sir, but she says she's your...wife."

"*Wife*?!" Trudy exploded.

****

"Who is the woman that had your child, Isaac?"

"Baby, that's not important."

"The hell it isn't! I want to know who she is."

"Cecily, there's absolutely nothing between that woman and me."

"Except the *child*."

"Well, yes, I guess so, but that's it. I am not having an affair with her. It only happened that one time. I swear."

"She must be someone I know since you don't want to tell me who she is."

"Who she is, is not important."

"Is this child going to be a part of our lives?"

"Yes, I guess she is. I haven't thought that far."

"Then don't you see *why* I need to know who the mother is?"

"Cecily, I....."

"Who is she?"

Isaac took a deep breath, then he said softly, "Cindy."

"Cin..." she started but her breath ran out. "Cindy?! Cindy Bates, my *secretary*?!"

"Yes."

Chapter 5

Going to Maria's funeral was the hardest thing Cecily has had to face since Cotton's death. Lillian sang a beautiful rendition of *Precious Lord, Take My Hand,* which comforted her a lot. Her baby was gone, and she never had an opportunity to really know her. All those wasted years she spent trying to find her little girl, and she was right under her very own nose. Funny how things turn out. Now she was going back to work with a large part of her heart missing. But she knew she had to go on with her life. Dr. Smiley had been great in helping her out, but he couldn't continue to handle his patients and hers indefinitely. After all, it *had* been two weeks. Now the biggest part to coming back to work was how to deal with Cindy. The bitch had betrayed her, and she *had* to go!

Cecily walked in her office and dropped in her chair. She had come to work early in hopes of talking to Cindy before Ruth came, but Cindy was not there. Cecily picked up a newspaper, propped her feet up on the desk, and read. *Barry Jett was voted MVP in last night's football game. Barry is sure to lead his team to the Super Bowl this year. He made an amazing five touchdowns out of the seven, scored by his team.* Cecily stared into space as her thoughts carried her to the past:

*   *Cecily walked into a small office where a huge man sat behind a desk. "Coach Tottelli?" she asked.*

"Yes," he said jumping up. "You must be Cecily Allen."

"Yes," she replied as they shook hands. "Coach Tottelli, I think you should know right up front that the only reason I'm here is to do a favor for my anatomy professor, because he loves football so much. I don't like wasting my time on some dumb jock who majors in football and minors in stupidity. Personally, I think they're all a bunch of air-headed meatballs."

"Then you take your little holier-than-thou attitude, Little Miss Half-breed, and go to hell!" an angry, base voice barked from the door, and Cecily turned around and focused on the angry, ebony, no-neck face of a solid 210 pound, six feet, four inches young man towering over her. "I don't need you!"

"Barry, take it easy," Coach Tottelli interjected.

"I could pick you up, little girl, and break you in two with just one snap!" the fuming young man added.

"Enough, Barry!" demanded the coach.

"Coach, I'll rather flunk before I let some snobbish little bitch like her help me do anything!" Barry was not to be controlled for he saw only red.

"Stop it, Barry!" the Coach yelled with one final plea to silence the angry jock. Barry finally zoomed in on the Coach, took a deep breath, then exited very quickly into the locker room, and slammed the door. Cecily swallowed hard. "Miss Allen, maybe I've better set you straight on some important facts, before you get your pretty little head bashed in by a dumb jock one day. Barry has a 3.8 GPA. He's majoring in Business Administration, with a minor in Sociology. Barry is only having problems in one subject, calculus. I know you have a 4.0 GPA, and I was hoping you could help

Barry with calculus. Barry's first priority is his studies, not <u>football</u>."

"I'm sorry," Cecily said weakly. "I guess I put my foot in my mouth, didn't I?"

"You get no arguments from me on that," smiled the Coach. "But, I'm not the one you should be apologizing to."

"Where did he go?"

"He's in the locker room," the Coach said pointing, "Right through there." She nodded then proceeded in that direction.

Cecily slowly walked into the locker room where Barry was pounding on a punching bag, releasing steam that Cecily had induced in him. She blew hard then stepped in his view. He looked at her and snapped, "I'm sorry, Miss, you're in the wrong place. This is the room for dumb Jocks, not High Society, high-yellow, stuck-up Debutantes!"

Chuckling, Cecily said, "Okay, I deserved that, but you couldn't be further from the truth about me. I came to apologize. I was out of line, and I'm sorry."

"There's no need to apologize for speaking your mind."

"Yes, there is. I was wrong, and I'm big enough to admit it. Are you big enough to accept my apology?" she asked, but he didn't answer. "What do you want me to do? Get down on my hands and knees and beg for your forgiveness."

"For starters," he snapped, so Cecily did just that, and he couldn't help but to smile.

"Please forgive me, Oh, kind sir," she said, then raised and lowered her

arms and hands as if she was bowing to Royalty.

"You're crazy," he laughed stopping with the bag.

Rising she asked, "Well, do you accept my apology?"

"Yes. I accept your apology."

"You know, Barry, I was wrong to make assumptions, and so were you."

"What're you talking about?"

"I am not some spoil little rich girl like you think. You would be surprised where I live,"

"I bet I would."

"So, when do we start your tutoring lessons?"

"Whenever you say."

****

He made love to her tenderly, and when it was over, he rolled off her and pulled her in his big, strong, muscular arms. Suddenly the door opened, and Cotton stood there, frozen in her tracks. Barry pulled the covers up, as he and Cecily lay entwined in each other's arms, speechless, and Cotton turned and left the room without saying a word.

"Holy shit!" Barry spat jumping up. "She's mad as hell."

"I know," Cecily said pulling on a housecoat as Barry threw on his clothes. "Damn, she's early!"

"We can talk to her together, Baby," he said. "She needs to know how much we love each other."

"No. I'd rather talk to her alone."

"Are you sure?"

"Yeah. I'm sure."

Planting a kiss on her lips he said, "I'll call you later." She nodded. "I love you."

"I love you, too," Cecily said, as he left quickly. Cecily took a deep breath then walked slowly to Cotton's room.

Cecily pushed the door open and walked in. Cotton was outstretched on the bed with a bra and half slip on, staring at the ceiling, smoking a cigarette. Cecily sat on the edge of the bed and asked softly, "How are you?"

"Fine," she nonchalantly replied.

"Those cigarettes are going to kill you."

"Gotta die of something."

"Cotton, I'm sorry. It's just that Barry and I love each other so much. Please, don't be disappointed in me."

"I am disappointed in you, Sissy," Cotton said sitting up. "When you gonna learn? Men ain't shit! They never been, and they never will be. Remember what that musician did to ya?"

"Barry isn't Rocky," Cecily defended. "He loves me. I know he does."

"You don't know shit!" Cotton stressed. "You too young to know!"

"I'm a grown woman, Cotton."

"And, you still don't know shit! As long as he fuckin' ya, he luv ya. He luv the hell outta ya!" she sarcastically stated.

"You're making it sound so dirty," Cecily said with tears rolling down her face. "Barry does love me."

"Listen, Honey. Barry is like all the rest! He ain't no different! He just a big, horny ass, hard dick jock!"

"What're you saying? That I can't have a man in my life?"

"All I'm saying is, don't jump in the damn sack wit' the furst damn horny ass man tha' com' around."

"Cotton, I finished high school, and I'll be finishing college soon. I've only had two men in my whole life, Rocky and Barry. I don't think I'm jumping in the sack with the first man available," she explained behind tears. "Do you?'

Cotton felt bad when she looked in Cecily's sad eyes, then she pulled the girl in her arms, "No, Baby, you didn' do tha'. I'm sorry. I just don't wan' you to mess up. I luv you, kid."

"Oh, Cotton, I love you, too. I don't ever want you to be disappointed in me."

"I'm not, Baby. I'm not. I'm just tired. Barry is a nice boy. Jus' be careful! No mor' babies!" she said then smiled.

"I'll be careful. I promise."

"I'm so proud of you, Sissy."

*"And, I'm proud of you, Cot...<u>Mama</u>," Cecily squeezed out still in tears, and Cotton pulled her in her arms, and they embraced lovingly. **

"Cecily," Ruth called bringing the daydreaming doctor back to the present.

"Hello, Ruth," Cecily said wiping the tears from her face.

"Anything wrong, Honey?"

"I'm all right," she said standing and putting on her white smock. "Is Cindy here?"

"She called. She isn't coming in today. Her daughter is sick."

"I see," Cecily said, thinking that the child belongs to her husband, too.

"Oh, Cecily, there's a man to see you," Ruth said looking rather strange.

"A man?"

"Yes. He said it's very important."

"All right. Send him in," Cecily said, and Ruth nodded leaving out.

 Cecily walked to the filing cabinets to get some papers. When she heard the door open, she said, without looking up, "I'll be right there."

When Cecily turned around, she dropped the papers that were in her hands, as she focused on a six feet, two inches, light brown tanned, African American man, with short, processed-wavy, jet black hair, and a winning smile, exposing his extremely rugged good looks. His slim body was covered in a Bonez navy-blue, three-piece suit with a matching hat in his hand, and a black fur coat thrown over his arm. He stepped forward in navy-blue, leather shoes, planted himself down in the chair in front of Cecily's desk, and propped his feet on her beautiful desk, then spoke very softly, in his deep, sexy, baritone voice, "Hiya, Babe."

"Spencer," Cecily squeezed out when she found her voice.

"Long time, no see," he said still with a smirk on his face.

"What're you doing here?"   she said again picking up the papers she had dropped, watching his every move.

"I came to see my best girl."

"I'm not *your* girl," she spat with venom. "I want you to leave. I want you *out* of my life."

"I don't think so," he smiled, pulling an envelope from under his coat, and tossing it on her desk.

"What's this?" Cecily asked, as she moved behind her desk.

With a slight tilt of the head, he said, "Open it."

Cecily picked the envelope up slowly and opened it so carefully, as if she was diffusing a bomb, because knowing Spencer, she didn't know what to expect.   When she focused on the content of the envelope, her breath momentarily left her body, and she dropped in her chair, covered her mouth, and squeezed out, "Oh, my God!" She was speechless as her eyes found his. "Where did you get these?"

"I have my ways," he smiled. Cecily couldn't believe what her eyes were seeing.   The photographer had captured the whole bloody scene of her planting a knife in the body of Rocky Simpson. Tears began to flow uncontrollably down her distraught face as she remembered that horrible day. "You killed a famous person, Dr. Wade. How do you think your patients would feel about coming to a doctor, sworn to save lives, if they knew she *took* a life then *left* the scene?"

"Then the person who took these pictures knows it was self-defense."

"He doesn't remember *details* too well," he sarcastically replied.

"How do you know he's dead? I never read it in the newspaper or anything."

"That's because I took care of it for you. Rocky Simpson is fish food. Everyone thinks he is out of the country on an extended vacation. What they don't know is that he will *never* return, and hell, nobody really gives a fuck anyway. Rocky is *old* news," Spencer explained with a slight chuckle.

"Why did you do that?"

"To help you of course."

"But, why? What do you want from me?"

"Nothing."

"What?"

"I don't want shit from you!" he spat with a melting smile. "You walked out on me, Bitch, and you *will* pay!" He grew upset and began to yell as he stood, banging his fist on the desk. "Nobody walks out on Carl Spencer! *Nobody*!" He focused on the nameplate on her desk and slammed it on the floor so hard Cecily cringed, and Ruth exploded into the office.

"Cecily, is everything all right?"

"Yes," Cecily squeezed out, then Ruth walked out slowly, looking back, strangely at Spencer.

"Doctor! Hah! You ain't nothing but a two-bit whore! A hooker! A bitch! A cocksucker! And you *always* will be!" he fumed on.

"You don't own me, Spencer!" retaliated the trembling doctor, finding courage from somewhere in her heart, as she dried the tears from her face.

"The hell I don't, Bitch!" he insisted. "I own that doctor's certificate, your marriage license, your whole goddamn whoring ass! I own *all* of you, Bitch! You wouldn't have *any* of this if it weren't for me! *Me*!" Cecily was sure that he would hit her, so she remained very still. She knew the rage this maniac possessed, and she was bitterly afraid. "It took me some time to find your ass, and to get something I could use on you, but I have it now, Bitch, and you *will* pay!"

"What do you want, Spencer?" she asked carefully.

"You, Bitch! I want *you*! Lock! Stock! and Barrow!"

"*What*?" she said wiping a tear from her face that she just couldn't hold back. He took another envelope from his pocket and threw it on her desk, and then he turned and walked to the window. Cecily opened it carefully again. She didn't know what else he could have that was worse than what he had already shown her. But she was wrong. She became face to face with her greatest fears. Pictures of one night of weakness with her best friend's husband. The photographer even captured the lust in her eyes. Her tears flowed heavily now, for she could not control them any longer. "What do you want from me?" she asked in between tears. He swirled around and stared blankly at the distraught doctor.   He felt a little satisfactory in seeing her in so much pain. He hated this woman so much for how she used and deserted him. It was a pleasure to see her hurt. But he wasn't finished with her yet. Not by a long shot! She would pay for walking out on him. Nobody walked out on Spencer! *Nobody*! The lying, stinking whore! *He wasn't finished with her yet*!

****

"Hi, Doris."

"Miss Miles, how are you," the lady said behind a desk with a big fan smile.

"Joe wants to see me," Trudy said removing dark sunglasses but leaving on the stylish feather hat.

"Sure. One moment," she said pushing the intercom button.

"Yes, Doris," a lady's voice answered.

"Gladys, Miss Trudy Miles is here to see Dr. Burke."

"Oh, okay. Send her back please, Doris."

"Sure," she said then focused on Trudy. "You may go back, Miss Miles."

"Thanks, Doris. You're a sweetheart," Trudy said then exited through a door.

As soon as Trudy walked through the door a two-hundred-pound black lady met her saying, "Hi, Miss Miles."

"Hi, Gladys."

"You may sit in Dr. Burke's office," she said showing Trudy in. "He'll be right in."

"Thanks, " Trudy said taking a seat in the huge brown leather chair in front of the doctor's desk. As the lady walked out, Trudy couldn't help but to smile. She had come a long way from Phoenix. She had come from being a fat, freckled face poor girl, to a slim, high-fashioned, rich fashion model.

She's so happy she did something about her weight *and* her freckles. Thank God for diets and cosmetic surgery. She might've ended up looking like Gladys. That was a revolting thought. She couldn't imagine letting herself go like that. Although, it was hard work to keep her body so lean and trim, it was worth it. If she was dreaming, she didn't want to wake up. She loved the way people fussed over her. She had always known rich people were treated special, but she never knew just how special, and she loved it. Now she wondered why the doctor had called to see her. She prayed she wasn't dying. Her life was too perfect now.

The door opened and a short, bald, graying black man walked in, extending a hand saying, "Hi, Trudy. How's my favorite model?"

Shaking his hand, she said, "That's what *I* was hoping you could tell *me.*"

"Relax, Sweetheart. It's nothing serious."

"Anytime a doctor calls and wants to see you, it's *serious*!"

Laughing he said, "All right, I'll come to the point, so you won't have a stoke trying to figure out why I wanted to see you." He took a deep breath. "How have you been feeling lately, Trudy?"

"Fine. Why?"

"No shortness of breath, nausea, vomiting?"

"What the hell are you talking about?"

 Laughing again he said, "You are so impatient."

"What is it, Joe? I've been a little tired lately, but I've had a very busy schedule. As a matter of fact, I'm getting ready for a leave of absence."

"Nine months I hope."

"*What*?!"

"Well, actually about seven and a half."

"You can't be saying what I think you're saying," she said, and he nodded. "But I'm on the pill."

"Pills are not one-hundred percent," he smiled. "There's no mistake about it, Trudy. You're pregnant."

****

"Hi, Baby."

"Alton, what're you doing home?" Lillian asked walking in the bedroom door and dropping her purse on the vanity chair.

"I left some papers home I needed," he said putting his arms around her waist. "Wanda got off to school okay?"

"Yeah," she said, and they kissed softly. "But I had a hard time getting home."

"Why?" he said putting some papers in his briefcase.

"There was a drunk man staggering in the middle of the road, stopping traffic."

"He was really drunk?"

"Yeah. A policeman had to get him out the road."

"I bet he was a sight."

"That's an understatement. I wonder how people let themselves get that low."

"Baby, sometimes circumstances will allow people to do things they don't usually do."

"But, Honey, there's no excuse for that kind of behavior."

"Well, Sweetheart, we have to be tolerant. We don't know what drove him to that point."

"There's always AA, rehab, or *something*."

"Oftentimes, the person with the problem is the *last* to know he has a problem."

"If you're falling all down in the streets, how can you *not* know you have a problem?" she chuckled. "Thank God for good sense."

"And," he said grabbing her around her waist again. "You can also thank him for beauty."

"Thank you, Baby," she said, and they kissed again.

"Umm," he cooed. "Let's go back to bed."

"I thought you had to get back to work."

"*I'm* the boss. Remember?" he said as he led her to the bed.

"Honey, have you seen Cecily?"

Freezing in his tracks, he said carefully, "No. Why?"

"I was just worried about her. She's been staying to herself since the funeral."

"Lillian, Cecily is a big girl. She can take care of herself," he said walking away, so she wouldn't see the guilt in his eyes.

"I know, but that doesn't stop me from being concern."

"Why don't you call her?"

"I did, but she seems so distant."

"When she's ready to talk, Lillian, I'm sure she will," he said picking up his briefcase.

"I suppose so," she said noticing that he was walking out the door. "Hey, I thought you wanted to fool around."

"You really know how to spoil the mood, Lillian," he said walking out. "See you tonight."

****

"What do you want Spencer?" Cecily asked, and he sat again.

"Business has fallen off now since all these damn diseases came out, especially AIDS. I need a new line of business," he spoke evenly, and she just watched him. "I need a supplier. Top grade stuff."

Cecily could not believe her ears. This man was sitting there talking about supplying him with drugs as if it was a cup of sugar. "No," she nonchalantly replied.

"Baby, it's up to you," he snapped. "It's either prison or business. Not to mention the newspapers, Mrs. Lillian Carter and your husband will be getting copies of these pictures. You won't have a friend in the world. I advise you to think it over. I believe the penalty for murder here in California is death. You better think it over *real* good."

"I will *not* supply you with drugs," she repeated with clenched teeth. "I will have nothing to do with you putting that poison on the streets!"

"It's up to you," he smiled, standing. "I'm a patient man, Dr. Wade. I'll expect to hear from you by noon tomorrow before I proceed with my plans."

"Why are you doing this, Spencer?"

"I told you. You owe me. I took care of you when Cotton died. You owe me."

"Yeah. You took care of me *real* good, by putting me on the streets to make money for you."

"You were a fucking whore anyway, Bitch. I just set it up so you would get paid, rather than giving it away free."

"I was *not* a whore until *you* made me one."

"Nobody can make you *anything* that *you* don't want to be," he said walking to the door.

"Just answer me one question, Spencer. Why did you kill Cotton?"

"I don't know what you're talking about, Bitch! I didn't kill Cotton."

"Yes, you did, you son-of-a-bitch," she replied, and he burst into laughter as he left her office, and Cecily dropped her head on the desk.

****

"Hello?"

"Lil?"

"Yes. This is Lillian."

"Lil, it's Trudy."

"Trudy?!" Lillian exploded dropping on the couch. "Where are you?"

"I'm in New York," Trudy said lying in a hospital bed.

"Tru, I can't believe it's you! It's been so long."

"*Too* long! That's why I'm taking a vacation and coming to see you guys!"

"What?! You're coming *here*?!"

"Yes, tomorrow," Trudy said sitting up. "I'll see you tomorrow about noon."

"This is great!" exploded Lillian. "And Cecily could really use *both* of us right now."

"Why? What happened?" Trudy asked, as Ramon entered in a navy, pinstriped suit carrying a dozen of red roses.

"We'll talk when you get here."

"Okay, Sweetie. Gotta go! See you tomorrow," Trudy said then hung up, as Ramon sat beside her bed.

"Where're you going, Baby," he asked in his deep, throaty Spanish accent.

"I told you, on *vacation*."

"Where?"

"I don't have to answer that. You are not married to *me*!"

"I suppose I deserved that," he said sadly. "How do you feel?"

"Fine."

"You didn't have to do this."

"It was *my* choice!"

"It was *my* baby, too, Trudy."

"And you didn't need *another* family."

"I love you, Baby."

"And where does that leave your wife?"

"You know why I stay. The kids! Our marriage has been over a long time. We go our separate ways. I haven't touched her in years."

"Yeah. Right. But you could've told me you were married."

"I didn't want to lose you, Baby."

"Well, anyway, you have a good life," she said turning her back to him.

"I'll find you, Trudy. I swear to God. I'll find you."

"I'm not hiding, Ramon. I'm just going on vacation."

"Then why can't I go with you?"

Jerking around to face him, she yelled, "Because it's over between us. Over! Finish! The End!"

"No, it isn't. I still love you."

"Get lost, Ramon," she said about to turn around again, but he grabbed her arm and jerked her up, frightening her.

"It's not over until *I* say it's over. Got it?" he insisted. "And, if you walk out on me, Baby, you'll be sorry."

****

A distraught Cecily walked into her big beautiful house slowly, with a sense of defeat that she'd never experienced before. She called out to her husband, but he did not answer. She dropped in a chair and let her head fall backwards. She couldn't help but to remember the events of the day. She knew she had to tell Lillian and Isaac about Alton and her one-time affair, because she didn't trust that double-cross, son-of-a-bitch Spencer. Even if she did what he wanted, he would probably still tell Lillian and Isaac, just to be mean and to hurt her. But first she had to talk to Alton. She picked up the telephone receiver and dialed. "Carter Construction Company," the receptionist answered.

"May I speak to Alton Carter, please."

"I'm sorry but Mr. Carter is in conference. May I have him return your call?"

"No. I'll call back. Thank-you," she said then hung up, as she heard the door open.

"Cecily!"

"In here."

Entering quickly Isaac blurted out, "Is anything wrong, Honey?"

"No. Why?"

"You're home so early."

"I finished early," she replied receiving a kiss from him.

"Hey, Darling, do you remember the Washington deal I worked on so long and hard?" She nodded. "Well, I *got* it, Baby. I *got* it! I got the contract!" he exploded pulling her up in his arms and dancing around with her, full of enthusiasm. He kissed her again, but this time, long and passionate. "Oh, I love you so much," he breathed in between kisses. "Don't push me away this time, Baby. It's been so long." He proceeded to unbutton her blouse. Cecily was in no mood to make love to her husband, but she went through the motions anyway, because she knew she owed him. She had denied him for months, and she knew that wasn't right. Isaac was so handsome, he could have his pick of women, but he chose her, and she must do the wifely thing by him. He couldn't wait to have her. He yanked her clothes off savagely, and she went through the motions of helping him out of his. Their lovemaking was divine to Isaac, but it was only a chore to Cecily, as she lay there praying it would soon be over, until her prayers were answered.   "I love you so much, Cecily," he breathlessly whispered in her ears softly, pulling her in his arms and squeezing her tight. Cecily's thoughts were on Spencer, and how she would have to break her husband's heart, a man who loved her unconditionally. "I'm sorry, Baby. That was too damned quick. I'll make up for it the next time," he said, and Cecily cringed. She didn't know if she could fake it a *second* time. Realizing they were on the floor, Isaac got up then helped Cecily up, and they pulled on their clothes. He planted a kiss on her forehead and asked, "Want something to drink, Baby?"

"Yes," she said, while he exited the room. She then sat on the couch, let her head drop backwards, and drifted into the past:

*   It was June, and Cecily was running in the apartment she shared with Cotton, waving a letter in her hands, full of excitement. She was yelling Cotton's name, laughing hysterically.   When she burst into Cotton's room*

she stopped abruptly, because Cotton's clothes were thrown on the floor. This seemed strange to Cecily, because Cotton was incredibly neat. Then she caught a glimpse of Cotton's leg sticking out from the other side of the bed. "Cotton?" she asked cautiously, as she walked around the bed slowly. Cecily was not prepared to witness Cotton's body lying on the floor, stark naked, soaking in her own blood. Cecily's heart seemed to stop right then and there at that very moment, for she froze in her tracks, then at no control of her own, Cecily suddenly released a horrifying, "NOOOO!" She dropped on the floor next to the body, seized the woman in her arms and cradled her like a baby, as two men exploded into the room.

"Sissy, what's wrong?" one man asked. Cecily didn't answer for she was in a dreamlike state, still crying. They walked around the bed slowly and witnessed the horrible scene. Cecily didn't seem to notice they were there because she was crying, yelling and screaming hysterically, trying to wake Cotton, but it was too late, for Cotton had no life left in her frail, cold, lifeless body.

****

Spencer walked into a hospital and to a doctor. "How is she, Doc?"
"Still the same I'm afraid. You may see her if you wish."
"Listen, Doc, I want Sissy to have the best. Money is no object."
"I understand, Mr. Spencer."
When Spencer opened the door to Cecily's room, she sat on the small

bed in a hospital gown, staring into space, twirling a lock of her hair. He walked to her and sat on the bed next to her. She did not seem to notice his presence. The doctor left them alone. "Hiya, Sissy," Spencer spoke to her softly, but she was unresponsive. "Sissy, you get well, girl. Cotton wouldn't want this for you. Stuck in a loony bin." He took a deep breath. "I'll take care of you, Honey. Don't you worry. Get well soon." He planted a kiss on her forehead, and then he walked out slowly, giving her one final glance.

****

Cecily was lying in the bed staring into space when an image appeared before her, calling her name. She looked up and realized it was Cotton, dressed in a white gown, speaking so soft and Angelic. Cecily sat up in bed and called, "Cotton. Cotton, I want to go with you."

"You can't, Sissy."

"I can't go on without you," Cecily whined, beginning to cry.

"Yes, you can," Cotton continued softly. "Sissy, you have to pull yourself together for <u>me</u>. I have always wanted the best for you. Make me proud of you. Become that great doctor you've always wanted to be." She began to fade away.

"Cotton, please don't leave me," Cecily cried running at the illusion.

"I love you, Sissy," Cotton said, as she faded into the darkness.

"No! Please don't leave me, Cotton!" Cecily yelled as a nurse rushed into the room. "Please don't leave me!" The nurse sat on Cecily's bed, pulled

her in her arms and cradled her like a baby.

"It's all right, Sweetheart," the nurse said trying to soothe the hysterical girl.

Soon Cecily regained her composure, lifted her head, and said very weakly, "I want to see the doctor."

****

Cecily walked into Cotton's apartment, followed by Spencer. She looked around slowly. She picked up a picture of Cotton and couldn't hold the tears back any longer. Spencer pulled her in his arms. "It's all right, Baby," he said. "I'm here for you as long as you need me."

"Spencer, I appreciate your kindness, but I would like to be alone now."

"I understand," he said then planted a kiss on her forehead. "I'll call you later, and if you need me, just pick up that phone." She nodded slowly, then he left.

Cecily sat on the couch and hugged Cotton's picture close to her chest as the tears flowed heavily now. Her thoughts traveled back in time to all the special times she and Cotton shared: the laughter, the playing, the joking, the zoo, the carnivals, the arguments, and the dinners. But most importantly, the <u>love</u>. The wonderful, special love. She loved that woman more than life itself, and now she was gone. She would be so lonesome without Cotton. Cecily felt as if a part of herself died with Cotton. Cotton was her mother, her friend, her confidant, her teacher, her provider, her _everything_. Why had God done this to her? Why did he take Cotton from her? Didn't he know how much she _needed_ Cotton? Did he care? Cecily's tears flowed hard.

****

Cecily was awakened from a sound sleep by a strange noise. She jumped up calling, "Cotton?" Then she realized Cotton was dead, so she must've been dreaming, but she heard another noise. She was sure this time she was not dreaming. There must be a prowler in the apartment. She didn't know if anyone knew she was back. A sense of nervousness over-powered her, but she got up anyway, and slowly pulled on a housecoat. She reached under the bed and pulled out a 45-revolver then cautiously walked into the living room. She saw a shadow, then flipped on the light, and focused on Spencer coming out of the kitchen with a newspaper in his hand.

Throwing his hands up in the air, Spencer yelled, "Whoa, little girl. It's only me, Spencer!"

"Spencer!" she shouted lowering the gun. "You scared the shit out of me! What in the hell are you doing here?!" she demanded. "How did you get in?"

"I came to check on you. Cotton gave me a key a long time ago. I have keys to _all_ my girls' apartments."

"Well as you can see, I'm fine. And since I'm not _your_ girl, you can leave that key before you go, which I prefer it to be _now_."

Sitting on the couch Spencer dropped the newspaper on the small, round table and asked, "What're you going to do now, Kid. I mean, I know Cotton was taking care of you, but now, how will you live?"

"I guess I'll have to get a job," she said, sitting on the couch also, but intentionally not telling him she will be starting medical school in the fall, and Cotton had left her an insurance policy that will pay her tuition for the entire four years.

"What kind of job?"

"I don't know. And, why are you so interested in what my plans are?!"

"I need a bookkeeper. I think you would be perfect."

"Why?"

"Because you're smart."

"Is there <u>another</u> reason?" she asked sarcastically.

"No."

"What kind of books do <u>you</u> keep?"

"I have several legitimate businesses. Will you do it?"

"I don't know, Spencer. Cotton has always said under no circumstances I'm to work for you,"

"She meant you couldn't go on the streets, Girl. She wouldn't mind if you kept my books,"

"I don't know. I'll have to think about it."

"Hey, can I have a cup of coffee?"

"Spencer, it's <u>late</u>!"

"Just <u>one</u> cup?"

"I don't even think I have any coffee. I haven't bought any groceries yet."

"I bought you a few things. I put them in the kitchen."

"You did?"

"Yeah."

"Why?"

"I care. Isn't that enough?"

"But, why, Spencer?"

"Damn, Cotton sure does have you paranoid about me. I'm a nice guy."

"But..."

"No buts. I'm here to help you. I promised Cotton I would."

"What're you talking about? Cotton has always said stay away from Spencer!" she laughed.

Laughing also he said, "And, you're sticking to that shit, ain't cha?"

"Spencer, may I ask you a personal question?" she asked, and his eyebrows rose as to say what. "Why do you do what you do? You don't seem the type."

"Why? Cause I ain't all stupid and shit?"

"I mean you can talk correctly and..."

"Hell, Girl, I went two years of college. Engineering."

"Wow, I'm impressed. Why did you quit?"

"I didn't. I got kicked out. I had a fucking 3.5, but a cracker said something I didn't like, and I knocked the hell outta him."

"They kicked you out for hitting another student?"

"No, he was the teacher. Professor Godbolt. Three stitches."

"Did he press charges?"

"No."

"How did you manage that?"

"I told him I would've fucking killed him, and he knew I wasn't playing."

"What did he say to make you so mad?"

"He called me a boy."

"I'm sorry, Spencer. Tough break."

"I'm doing okay. Now what about that coffee?"

"Okay, <u>one</u> cup, then you've got to go, so I can get some sleep." she said as she stood, knocking the newspaper on the floor. When she bent to pick it up, there was a picture of Barry and a lady on the cover, and the print read, <u>MVP running back, Barry Jett to wed Valerie Melton, his coach's daughter.</u> Cecily threw the paper down and ran in the bedroom. She lay on the bed crying softly. Spencer took a deep breath then followed her. He sat on the edge of the bed then pulled her up and cradled her in his arms.

*"Shhh," he cooed. "He's not worth it." He raised her head and wiped her tears gently. "You don't need him, Baby." He planted a kiss on her lips softly. Then she surrendered to his affection, and he made love to her so passionately, she imagined it was Barry instead of Spencer. ***

The constant ringing of the doorbell brought Cecily back to the present. "Cecily," Isaac yelled. "Get the door, Honey."

"All right," she called back jumping up. When she opened the door,

Lillian was standing there.

"Hi, Cis."

"Hey, Girl. Come on in."

"I have great news," Lillian said bubbling over with excitement, as they walked into the den.

"What's up?" Cecily asked sharing in on the enthusiasm.

"Trudy called me. She'll be here tomorrow."

"Tomorrow?!" exploded Cecily, and Lillian nodded. The two women hugged, jumped and cheered like teenagers, as Isaac entered.

"What's going on?" he wanted to know.

"Honey, Trudy's coming for a visit," Cecily announced. "She'll be here tomorrow."

"That's great, Sweetie," Isaac said trying to share their enthusiasm. "Hi, Lillian."

"Hi, Isaac."

"Listen, Sweetheart, we're out of coffee creamer. I'm going to run out and get some."

"Okay," she said as their lips touched softly.

"See you, Lillian," he called back.

"All right," Lillian responded, as he left. "You have a great guy, Cis."

"He's wonderful," Cecily agreed, and Lillian could see a hint of sadness in her eyes.

"Have you thought any more about finding David?"

"No, and I'm not going to. That's history. Water under the bridge! Isaac is my husband now, and I must make the best of it."

"You're right to make it work, Girl. Good men are hard to find."

"So, we're *both* lucky," Cecily said as they sat.

"I don't know," Lillian said, and this time, Cecily could see sadness in *her* eyes.

"What's up, Girl?"

"Alton was unfaithful to me."

"What? When?"

"It was a long time ago. He used to go on a lot of business trips, and he would act differently when he returned. I never had any proof, but I'm sure it was another woman."

"You might be wrong, you know."

"No, I don't think so," Lillian stated matter-of-factly. "And, now, I think he's doing it again. Two weeks ago, he stayed out all night. He said he was in a business meeting, but what business meetings do you know of that stay in section *all* night?"

"I'm sorry, Lil," Cecily said pulling her friend in her arms.

With tears flowing down her face Lillian squeezed out, "I love him so much, Cecily. I don't know what I would do if he left me for another woman."

"That's not going to happen. Don't you trip like that, Girlfriend!" Cecily insisted. "Alton loves you. He would never leave you for anyone!"

"I'm so glad we're together again, Cis. I've missed you so much. You're the *one* person in this whole world that I can truly trust and confide in."

With tears rolling down her face Cecily replied, "I'll always be here for you, Kid. You know that." And Cecily knew that whatever happened, she could never let Lillian know that *she* was the other woman. Spencer had won. She had no other choice but to supply his drugs. The son-of-a-bitch has won ...*for now*! But she would get even with the low-life, snake-in-the-grass, if it's the last thing she ever does, she *would* get even with Mr. Carl Spencer!

Chapter 6

Cecily walked into her office and to Cindy's desk. "I want to talk to you," she stated. Cindy stood and followed Cecily in her office.

"What's up?" Cindy asked closing the door.

"Isaac told me about your daughter."

"I see."

"How could you do this to me, Cindy? I trusted you!"

"It wasn't like that, Cecily. I didn't *know* you then."

"But you did sleep with my husband?"

"Yes, but I didn't betray you. I didn't *know* you."

"So that makes it right? Because you don't know the wife?"

"I loved Isaac, Cecily," Cindy explained. "It was not some cheap affair. I really did love him."

"And, now, Cindy? How do you feel about my husband now?"

Cindy took a deep breath then continued, "I met Isaac in a restaurant. I was having lunch with a friend who knew him. Her husband had done some business with Isaac's company, and she introduced us. He wasn't wearing a wedding band, so I thought he was single. I invited him to have a drink at the bar when my friend left, and he accepted. I didn't have a car, so Isaac took me home. I invited him in, and we had a few more drinks, then he told me that he was married, and that he loved his wife very much, but she was in love with her career. He let me know that we could only be friends and *nothing* more. But I think I fell in love with him that first night. He was so handsome and so caring and so honest, but I lied and told him that that was all I wanted, too. So, we became friends and kept in touch with each other. And one night he came to my apartment very upset. I've never seen him like that. Something about your breaking a date with him to go and take care of someone. I don't remember the exact details, but he was so hurt he needed someone that night, and I was there. So, we drank a whole bottle of wine and ended up in bed. It wasn't planned. It just happened, but it was the most beautiful thing I had ever experienced in my whole life. I saw Isaac one more time after that, and that's when he apologized to me and said that that would never happen again, and it didn't, but then, I found out I was pregnant. I begged him to tell you, but he was too afraid of losing you. So, after Angela was born, I had gotten up enough courage to tell you myself. When I came here that day Ruth thought I was coming for the receptionist job, and after I met you, I really liked you, so I took the job, since I hated my other job anyway. Isaac was furious when I told him I was working here, but I told him that I liked the job, and I was staying. I never meant to hurt anyone, Cecily, especially *you*."

"You never answered my question, Cindy. Are you still in love with my husband?"

"I would be lying if I said no. The truth of the matter is that I care for Isaac very much," Cindy admitted, and then she took a deep breath. "Am I fired?"

"Good secretaries are hard to find," Cecily said with a slight smiled. "No. You're not fired." She paused. "And, Cindy, thank-you for your honesty."

****

"Put them there," Trudy told the bellboy in the luxurious blue and white suite, and he did, so she handed him a twenty-dollar bill.

"Gee, thank you, Miss Miles."

"Thank *you*."

"If you need anything, you just let me know."

"I sure will. Thank you," she said, then he left closing the door. Trudy removed her big hat, and then sat at the vanity mirror and removed her dark sunglasses slowly. She rubbed off a little makeup, exposing a dark bruise right under her left eye. "Son-of-a-bitch." she said aloud.

****

"You want to see me, Pastor Graham?"

"Yes, come in Lillian," the man of five feet, nine inches, one hundred seventy pounds, most of which was his protruding stomach, said, standing. He kissed her cheek and guided her to a chair in front of his small desk in the five by seven paneled office.

"What can I do for you?"

Sitting on the desk in front of her he said, "Lillian, I'm very expressed by the way you took over Mrs. Lamont's job with the youth of the church at her untimely death. The Lord sent you here right on time."

"Thank you, Pastor, but I was more than happy to do it. Young people are very important. They're our future."

"I'm glad to hear you say that, Lillian," he smiled. "The reason I asked to see you is to ask you to take over the job of Youth Director."

"What?"

"You will do a great job, and we desperately need to fill that position."

"I don't know what to say."

"Just say yes."

"But I don't know if I know *how* to direct a whole youth department."

"You'll do just fine, and you'll have help from my wife and the other people in that department."

"I'm so new here. Are you sure you want *me*?"

"Very sure."

"Then I guess I'll take it," she said getting up. "Thank you, Pastor Graham for your confidence in me."

"Thank *you*, Madam Directress," he said extending a hand to her, but she was so excited she hugged him instead, as a lady stood, watching at the door.

****

Cecily walked in her office and pulled off her white smock. As she sat at her desk and began looking at some charts, Ruth stuck her head in the door. "Goodnight, Cecily," she said.

"Goodnight, Ruth," Cecily smiled. As Ruth left a buzz came from Cindy, and Cecily pushed the button. "Yes, Cindy."

"You have a call on line one. See you tomorrow."

"Thanks, Cindy. Good-night," Cecily said pushing the button, as she picked the receiver up. "May I help you?"

"Dr. Wade, how are you," a voice said, and she recognized it to be Spencer's.

"I don't want you to call me here at work, Spencer."

"I don't give a damn what you don't want, lady!" he snapped. "When in the hell can I expect my first shipment?!"

"In four weeks."

"In *four* weeks?! You *gots* to be crazy, Sissy, if you think I'm waiting four goddamn weeks for my stuff!"

"Let me explain, I…"

"One week."

"*One* week?!" she exploded. "I couldn't possibly get it in a week!" She took a deep breath, to calm down. "Listen, Spencer. I make my orders out every other week. My supplies don't come in until another two weeks."

"Don't fuck with me, Sissy!" he demanded. "I'll give you *two* weeks, Baby! That's *all*! Two weeks! Take it or leave it!" Before she could protest any further, the phone went dead to her ears.

"Spencer!" she called but he was no longer on the line. Cecily slammed the receiver down. "Damn! You son-of-a-bitch!" She took a deep breath to calm down again. "How could I have *ever* been in love with that *man*?" She dropped her head back and drifted into the past:

*   *Cecily sat across the big, white oak dining room table from Spencer while they ate dinner. A lady in a maid's uniform entered and refilled their wine glasses. Cecily's hair was secured in a bun on the top of her head. Diamonds caressed her neck and ears, and sequins dazzled her beautiful black Lorenzo de Vaughn formal dress. "You look very stunning, Baby," Spencer breathed softly, hypnotized by her beauty so much that he couldn't take his seductive eyes off her.*

"Thank-you," Cecily replied with a smile that confirmed that she was <u>his</u> tonight.

"I'm glad you finally decided to move in with me, Baby."

"So am I."

"We better get a move on," he said standing, exposing a dazzling black Mario Van Def tuxedo. "The opera will begin shortly." He walked to her and pulled her up gently by the hand. She melted in his arms, and their lips met passionately. "Ummm, if you don't cut it out, pretty lady, we will never make it for the opening."

"Oh, <u>yes</u> we will," she chuckled. "I've waited all year to see this opera. I'm not going to let you worm your way out of seeing it <u>this</u> time."

"I'll do anything for you, my beautiful princess," he cooed nibbling on her ear. "You name it. You got it."

"I love you, Spencer," she said breathlessly, and their lips found each other again.

"I love you, too, Baby," he added in between kisses.

Breaking away, Cecily said, "Let's go." As she walked away, he stood looking at her swaying body and feeling very warm. He had to smile at himself when she looked back at him and said, "Hold that thought." Then he burst into laughter.

"Oh, I will," he said following her. "Indeed, I will."

****

Later that night, Cecily and Spencer walked into the bedroom laughing. "It wasn't as boring as all that," she laughed.

"What do you get out of those things?" he laughed also. "That was boring as hell!"

"You'll get used to it, Big Boy."

*Grabbing her in his arms, he declared, "<u>You</u> are the only thing I want to get <u>used</u> to." They kissed hard, as he tore her clothes off savagely. He took her there on the floor, too excited to reach the big king-size bed. Cecily was in awe because he had literally ripped her beautiful eighteen-hundred-dollar dress off her body. But she couldn't complain too much since he bought all her clothes anyway.   **

Cecily held up, wiped a tear from her face and stood. She could not help but to wonder how she could've ever been taken in by Spencer. Cotton had warned her to stay away from him, but when Cotton died, she was putty in his hands because of her vulnerability, and he knew it. She had no idea that loving care he was giving her was his way of preparing her for the streets. She actually thought she was special to him. That he wanted nobody else to have her but him. What a joke! Oh, how she hated that man! It's so strange how you could love someone so much at one time and hate him so much now. And she honestly loved Spenser once. It all seemed so long ago. Suddenly Cecily jumped up and said aloud, "Trudy should be here by now. I've got to go! I'll deal with you later, Spencer!"

****

When Cecily arrived home, Isaac met her at the door. "Hi," he said, planting a kiss on her lips.

"Hi," she said walking into the den. Cecily froze in her tracks when she focused on Lillian, Alton and Trudy talking and laughing.

"Hiya, Cis," Trudy said smiling in her very tight blue jeans and over-sized T-shirt, with all her hair pulled back in a ponytail. Then, suddenly she and Cecily simultaneously ran into each other's arms and embraced lovingly as tears rolled down their happy faces. "What's happening, Girl?"

"Look at you," Cecily exploded holding Trudy at arm's length to inspect her. "You are beautiful."

"Not as beautiful as you and Lil, but I try."

"Lillian and I ain't on the cover of *Fashion and Glamour Magazine*!" Cecily joked. "Who would've thought that our chubby little, freckled-face friend would turn out to be such a big, beautiful celebrity?"

"Not me," Trudy said holding up her hand like she was in school, and everyone burst into laughter.

"What happened to your freckles?" Cecily wanted to know.

"Cosmetic surgery. It does wonders."

"How long are you staying?"

"I don't know. Probably until the summer."

"Oh, that's great!" Cecily said, and they hugged again. "Hiya, Lil," Cecily added. "Alton." They greeted her back.

"Cecily, I told Trudy she could stay here," Isaac said.

"Oh, that's great!" exploded Cecily again.

"Now, Cecily, don't hog. She's staying with *us* some, too," Lillian spoke up, and they all laughed again.

****

"Angela, how would you like to spend some time with your daddy?"

The little five-year-old, blonde-headed, blue-eyed girl, lying on a Cinderella canopy bed, looked up in her mother's face and asked, "My *daddy*?"

Sitting on the child's bed Cindy added, "Yes, Sweetheart. Things have changed. You'll be able to spend more time with daddy. You can go to his house and spend the night if you wish. His wife is very nice. They have a swimming pool. What'd you say?"

"Do I have to?"

"Don't you want to, Sweetheart?"

"Not really."

"But, why? Isaac is your daddy."

"I don't know."

"You must have a reason, Angela."

"I like Bobby."

"I'm glad, Sweetheart. Bobby is very nice, but Bobby is just Mommy's friend. Isaac is your daddy."

"Couldn't Bobby be my daddy?"

"I'm afraid it doesn't work like that, Honey."

"Well, I don't like him!" Angela blurted out.

"Who? *Isaac*?! You don't like your *daddy*?!"

****

"Are you all right?"

"Yes," Cecily said, picking up the silverware from the floor, and Alton bent down to help her. "Did you come to check on me?"

"Yes. Isaac went upstairs for a moment, and when we heard the crash, Lillian asked me to check on you."

"I'm fine. I just dropped the silverware," Cecily said, then her eyes caught his for the first time, and she added. "Alton, we have to talk."

"About what?"

"About the night we were together."

"I thought that was in the past."

"I thought so, too, but it has resurfaced."

"What'd you mean?"

"Spencer had someone follow us that night. He has pictures," she whispered.

"What?!" Alton exploded trying to keep his voice low. "What kind of pictures?!"

"Everything."

"He has us...?" Alton couldn't finish, and Cecily nodded. "How?"

"I don't know."

"Damn!" he snapped walking away. "That son-of-a-bitch!" Then he took a deep breath to calm down. "What does he want?"

"Me! He wants *me*. You're just an innocent bystander who was caught in the crossfire. I'm sorry," she said very weakly as tears rolled down her face.

Chuckling he said, "I'm not so innocent." He took another deep breath. "What is he demanding? Knowing him he's asking for *something*."

"He's blackmailing me to...." Cecily started but was interrupted by Lillian entering.

"Is everything all right?" she asked.

"Yes," answered Cecily very quickly, turning away from her friend to wipe her tears. "I dropped some silverware." Lillian could feel the tension between her best friend and her husband, and it puzzled her. Alton walked to his wife.

"Come on, Darling. Everything's fine now, " he said, and she gave Cecily one final glance before following her husband.

****

"Where in the hell is she, Mike?" Ramon burst into a medium-sized, moderately decorated office demanding to a man behind a desk. "She's not answering her damn cell phone!"

"Ramon, what's the meaning of this?!"

"I know you know where she is! You're her agent!"

"I thought *you* would know. Trudy didn't tell me anything," he said picking up a note off his desk. "She only left me this note." Ramon grabbed the note from him. "All it says is that she's taking a leave of absence indefinitely." He looked at Ramon's sad face and added, "Did you two have a fight?"

"Yeah. Something like that," Ramon said dropping the letter on the desk then turning to leave.

"If you hear from her please tell her to call me."

Turning around abruptly to face the man, Ramon insisted, "Oh, I *will* find her! You can count on that! The ungrateful little bitch! And may God help her when I do!" He tore out the office, leaving a stunned Mike, who dropped down in his chair.

Mike buzzed his secretary. "Yes, Sir, Mr. Ballentine," she said.

"Leonora, get Trudy Miles on the phone for me please."

"Yes, Sir."

"And the next time Ramon Perez comes into this office, call security. That man's crazy!"

****

"I'm glad the men are gone. Now we can talk," Lillian said laughing with Trudy and Cecily while they sat on pillows in front of the blazing fireplace. "Tru, whatever happened to that man you were engaged to marry?"

"Ramon? Oh, Girl, let me tell you. He turned out to be a first class, grade *A* bastard," smiled Trudy. "I thought we were going to live happily ever after. He didn't tell me his wife came with the deal."

"He was *married*?!" exploded Cecily.

"With two kids."

"Dag!" added Lillian.

"So, is this the reason for your long visit?" Cecily wanted to know.

"Partly," confessed Trudy. "But I do need a vacation. I've been working sixteen hours days for the past year and a half. "Girlfriend, I need a break."

"I heard that," chuckled Lillian.

"But you heifers got it going on; those two gorgeous hunks you have."

"Sometimes gorgeous men are more trouble than they're worth," Lillian said very seriously.

"I bet you don't say that in bed, Girlfriend," Trudy blurted out, and they all burst into laughter.

"Get outta here, Girl," Lillian shoved her. "I'm serious."

"Come on, Lil, on a scale of one to ten, how is he?"

"A *twelve*," answered Lillian, then she and Trudy burst into laughter again. Cecily didn't find it amusing, but Lillian and Trudy noticed that.

"Cis, what's up?" Trudy wanted to know.

With a sad face, Cecily squeezed out, "I'm in trouble." Lillian and Trudy were stricken with surprised; therefore, they simultaneously focused on their friend.

"What kind of trouble?" was Lillian's question.

"It's Spencer. He's blackmailing me to supply him with drugs. I don't know what to do."

"Spencer?! The *pimp*?!" Trudy asked, and Cecily nodded.

"He's threatening to reveal your past?" Lillian asked.

"And more," Cecily said. "A whole lot more."

"Like what?" Trudy asked.

"Let me tell you the whole story," Cecily said, as she drifted into the past, telling her story:

* *Cecily sat at her desk when Cindy buzzed. "Yes, Cindy."*

"You have a call on line two, Cecily."

"Thanks, Cindy," she said, then picked up the telephone receiver, pushing the button. "Dr. Wade. May I help you?"

"Dr. Wade," a man's voice said, but Cecily didn't recognize the voice. "I

always knew you were special."

Growing impatient Cecily asked, "Who is this?"

"You've forgotten me already?" he went on. "It's only been fifteen years. And even after we had a child together. I'm deeply hurt."

"Rocky?" her breath ran out.

"In the flesh," he smiled. "I want to see you, beautiful."

"I'm sorry. That part of my life is over," she said sternly.

"Please don't make me beg."

"Rocky, I could care less what you do."

"Please, pretty lady. I want to see you so bad," he pleaded. "I worked long and hard to find you." She did not answer. "I'm staying at the Waldenburg Hotel. Suite 7T. Please come. "I'll be waiting for you." The telephone went dead in her ears.

As Cecily replaced the receiver, she couldn't help but to wonder why this man wanted to see her. Her curiosity got the best of her, and she decided to go and confront the man who had broken her heart so deeply, many years ago.

****

"Wow! You are beautiful," Rocky said staring at Cecily at his hotel room door. He stepped aside. "Please come in."

Stepping inside the room Cecily asked, "Where's your bodyguard?"

"Who Clarence?" he chuckled closing the door. "He's around

somewhere" He couldn't take his eyes off her.

"What'd you want, Rocky?" she asked looking at this man as if he was a stranger, for she couldn't see what attracted her to him in the first place. He wasn't even good looking with his greasy, shiny looking hair, which was slick down on his head, combed to the back, exposing his receding hairline. He looked old and frail. His once lean and muscular body was now a patchwork of skin and bones. He even looked shorter. The drugs had really done a job on this man, and she even felt a little sorry for him.

"How is our child?"

"I thought you were sterile," she sarcastically replied.

"That was Clarence's way of protecting me. I'm sorry," he said weakly. "Well, how is the child?"

"I have no idea."

"I don't understand."

"You <u>should</u> understand," she yelled growing very angry. "You denied her, and I was forced to give her away, you lousy, son-of-a-bitch!"

"I'm sorry about that, Cecily."

"Yeah, right," Cecily sarcastically replied. "Are you still doing drugs?"

Laughing, he said, "Nobody's perfect, Babe."

"Get to the point, Rocky. Why did you ask to see me?"

"I wanted to see if I could make amends for the baby. As I said, Clarence makes all decisions for me. He's responsible for me. I trust his decisions, and he made <u>that</u> one. I'm so sorry."

"It was <u>your</u> baby, <u>not</u> Clarence's!" Cecily exploded, now very angry *with this pathetic shell of a man. "Your apology ain't worth shit, Mister! My baby was taken away from me because there was no one to give a damn!" Tears flowed down her face now, but she was too angry to stop. "I have suffered the consequences for loving you. I can do nothing but wonder what happened to my only child! I hate you for what you did to me! And I hate you even more for what you did to our daughter! I will always hate you " She quickly turned and headed for the door to leave, but he grabbed her arm.*

"Cecily, please don't go," he begged as sweat began to pop out his already moist skin.

Jerking away from him, she yelled, "Take your hand off me!" Suddenly he headed for the bedroom. Curiosity guided Cecily in that direction also. When she reached the bedroom, it was Deja vu as she witnessed the famous singer setting up his dosage with a rubber tubing around his arm, desperately seeking a vein in his track-bearing skin.

"Don't do it, Rocky," she said weakly and received a blank stare from him momentarily, before he proceeded on with his deed. She walked to him. "You can beat this thing, Rocky, if you try. Then we can find our daughter together. I need you to help me to do that. Please."

"This will only take a second, Baby," he squeezed out aiming the syringe towards his vein.

Cecily just couldn't stand by and do nothing while this pathetic junky kill himself. "No!" she yelled grabbing the syringe. Before she knew what was happening, he was all over her, reaching for the syringe with one hand and

encircling her neck with the other hand. She couldn't breathe, and what's worse she knew he was totally unaware of what he was doing to her. The oxygen could not enter her body, and she couldn't let the syringe go even though she wanted to. He was out of control, and they fell to the floor, his body covering hers. Then she realized that he was actually trying to kill her, *for he now had both of his hands around her neck. She fought for every breath, but he would not let her go. She couldn't believe this was happening to her. She knew she could not stop him, for he was much too strong and much too angry. Suddenly with her eyes slowly seeing black, she spotted a knife on the floor. She outstretched her hand and tried to seize it. She couldn't breathe anymore, and then she felt the knife in her hand. She raised it as high as her weak, breathless body could and found the strength from somewhere to bring it down as hard as she could in his back. He jerked up and froze then collapsed on her weaken body. She gasped for air, as she coughed and wheezed, trying to fill her lungs again. Then she managed to push him aside, stumbled to her feet and breathed as deeply as she could.*
*

Cecily came out of the past, wiped her tears and focused on her friends. "I didn't mean to kill him," she squeezed out. "But I swear to you, it was self-defense."

"Why didn't you call the police?" Trudy asked.

"I don't know. I was scared. I panicked. Rocky's a big star. They would have locked me up and thrown away the key."

"Rocky *used* to be a big star. He ain't shit now," added Trudy.

"How does Spencer know all this?" was Lillian's question.

"He has pictures of the whole thing. He conveniently left out the pictures of me struggling for my life. They just look like I killed Rocky in cold blood."

"But I remember reading something about Rocky's being abroad on some extended vacation," added Trudy.

"Spencer fixed that. He said he moved the body and dumped it in the ocean."

"What about Clarence?" Lillian asked. "Have you heard anything from him?" Cecily shook her head. "It doesn't make sense. How can a famous person like Rocky be missing, and his manager doesn't report it? I would think there would be an all-point bulletin out on him."

"I got the impression that Rocky and Clarence had had a fallen out," Cecily said. "Rocky was very nonchalant about Clarence's where-a-bouts. And you don't know what Spencer is capable of. He has mob connection with a family named Romalotti."

"And now Spencer's blackmailing you." Trudy stated, and Cecily nodded. "That son-of-a-bitch!"

Patting Cecily on the shoulder Lillian said, "Don't worry, Kid. We'll think of something." Cecily nodded as the telephone rang, and Trudy picked it up.

"Hello?" She paused. "Sure. Hold on." She looked at Lillian and covered the telephone. "It's your husband. He wants you to get your black ass home and give him some of that down-home loving!" She burst into laughter, as Lillian grabbed the phone.

"You never quit," Lillian said laughing with her. "Hi, Darling. What's up?"

"*I* am," Alton said, lying his muscular, lean body between deep, hunter green, silk sheets. "What can you do about it?"

Lillian's face felt warm. She couldn't believe as dark as she was, she was actually blushing. "I'll be right there," she smiled, speaking softly.

"Hey, don't let *things* go *down* before you do," he whispered seductively soft. As Lillian hung up the phone, she felt a warm, wet feeling in her groins. She couldn't believe that after ten years of marriage, Alton still had that kind of effect on her, by just hearing his sexy voice.

"Ah, that's a woman in lust if ever I saw one," Trudy joked, and Lillian shoved her. "What'd I tell ya?! He's horny as hell, ain't he?"

"Do you ever quit?" Lillian laughed, getting up. "Girls, it's been real, but I've got to go," Then she looked at Cecily. "We'll talk some more tomorrow. We'll think of something. Let's pray about it. Maybe you should call his bluff and let the chips fall where they may. The Lord will bring you out all right if you just *ask* him then *trust* him." Cecily nodded, then she and Lillian hugged lovingly. "Don't worry."

"Check you later, Girlfriend," Trudy added as she and Lillian hugged.

"It's good to have you here, Girl," Lillian added.

"It's good to be together again," Trudy smiled. "Now go and take care of that horny husband." Lillian punched her on the arm again as she left.

"Ahhh, true love. They've been married over ten years, and they're still in love. That *is* super." She focused on Cecily who seemed to be a million miles away. "Cis, I think Lillian is right. Maybe you should call Spencer's bluff."

"Spencer doesn't *bluff*, Trudy."

"Then why don't you call the police yourself?"

"I can't, Tru."

"Why not? You can explain what happened, and if Spencer moved that body, his black ass is in just as much trouble as you are!"

Standing, Cecily took a deep breath and said, "It's not that simple, Tru. I wish it were."

"What're you talking about?"

"There's more."

"What? What do you mean?"

Cecily took another deep breath then started to explain, "Tru, do you remember David?" Trudy didn't appear to remember. "When I was hooking, he was the client I fell in love with."

"Oh, yeah. I remember him. I think he was the *only* man you ever loved besides Barry."

"Yeah. That's him."

"What about him?" Trudy wanted to know. "He was married, wasn't he?"

"Yes. *Very* married."

"What's he got to do with this?"

"I saw him again recently."

"Yeah? Is he still married?"

"Yeah, but a couple of weeks ago, we slept together again," Cecily confessed, taking another deep breath. "Spencer has pictures of that also. He's threatening to show the pictures to David's wife and Isaac."

"Oh, Cecily."

"We didn't plan it, Tru. I swear. It just happened."

"Are you planning to see him again?"

"No. Not like that. We both agreed it was a terrible mistake, and it would never happen again,"

"Then tell Isaac the truth. He loves you," Trudy replied sadly. "It's not the end of the world, Cis. I'm sure Isaac will forgive you, and this man's wife, well, they've been married a long time, maybe she will forgive him too."

Cecily locked eyes with Trudy and announced very softly, "It's Alton. David is Alton. Lillian's husband."

"*What*?!"

"David is Alton. I didn't know until they moved here a couple weeks ago."

"You're kidding, right?" Trudy exploded, jumping up. "You're fucking kidding?!"

"Tru, please understand...."

"Cecily, how in the hell could you sleep with *Lillian's* husband?!" she yelled. "She's your *best* friend!"

"I didn't know he was Lillian's husband when I fell in love with him."

"Well, you sure as hell knew it when you slept with him a couple weeks ago!"

"Tru, please try to understand!" Cecily was on her feet now. "I have loved this man for so long. We haven't seen each other in years! The night that we slept together, there were extenuating circumstances. I'm not trying to justify what I did. I know it was wrong. But that day, I had just learned that the daughter I was forced to give away was a patient of mine, and four hours later she was dead in my arms. Then to top it off, Isaac told me of a daughter he had with my secretary five years ago. I got drunk and as faith had it, Alton was the one to come to my rescue." She took a deep breath as tears flowed down her face. "I love him, Tru. I have always loved him. And, it's killing me for him to be so close and yet so far away."

"Are you and Alton having an affair or was it just that one night?'

"It was just that one night. We decided it couldn't happen again."

"Can you do that?"

"I have to. Lillian is my best friend."

Chapter 7

Cecily walked out the operating room and pulled off her surgical mask. She walked to a nervous couple and announced, "Mr. and Mrs. Bigelow, he's fine."

"Oh, thank God!" the woman exploded in her husband's arms. "May I see him?"

"Yes," Cecily said pointing, "Go right through there. They will be bringing him in soon."

Taking Cecily's hand and squeezing it lovingly, the lady said, "Bless you, Doctor. Bless you."

****

Cecily walked into the doctors' lounge, poured a cup of coffee, then sat at the table. The door opened, and Mr. Bigelow walked in. "How did you do it?" he asked softly.

"Excuse me?"

"I've never let on because I wasn't sure. Now, I know I'm right. How did you do it...." he said, then paused and added, *"Sissy?"*

She exhaled deeply then replied, "Hard work, Mr. Bigelow. Hard work."

"You've got to be a *very* smart young lady," he smiled. "Can we get together sometimes? For old time sake?"

Walking to the door Cecily said, "I don't think so. My hands are quite full."

"Yes. I remember how *good* you were with your *hands*," he sarcastically cooed with a smirk on his face.

"That was the *past*," Cecily stressed growing a little annoyed at this man. "This is *now*."

"Have you changed *that* much?"

"I just saved your little boy's life. What do *you* think?"

"I'm sorry," he said walking to the door. He stopped in front of her and focused on her full, rounded breasts and sighed deeply. "Um! What a waste!" He walked out, and Cecily had to smile as she thought, *Men!* She sat to finish her coffee, as she drifted into the past:

*   *Cecily strolled into a hotel room in a long, blonde, wavy wig, and a short, black, mini dress, with a neckline so low it left little to the imagination. She sat in a chair and crossed her long, smoothed legs, exposing black, fishnet stockings. The door opened, and Mr. Bigelow stepped in wearing a pair of dark sunglasses and a big Indiana Jones hat. "Hi. I'm Sissy," she cooed seductively in her highest pitched, bimbo, soprano voice, as she stood and swayed towards him.*

*"Wow! You're beautiful, Sissy," he glared, taking off his hat and sunglasses. "I'm Rudy." Suddenly he grabbed her and kissed her hard and savagely, and then he swept her up in his arms and carried her to the bed. She had a feeling he was going to be rough. She was right. She hoped it would be over quickly, and it was.   **

Cecily picked up the telephone and dialed a number. "Information. What city please?" the voice asked on the other end.

"LA."

"May I help you?"

"Carl Spencer."

"Hold for the number please," the lady said. In a moment, Cecily wrote the number down. She then hung up and dialed.

"Hello?" a young, blonde, cute white lady answered, lying in bed with Spencer sleeping beside her.

"Spencer please."

"Who's calling?"

"His *doctor*," Cecily sarcastically replied.

"Hold on," she said then shoved Spencer a little. "Honey, your *doctor* is on the phone."

"My *what*?!" he exploded, sitting up.

"Are you sick, Honey?"

Grabbing the phone, he snapped, "Give me that!" Then into the receiver, "Yeah, Spencer here."

"Isn't it a little early for *bed*, Spencer," Cecily teased. "Oh, but I do recall you were one who *loved* to go to bed early."

Catching her voice, he looked at the woman and demanded, "Get me a cup of coffee, Honey." She slipped on a housecoat, planted a quick kiss on his lips and walked out. "Now I *know* a busy doctor like you didn't call just to check up on my bedtime habits."

"You're right. We need to talk."

"When?" he yawned.

"What about lunch?"

"*Today?*"

"Yes, today!"

"I'll have to check my schedule."

"And you said business was falling."

Looking at his calendar he said, "I can make it at two."

"The Brigade."

"Right."

"And, Spencer, don't hurt yourself," Cecily added. "She sounds very young." The phone went dead to his ears.

"Bitch!" he chuckled. Spencer sat back, lit a cigarette, and drifted into the past:

** A man handed Spencer a picture and said, "I couldn't get any closer."*

Spencer felt the life momentarily leave his body when he focused on the picture of Cecily, in a brown full length mink coat and matching hat, that he had bought, standing in front of a hotel room door, in a bath-robed Barry Jett's arms, kissing him as she had done to him just a couple of hours before. "How long did she stay?" he asked weakly.

"I don't know. I had to leave. Remember I told you I had another gig?" the man said, and Spencer nodded slowly. "Are you all right, Spencer?"

"I'll check you later, Man."

"You really do love her, don't you?"

*"Bye, Charlie!" Spencer finalized, so the man turned and walked out, and Spencer wiped his eyes hard to keep tears from rolling down his face. Then he sniffed and began savagely ripping the picture to shreds, as he yelled, "You wanna fuck around, Bitch?! I'll let you fuck! I gave you everything, but you bitches are all alike! You're never satisfied unless you have more than one dick.   Well, Baby, you got it! I'll show your little red ass! You don't fuck with Spencer!"   ***

"Here is your coffee, Baby," the lady said bringing Spencer back to the present.

****

Cecily stared into space as she drifted into the past:

*   Cecily sat in a bathtub full of bubbles as Spencer entered removing his tie. "Hi, Baby" she smiled.*

"Hi," he said bending down to kiss her.

"What's wrong? You look tired."

"I'm frustrated. Candy's sick," he said. "She has a big fish tonight, and I don't know who I can get to replace her." He took a deep breath. "This client is special. He doesn't fuck. He just likes to have someone to talk to."

"You mean a man pays good money just to <u>talk</u>?"

"That's right," he said drying her off with a towel, as she stepped out the tub. "Hey, darling, why don't you do it?"

"Do <u>what</u>?!"

"Entertain this client."

"Are you <u>crazy</u>?!" she yelled, grabbing the towel from him.

"Baby, you don't have to fuck him. I just don't want to lose his business."

"I can't believe you'd ask me to do this, Spencer!" she raged securing the towel around her body.

"Darling, you know I don't want anyone else to have you. You're mine. I'd never ask you to do this if there was the slightest chance that you'd have to fuck him. Never."

"I don't want to spend my time with some freak."

"He's not a freak. He's a nice old man who lives out of town. I promise you, Baby. I wouldn't put you in danger. Trust me!"

"I don't know, Spencer."

"Honey, I love you," he cooed, planting a kiss on her lips.

"I love you, too, Baby, but..."

"But, what?" he cooed again, planting another kiss on her lips.

"Are you sure he won't expect me to have sex with him?"

"I promise, Baby," he said softly. "Will you do it for me, Baby? I'll buy you something real special tomorrow."

"All right," she gave in.

"That's my girl!" he smiled, grabbing her up in a big bear hug.

****

Cecily nervously knocked on a hotel room door. The door flew open and a tall, completely bald, three-hundred-fifty-pound, jet black man stood there, wrapped in a towel, with fire breathing dragon tattoos covering his chest and arms. Cecily grew frighten and started to change her mind and run away but he barked in a gruff, raspy voice, "Sissy?!"

"Yes," she replied, finding her voice. "I'm here to see Roy."

"Well, you got him, Baby!" he smiled, exposing three empty tooth sockets, while barbarously pulling her in the room by the arm. He closed the door with his bare foot, staring at her so hard, she knew he was undressing her with his large, bulging eyes, and she felt very uncomfortable. "I was disappointed to hear about Candy, but you'll do just fine. Just fine indeed." He dropped his towel leaving <u>nothing</u> to the imagination, and Cecily swallowed hard. He grabbed her breasts with his huge hands, and she backed away.

"There must be a mistake. Spencer said all you wanted to do was talk."

Bursting into laughter, he said, "Spencer told you that?! Damn, Baby, Spencer know I'm the horniest nigger in all of Texas, and when I'm in New York he always get me a special lady to fulfill my needs."

Backing away Cecily squeezed out, "I don't understand."

"What don't you understand, Sugar. You're a woman and I'm a man. You came here to service me, didn't you?"

"Yes, but..."

"No buts!" he said jumping to her like a vulture, ripping off her clothes with one jerk and laughing hysterically, like a crazy man. As she cried and begged him to stop, he threw her on the floor and forcefully had his way with her. The more she screamed, the more he seemed to like it. She wondered why Spencer had betrayed her. She thought he loved her, but she was sadly mistaken. But it was her <u>own</u> fought. Cotton had warned her about Spencer; that the most important thing in his life was <u>money</u>. Cecily couldn't believe this was happening to her. She closed her eyes and wished it would soon be over. After he was satisfied <u>several</u> times, then he finally rolled off her and went to sleep right on the floor. She prayed that God would take her right now. She wanted to die! Cecily's entire body ached with unbearable pain as this man snored like a bear in hibernation. No one had ever treated her so savagely before. She hated this man, and even more than that, she hated <u>Spencer</u>. While he slept, she struggled to find her footing, and then she tipped around collecting her torn clothes. She was so afraid she would wake him, and she knew she just couldn't bear to take that kind of abuse anymore. She'd rather die than to have him touch her again. She pulled on her clothes softly and quietly, and then she tipped out.

****

Cecily walked into the house that she shared with Spencer, and he was cuddled on the couch with another woman in their bathrobes. Cecily paused briefly then walked pass them and started up the stairs. "How was it?" Spencer asked with a smirk, and she did not answer. "Hey, Bitch, I'm talking to you!" he yelled, springing to his feet and moving behind her up the stairs. She turned around slowly to face him.

Indicating the woman Cecily said, "I thought she was sick."

"All Candy needed was Dr. Spencer," he joked. "How was your outing?"

"How do you <u>think</u>?" she snapped. "You lied to me. How could you do that to me? I thought you loved me."

"The only thing I love, Babe, is the almighty dollar!" he snapped back. "What're you complaining about? You ain't no damn virgin. You've been around."

Tears ran down Cecily's face as her lips curled up, and her hand flew back and aimed at Spencer's face, but he caught it in mid-air then pushed her down the spiral stairway. Candy screamed as she jumped up, while Cecily's weaken body tumbled down the stairs until it reached the bottom. Spencer ran to Cecily, picked her up, and slapped her in the face as hard as he could as he yelled, "Bitch, don't you ever raise your hand to hit me again!" Spencer's rage knew no limit as he pounded on Cecily's weaken, semi-conscience body. Blood splattered everywhere until Candy ran to Spencer and caught his hand.

"Stop, Spencer! You're killing her!" she yelled, and he took control of his senses again, and Cecily's head dropped to the floor, and all she saw was darkness.

****

*Cecily opened her swollen, black and blue eyes, and Spencer was standing there, and she cringed at the sight of him. He walked to the bed and said very business-like, "I want you to move back into your apartment. It's bad for my business to have any of my bitches staying here." Cecily couldn't believe her ears. This man whom she shared a life with intimately for three years was tossing her aside like an old shoe. And, to top it off, he sounded as if he wanted her to be one of his whores. And, as if he was reading her mind, he added, "And, don't you even <u>think</u> about skipping out on me, Bitch! Wherever you go, I'll find you, and I swear to God, I'll make you sorry you ever heard of Carl Spencer! Nobody <u>skip</u> out on Spencer! <u>Nobody</u>!" He walked out slowly, and Cecily's tears burned her swollen, bruised eyes, but she couldn't hold them back. She had only one more year left in medical school, and she would make it. She was tough. Thank God she had never told the son-of-a-bitch she was in medical school. She had wanted to surprise him when she was finished, but now, he'll <u>never</u> know. But, one day, she would get even with this bastard! <u>One day</u>!   **

Cecily came from the past and wiped her tears. "I be damned if I'll let you screw me again, Spencer." She walked over to the closet and retrieved a small, metal box. She opened it and took out a 22-caliber pistol. "You son-of-a-bitch! It's *my* turn!"

****

Trudy lay on the bed and looked at one o'clock on the bedside clock. She knew she had to be at the restaurant about two thirty. She hoped Cecily's plan worked. Cecily was right about *one* thing; Lillian must *never* find out about Cecily's affair with Alton. That would kill her. They all had a bond stronger than some sisters. She didn't understand how Cecily could have crossed that line and slept with Lillian's husband, but love is a strong potion, and she knew Cecily has always loved this man called David, a.k.a. Alton. She prayed Cecily would get over Alton. She felt sorry for her, loving a forbidden man so much. That must be pure hell. But if Cecily's plan worked, maybe at least, Lillian would never find out about Cecily and Alton. Although she was taking a risk, she knew she *had* to do this for Cecily, because Lord knows, Cecily had taken risks for her before. Trudy drifted into the past.

*   *"Are you sure, Trudy?" Cecily asked standing over Trudy as she lay on a surgical bed.*

"Yes, I'm sure, Cecily. I <u>can't</u> have this baby. I'm just starting my career. I've just signed a major modeling contract. They won't wait until I have this baby," Trudy explained.

"You don't know that, Tru," added Lillian. "You could ask."

"Get real, Lillian. They won't wait for me. I'm an unknown. A nobody.

I can't blow this. This is my big chance."

"But, Trudy, an <u>abortion</u>?!" Cecily insisted. "Think about what you're doing."

"Cecily, I've thought about nothing but this for the past month. Please, no lectures! Just do it. I know what I'm doing."

"I'm afraid, Tru. What if you have complications?" was Lillian's question.

"I'm only in my second year of Med School. I could lose everything if this gets out. I could even go to jail. But none of that matters as much as how I could live with myself if something happens to you?" Cecily added. "I'm taking a big risk here, Trudy."

"If there are complications, I'll handle it. I promise. There's no risk to your career. You will be left out of it completely. And if something happens to me, I want you to feel good that you tried to help a friend. And know that if you don't do it, <u>somebody</u> will. I <u>cannot</u> have this baby."

Cecily smiled at her determined friend lovingly as she gently wiped the perspiration from her forehead gently, and then she took a deep breath, looked at Lillian and asked, "Ready?" Lillian nodded slowly. "Let's do it."

*

Trudy came out of the past, wiping the tears from her face, as she stood and went to her vanity table. When she opened a makeup bag a picture of her with Ramon fell out. She drifted into the past again:

*   *"Ramon! What're you doing here?"*

Walking pass her into her apartment he said, "We need to talk, Trudy."

"About <u>what</u>?" she asked, closing the door. "We've already talked."

"No! <u>You</u> talked!" he said removing his Chaucer Holloman coat. "Trudy, I love you. Don't you get it? I love you. I don't want to lose you." He put his arms around her waist. "Please don't push me away."

"What about your wife, Ramon?"

"I asked her for a divorce."

"You <u>what</u>?!" she exploded, breaking away from him.

"You heard me. I asked my wife for a divorce. I want you, and hell, I can still help with the kids. You don't have a problem with that, do you?"

"Of course not. I love kids."

"I don't ever want you to kill my child again, Trudy. I want us to have a lot of babies."

"Oh, Ramon, I love you," she said as he pulled her in his arms, and they kissed long and hard.

"I don't just want an affair with you, Trudy. I want you to be my wife just as soon as my divorce is final, if you'd have me."

"Oh, yes, Baby. Oh, yes," she said smiling big, and they kissed again.

Sweeping her up in his arms, he said, "Let's celebrate." They kissed long and passionately as he carried her into the bedroom.

****

Trudy and Ramon were awakened by the ringing of the doorbell. "Damn!" Trudy grumbled. "I wonder who that is."

"Maybe they'll go away," he mumbled squeezing her close in his arms from the rear, but he was wrong. The persistent intruder continued to ring the doorbell.

Rolling off the bed to her feet she said, "It must be important."

"Hurry back," he said smiling, patting her bare behind, then turned over to go back to sleep. Trudy grabbed a housecoat then walked out pulling it on.

When Trudy got to the door, she yanked it open, and a lady of Spanish decent stood there with stringy, dirty, black hair, torn check-a-board dress, granny boots with a toe sticking out of one, a swollen lip and black eyes, where she appeared to have been beaten or hit by a Mack truck. "May I help you?" Trudy finally asked, once she found her voice, for the woman's appearance shocked her so much, it left her speechless.

In broken English the woman said very weakly, "I come to git me husben, Miss Miles."

"Excuse me?" Trudy said not believing her ears, as she thought to herself that even if this pathetic woman had a man, surely, <u>she</u> wouldn't be interested in him. She doubted if she and this woman shared the <u>same</u> taste in men.

"Ramon Perez. He me husben. He here. No?"

"What?!" Trudy blurted out. "Surely, you're not…" her breath ran out as she added, "…his wife?"

"Si. I he wife."

"There must be some mistake," Trudy said stepping aside. "Please, come in." She closed the door behind the lady. "I'll be right back." She went into the bedroom and shook Ramon slightly. "Honey, wake up."

"What is it, Baby?" he yawned, pulling her in his arms. "You're ready for seconds." He smiled planting a soft kiss on her lips.

"Ramon, you need to get up. We have a guest."

"Get rid of them, Baby."

"She says she's your wife," Trudy announced, and he froze solid.

"What?!" he exploded out of bed, throwing on a robe. He rushed into the living room, followed by Trudy, and came face to face with the woman. "What in the hell are you doing here?!" he demanded.

"The children hungry, Ramon. No food," she said, then Ramon said something back to her in Spanish, so she replied also in Spanish. Trudy didn't know what they were saying, but she knew Ramon didn't like it because he was growing very angry.

"Ramon, is this woman really your <u>wife</u>?" Trudy finally asked. He walked to her and held her face in his hands.

"Baby, she doesn't want to give me a divorce. I saw a lawyer, and he's gotten the papers started," he sincerely said. "You know how much I love you." Tears rolled down the sad woman's face as she witnessed her husband confessing his love to another woman, but his concerns weren't with his wife at the moment as he continued trying to soothe Trudy, "You will be my wife with or without that divorce. I promise. I love you, Baby." Then he

planted a kiss on her lips and wiped her tears with his fingers. "Don't cry, Baby. I will always be with you. I love you." He kissed her again so tenderly it surprised her when he turned to his wife and did a Mr. Hyde on her as he yelled, "Get the hell out of here! I swear to God if you ever come near us again, I'll kill you!"

"I no want to come. The children hungry. We have no food. No clothes," she explained wiping tears from her face.

"And, what about the divorce?" he wanted to know. "I'll set up whatever I need to in financial support for you and the kids if I get my divorce."

"No divorce, Ramon. We marry in church. No divorce."

"You're crazy, woman."

"You got me good years."

"Shut up!" he demanded, but she was not to be denied her chance to speak, no matter what he did to her.

"I work. You went college. Now, I no good enough for you."

"I said shut the fuck up!" he yelled again moving towards her, but again, she was not going to be intimidated by this man.

"I pretty one time. He beat me mucho. Now, I ugly."

"I owe you nothing!" he snapped, slapping her so hard, she landed on the floor, while Trudy screamed. He ran to Trudy and pulled her in his arms. "I'm sorry, Baby. This woman makes me crazy."

Struggling to regain her footing, the woman squeezed out a bloody mouth, "I pregnant."

"What?!" Trudy exploded, jerking her head off him.

"Baby, I was drunk one night, and she took advantage of the situation," Ramon talked quickly to explain.

"No talk true," the lady said. "You raped me."

"I <u>despise</u> you," he shouted turning to her. "If I wasn't drunk, you'd have <u>never</u> gotten me in bed, and you know it. Now, get the fuck out!"

"What about baby?"

"I don't give a fuck about you or those bastard kids!" he yelled opening the door. "Get the fuck out before I throw you out!"

She walked to the door slowly then turned to look at Trudy and said, "You see me. This you when he tired of you." He pushed her out the door and slammed it. Trudy dropped on the chair, and he ran to her.

"Baby, I'm sorry I didn't tell you about the baby. I didn't think you would understand. I love you. Please, don't let that bitch come between us."

"Get out, Ramon."

"What?"

"I want you out of here."

"You can't mean that, Baby. We have such a good thing here."

Growing angry Trudy jumped up and yelled, "I want you the hell out of my damn home! That woman wasn't lying on you! What kind of animal are you?! To let your wife and children go hungry and without clothes, while you wear five hundred-dollar <u>shoes</u>! What kind of animal would do that to his <u>family</u>?!"

"She was lying, Trudy!"

"She was <u>not</u> lying!" she yelled, and suddenly his hand came crushing

down hard on her face, knocking her to the floor. He rushed to her and picked her up.

*"Baby, I'm sorry. I didn't mean to. You just made me so angry, saying that <u>she</u> was telling the truth, when I know she wasn't. Please, forgive me," he pleaded bathing her face and neck with kisses. "Oh, you are so beautiful. I love you so much." He laid her on the couch, pulled up her housecoat, and made love to her so gently, it was hard for Trudy to believe he was the same monster his wife described, but she knew he was. She had seen the rage, and it frightened her. Trudy didn't want his hands on her and wanted to protest so badly she ached, but she didn't dare to. She couldn't afford to make him angry enough to ruin her face like he had done his wife's. Unlike his wife, <u>her</u> face was her life, so she lay there, suffering in silence, letting him have his way with her, hoping that it would soon be over. She knew what she had to do. She would change the locks then take a long vacation with her friends, and maybe by the time she returned, he would have hooked on to someone else, and that will be the end of that.   ***

Trudy came back to the present in tears. She wiped her tears, looked at the clock, and started getting dressed. She knew it was time to go. She hoped Cecily's plan worked because if it didn't, it could destroy *all* of them.

****

Cecily walked into a very eloquent restaurant and asked for Spencer. The

Maître d' showed her to Spencer's table. "Mr. Spencer," she said very formal as she sat.

"Dr. Wade."

"May I get you something from the bar, Madam?"

"White wine," she said dropping a magazine on the table.

"Bring me another scotch," Spencer added.

"Very well," the waiter said handing Cecily a menu then left.

"Have you ordered, Spencer?" Cecily asked, noticing that he was looking at a picture of Trudy on the cover of the *Fashion and Glamour Magazine* she had laid down.

"No," he said, picking up the magazine. "I was waiting for you."

"How noble."

"This is one *foxy* chick," he drooled over Trudy's picture.

"I doubt she's for sell, Spencer, so put your eyes back in your head,"

"*Everyone* has a price," he stressed. "But a chick like this, I would keep all to myself."

"Until you got tired of her, then you'll put her on the streets like all the rest."

"*Everyone* has a choice, Baby."

"Where the hell was *my* choice when you threw me out on the streets to make you money?"

"You made your choice! I didn't say there wouldn't be consequences!"

"God, I hate you," Cecily replied through clenched teeth.

"The feeling is mutual, my dear. I assure you. The feeling is mutual!" he said bringing forth silence between them. Soon the waiter returned, breaking the cold silence of hatred that Spencer and Cecily shared.

"Are you ready to order?" he cheerfully asked.

"I'll have the lamb chops," replied Cecily handing him the menu.

"T-bone for me," added Spencer.

"Very well," the waiter said receiving Spencer's menu then walking away.

"Does he satisfy you, Sissy?" Spencer nonchalantly asked.

"Who?"

"Your *husband*!" he snapped. "Remember *him*?"

"That's none of your goddamn business!"

"Obviously *not*," he replied with a smirk. "Or you wouldn't need lover boy Carter."

"I don't need *anyone*."

"I remember very clearly when you and he needed each other very much. He would never accept any other girl. And, when you skipped out on me, I never saw him again."

"Pity," she sarcastically replied. "And, I didn't *skip* out on you. You forgot our deal. I was to work for you until something better came along, and something did."

"You didn't even have enough guts to tell me you were in medical school. I would've helped you."

"Yeah, then I'd owe my *medical degree* to you as well. No thanks!"

"Well, that's in the past. Now, let's get down to business. I am expecting my first shipment next Friday, Sissy."

"I told you I can't get it *that* soon."

"Then you better put a rush on it, Baby!" he insisted as the waiter brought their food.

"May I get something else for you?" he asked, and they shook their heads, then he left.

"Can't we work something out?" Cecily smiled thinking of the gun in her purse.

"Like what?" he said and thinking, *This bitch is up to something.*

She took off her shoe and rubbed her foot up his leg until it reached his crotch. She felt his excitement grow at her touch. "I'm sure we can think of something," she said thinking that as soon as they got to a hotel, she would blow his fucking brains out.

"Where?" he asked still wondering what she was up to. He had to find out, so he would play along with her little game, because if it turned out that she was for real, they could have a great time together, like they used to do. And Lord knows they *did* have some *really* good times together. His excitement grew even more just thinking of being with her again. But, if she was playing with him like he thinks, Lord help her.

"Don't you have a hotel room?" she asked, and he didn't answer. He just gulped down the last of his scotch and stood up.

"Let's go."

****

"Wanda!" Lillian called stepping out of the shower, wrapped in a towel, but the child didn't answer.

"Will *I* do?" Alton peeked his head in the door with a smile.

"Alton! What're you doing home this time of day?"

"Well, I'll tell you," he said wrapping his arms around her. "I just knew my beautiful wife would be stepping out the shower right about now." He smiled loosening her towel and letting it fall to the floor. "And I just couldn't resist coming home." They kissed long and passionately. Then he swept her up in his arms, carried her into the bedroom, and laid her on the bed. She couldn't believe how passionate their lovemaking still was after all those years of marriage. Then when it was over, he pulled her in his arms and whispered softly in her ear, "I love you, Baby."

"And, I love you, Sweetheart," she said, and they kissed again.

"Lillian, I was just thinking. Wanda's five now. Don't you think it's time for us to work on giving her a little brother or sister?"

With widen eyes she said, "What?! I thought you didn't want any more children!"

"I changed my mind. I want to have a house full of children with you, Baby."

"Oh, Alton!" she exploded, attacking him with tender kisses, as he laughed.

****

Spencer dropped some money on the table, turned quickly, and crashed into Trudy. "Oh, I'm sorry," he said.

"No. It was my mistake," Trudy replied taking off her big, hat, which almost covered her face, exposing her long, beautiful, free-flowing, auburn hair.

"Are you all right, Miss Miles?" the Maître d' ran to her asking.

"Yes, I'm fine," she smiled then turned to Spencer. "I wasn't looking where I was going. Please excuse me."

Admiring her shapely body in that skin-tight, black dress, Spencer said smiling, "There's no need to apologize. I assure you." He also recognized her to be the gorgeous creature on the cover of that magazine he had just seen.

"Your table is over here, Miss Miles. You're dining alone? Is that correct?"

"Yes, thank-you," Trudy said sweetly then focused on Spencer. "Are you leaving, Mister…?"

"Spencer," he finished. "Carl Spencer." He paused. "A beautiful lady should never dine alone. May I join you?"

"I would deem it an honor if you and your friend would join me."

"She's not my friend. She's a business associate."

"I see," Trudy said then focused on Cecily. "Please join us, Ah, Miss…."

"Dr. Wade," Cecily finished. "No thank you, Miss Miles. I need to get back to work."

"Very well," Trudy said then stuck her elbow out to Spencer. "Shall we, Mr. Spencer?"

"Yes, Ma'am," he said taking her arm and leading her to her seat. "We'll talk later," he called back to Cecily with a fake smile. Cecily had to smile at witnessing what a pro her friend was. She had Spencer groveling like a puppy, and he never knew what hit him. The pathetic little shit. He's lucky Trudy showed up when she did, but there'll be another time. Her plan had better work or she'll take care of Spencer herself. Cecily knew she and Alton were wrong for what they did, but she would never let Spencer hurt Lillian and Isaac just to get back at her. *Never*!

As Cecily walked out, she said aloud, "I be damned if I'll be victimized by you again, Spencer. You have pushed me to the limit, and *this* time, I'm *fighting* back!"

Chapter 8

It has been two months now and Trudy and Spencer were a hot new item according to the media. He attended different events with her, so they were linked as the hottest couple in show business. Spencer moved into a condominium, and Trudy moved back into the hotel to avoid his making any connections between Cecily and herself.

The three friends' meeting place was Lillian's country house on the lake, which is where Cecily, Lillian, and Trudy sat today drinking tea under a big shady tree in the beautiful, landscaped yard. "Do you think he suspects anything?" Lillian asked Trudy.

"No. I don't think so, but I'm running out of excuses why we can't sleep together. He's getting very horny, Girl," Trudy laughed.

"What about *you*?" asked Cecily.

"What'd you mean? What about *me*?!"

"I know how *charming* Spencer can be."

"Yeah, he's *very* charming and handsome and suave, but I know what I'm here to do, Cecily. I'm not stupid!" Trudy insisted growing a little annoyed.

Bursting into laughter Cecily said, "I'm just kidding, Tru. Dag! Don't be so serious!"

"That ain't funny, Cecily," Trudy said and laughed also, then Lillian joined in.

"But seriously, Tru, he hasn't told you *anything* yet?" Lillian asked.

"Not a thing."

"You have to win his trust," added Cecily. "Once you do that, he'll tell you anything, but winning his trust is the hard part. Spencer trusts no one!"

"What exactly am I looking for, Cecily?"

"Anything and everything that will incriminate the bastard. Believe me, there's *plenty*. I need something to hold over his head to get him off my back," Cecily explained. "And if possible, I wish you could find something to prove the bastard murdered Cotton."

"Just how dangerous is this man, Cis?" Lillian asked.

"*Very* dangerous. And, Tru, whenever you feel uncomfortable, you pull out."

"I can take care of myself."

"Yes, but you've never had to deal with anyone like Spencer before," added Lillian.

"I'll be all right."

"Just keep one thing in focus," insisted Cecily. "We have to nail the son-of-a-bitch!"

****

Trudy walked into her hotel suite, kicked off her shoes, and then stopped suddenly when she heard a noise. "Who's there?!" she called heading for the door.

"It's me, Darling," Spencer said, entering from the kitchen, wrapped in a towel, exposing his broad, hairy chest.

"How did you get in?" Trudy asked, while thinking to herself, *Damn, this man is fine.*

"The maid. She knows about us," he said kissing her neck. "Umm, you smell good."

"I didn't expect you," she said with trembling lips. "Did you take a *shower?*" She thought, *I'm in trouble. Help! Someone! Anyone!*

"Ugh-humm," he coed, turning her around, and kissing her lips softly. "I ordered lunch. Are you hungry?"

"Starved," she replied, walking away from him and into the kitchen. He walked behind her. When she entered the kitchen, she was shocked to see the table was arranged beautifully, with china, wine, and fresh cut flowers. "Wow, the table is beautiful."

"Not as beautiful as you are," he smiled, and she knew he was undressing her with his eyes, and *that* made her feel very uncomfortable, so she turned away from him. "What's wrong, Baby?"

"I had a rough day. That new job I took had me in retakes all day."

"Come on," he said taking her hand and leading her to the bedroom.

"Carl, what're you doing?" she chuckled, reluctantly, following him.

"Lie down, baby. I'm going to give you a massage you'll kill for."

"I just need to take a shower and relax."

"And, you will, after I give you one of Spencer's famous massages."

"But..."

"No buts," he cut her off. "Lie down." She obeyed because she didn't want to make him suspicious. He got some oil and began to massage her body, starting with her feet, and working his way up. She felt him pulling off her pantyhose and panties simultaneously.

"Do we have to...."

"Shhhh," he coed going on with his business. "Relax. You're so tense." Trudy tried to relax because he was right, his strong hands felt so good, but she couldn't allow herself to become intimate with this man. A murderer, Cecily called him. Scum of the earth for what he was making Cecily do. She loathed this man, but how in the heck was she going to get him out tonight without...? She didn't want to think about it, but wow, his massage felt sooooo good!

****

Cecily walked into her office and pulled off her white smock. She then ran to the toilet, just in time, before she relinquished all her lunch to it. She held up momentarily, closed her eyes and sat on the floor. "Oh, my God, what is wrong with me?" she said aloud, and then she felt the swelling in her mouth again and barely made her head over the toilet this time. When she finished, she dropped on the floor again, and an image of her in Alton's arms appeared before her causing her to gasp. "Oh, no. I can't be...." she stopped abruptly for she didn't want to hear it aloud. She didn't even want to *consider* the possibility of being.... *pregnant*, because if she was, she wouldn't know who the father was, Isaac or *Alton*. She just *couldn't* be pregnant. Not *now*! "Lord, God, please be merciful," she prayed as Cindy buzzed her. She stumbled to her feet slowly, made it to her desk chair, and pushed the button. "Yes, Cindy."

"Cecily, Mr. Carter is on line one."

Alton? Cecily thought then responded, "Thanks, Cindy." She picked up the phone. "Alton?"

"Hi, Cecily."

"What's up?"

"We need to finish our conversation about Spencer."

"I'm taking care of that situation, Alton."

"We still should talk. This involves me, too," Alton added. "Can we meet somewhere?"

"Now?"

"If you can."

"No. I'm afraid I can't right now. I'll call you later."

"Are you sure, Cecily. We need to talk about this."

"Yes. I'm sure. Talk to you later," she said hanging up. She sat back in her chair and felt ashamed of the feeling that came over her just by hearing Alton's voice. "Oh God, I've *got* to get *over* this man! But *how*? He's my best friend's husband. How do you fall *out* of love with someone?" So, to get her mind off Alton, she focused on Trudy and wondered how she was doing with Spencer. Although Trudy had made it clear that she could take care of herself, Cecily still worried about her. She knew what Spencer was capable of. She drifted into the past:

** Cecily was buttoning her blouse when a man entered from the bathroom, zipping up his pants. He kissed the back of her neck and cooed, "That was good, Baby. I needed that. I didn't think Spencer would find me anyone as good as Cotton, but he did. I do miss Cotton, though. Spencer should've never rubbed her out."*

"What?!" Cecily exploded. "What'd you mean, he should've never rubbed her out?"

"It's common knowledge Spencer put a hit out on Cotton. She was about to turn state. Spencer has mob connections, you know."

"I don't think you know what you're talking about," she chuckled.

*"That's what's out on the streets," he finalized. "I hear it all started when Spencer wanted to put Cotton's niece on the streets, and Cotton wouldn't let him. I'm sorry you didn't know, Baby." Cecily couldn't believe her ears. <u>Spencer</u> killed Cotton and probably because of <u>her</u>. Cotton had lost her life trying to keep her off the streets and look where she is today. She knew right then and there that she was getting far away from this life. Spencer would just have to find her, but she was leaving <u>now</u>!   **

Cecily came back to the present, wiped her tears, and then stood up. She had to go and have a pregnancy test done. She had to know if she was pregnant or not. And, may God help her if she is carrying Alton's baby.

****

The water splashed on Trudy's body from the shower as she wondered what Spencer was thinking about her since she jumped out of bed like a teenager on her first date, just as he was about to make love to her. She just couldn't do it. She had to stay focus like Cecily said. She can't let herself get too involved with this man Cecily called a murder, although she couldn't imagine Carl killing anyone. He was so gentle with her. She heard the shower glass push open then focused on Spencer's gorgeous, lean body stepping in with her. "Carl!" she exploded. "I told you I wouldn't be long."

"I couldn't wait," he smiled, grabbing her in his arms, and giving her a long, passionate kiss. "Why are you afraid of me, Miss Miles?"

She chuckled, "Afraid?! I'm not afraid of you."

"Then why do you keep pushing me away?"

"Because I still don't know you very well."

"You know *everything* you need to know right now."

"Like what?"

"Like, I love you," he confessed, and Trudy's mouth dropped open. "Yes. I love you, Pretty Lady. *I'm* surprised, too. I've never fallen for anyone this quickly, but I do love you, and I want to share everything with you." He planted his lips on hers again, very gently, breaking her resistance; until she gave in to his desire and let him take her right there in the shower, making wild, ecstatic love to her, with the water caressing their clinging bodies. She had never known a man to be so tender but yet so exciting. He touched buttons in her emotions that she didn't know she had, and it was wonderful.

"I love you, Baby," he whispered in her ear.

She was putty in his hands, and she heard a voice say, "I love you, too, Carl," And she realized it was *her* voice, and what's more, she realized it was *true*. Oh God, what was she going to do now? She had a decision to make. Cecily was one of her best friends, but she truly loved this man whom she was deceiving. What was she going to do?

When he finally released her, he turned off the shower, led her to the bed and sat her on it softly. He handed her a bathrobe and wrapped a towel around himself. Then he sat on the edge of the bed, opened the drawer to the nightstand, pulled out a small, black velvet box and handed it to her. "What's this?"

"Open it," he said softly, and when she did, her breath ran out, for it was the most exquisite, five-carat, sparkling, marquise diamond ring she had ever seen in her life. "Trudy, Baby, I'm not much on formalities and all that. I know we've only known each other a couple months, but I know what I want, and I want *you*. Will you marry me?"

"Carl, I don't know what to say," Trudy finally said after finding her voice. "You've completely knocked me off my feet." She paused, thinking of what to say. "I do love you, but I don't know if we're ready for marriage yet."

"Why not? I love you, and you love me. What else is there?"

"There're a lot of things to consider. I mean, I don't even know how you make a living."

"That's not important."

"It is to *me*. When I marry a man, I want to know *everything* about him, not just what he *thinks* I should know."

He dropped his head and said very softly, "If I tell you what I do, you might not want to marry me."

"I can't marry you if you *don't*."

"Baby, I'll tell you anything you want to know but keep in mind, I can change *anything* for you," he said so sincerely, that Trudy felt absolutely terrible for what she was trying to do to him. She took a deep breath. Here comes the big moment. What she had been working towards for two months now. She didn't know if it was worth it. She really loved him, and he trusted her, but Lillian and Cecily were her *best* friends. She didn't know what she would do now.

****

"All right, I need suggestions on what you want to do."

"Mrs. Carter, what about a talent show?" one teenage boy spoke from the crowd of teenagers sitting on a carpeted floor in the church with Lillian and Wanda.

"A talent show. That's a good idea," Lillian said.

"Will Pastor Graham let us do one?" a girl wanted to know.

"I'm sure he will. He said to get the young people in the church involved, and a talent show definitely will do that."

"What about a fashion show with it? I can model, but I don't have any talent," another girl added.

"Juleps, God gives us *all* at least *one* talent, so don't say you don't have any," Lillian said. "But a fashion show is good, too. So, let me run this by Pastor Graham, and we'll meet again next week. Okay?" The young people agreed very enthusiastically as they stood, while Pastor Graham entered. He greeted them as they left.

"They're very excited. You're a hit, Mrs. Carter," Pastor Graham said smiling as he walked to Lillian.

"They're great kids. I'm going to enjoy working with them."

"And I know *they* will enjoy working with *you* as well. That's why I chose you for this position. I just knew you would do a fine job."

"Thank-you, Pastor," Lillian smiled, as Alton entered.

"I thought I would find you here."

"Daddy!" Wanda exploded, jumping on him and receiving a big bear hug.

"Pastor," Alton greeted.

"Hello, Alton. Lillian's doing a fine job with our young people already."

"That's great," Alton said then planted a kiss on Lillian's lips. "Hello, Mrs. Carter."

"Hi," she smiled, and Pastor Graham could see he was no longer needed.

"Well, you two have a blessed day," he said.

"Pastor Graham, I need to talk to you about some plans the kids and I discussed," Lillian spoke up.

"Very well, Lillian. My door is always open to you."

"Thank-you," she said, as he left. "Don't forget about dinner Friday."

"We won't."

"Dinner?" Alton asked when the Pastor had gone, as he put Wanda down to run to the toys in the corner.

"Yes. Don't you remember? Pastor and Mrs. Graham are going out of town Saturday morning, so I invited them to dinner Friday night."

"Oh, yeah, I remember. Who else is coming?"

"Cecily and Isaac, and Trudy and Carl I guess."

"Should I be worried?"

"About what?"

"About how *cozy* you and the *Pastor* are getting."

"Oh, Alton!" she exploded in laughter, and he laughed also.

"Where're you off to?"

"To meet with Cecily and Trudy."

"What're you women up to? All these secret meetings. What's up?"

"It's just something we have to do, Baby. That's all."

"I hope you ladies aren't doing anything *dumb*."

"We have it all under control, Sweetie. Trust me," she cooed with a sweet smile.

"All right now. I don't want to find your black ass in a ditch somewhere."

"Alton, you're in *church*," she exploded.

"I'm serious, Lillian. You ladies are all grown up now. You shouldn't be playing silly little kid games anymore!"

"It's all right. I promise," she cooed again. "Now will you take Wanda on home with you, *pleaseee*?"

He had to chuckle as he replied, "You're full of crap, Lillian."

"But you love me, don't you?" she smiled grabbing him around his waist, and they ended in a long kiss.

"You know I do," he said pulling her in his arms again, as he thought, *I bet this has something to do with Spencer blackmailing Cecily. I can't let Lillian know I know Spencer, or she'll wonder <u>how</u> I know him. But I have to warn her about how dangerous he is.* Then he added, "But if I hear of you trying to mess around with some crazy mutherfucker out there, *I'll* kill you my damn self!"

"I hear ya, Daddy," Lillian laughed. "I'll see you later. I've got to check something out with Pastor Graham. The kids want to have a talent show."

"All right, Baby. I'll see you later," he said then called Wanda, and she came running.

Bending down to kiss Wanda, Lillian said, "Daddy's taking you with him, Honey. I'll see you later."

"Okay, Mommy," she agreed smiling.

"Love you, Baby," Lillian told Alton.

"I love you, Sweetheart," he replied, and they kissed one more time before he left with Wanda.

Lillian walked into the stock room to see what equipment they had for the talent show. She saw a picture of a group dancing, and she drifted into the past:

*   *Fifteen-year-old Lillian was on a decorated stage, with a banner up which read <u>Talent Show</u>, singing <u>God</u> <u>Bless</u> <u>the</u> <u>Child</u> <u>That</u> <u>Has</u> <u>Its</u> <u>Own</u>. The people in the audience were in awe of the musical talents of Lillian's trained voice. When she was finishing, she received a standing ovation, while she was still holding that last note so long, it would have shattered a glass vase. Cecily and Trudy stood on the floor in the front row of the auditorium, yelling louder than anyone. Then when all the contestants came back on stage, they announced the winner, and it <u>wasn't</u> Lillian. It was a teacher's daughter. Lillian was so devastated she ran out the auditorium before she received her prize for first runner-up, and without her coat, into the freezing rain. Cecily and Trudy jumped up and ran out also.*

When Cecily caught up with Lillian, Lillian collapsed under a tree, crying hysterically on the cold, wet ground. Cecily sat beside her and pulled Lillian in her arms. "I didn't win," Lillian cried.

"It's okay, Lil," Cecily cried with her friend. "It's not the end of the world. And everybody knows Rebecca won because of her <u>mother</u>."

"But I was counting on that money to help Mama pay a bill."

"Something else will come along, Lil. I promise. And if it doesn't, I have some money saved. It's <u>yours</u>. So, don't worry so much." Cecily consoled her friend. "You were so terrific on that stage, Girl, <u>I</u> even got religion." That made Lillian laugh, as Trudy ran to them carrying Lillian's coat and trophy.

"What in the hell are Y'all doing sitting in this cold ass rain on that cold ass ground?!" Trudy shouted, then Lillian and Cecily burst into laughter.

"Thanks, Cis," Lillian said softly.

"There's no need to thank me. I love you, Girl," Cecily said, then pulled Lillian in her arms and hugged her tight, as Trudy threw Lillian's coat over them.

"Y'all some sick ass heifers! It's freezing out here!" Trudy spat then Lillian and Cecily jumped up and grabbed Trudy down with them, and they all laughed hysterically. *

"Are you all right?" a lady asked, bringing Lillian back to the present.

Lillian wiped her tears then turned around to face the intruder. "Oh, hi, Joyce," Lillian said. "I'm fine. Just reminiscing." The short woman stood there just as she stood at the door of Pastor Graham's office, watching Lillian hug him the day he gave Lillian the appointment.

"How's it going, Lillian?"

"Fine."

"How're the children behaving?"

"There're great."

"Good. I'm glad we have some new blood around here like you and Alton. The children need someone they can relate to."

"Thank you, Joyce."

"If there's anything I can do to help, just ask," Joyce offered walking away, as she thought, *Don't hold your breath, though. Cause I know you are going to fall on your face. The only reason the Pastor gave you that position in the first place is because you're young and pretty.*

"Thank-you. I appreciate that," Lillian replied sweetly but thinking, *I hope I don't need you, though. You're strange. You don't fool me with those smiles. I know you want me to fail. I wonder why? Maybe I'd better keep my eyes open when it comes to you, Joyce.*

Chapter 9

"Carl asked me to marry him."

"What?!" Cecily exploded.

"What did you say?" was Lillian's question.

"I told him I needed to know him better, so he told me all about his business."

"He *did*?!" Cecily asked.

"Yes. But he left out the part about his blackmailing you, and I don't know how to get around to it without tipping him off."

"You have to be very careful, Trudy. Cecily said this man is dangerous." warned Lillian.

"He *is* dangerous. He killed Cotton!" Cecily insisted.

"How do you know that, Cecily?" Trudy asked.

"I *know* Carl Spencer."

"Has he ever said he killed Cotton?" Trudy wanted to know.

"Do you expect him to *admit* it?"

"People do change."

"Why are you defending *Spencer*?!" Cecily exploded. "You would think...." She froze in her tracks. "Oh, my God, you're in love with him." The room grew so silent you could hear a pin drop as Lillian and Cecily focused on Trudy.

Breaking the silence, Lillian finally asked, "Is that true, Trudy?" She didn't answer. She just turned away.

Jerking her around, Cecily demanded, "Are you in love with Spencer, Trudy?!"

"Yes!" Trudy finally exploded. "Yes. I'm in love with him!" She dropped in a chair.

"Oh my God," Cecily's breath ran out, as she dropped in a chair also.

"*He* loves *me* too."

"Huh!" Cecily responded. "Carl Spencer doesn't love anybody or anything, but the almighty *dollar*. And don't you forget that!"

"Well I believe he loves me."

"You're so naive. Wake up and smell the coffee, Woman! Because he's good in bed doesn't mean he loves you! I thought Spencer loved me once, but I was wrong. The only thing he wanted was to get me on the streets, and he used whatever means necessary to do it. Spencer does nothing without a reason! And the moment you forget that, you're through!"

"Well, *I'm* not *you*, Cecily, and I believe he has changed!" Trudy retaliated.

"*Changed*?! He didn't even tell you about blackmailing me, and yet he was *supposed* to have been telling you *everything*. He's a lowlife, son-of-a-bitch, and he always will be!"

"Maybe Carl put you on the streets because *you* wanted it!" Trudy yelled out of control, and Cecily's hand flew up and handed on Trudy's face. Then Trudy jumped back at her, and they tumbled to the floor fighting like wild, barbaric animals, while Lillian tried to separate them.

****

"Hello?"

"Isaac? Cindy."

"What is it, Cindy?"

"Angela needs you, Isaac."

Taking a deep breath, he insisted, "Cindy, I told you I'll pick her up soon. Please don't do this. Don't use that child to get to me."

"I would *never* do that!" she insisted, growing angry. "I'm afraid, Isaac, if you don't start being a daddy to your little girl, it might be too late. She thinks you don't love her."

"I'm sure you're overreacting, Cindy."

"Oh, yeah? Then why did she tell me she hates you?"

"She said that?"

"Yes, she did. You used to say you couldn't spend much time with Angela because Cecily didn't know about her. Well, now Cecily knows, so what's your excuse *now*, Isaac?"

"Cindy, you act like I never see Angela. I come to see her."

"But not *nearly* enough."

Taking a deep breath, he said, "I'll talk it over with Cecily to see if Angela can stay the weekend."

"When will you call me back?" she asked as Isaac focused on Cecily entering with her hair wild, her clothes torn, and her face red.

"Gotta go," he said hanging up the phone quickly then rushing to Cecily.

"Honey, what happened? Were you attacked?"

"No. I'm fine," she said kicking off her shoes.

"What happened?"

"I was in a fight," she said then burst into laughter.

"What?"

"Tru and I had a fight. We haven't done that since we were kids."

"Are you standing there telling me that two intelligent, grown women had a *fist* fight?" he asked, but she was laughing so hard, all she could do was nod, and he laughed also. She dropped on the bed and grew serious.

"Isaac, I'm pregnant," she announced, but thinking, *How in the hell do I tell you this baby may not be yours?*

****

"Hi, Darling," Lillian greeted, entering Alton's big, beautiful. paneled office.

"Hi, Sweetie," he said as they kissed.

"New secretary?"

"No. She's just filling in."

"She's very young."

"So what?"

"And beautiful."

"So are *you*, Mrs. Carter," he said, planting another kiss on her lips, and she laughed.

"I was on my way to get Wanda some shoes and realized I don't have any checks in my checkbook. Do you have any?"

"I think so, but why don't you use your debit card?"

"I don't have that either."

"Credit card?"

"Interests."

"My wife, the penny pincher," he laughed, handing her his checkbook.

"Hey, I grew up poor. Habits are hard to break," she smiled.

"Try," he encouraged then kissed her again.

"Thanks, Baby," she replied, walking to the door. "Let me get out your way so you can make us some money." He opened the door for her as they laughed. They kissed again, and she left. Then, for the first time, Alton noticed the young lady sitting at the desk and thought how pretty she really was, with her jet black, smooth skin and very short hair, jelled down on her head like a cap. She looked up at him and smiled sweetly, but he knew that *I'm available* look, so he made a quick exit into his office. He didn't need *that* kind of trouble, as he thought, *Where in the hell is Patty anyway?*

Chapter 10

"I'm glad you decided to move in with me, Baby, even though you won't marry me yet." Spencer told Trudy as they lay cuddled in bed. "This has been the best month of my life, having you here."

"It's been great for me, too, Sweetie," she replied, snuggling even closer to his smooth body.

"I saw my lawyer today. I had him to redo my will, making *you* my beneficiary. I didn't want anything to happen to me without taking care of you first."

"Oh, Carl, that's so sweet," she smiled, kissing his lips. "But you do know that I am very comfortable financially."

"I know, but that's *your* money. I just want to leave you something from *me*."

"That is so sweet," she cooed, kissing him again.

"I need to show you something," he said getting up, and she followed him. He went to the closet, pulled back his clothes and exposed a safe in the wall. "The combination is 30-18-65, right, left, right. Remember that. If anything happens to me, you need to know how to get in this thing."

"I'll remember. 30, 18, 65," she repeated, as he opened it. He pulled out some papers.

"These are stocks and bonds. Deals to property, business contracts, and some other shit," he explained as an envelope dropped on the floor, and he tried to pick it up before she could see it, but she noticed one thing immediately, Cecily's name on the envelope. "Don't be concerned with this. It's just a little insurance I have."

"What kind of insurance?"

"The kind you get to let niggers know you mean business, so they'll cooperate with you. Don't you worry about that, Baby. I'll handle it," he explained, putting everything back in the safe. Trudy knew that those must be the negatives he was holding over Cecily's head. She realized that she had let her friend down, and Cecily would *never* have done that to her. She *had* to help Cecily, and may the chips fall where they may, even if it meant *death* for her, because she had no doubt that Spencer would kill her if she ever betrayed him...*just like Cotton!*

****

"Hello, Doctor."

Cecily looked up in Alton's face and said, "Hi." She started back feeding the pigeons, as he sat beside her on the park bench.

"What's with the park?"

"Hotel rooms aren't safe for us. That's why I asked you to meet me *here*."

"I see," he smiled shyly. "What's up?"

"I'm pregnant," she said, not looking at him.

"Yeah. Lillian told me. I was wondering when you'd get around to telling me," he said then took a deep breath. "Is it mine?"

"I don't know."

"Are you going to have it?" he asked and drew her attention now.

"Yes!" she stressed. "Of course!"

"If this is my baby, Cecily, you know my marriage is history?"

"And I lose my best friend, so what's your point?"

He knew this was a no-win situation. She would never consider an abortion, and he said softly, "No point. None at all." He knew he was dead meat! He knew what he and Cecily shared would eventually catch up with him, and now it has. He thought to himself, *Lord, please be merciful and don't let me lose my family.*

****

Trudy rolled over and viewed one thirty on the clock. She slipped out of bed and pulled on a big nightshirt, while Spencer slept on. Trudy went into the den and curled up on the couch, staring blankly at the fireplace until she drifted into the past:

*   *"How much do you need, Tru?" Cecily asked over the telephone.*

Crying hysterically, Trudy said, "Two thousand dollars."

"Listen, Tru. Stop crying. In about an hour, go to the nearest Weston Union and the money will be there for you."

"I can't let you do that, Cecily. You're in Medical School. I know how expensive that is."

"You can pay me back. It's just a loan. Okay? " Cecily said, but she didn't answer. "Trudy, do as I say. I won't let you lose everything because of a sorry ass man!"

"Thank-you, Cecily. I promise, I'll pay you back. I just can't let him hit me anymore. I've got to get away from him. If he messes up my face, I'll never get a modeling job."

"I know, Honey. I know. Take care of yourself and call me tomorrow."

*

Trudy rolled out of the past with tears running down her face. She picked up the telephone and dialed. "Hello?" Cecily answered in a sleepy daze.

"Cecily, I'm sorry," Trudy cried.

"Trudy?" she asked sitting up.

"I'm sorry I let you down. You've always been there for me."

"Tru, calm down," Cecily said getting out of bed.

"Anything wrong, Sweetheart?" Isaac asked.

"No, Darling. Go back to sleep," she said, and he turned over and quickly drifted back to sleep. "What's wrong, Tru?"

"I know where the pictures and negatives are. I'm going to help you."

"Are you sure about this, Tru?"

"You're my best friend. I can't let you down, and I can't just stand by and do nothing while Carl cause you so much pain."

"Tru, where are you?"

"At home?"

"With *Spencer*?!"

"Yeah. Why?"

"Where is Spencer?"

"He's asleep."

"Tru, you shouldn't have called me from there. Hang up this phone and go and see if he's still asleep. We're talk tomorrow."

"Okay, but don't worry. He's asleep."

"Make sure," Cecily demanded. "Good-night."

****

Spencer replaced the telephone back on the hook and stared into space. He could not believe what he had just heard. The woman he loved most in this world had betrayed him, and for *what*? A two-bit whore like *Sissy*. He wiped a tear from his face and remembered that only two women in his whole life have ever made him cry, and *they* were teaming up together to destroy him. "You will live to regret this, Miss Miles," he spat aloud. "You *will* live to regret this. I promise you that." He paused, then added, "And you, Dr. Wade, will be dealt with *severely*." He heard Trudy's footsteps, so he quietly eased back down, pulling the covers up. She slid in bed, put her arm around him from the rear, and cuddled up closed to him. His lips curled up with intense anger, and he wanted to grabbed her little, narrow, red ass out the bed and beat the living daylights out of her, but he knew he had to keep his cool if he wanted to beat these bitches at their own game. He *knew* how to play hardball. They were only amateurs trying to play *his* game. *They will pay!*

****

"Cis, I'm telling you, he was fast asleep," Trudy insisted as she sat in Lillian's lake house with Lillian and Cecily. "When I returned to bed, he was still fast asleep."

"I don't trust him," Cecily said.

"Cis, don't upset yourself. Remember the baby," Lillian said.

"Baby?!" exploded Trudy.

"Yeah. Didn't I tell you?" Lillian smiled. "Cecily's pregnant. Isn't it great?"

"Yeah. Congratulations, Cis," Trudy replied, wondering who the father was.

"It doesn't matter if Spencer knows or not," Lillian added.

"What'd you mean?" Cecily wanted to know.

"If he does know, he only found out last night. I don't think that'll give him time to plan anything. We can plan something for *tonight*." Lillian suggested.

"You don't know Spencer," replied Cecily.

"*He doesn't know*," insisted Trudy. "He loves me, and he trusts me."

"When are you going to get it through your thick head?!" Cecily exploded. "Carl Spencer loves *nobody*!"

"He loves *me*!" insisted Trudy.

"Hey, let's not start *that* again," Lillian intervened. "Tru, after my dinner party tonight, do you think you can get Spencer to take you to a movie or something?"

"Yeah. No problem."

"Give us the combination to the safe, the code to inactivate the alarm system, and a key to the house," Lillian explained. "Cis, you and I are going to break in tonight. Once we have those negatives, he can't blackmail you anymore."

"Those negatives aren't the only way to stop Spencer, Lil," Cecily replied. "Knowing Spencer, he has the negatives some other place too. I'll be looking for something to incriminate the bastard in that safe, and I know there is plenty. That's the only way to stop someone like Spencer!"

"Think positively," Lillian added, patting Cecily on the shoulder.

"I've got to go," Trudy said, handing Lillian the paper. "I don't have a spare key on me, so I'll give you that tonight at dinner."

"Okay, I'll see you at seven," Lillian finalized, and Trudy nodded.

"Tru, did Spencer get suspicious about Lil asking you to dinner?"

"Oh, no. I get invitations from people all the time. Some I know and some I don't."

"Cecily, Tru's *famous*," Lillian smiled.

"I don't know about all that," Trudy laughed. "See you guys later." She left, as Cecily and Lillian said good-bye to her.

Cecily looked at Lillian and said, "Tru's in love. She doesn't believe she's in danger. Do you have a gun?"

"A *gun*?!"

"Yeah. Spencer is *dangerous*. I know that only too well. Do you have a gun?"

"Alton has one."

"Do you know how to use it?"

Nodding, Lillian said, "A little. Alton showed me how a long time ago."

"Bring it tonight."

"Cis, do you really think...?"

"Just *bring* it. Better safe than sorry," Cecily said, cutting her off, and Lillian nodded.   "Spencer is a *crazy* son-of-a-bitch, and we've got to be willing to get just as *crazy* as he is, or we need to back out *now*!"

****

"Hello?" Trudy said into the Bluetooth in her ear, breathing hard in tights and leotards, as she stopped running on the treadmill.

"Hi, Darling," Spencer said on the other end. "What're you doing?"

"Trying to keep in shape. I've been exercising," she said catching her breath. "What's up?"

"Listen, Sweetie, I have to go out of town tonight. Could you throw some clothes in a suitcase for me? I'll be home in about an hour."

"Sure, Baby, but you're going to miss the Carters' dinner party tonight."

"I know, Baby. It can't be helped. But you can still go."

"It won't be any fun without you," she cooed. "Maybe *I* can go with *you*?"

"No, Baby. It's just business. You'll be bored stiff. I'll be in meetings for two days."

"All right. I'll see you soon," Trudy said then hung up, and she said aloud, "Spencer's going out of town. This is *perfect*."

****

"Hello?"

"Lil, Tru just called me," Cecily said. "Spencer's going out of town today."

"Wow! That's perfect!" Lillian smiled.

"Yeah, *too* perfect."

"What'd you mean?"

"Just make sure you have that gun," Cecily insisted, "I have a feeling he knows! And if I'm right, *God help us*!"

****

"Hi, Isaac, Cecily," Lillian greeted them at the door with a hug, in her Margo Beatty blue suit with sequins spread about the collar, cuffs, hemline, and buttonholes. Her beautiful hair hung loosely to her shoulders with a sequined blue barrette sweeping it behind her left ear.

"You look beautiful, Lillian," Isaac admired in his black Leonn Poultrie pinstriped suit.

"Thank-you, Isaac," Lillian smiled.

Handing her a bottle of wine, Isaac said, "Something to go with dinner."

"Thank you, Isaac. You didn't have to."

"Where's Wanda, Lil?" Cecily asked in her black, body fitting dress, outlined with pearls around her neck, on her ears, and on her wrist. Her hair also hang loose, down her back, with two pearl barrettes securing it behind both ears, and Shirley Temple curls draping down in front of each lobe.

"She's in the den with Alton, Pastor and Mrs. Graham," Lillian said as the doorbell sounded again. "That must be Trudy. Isaac, you know the way."

"Cecily?" Isaac offered.

"You go ahead, Darling. I'll be right there," she said, and he nodded then exited.

When Lillian opened the door, Trudy stood there in a Cardene Myers olive pantsuit, with fine embroidery down each lapel. Her long hair was secured in a French braid down the center of her head, and a small olive barrette rested on the end of the braid that hung just below her shoulders. "Okay, the party can start now. I'm here!" Trudy joked.

"What's up, Girl?" Lillian smiled grabbing her in a hug.

"Did Cecily tell you? Spencer's out of town tonight!" added Trudy.

"Yeah, I told her."

"So, we can leave here tonight, go to my house, and take our time looking for everything,"

"Sounds good," Lillian said.

"Did you *see* him get on the plane?" was Cecily's question.

"Yes, I *saw* him get on the plane," Trudy mocked sarcastically. "Dag, Cis, you're so damn paranoid."

"I've got to get me some more friends. You two *swear* too much," Lillian announced, throwing her hands up in the air. "You guys, be cool. My Pastor is here!"

"Oooooo, her Pastor is here," Trudy jokingly purred like a little girl, and Lillian shoved her, and they burst into laughter.

****

"How large is your congregation, Pastor?" Isaac asked during dinner.

"We have about five hundred members right now, but that number is rising every day," Pastor Graham announced proudly. "But I don't worry too much about numbers, as long as I'm doing the work of the Lord. If I can help just *one* person accept Christ in *my* lifetime, then my living won't be in vain."

"We had six to join Sunday," added Lillian.

"It must be tough being the wife of a Minister," Trudy directed her question to the distinguished looking, one hundred-seventy-pound woman.

"Not at all," she answered in her deep *Louise Jefferson* voice. "I believe in my husband's work, Miss Miles. When you're following a man of God, it's never hard. Sometimes people try to make it challenging, but if you're doing the will of the Lord, God said, I will remove all your stumbling blocks and make your enemies your footstool."

"Amen," Pastor Graham agreed, looking at his wife in the most admirable way.

"Hallelujah," added Lillian.

"Dr. Wade, I've heard a lot of great things about you," Pastor Graham said. "What church do you attend?"

Taking a deep breath, Cecily said, "I'm afraid to say, Pastor Graham, but I don't attend *any* church on a regular basis."

"That's too bad," he said sadly. "May I ask why?"

"Well, I question the existence of God. I've had so much pain in my life until I can't see why a God as good as you say would allow that."

"God allows us to go through things, Dr. Wade, so that we can grow spiritually, and learn how to serve him and trust him," Pastor Graham explained. "God hears *all* of our cries. He not only hears them, but he weeps with us, but he gives us free will, and a lot of times we get ourselves into difficult situations and just expect God to come to our rescue. He doesn't work like that." He smiled lovingly at her, and she returned it. "I would like to invite all of you to come to our little church one Sunday morning, and maybe if you have time, to Bible Study, Sunday School, and Prayer Service. I promise, you won't be disappointed." He reached in his pocket and took out some business cards and handed one each to Isaac, Cecily, and Trudy. "I'll be looking for you."

"Missionary Fellowship Church," Isaac read then chuckled. "I didn't know Preachers had business cards."

"Helping people to receive Christ as their personal Savior *is* a business, Mr. Wade. *God's* business." Pastor Graham smiled also. "And a very *rewarding* business, too."

****

"Come on in," Trudy said, letting Lillian and Cecily into the house. "The safe is upstairs. What took you so long?"

"We had to change," Cecily said then noticing that they all had on blue jeans and ponytails, she added. "And it looks like we *all* had the same idea." They laughed.

"What're you going to say if he notices there're missing?" Lillian asked.

"I'll take them to the office tomorrow and copy all of them, and I'll bring them right back. He won't ever know there're missing," Cecily said.

"That's a good idea. He won't be back until Sunday," Trudy said, heading for the staircase. Just as she was about to take the first step, she stopped abruptly, for the women stood, staring eye to eye with an angry Carl Spencer, standing at the top of the stairs.

"Darling, you have guests," he spoke calmly.

"Carl!" exploded Trudy. "When did you get here?"

Ignoring her question, his attention landed on Cecily, "Well, if it isn't the prominent Dr. Wade." Then his eyes fell on Lillian. "And, the beautiful,

Mrs. Alton Carter. What a pleasure it is to finally meet you, Mrs. Carter. I know your husband from numerous business acquaintances." He paused, walking down the stairs. "Shall we sit and chat, ladies?" He motioned for them to go into the den, and they did. Spencer sat at the bar, Cecily sat in a chair, and Lillian and Trudy shared the couch. "Well, Darling. Tell me about your little party. And, I'm very disappointed that I wasn't invited."

"There's nothing to tell, Baby," Trudy answered with a trembling voice, wringing her hands.

"And, Dr. Wade," he said, turning to Cecily. "I've underestimated you terribly. I had no idea you knew such prestigious people as Miss Miles."

"Cut the bull, Spencer!" Cecily demanded, finding her courage. "What in the hell are you planning to do?!"

Focusing on Lillian, he asked, "Mrs. Carter, are you a *friend* of the good doctor?"

"Yes," Lillian replied, clearing her throat.

"This *woman*!" Spencer said, pointing a finger at Cecily. "And, I use the term loosely, does not *deserve* to have a friend like *you*." Cecily's eyes stretched for she knew Spencer would tell *everything* before this night were over, but she couldn't let that happen. The sound of the doorbell silenced him. "Get that, Darling," he said to Trudy. "I'm expecting guests, too." Trudy stood and walked to the door slowly, still looking back at Spencer.

Soon Cecily cringed as she saw Alton and Isaac rush in. Alton ran to Lillian asking, "Honey, what's wrong?"

"What're you talking about?" Lillian asked.

"I received a phone call saying you were hurt."

"I'm fine."

"I received a phone call saying *Cecily* was hurt," Isaac added. "What's going on here?"

"I'm sorry, gentlemen, " Spencer said. "I didn't know of any other way to get you to my little party."

"What's going on, Spencer?" Alton wanted to know.

"You remember me, Mr. Carter," Spencer sarcastically replied. "I'm flattered that a big business tycoon like yourself would remember a small businessman like me."

"Will someone please tell me what's going on," Isaac asked again, sitting on the arm of the chair that Cecily occupied.

"Spencer was blackmailing Cecily," Trudy spoke up, sitting on the couch next to Alton and Lillian. "We tried to help Cecily, and Spencer caught us. He'll have to tell you why he asked you to come." The men focused on Spencer now.

"Let's hear it, Spencer," Alton insisted.

"Mr. Wade, let me introduce myself," Spencer spoke, walking in front of the bar and towards Trudy. "My name is Carl Spencer. I'm what you people might call a pimp." Isaac's eyes stretched. "That's right. I own girls, bitches, whores!"

"Spencer, it's *me* that you want," Cecily said softly. "Let everybody else go, please. This is between *you* and *me*!"

"Now that's where you're wrong, Dr. Wade," he chuckled. "My Darling

Trudy made it *all* our business." He walked to the door that led to the kitchen, and called, "All right, Boys!" Suddenly two big, black, muscular, hulking, *Mr. T* look-a-likes hopped in, whipping out sawed-off shotguns. Trudy and Lillian screamed while the others just cringed. "Now let me finish introducing myself to Mr. Wade." He paused. "You see, Mr. Wade, one of my bitches was your *wife*!" Cecily's head dropped.

"What?!" Isaac exploded, then chuckled and added, "Mr. Spencer, my wife is a respected doctor."

Growing upset, Spencer yelled, "Your wife is a lying, cheating, stinking, two-bit *whore*! I owned the bitch for years! I still own her, and I will *always* own her!"

Looking at Cecily, Isaac asked weakly, "What is this all about?"

Raising her head, Cecily replied weakly, "It's true. While I was in medical school, I lived with Spencer for three years as his lady, then he put me on the streets for one year, then I left."

"*What*?" Isaac said. "You were a…*prostitute*?"

"He forced me," Cecily said with tears running down her face then she yelled, "Spencer *forced* me!"

"Why didn't you tell me?"

"I tried to tell you many times, but you would always say the past wasn't important."

"But you should've told me *that*, Cecily."

"I'm sorry," Cecily cried, and he pulled her in his arms.

"It's all right, Darling," Isaac replied softly. "That *was* in the past. It doesn't matter."

"Touching," Spencer sarcastically replied. Part one of his plan had failed. He wanted Isaac to scream, yell, hollow, hit the bitch, *something*! Instead he acted like a little *wimp*. But, that's okay. He had another ace in the hole to bring the bitch down to her knees! Then he turned to Lillian, and Cecily cringed as her eyes locked with Alton's.

****

Ramon frantically searched through every drawer, every closet, every cabinet, wildly dropping everything on the floor. He had made a mess of Trudy's New York apartment, but he didn't care. He just wanted to find her. He *had* to find her. She was not going to brush him off that easily. Who did the she think she was? Changing the damn locks on him. Didn't she know he could get in *any* room, building, or vault, if he *wanted* to? He stopped suddenly as he spotted a picture of Trudy with Lillian and Cecily, on the beach, smiling big. "Of course!" He said aloud. "Of course. She's with her friends." Thinking hard, he repeatedly bumped his head with his fist. "Where in the hell did she say they lived?" He dropped on the bed momentarily, then suddenly he jumped up yelling, "California! That's where she is. Cali-fucking-fornia!" He grabbed his coat. "Wait till I get my hands on you, Bitch!"

****

"Mrs. Carter, I think you should know that Sissy's best customer was..."

"Be careful, Spencer!" Alton warned. "I know a lot of people."

"Fuck you, man!" Spencer yelled, growing very angry now. Who does this son-of-a-bitch think he is, to tell *him* what to do? He would fix this high and mighty, executive asshole. "Or should I say fuck *Sissy*? Oh, excuse me...*Cecily*." Lillian jerked around to face her husband.

"What is he talking about?" she wanted to know.

"I'm talking about your husband and your *best* friend. She was *all* he wanted whenever he came to New York."

"Is this true, Alton?" Lillian inquired weakly, but her husband didn't answer. Then she focused on Cecily. "Is this true?" Her voice was a low whisper now, for she was too choked up with anguish and pain to speak any louder.

"I didn't know he was your husband, Lil," Cecily squeezed out wiping her tears. "And Alton didn't know I was your friend. Neither of us used our *real* name."

"Well you sure as hell know *now*!" Spencer fumed on.

"Spencer, please," Cecily begged in a low whisper, closing her eyes. "This is unnecessary."

"What was that, Dr. Wade?" Spencer said sarcastically. "Do my ears deceive me? Is the great and mighty Dr. Wade begging a *pimp* like me for mercy?" He enjoyed this because he hated this woman so much. Although he didn't want to hurt a classy lady like Lillian, he took great pleasure in seeing Cecily squirm. He knew Lillian didn't deserve this, but she just had to be a casualty of war, because he *had* to get even with that lying, conniving, whoring Cecily!

"Yes, I'm begging you!" Cecily confirmed. "Please, don't do this. These people have done *nothing* to you. It's *me* you want, not *them*. Please don't do this."

"Well, your begging don't mean shit to me, Sissy!" he snarled. Then, all of a sudden, Spencer jumped and grabbed a lock of Trudy's hair, jerking her head back, as she screamed with pain. "Is *she* worth breaking my heart, *Darling*?!"

"Carl, I *had* to. You have no idea how Cecily has always been there for me," Trudy cried. "But I do love you."

"I loved you, and you deceived me for this piece of trash," he spat, indicating Cecily with his head.

"I'm sorry," Trudy wept. "It started out that way, but I fell in love with you. This was the hardest thing I've ever had to do in my whole life."

"Let her go, Spencer," Alton demanded on his feet, and Spencer waved to the big men, and then their guns aimed at Alton, and Cecily bellowed out a loud, screeching scream.

"Sit the fuck down!" Spencer raged on. "Before I have my boys blow your fucking balls off!" Alton sat slowly. Spencer then let Trudy's hair go, stood over her, and snarled. "I will deal with you later!"

"Carl, you can do whatever you want with me. It still won't change the fact that I love you," Trudy squeezed out in tears. Spencer couldn't believe this woman; sitting there talking about she loved him after she plotted to destroy him with her friends. What kind of fool did she think he was?

"Shut the fuck up!" he yelled, raising his fist up high, and bringing it down on her face as hard as he could, causing her whole body to jerk backwards with blood squirting out her nose. He walked over to Cecily and asked, "Tell me, Sissy, is your baby going to be… white… or black?"

"Shut up, Spencer!" Cecily yelled.

"Tell us all, Sissy," Spencer chuckled. "Tell us about your little bastard baby! Tell your *husband* and your *best* friend who your baby daddy is!"

"Spencer, please," Cecily begged.

"That's right, Bitch!" Spencer fumed. "I *want* you to beg. Get on your fucking knees like a fucking dog and beg!" She did not obey, and he took a step towards her and yelled, "Do it, Bitch!" She dropped to her knees, crying hysterically.

"Cecily, no!" Isaac yelled, starting to pick her up.

"Stay where you are!" Spencer demanded, and the guns pointed towards Isaac now.

"Can't you see how upset she is?" Isaac said as he picked her up anyway and sat her back in the chair.

"Isaac, he will kill you," Cecily replied. "He's dangerous. He killed Cotton."

"You're crazy, Bitch!" Spencer yelled. "I didn't kill Cotton."

"You never denied it," confronted Cecily.

"I didn't have to. I owe you *nothing*," Spencer insisted. "It was good for people to think I killed Cotton.   Hell, I started the rumor my damn self. That way they knew better than to fuck with Spencer.   Cotton was my *best* girl. Why in the hell would I kill her?"

"To get to *me*."

"I *never* wanted to put you on the streets," he yelled. "I *loved* you! But after I saw you fucking around with that football jock, I knew all those late nights you were out the house, you were with *him*. That's why I put your red ass on the streets. I gave you *everything*. You didn't need *him*."

"I wasn't *sleeping* with *Barry*!"

"I got pictures of that, too, Sissy, so don't try to deny it."

"Oh my God. You put my life through hell because of a *lie*," Cecily insisted. "Spencer, I only saw Barry *one* time and that was when I told him how much I loved *you*. He kissed me goodbye and I never saw him again. It was meant to be a goodbye *hug*, and *Barry* turned it into a *kiss*. He apologized to me and that was that!"

"What about all those late nights?"

"I was at the *library*. I didn't want you to know I was in medical school. It was hard trying to keep that from you. At first, I didn't trust you enough to tell you, and then I wanted to surprise you with my graduation," she wept hard. "You made my life a living hell because of a lie."

"Why didn't you tell me what happened between you and the jock when you came home that night?"

"I didn't think you would've understood if I had told you that I had gone to Barry's hotel room to see him. I didn't even go *in*," she explained. "Your snitch should've told you *that*."

"Well, he didn't stay. He had another job to do," Spencer said then added. "Well, that's not important now."

"It *is* important," Cecily continued. "You hated me all those years because of a *lie*."

"And *you* hated *Spencer* because of a lie, also, Cecily," Trudy added. "He didn't kill Cotton."

"That's what *he* said," Cecily spat. "But I know what a liar Spencer is."

"And *you're* not, Dr. Wade?" he chuckled. "Mrs. Carter, I think before you help this bitch any further, you need to know that the father of her baby is...."

"Spencer!" Cecily yelled, but he was not listening.

"Your *husband*!" he yelled on. "The bastard cheated on you! And *she's* no friend!" he raged on as all eyes fell on Cecily, especially Lillian's. Spencer nodded his head and the big, burly men grabbed Alton and Isaac up then threw them in two separate chairs, handcuffing them each to the chair.

"You ladies will pay for what you tried to do to me," Spencer raged on. "You'll see your husbands die, and then I'll put all three of you bitches on the street. You will belong to me *forever*!"

"Is this true, Cecily?" Lillian asked, finally finding her voice, oblivious to everything else going on. "Is *Alton* the father of your baby?"

"He's crazy," Cecily spat.

"Am I?" Spencer insisted as he threw a brown envelope in Lillian's lap.

"Nooo!" Cecily yelled as she ran to get the envelope, but Spencer caught her in his arms and held her. Lillian opened the envelope slowly, as Cecily begged her not to, while Spencer held her in his grasp.

When Lillian came face to face with the realization of her husband's *very* intimate affair with her best friend, she felt as if her whole world had just tumbled down around her, as sad, disappointed, confused tears immediately flooded her pitiful, heartbroken face. Her head dropped, as Spencer released his hold on Cecily, and Cecily fell on the floor in tears.

"How could you do this to me, Cecily?" Lillian squeezed out in tears. "I *trusted* you. I *loved* you. You were like a *sister* to me!"

"I'm sorry, Lil," Cecily squeezed out as she rose from the floor.

"Sorry? That's all you can say, you're *sorry*. How could you betray me like this? How could you?" Lillian continued to weep.

Crying also Cecily said, "I never meant to hurt you, Lil. It wasn't planned. It just happened. I love you." Then Cecily focused on a smiling Spencer, and she knew she couldn't let him get away with this. Witnessing the hurt in Lillian's eyes was more than Cecily could bear. And, more than that, she couldn't let Spencer kill Isaac and Alton like he had threatened to do. "You bastard!" Cecily screamed as she opened her purse. "I hate you! I hate you! You bastard!" Spencer's eyes focused on a gun that Lillian was pointing towards Cecily, and he jumped towards Cecily while Trudy dived towards Lillian, but shots filled the room anyway, and then hysterical, loud, screeching screams echoed. The next sight was blood, blood, and more blood, as gunshot sounds exploded in the atmosphere over and over and over again.

Part Two

Five Years Later

June

Chapter 11

"Mommy!" a little walnut-colored girl with curly, jet black hair that hangs in the middle of her back, yelled as she exploded into the bedroom of a sleeping person, under loads of black, silk sheets. "Mommy, wake up. You're late for work!" The little girl jumped on the bed trying to find her mother, under the abundance of covers on the king-sized bed.

"Keisha!" a lady's slurred, sleepy voice replied very annoyed.

"Get up, Mommy. You're late for work."

"What time is it?"

Focusing on the bedside brass clock, the little girl said, "7-1-5."

"7:15!" the lady exploded throwing the covers off her head. "You got me up at 7:15?!" She attacked the child with tickles. "You'll pay for this, young lady!" The child laughed hysterically as a 200-pound ebony lady entered in a plain black dress.

"Excuse me, Dr. Wade," the lady spoke. "You have a telephone call."

"Thanks, Mae," Cecily said, seizing the attack on her laughing little girl. Cecily rolled over, pushed her shoulder-length, dyed light brown, wavy hair out her face, and picked up the telephone receiver. "Hello?"

"Good-morning."

"Hi, Alton. How...." Cecily started but was forced to stop abruptly, because Keisha grabbed the telephone.

"Hi, Daddy!" the child exploded.

"How's my girl?"

"Fine. Are you coming over today?" Keisha asked as Cecily got up and exited into the restroom.

Cecily closed the bathroom door, tuning the excited child out of her thoughts. She opened the medicine chest, took out a bottle of pills and dropped a couple of them down her throat, then followed by a handful of water from the sink. She held her head back momentarily, trying to feel the effect of the pills as Keisha's voice found her ears again. Cecily walked back into the bedroom, turned on the radio and began swaying her hips to a song by Alicia Keys. Keisha began to giggle as she said, "Mommy's trying to dance." She giggled some more then said, "Okay." She pointed the phone in Cecily's direction and added, "Mommy, Daddy wanna talk to you."

Sticking her tongue out at the still giggling little girl, Cecily grabbed the phone out of her hand, and Keisha fell back on the bed still laughing. "Yes, Darling."

"I'll be over about five to pick Keisha up for the week-end."

"What about *me*?" Cecily cooed pulling clothes out of the closet.

"Huh?"

"I wanna goooo," Cecily purred like a whining child.

"Are you all right?"

"Couldn't be better," she giggled. "Can't we go away for the weekend?"

"What about Lillian?"

"What about her?"

"You know what I mean. What will I tell her?"

"Tell her what you usually tell her. Hell! I don't know! You can think of *something* to tell the snobbish bitch!"

"Why are you getting so upset? What's up with you?"

"Why do you keep asking me that? I'm fine. So, *we* will be ready about five," she insisted then quickly hung up and turned to Keisha. "Last one downstairs is a rotten egg!" She took off, and Keisha rushed off behind her laughing hysterically.

****

Turning over in bed with a very short hair cut that is straight and smoothed down on her head, Lillian looked at Alton, who was tying his necktie as the finishing touches to his attire, and asked, "Are you leaving?"

"Yes, Baby," he replied, sitting on the edge of the bed and planting a kiss on her forehead. "I'm going out of town tonight."

"Where?"

"Los Angeles."

"I want to go."

"Not this time, Honey."

"What'd you mean, not *this* time?" she snapped, growing upset. "I can *never* go!"

"I'll be in a lot of meetings, Sweetheart. You'll be bored."

"I wish you'd never started those business trips back up again. You're the boss. Can't you send someone?"

"Not this time."

"Not *this* time?!" she said sarcastically. "Not *any* time!" She leaped from the bed and slipped on a housecoat. "I thought Keisha was coming over this weekend."

"We'll have to change it," he said standing. "See you later. I'll be home early to pack." He planted a kiss on her forehead then left. Lillian frowned then walked over to her vanity chest. She opened it, took out a pint of vodka hiding under her underclothes, then turned it up to her mouth with trembling hands and gulped a big swallow down her throat. Then she gulped down another swallow before replacing the bottle just in time before ten-year-old Wanda entered, looking very mature with her shoulder-length, dark-brown hair, hanging loosely in a silky wrap.

"Bye, Mom," Wanda said as Lillian turned away, immediately spraying her mouth with breath mint.

"You're leaving, Darling,"

"Yeah. Daddy is ready to go," Wanda said receiving a kiss on the cheek from her mother. "I'm going to the library after school. Pick me up about four. Okay?"

"Okay, Sweetie."

"Don't forget," Wanda replied walking out, as Lillian nodded.

****

"Cecily, got a minute?" Cindy asked poking her head in Cecily's office.

"Sure. What's up?" Cecily said, then Cindy came in and closed the door.

She sat in front of Cecily's desk.

"I need to talk to you about something."

"Shoot."

Cindy took a deep breath then said softly, "Isaac is going to move in with me. I wanted to know how you felt about it."

"Cindy, that's very nice of you, since Isaac and I have been divorce for over three years. He's a free man."

"I know, but I don't want any hard feelings between *us*."

"There won't be any. I can assure you," Cecily stressed. "You've wanted Isaac for a long time. I'm glad things are finally coming together for you. He's a good catch. Go for it, Girl."

"Do you really mean that, Cecily?" Cindy smiled big as the telephone rang.

"Yes, I do," Cecily said while Cindy stood. "I got it."

"Thanks, Cecily."

"Take care of him, Cindy. Lord knows he needs someone to love him."

"That's no problem for me," Cindy said then walked out.

"Hello?" Cecily said into the receiver.

"Cecily?"

"Isaac?" Cecily said smiling. "Well, speak of the devil."

"What's that supposed to mean?"

"Never mind."

"Well, I never expected for the doctor to answer her own phone."

"I do work sometimes," Cecily chuckled. "What can I do for you?"

"Is Cindy around?"

"Yes, she is. I'll get her for you," she said. "And, congratulations. I hear you've found yourself a roommate."

"She told you, Huh?"

"Yes. I think it's wonderful."

"Cindy's a nice lady."

"You get no arguments from me on that," Cecily smiled. "Hold on. I'll get her."

"Cecily."

"Yeah."

"When was the last time you talked to Lillian and Trudy?"

"It's been a while. Why?"

"That's a shame. You were such good friends."

"Well that's in the past. Lillian hates me because of Keisha, and Trudy hates me because of Spencer."

"She still blames you for his death?"

"Yes, but I'm cool with it. If they want it that way, they got it."

"What about you and Alton?"

"What about us?"

"Are you seeing him now that you're no longer friends with Lillian?"

"Alton is the father of my child. No more! No less!"

"I find that hard to believe, Cecily."

"Why?"

"Because I know how much you had the hots for the guy. This is *me* you're talking to, Kid. Not some stranger on the streets. What Cecily *wants*? Cecily *gets*. Poor Lillian doesn't stand a chance," he laughed.

"You don't know what you're talking about, Isaac, so I'll get Cindy for you."

"Yeah. Right!"

****

A little boy of about five years old ran into Spencer's big, beautiful, newly decorated house. His curly, sandy colored hair glowed with his golden, bronzed skin as he called, "Mommy!"

"In the kitchen, Darling," a lady's soft voice called back. He ran towards the kitchen and burst through the door, and the refrigerator was opened, with a person behind it.

"Mommy, can I go to the park with Hakim?"

Closing the refrigerator door with a chicken leg in her mouth, the lady jerked her head back to rid her face of her long, auburn colored braids, that hang to the center of her back, as she placed a big bowl of potato salad and a pan of apple pie on the porcelain topped counter. Then she sat with her whopping 220 pounds on the stool, bit a big chunk out of the chicken, and focused on her son and mumbled with a mouthful of food, "I don't know, Honey. Who else is going?"

"Darrell, Hakim big brother."

"Carl, Sweetie, what time did Florence say she was coming back to make dinner? I'm starving," the huge woman said, preoccupied with food instead of her son's answer.

"I don't know, Mommy. Please, can I go?"

"*May* you go?"

"May I?"

"What time?" she mumbled again to speak, because her mouth was still packed with food.

"They're leaving now."

"What time will you be back?" she asked again, still wolfing down the food.

"I don't know. Come and ask them. They're outside," he said trying to pull her up. "Come on."

"All right! All right!" she said getting up and grabbing another piece of chicken.

"Hi, Miss Miles. You're up," a tall, thin lady in a plain white dress said entering with two bags of groceries.

"Hi, Florence. I hope you bought something good to eat. I'm starving," Trudy said.

"Yes, Ma'am. I'm sorry it took me so long to come back. I'll have dinner ready in a moment," the lady said as the boy pulled his mother on out the door.

"Hi, Miss Miles," the teenage boy spoke, standing on the porch.

"Hi, Darrell," she answered. "You're taking the boys to the park?"

"Yes, Ma'am," he said then indicating the car. "Me and my Mother."

"Hi, Trudy!" a lady called sitting on the passenger side of the black Cadillac SUV."

Wobbling to the car, Trudy asked, "Maggie, you're going with the boys?"

"Yes. Don't worry. We'll take good care of Carl."

"I know you will," she said then planted a kiss on her son's forehead and added. "Have a good time, Sweetheart." He ran and jumped quickly into the car. "Maggie, let me get some money for Carl."

"It's on me today, Trudy. Bye," the lady said, as Darrell drove off, and Trudy waved.

Trudy wobbled back into the house, grabbed a handful of cookies out the cookie jar, then dropped on the couch, and propped her fat legs up on the beautiful, gold-trimmed walnut colored table, then drifted into the past:

* *"Noooo!" Trudy screamed as she dived on Lillian, but Lillian's gun went off anyway over and over, dropping Spencer's bleeding body to the floor, as he shielded Cecily from the line of fire.*

"Let's go! We on parole!" one of the hulking men yelled to the other one, and they tore out of the house like two scared rabbits, dropping their guns on the floor.

"Cecily, look in Spencer's pocket for the key to these damn handcuffs!" Isaac demanded, and she bent down to Spencer's body, while Trudy cradled him in her arms, crying hysterically, begging him not to die, and took the key from his pocket, then ran to Isaac. She fumbled with the lock until he

was free, then he unlocked Alton who immediately ran to Lillian, who had dropped on the floor, numb, in a lifeless state. He picked her up, carried her to the couch and sat her down, while Isaac called an ambulance.

"Cecily, please, do something," Trudy begged her friend then focused back on Spencer. "Carl, I love you so much. Please, stay with me, Darling. Please."

"Trudy, he was going to <u>kill</u> us," Cecily insisted.

"He wasn't," Trudy replied. "I know him. He was only trying to scare us. He could never kill <u>anyone</u>."

"He killed Cotton," Cecily said.

"I didn't kill Cotton," Spencer squeezed out.

"The ambulance is on the way," Isaac announced.

"Sissy..." Spencer squeezed out again very weakly.

"Don't talk, Sweetheart," Trudy insisted. "Conserve your strength. The ambulance is on the way."

"I need to talk to Sissy," he squeezed out again.

"I hear you, Spencer," Cecily snapped.

"I didn't---kill---Cotton," he said growing even weaker, frowning his face with pain. "Sissy, look----in---my---safe. A letter----to----you---from---Cotton."

"What're you talking about, Spencer?"

"Cotton gave---it---to---me---before----she –died."

"Why would Cotton give you a letter to give to me?" Cecily wanted to know. "She hated you."

"No," he said. "She didn't. Read----" He coughed a little, and Trudy saw a trace of blood in his mouth, as he focused on her now. "I----love---you." Those were his final words before his head dropped to the side for the last time. Trudy released a scream so loud, it drowned out the sirens of the approaching ambulance. *

"Miss Miles," Florence said, bringing the weeping lady back to the present.

Wiping her face, Trudy asked, "Yes, Florence."

"I fixed you a snack while you're waiting for dinner," she said placing the tray of cheese, crackers, and cut up fruit on the table.

"Thank you, Florence. That's very nice of you."

"Are you all right, Miss Miles?"

"Yes, Florence. I'm fine. Thank-you."

"Let me know if you need anything," the lady said, and Trudy nodded because her mouth was already full of crackers, then the lady walked out slowly.

****

Wanda walked out of the library and looked for her mother's car, but it was not there. Her plaid mini skirt blew in the wind as she brushed her hair out of her face, growing frustrated. Her long pearl earrings caressed her small earlobes. Her silk blue Vanburen blouse swept her small frame gently, ending inside her skirt. The sun shone brightly in her eyes as she watched for her mother. Suddenly her mother's tan Rolls Royce pulled up in front of her, but Lillian was not in it. A man behind the wheel said, "Hi, Wanda. Get in." She recognized it to be Louis, the man who helps around the house with odd jobs. Louis' father was a foreman on one of Alton's crew.

Looking in the car, Wanda asked, "What're you doing here, Louis?"

"I was doing some work around the house, and your mother asked me to pick you up because she didn't feel good," he explained. Hesitantly, Wanda jumped into the car. She felt very uncomfortable around Louis, because he stared at her a lot. She wished her mother hadn't put her in this situation. She would have to talk to her mother about this, or better yet, maybe she'd better talk to her father. "How old are you, Wanda?" She heard Louis ask.

"Ten," Wanda answered clearing her nervous throat. She didn't trust this man at all. Her mother might trust him, but she sure didn't. She would keep an eye on this sneaky-looking white man.

"That's *all*? You look older," he smiled, as his big, blue eyes focused on her smooth legs.

"I know."

"Do you have a boyfriend?"

"No. I'm too young."

"No, you ain't," he chuckled. "I know lots of girls your age with boyfriends."

"Not me," Wanda replied, very happy to be entering her neighborhood.

This man made her very uncomfortable.

Wanda barely waited for the car to stop before she jumped out and ran in the house. When she entered her mother's room, Lillian was outstretched on the bed. "Mommy!" Wanda called shaking Lillian. "Mommy, wake up!" Lillian groaned but did not wake up, then Wanda spotted an empty bottle of vodka lying on the floor beside the bed, and she knew her mother was drunk.... *again.* She knew her daddy had to be out of town, because her mother didn't hide her liquor bottles when her daddy was out of town. Wanda shook Lillian harder and yelled, "Wake up, Mommy!"

Jerking away from her daughter, Lillian snapped, "Get away!"

"Mommy, wake up," Wanda tried again.

"Get the hell out of here!" Lillian jumped up yelling.

"No, Mommy. I want to help you!" Wanda yelled back. Suddenly she felt a sharp pain sting her face as her mother's fist handed on her tender skin.

"Don't you yell at me, young lady!" Lillian shouted, and then Wanda ran out in tears.

Wanda entered her bedroom, locked the door, and picked up the telephone receiver on her disco-typed, multi-colored cordless phone. She dialed the number slowly. "Carter Construction Company," the lady said on the other end.

"Alton Carter, please," Wanda squeezed out in tears.

"I'm sorry. He's gone for the day."

"This is his daughter. Do you know where he is?"

"Oh, hi, Wanda," the lady replied.   "I didn't catch your voice. He's going out of town this weekend. He said he was going home early to pack."

"Thank-you," Wanda said then hung up. She picked up a teddy bear from her bed and walked to the window slowly. She hugged it close to her body as tears rolled down her sad face, as she muttered softly, "Daddy, where are you?"

****

Alton planted a soft kiss on Cecily's lips, then rolled off her and pulled her in his arms. Fighting to catch his breath he chuckled, "You're going to kill me."

"Then you'll die happy," she laughed also.

"That's for sure."

Sobering, she looked into his beautiful brown eyes and said very softly, "I love you, Alton." He held up over her with a sweet smile and kissed her long and passionately, then pulled her in his arms again.

"I've got to get home and pack if we're leaving for the week-end."

"Where're we going?" she asked excitedly, holding over him on one elbow.

"Wherever you want, beautiful," he laughed sharing her enthusiasm.

"The beach!"

"Fine," he said getting up. "I'll be back as soon as possible."

"We'll be waiting."

"Where is Keisha?"

"She went somewhere with Mae," she said getting up and pulling on a housecoat. "You didn't think she was *here*, did you?"

"I guess not," he said smiling, walking into the bathroom. Alton turned on the shower then stepped in. He reached for the soap, but there was none. "Damn!" he spat. "Cecily, Honey, bring me some soap please!" Suddenly she opened the door and stepped in the shower with him.

"You need someone to scrub your back, Big Fellow?" she winked. He laughed pulling her in his arms, and they ended in a long, passionate kiss, under the warm, flowing water.

****

"Oh, Mommy, look!" Carl said running in the big mall to a clown, and Trudy wobbled along reluctantly. She hated going to the mall, but she *had* to take Carl some place sometimes, and he loved the mall. Her feet were killing her and all she wanted to do was curl up on her couch and watch one of those silly reality shows on television with a big bowl of ice cream. Trudy stopped at a bookstore window and focused on a beautiful girl on the cover of *Fashion and Glamour Magazine*, then she soon imagined it was her again, thin, desirable, and beautiful; but reality soon set in when she caught a glimpse of her reflection in the store window, and she immediately wanted to leave.

"Carl, let's go!"   she snapped, turning around abruptly, but to her surprise, her son was nowhere in sight. Hysterics took over and she bellowed a scream so loud it seemed to shake the roof, "Carl!!!!" Then panic immediately set in and she raced around incoherently searching frantically for her son, hysterically screaming his name over and over. "Oh my God. Where is he?!" She caught the eye of a security guard and he ran to her.

"What's the problem, Ma'am."

"My son is *missing!*" she babbled. "Oh God, my little boy is *missing!* He's *missing!* He's *missing!*"

****

"Hi, Pumpkin," Alton said poking his head in Wanda's bedroom door.

"Daddy!" Wanda exploded, running to him and hugging him tight. "I'm glad you're home."

"What's wrong, Pumpkin?"

"Daddy, please don't go out of town this weekend!" Wanda pleaded with tears rolling down her face.

"Hey! What's this?" he said as he led her to the bed and sat her down. "What is it, Sweetheart?"

"Mommy was drunk again today."

"*Drunk*?!"

"Yes, and she sent that weird Louis to pick me up from the library. I don't trust him, Daddy. He stares at me."

"He's harmless, Baby."

"Daddy, please don't go."

"All right, Sweetie. All right," he said wiping her tears with his fingers. "Don't cry. Daddy's here for you, Baby. Daddy will *always* be here for his little princess. I promise." He kissed her forehead. "I love you, Pumpkin."

"I love you, too, Daddy."

"Now, go and wash your face, and let Daddy make a phone call."

****

"Jimmy, we have a five-year-old boy missing at point twelve. Can you seal off all the exits, then give me a hand down here please," the security guard spoke into his walkie-talkie.

"Roger that, Leo."

Turning to a weeping Trudy, he said, "Don't worry, Ma'am. We'll find him."

"Oh, please," she cried. "He's all I have. Please." As the caring man pulled her in his arms, through wails of tears, she caught a glimpse of what she recognized to be Carl coming towards her. Trudy jerked off the man, wiped her eyes and the picture of her son became clear to her. "Carl!" she yelled, running to him, as he walked hand in hand with an extremely tall man. She grabbed the child up and squeezed him tight. Carl's eyes bulged, because he couldn't understand why his Mommy was acting so strange. "Carl, where've you been?" she finally asked releasing her hold on him.

"Mommy, why're you crying?"

"I couldn't find you!" she said still crying. "I was worried sick. Where have you been?"

"Playing the games!"

"What *games*?"

"Miss Miles, we'll release security now. I'm glad he's safe," the security guard spoke.

"Thank you so very much," she said then opened her purse. "Here, let me give..."

"No, Ma'am. Just doing my job."

"Thank you," she said again as he left.

"Miss Miles, I'm Maurice Campbell. You don't know me, but I'm an attorney, and my law firm handled some contracts for you a few years ago," the six feet, ten inches, slender, pecan tanned man spoke. "Carl was in the arcade room looking at me ride the motorcycle. He was enjoying it so much; I gave him some coins to ride himself. I thought his mother knew where he was. Then when I heard the commotion, I asked a guard, and he told me they were looking for a boy named Carl. That's when I asked this little man his name, and when he told me, I brought him straight back. I'm sorry you were upset."

"Oh, thank-you, Mr. Campbell."

"*Maurice*, please" he said, and thinking, *This is Trudy Miles, the <u>model</u>! Damn, what happened to her? She used to be so fine.*

"Thank you, Maurice. I don't know *how* to repay you."

"No need to, I assure you."

"Have you eaten?"

"No, I haven't."

"Would you like to have dinner with Carl and me. *My* treat."

"I would love to, but really, there's no need to pay me."

"I insist. It's the least I can do."

"Well, if you insist, I can't possibly refuse," he said smiling sweetly, as he thought, *Maurice, ole boy, you hit the jackpot. Your money problems will soon be over. Fat or thin, this brad is loaded.*

****

"Hi, Baby. We're ready."

"Cecily, I have bad news, Sweetheart," Alton said talking on his cell phone standing on the pool deck. "I can't make it this weekend. Wanda's very upset."

"What's wrong with her?"

"I don't want to get into it over the phone. I'll tell you about it later."

"All right."

"But, anyway, I think I've better stay home and keep an eye on things," he explained. "I hope you understand."

"Of course, I do. I care about Wanda, too."

"Rain check?"

"Sure."

"Maybe I'll be able to get away for a little while tonight after Wanda goes to sleep."

"Okay, Baby," she said then hung up, as Keisha walked in.

"Was that Daddy, Mommy?"

"Yes, Darling. Daddy can't take us to the beach like we planned. Wanda is sick."

"Ahhh."

"Hey! I have an idea," Cecily exploded, trying to cheer up the child. "Let's get all dressed up and go to a fancy restaurant, and then to a movie."

"Yeahhh!" the child exploded in laughter. "I'll get Mae to help me!" Keisha skipped out humming.

Cecily walked to her closet to pull down a dress and tipped over a box. "Damn!" she snapped then bent to pick up the contents that had fallen on the floor. When she picked up an envelope, she froze and drifted into the past:

*   *Cecily's trembling hands opened Spencer's safe carefully. She moved some things around until she saw an envelope with her name on it. She picked it up slowly, for she knew her name was written in Cotton's handwriting. Her trembling, sweaty hand could barely hold the envelope, "Why am I so damn nervous?" she said to herself, as Isaac entered the room.*

"Cecily," he called, and she jumped. "Are you all right?"

Taking a deep breath, she said, "Yes. You just scared me."

"I think you should know that the guns the two thugs had weren't loaded."

"What?!" she exploded. "That doesn't make sense!"

"Apparently Trudy was right. Spencer never meant to kill anyone. He just wanted to scare us."

"Spencer was a lunatic!"

"Did you find the letter?"

"Yes.,"

"I'll leave you alone," he said, and she nodded. He planted a kiss on her forehead then walked out. Cecily sat on the floor where she was and began reading the letter, written in Cotton's handwriting:

My Dearest Sissy,

Words can't express the many feelings I'm experiencing right now. Of all the mixed feelings I'm having, there's one that I'm very sure about, and that's my love for you. I love you very, very much, my Darling. I love you more than I ever thought possible to love anyone. When I met you, you were a frightened little girl, running away from a past that you thought was unjust to you. Now, you're my beautiful, intelligent, confident, young lady, and I'm so very proud of you. And, that makes my decision so much harder. Sissy, about a month ago, I saw a doctor, and he gave me some very bad news. I'm dying, Sissy. I'm dying. I have stage four stomach cancer. I wanted to see your dreams come true so badly, but that's impossible now. But I know you will make it. I'm hoping that the teachings you had from me *and your grandparents are enough to keep you strong enough to keep your dreams. You did a lot for me, also. If it weren't for you, I wouldn't have been able to write this letter. Thank-you. Sissy, don't ever get in the streets. Spencer can help you a lot, but don't ever let him get too close, because I know he wants to get you in the streets bad. It's every pimp's dream to get a girl as pretty and young as you. Please, don't ever let Spencer fool you into the streets. He's very smart and conniving. Sissy, I hired a hit man to kill me. I was too chicken to do it myself. I just can't sit around waiting to die. And, when it does happen the natural way, I would suffer so much. I can't put that burden on you, either. I must do it this way. I can't tell you because I know you'll talk me out of this. Spencer has tried to talk me out of it, so I let him think that he has, but he hasn't. I don't want him to interfere. I'm asking Spencer to take care of you, but, Sissy, don't you dare let him trick you into hooking. He's been good to me, but he's still a <u>pimp</u>. Take care of yourself, my beautiful baby. I hope that one day you'll find it in your heart to forgive me. Don't worry about not being able to say goodbye. I know you love me, just as much as I love you. Goodbye, my beautiful, sweet, precious daughter. I love you so very much.*

Your Mother, Cotton

Cecily dropped the letter and melted to the floor in soft, agonizing tears.
*

Cecily came out of the past and wiped her tears. She walked into the bathroom, popped a pill in her mouth, and then held her head back to gather the effects.

****

"Hi, Baby," Cindy said greeting Isaac at the door with a kiss.

"Hi," he smiled, putting his briefcase down. "I'm beat!"

"Sit down and relax. I'll have dinner ready soon."

"Where's Angela?"

"In her room."

"I think I'll go and say hello," he said walking up the stairs, as she nodded with a big smile.

When Isaac reached Angela's room, he knocked on the door. "Yeah," she yelled above the extremely loud rock music.

"It's me. May I come in?"

"It's open," she called back, and then he opened the door and walked in.

"Will you please turn the music down, Sweetheart?" he said, and she obeyed, with a frown, by turning it all the way off. "How are you?"

"Fine," she answered shortly lying across her Cinderella Castle bed, not facing him.

"How was school?"

"Fine."

"What did you do today?"

"Work."

"Angela, talk to me, Honey. I'm your father."

"I don't have anything to say."

"Don't you like having a daddy in the house?"

"Not really."

"Why?"

"Because I never had one. What you never had; you don't miss."

"That's true sometimes. However, I'm here now," he said moving to sit on her bed. "And, I want us to be a family." She didn't respond. "Would you please meet me halfway?" Still no response from the child. "I love you, Angela."

"You don't even *know* me."

"I know you're my daughter. That's enough for me right now," he said then paused for her to respond, but she didn't. "Mama said dinner will be ready soon. Okay?" She only nodded. "See you later, Sweetheart." He stood and walked out slowly, closing the door.

"Bastard!" Angela spat under her breath, as she through a teddy bear at the door.

****

As Cecily and Keisha sat in the fancy, luxurious restaurant, they were the focus of everyone's attention. They were indeed the loveliest females there. Cecily's hair was swept to one side, secured by a big gold barrette.

Her Anna Corbona deep pink dress hugged the top part of her body, down to the waist, ending with a gold belt   encircling   her twenty-four inch waistline, then the dress flared out just below her knees, where her bone colored heels finished the mode of perfection. Keisha dazzled in a sky-blue dress with lace accenting its glory. Her hair hang loosely down her back with a blue ribbon on each side of her ears, securing the hair out of her cute little bronzed, oval face, where her bangs hang just above her eyebrows. The waiter serviced their table many times more than he had to, for it was a joy focusing on such beauties.

"Would you like dessert, Honey?" Cecily asked Keisha.

"Can I have ice cream?"

"Yes, you *may*," Cecily said as Keisha beamed with excitement. "And, I think I'll have some, too." A shadow appeared over their table and without looking up, Cecily assumed it was the waiter and added, "We'll both have ice cream for dessert."

"Sounds good to me," a deep, baritone voice replied, and she knew it wasn't the waiter's voice, so she looked up and locked eyes with a brown-eyed, hunk of a man, in a deep blue tuxedo. "Hello, Cecily."

Her eyes widen, for she could not believe who was standing before her, and she replied in a soft whisper, "Barry?!" But before she could regain composure, he had yanked her up and was squeezing her in a big, tight, bear hug. All she could do was hug back, as a very thin, tall lady stood by, with a slight trying-to-be-friendly-but-I-hate-your-guts smile.   Then she recognized the lady to be Barry's wife, and she broke away from him gently.

"It's good to see you, Cecily," he finally said, releasing her and staring into her eyes, thinking, *Damn, you're fine!* He added, "It's been a long time."

"Yes. It has been," Cecily replied, thinking, *Damn, you're fine!* She had to do something to release his obvious undressing-her-with-his-eyes look, which she knew his wife was well aware of also, so she zoomed in on Keisha. "Barry, this is Keisha, my daughter."

Bending to the child, he extended a hand to her. "How are you, Keisha," he said.

"Fine," the child smiled wide shaking his hand.

"My. My. You're a pretty girl," he said, then stood and focused back on Cecily, and added, "just like your mother." Barry heard someone clearing her throat, and that brought him back to earth, as he realized it was his *wife*. He pulled her in front of him. "Valerie, this is Cecily Allen, a very old and dear friend from College. Cecily, this is my wife, Valerie."

"How do you do?" the light brown tan lady replied, forcing a smile.

"It's nice to meet you," Cecily smiled as they shook hands. "And, it's Cecily *Wade* now."

The waiter came to their table and asked, "Dr. Wade, will you be having guests joining you?"

"*Doctor*!" Barry exploded. "I'm impressed, but then, you've always had that dream. You deserve it."

"Thanks, Barry," she replied then motioned to the empty seats. "You're welcome to join us if you like."

"No, thank you," Valerie spoke up quickly before Barry could answer. "Our table is ready."

Then Cecily looked at the waiter and said, "You may bring my daughter and me some ice cream, please."

"Yes, Ma'am," he said. "What kind would you like?"

"Chocolate!" Keisha blurted out.

"Make that two," Cecily laughed, then the waiter smiled and left.

Barry noticed another couple coming in, and he waved to them to come over, and they did. After greetings were extended from both couples to each other, Barry introduced the couple to Cecily and Keisha as William and Laura Benton, and the lady made a big deal about how pretty Keisha was.

Boiling Valerie couldn't stand it any longer. She knew this woman was *more* than just an *old* college classmate of her husband's, and she wondered if this child could possibly be his. She hadn't seen her husband drool like this with so much lust and sparkle in his eyes since their wedding night. "I hate to break up this friendly little class reunion," she announced very sarcastically. "But, shouldn't we get to our table before the restaurant closes?"

"Cecily, would you like to join *us*?" Barry asked, and his wife jerked her head back to confront her overly excited husband, eye to eye. Was he insane asking this woman, whom he obviously had the hots for, to join them, and force her to watch him drool over her like a naive little schoolboy all night?

Catching an evil eye from Valerie, Cecily replied with a slight chuckle,

"I don't think so, Barry, but thanks anyway. After we finish our ice cream, we'll be leaving. I promised Keisha a movie." Then she thought, *Now put your fangs back in, Valerie!*

Waving the others along, Barry said, "Go ahead and order. Valerie, you know what I want."

"Bar..." his wife started to protest, but his decision was not up for debate.

"I'll be right there, Honey!" he insisted, and the other couple extended final greetings to Cecily and little Keisha then walked off, and Valerie reluctantly followed, looking back at her husband, as he took a seat at Cecily's table.

As the waiter placed their ice cream down, Keisha said, "Mommy, I have to use the rest room."

"Come on, Sweetie," the waiter said as he waved for a lady, and she came over. "Joanne, escort this little lady to the ladies' room, please."

"Come on, Precious," the lady said as Keisha caught her hand, and they walked off.

"Will that be all, Dr. Wade?" the waiter confirmed.

"Yes, thank you," she said, and then he left with a slight nod.

"It's really good to see you, Cecily," Barry said, finding it hard to take his eyes off her.

"Barry, I want you to leave."

"Why?"

"Not to mention the angry stares I'm getting from your jealous wife, I simply don't want to see you again, after what you did to me."

"What did I do?" he asked. "*You* were the one who never wrote *me*."

"*Me*?! I wrote you *every* week," Cecily exploded, trying to keep her voice low. "Until you got *married*. And, you never once wrote me back."

"There wasn't a week that went by that I didn't write you, Cecily!" It was his turn to explode. "You never answered my letters, so I had to go on with my life. That's when I met Valerie."

"I *never* received any letters from you."

"And I never received any from *you*."

"I don't understand," Cecily said in a daze. "I wrote you faithfully." Then her eyes stretched, and she said weakly, "Cotton."

"Cotton?"

"Yes. Don't you see? Cotton didn't want me to ruin my life by marrying you and ending my dream of becoming a doctor," she explained then looked in his eyes. "And, all those years I thought you just left and forgot about me."

"And, I thought *you* dumped *me*."

"And, when you came to see me after Cotton's death I was already involved with Spencer, and it didn't matter anymore, so we never talked about it."

"Our lives could've been so different."

"Especially *mine*," she stated matter-of-factly.

"Where's your husband, Cecily?"

"Divorced."

"I'm sorry."

"It's okay. It was *my* fault."

"You never change, do you?" he chuckled. "May I see you later?"

"*Tonight*?!"

"I'm leaving in the morning."

"I won't get home until around eleven. I don't think Matron Valerie will let you break out of her prison that late," she laughed.

"What's the address," he laughed also.

"215 Golden Manor."

Standing, he said, "See you later." He touched her hand lovingly then walked away. A warm, excited feeling ran through Cecily's entire body, and she couldn't believe it. How can this man still turn her on with just a touch after all those years? Maybe seeing him later isn't such a great idea after all. She sighed deeply as Keisha ran back to the table.

****

Alton peeked in Wanda's dark room and watched her sleeping for a few moments, then he closed the door quietly and walked downstairs, where Lillian sat curled up on the couch. "Is she all right?" she asked.

"Yes. She's asleep," he said pouring himself a drink at the bar.

"Fix me one, please."

"Don't you think you've had enough?" he snapped.

"Don't *think* for me! Damn it!" she exploded jumping off the couch.

"Keep your voice down before you wake Wanda. Haven't you done enough damage to that child for one day?"

"*Damage*?! What damn damage?!"

"You had no right sending Louis for her, but I guess in *your* condition, you had no other choice."

"Don't you dare lecture me, Alton!"

"Well, *someone* needs to, Lillian! Then for you to let her see you *drunk* and, to top it off, you *hit* the child for Christ's sake. That's inexcusable!"

"You can't tell me shit, Alton. While I'm taking care of this damn house and Wanda, you're out screwing that slut, Cecily!"

"Don't change the subject, Lillian! This has nothing to do with Cecily! And furthermore, you don't know what you're talking about!"

"The hell I don't! I know you're fucking the bitch! That's the only thing wrong with your black ass tonight, is that your plans with the bitch were canceled because Wanda got upset."

Alton threw his hand up in the air as if she was crazy, and retaliated, "I can go anywhere I damn well please, Lillian.   I don't need Wanda's permission or *yours*! And, I sure as hell don't need *this* damn shit!"

"Then why the fuck are you here, Alton?! It's obvious it's the bitch you want and *not* me. Why the fuck don't you just go the hell to her and leave me the hell alone?!"

"Look at you, Lillian? You used to never use words like that! You don't even go to church anymore. You used to be so beautiful. Now, you're nothing but a goddamn, sloppy drunk!"

"Well, that's better than being a fucking whore like your bitch! She'll open her damn legs to anything as long as it has a fucking dick!"

"You're crazy," he said then walked away.

"Don't you call me crazy, you sorry ass bastard!" she yelled striking at him, catching him by surprised, so her fingernail contacted the side of his neck causing blood to gush to the surface.   He did all he could to just restrain her. Then, suddenly he was forced to push her on the floor to take his exit before he would be forced to hurt her, and *that* would definitely cause more problems.

****

"Hello?" Trudy said into the telephone receiver, but there was no answer. "Hello?"

"Who was that?" Maurice asked coming into the bedroom with two tall glasses of tea.

"I don't know. They hung up," she said sitting up and receiving one glass from him and a kiss, as the telephone rang again.

"I'll get it," he said grabbing the telephone receiver up, while Trudy exited into the bathroom. "Hello?" Pause. "Why did you hang up?" Pause "I see." Pause. "I'll be right there." He hung up, as she reentered the bedroom. "Honey, that was a client. He's in trouble. I need to go out for a while."

"*Now*?!"

"Yes."

"But, it's eleven thirty!"

"He needs me, Baby," he said taking off his pajamas and putting on his clothes. "It's my job."

"But, Honey..."

"I'll go on home when I finish," he said. "Do you have any cash? I didn't get to the bank today."

"Yes. Look in my purse," she said, and he opened her purse and took out two hundred dollars.

"I'll see you tomorrow," he said then planted a kiss on her lips and left.

Trudy looked in her purse. "Why in the hell would you need two hundred dollars, Maurice, just to meet a client?" she pondered aloud.

****

Cecily sat curled on the couch in a long white shirt and tight, black knit pants, drinking tea as she drifted into the past:

Barry opened the door, wrapped in a towel, and Cecily was standing there in a white mink coat. "Cecily, hello,"

"Hi, Barry," she smiled.

"Please, come in." he offered, and she accepted.

"I can't stay. I'm on my way to the library. I just came to tell you not to call me anymore. I'm involved with someone, and he might not understand."

"I'm sorry. I never meant to cause you any problems."

"I know," she said. "Well, let me go, so you can finish your shower."

"Are you in love with him, Cecily?"

"Very much, just as I'm sure you're in love with your wife."

"May I ask who he is?" he inquired. "He's obviously taking <u>good</u> care of you."

"Yes, he is. It's Spencer."

"Spencer!" he exploded. "The <u>pimp</u>?"

"Yes," Cecily laughed. "Spencer is very good to me, Barry, and I love him with all my heart."

"Will you marry him?"

"I don't know yet. I hope so."

"Well, I'm happy for you, Cecily. I know you have to go, but can I get one hug first, for old times' sake?"

"Sure," she said, then they hugged lovingly, and <u>he</u> added a kiss.

"I'm sorry. I should've done that."

"It's all right. No harm done. Goodbye, Barry."

"Goodbye, Cecily."   *

The ringing of the doorbell brought Cecily back to the present.

****

Trudy lay in bed, staring at the ceiling, and drifted in the past:

*   *Trudy dried her eyes then walked to the door.   When she opened it, Ramon was standing there with a dozen of red roses in his hands. "Hi, Baby," he said smiling.*

"Ramon, what're you doing here?"

"I missed you, Baby," he said walking in and closing the door.

"Ramon, I really don't need this right now."

Noticing the tears coming from her eyes, he asked, "What's wrong, Sweetheart?"

"I just had a terrible lost, Ramon. I don't want to talk about it."

"Hey, Baby, I'll take care of you."

"I don't need you to take care of me, Ramon. I just need to be alone. Please understand."

"Trudy, I came a long way to be with you, Baby. Please let me stay."

"You can stay the night, but you have to go tomorrow."

"No, Trudy. We belong together."

"Ramon, please..."

"I love you, Baby," he said again. "I have a lawyer working on my divorce."

"Ramon, you can't get a divorce. Your wife is pregnant."

"Yes, I can, Baby. You'll see," he said taking her in his arms and holding her tight. "I love you so much. I can't live without you."

Then she remembered two days later, the beatings started, and she had to have him forcefully removed and arrested, and that was the end of that.

*

Trudy came out of the past, wiped her tears then laid back down to get some sleep, but she couldn't help but to wonder what Maurice's story was. Was he *another* mistake? She was very good at picking *losers*!

****

"That's a shame what Spencer did to you. I feel responsible. If I hadn't kissed you, none of that would've happened."

"Barry, somehow I have a feeling that Spencer would've used any excuse to put me on the streets when he was ready to do so," Cecily explained, sitting on the carpet by the fireplace, with Barry, in a warm-up suit.

"Well, I'm glad you came out of it a champ. Not too many people could've done what you did."

"If it weren't for Cotton, I wouldn't have been able to do it either," Cecily said passing him the bowl of popcorn they were sharing. "She gave me my start in life."

"And, she didn't take any junk, either," Barry laughed. "I thought she was going to kick my butt *plenty* times! She couldn't *stand* me!"

"It wasn't that she didn't like you. She just didn't want anything to ruin my future. I don't know, but I think I was a project of some sort to Cotton. I've never understood why she was so protective of me."

"She loved you."

"Yes, but it was more than love. I guess I'll never know," she said looking at the wall clock. "Look at the time. Your wife is going to kick your butt!"

"She probably will, but it's worth it. I don't know when I've had a more relaxing and enjoyable evening with anyone. Thank you."

"Me, too, Barry. Thank *you*."

"So, does Keisha's father spend time with her even though he has a wife?"

"Yes. He's very good to her as well as his other daughter."

"That's great," he said. "Are you still seeing him?"

With a smile, Cecily nodded as she said softly, "Yes."

"Oh, what tangled web we weave...."

"I love him, Barry."

"Do you think he'll ever leave his wife?"

"Yes, *one* day."

"You're not living in a dream world, are you, kid?"

"No. I know he loves me, but it's his *daughter*. He can't leave her. She needs him, and I love the little girl. I don't know if I could live with myself if I hurt her."

"Well, maybe things will work out."

"Enough about me. What about you. Are you happy?"

"Cecily, I married Valerie because she was pregnant. The truth of the matter is we've never really been madly in love. At the time I married her,

I still loved *you,* but I thought you didn't want me anymore. Valerie is a wonderful woman, but we are just not compatible. She knows it, and I know it. I know what your friend is going through because if it weren't for the kids, Valerie and I would've split long ago. I love my kids, and I would go through hell for them."

"Do you think you will ever get a divorce?"

"I'm sure we will. It's just a matter of time."

"Do you have someone else?"

"No, but I can't say I never have. When I played ball, there were women everywhere. I'm not proud of it, but I have had my share of women during my marriage. But I think it was largely because I wasn't happy."

"Does she know about the women?"

"Oh, yes."

"How did she find out?"

"I told her."

"*You* told her?!"

"Yes. I just couldn't keep it from her. And, to my surprise, she had an affair also, which she admitted to me."

"She did?"

"Yes."

"And you didn't split up?" Cecily chuckled. "Maybe you have something more special than you think, Barry."

"I'm trying, Cecily. I really am. I haven't been unfaithful in over three years."

"That's great."

He took a deep breath. "As bad as I hate to leave you, pretty lady. I've got to go. My plane leaves at seven in the morning," he said standing then helping Cecily up, and they stared in each other's eyes for a while until their lips met long and passionately. "I'll always care for you, Cecily."

"You'll always have a special place in my heart, too, Barry," she said softly, and they kissed again as the doorbell rang. "Saved by the bell."

"You sure you want to be saved?" he asked, and their eyes locked until the doorbell rang again. "You are so beautiful."

Clearing her throat Cecily said, "I've better get that before it wakes Keisha." He nodded.

When Cecily opened the door, Alton walked in asking, "What took you so long? Whose car?"

"Alton, what're you doing here? It's one o'clock in the morning!"

"I told you I was coming."

"You didn't tell me it would be one in the morning," she said closing the door.

"What time did you get home? I called twice."

"I was home. I just didn't answer the phone."

"Why?"

Taking a deep breath, Cecily said softly, "I have company."

"What?"

"I have company," she said turning to avoid his eyes.

"What in the hell do you mean? You have company!"

"A very old and dear friend stopped by. That's all."

"Is he still here?" he asked cautiously, and she nodded slowly. "So that's his car outside? Where is he? In your *bed*?"

"*No*! Of course *not*! What kind of woman do you think I *am*?!"

"I'm sorry, Baby. Lillian just makes me so crazy," he said pulling her in his arms, as Barry entered, pulling on his coat.

"Alton?"

"Barry?"

"So, you two know each other?" Cecily asked.

"We *should*. My mother and Alton's father are sister and brother," Barry stated. "How the hell are you?"

"Fine, man, and you?" Alton replied as they greeted each other with a hug.

"Just great," Barry said, then added. "Keisha. *Yours?*" Alton nodded. "What a small world."

"So, I hear you're giving it up to coach."

"Yes. My old knees won't let me play any longer," Barry smiled then looked at Cecily, "Hey, I've gotta split. My plane leaves in a few hours and Boston Airlines don't wait for *no* body." She nodded. "It's been great seeing you again."

"Same here," she replied.

"Take care of yourself," he said then planted a kiss on her forehead, "Let's keep in touch." She nodded, then he focused on Alton. "Later, man." They slapped hands.

"Later," Alton replied, and then Barry left, and Cecily walked into the den, followed by Alton. "So, how *close* are you and my cousin?"

"Alton, don't start."

"Don't start what?"

"Don't give me the third degree. I'm free, black, and over twenty-one. Nothing happened between Barry and me, but if something *had*, you don't have a damn thing to say about it.   You have Lillian to soothe you when you're horny, lonesome, or *whatever*. I have *no* one.   How long am I supposed to wait for you?" she snapped.

"I'm sorry. I guess I've been very unfair to you. But, you're wrong about one thing. Lillian and I haven't made love in months. Lillian is relying on the bottle for comfort."

"What *bottle*?"

"The *liquor* bottle. What else?"

"*Lillian, drinking*?!" exploded Cecily, and Alton nodded. "I can't imagine *Lillian* drinking. She *never* would before. She never did *anything* before."

"Well she is *now*, and I have to do something very soon, because it's affecting Wanda."

"I'm sorry."

"So maybe we should cool it. Lord knows I can't give you what you want right now, and there's no need for me to lie about it," he said and there was a long silence, until he finally broke it. "I've got to go. I'll see you later." He rushed out so quickly, Cecily didn't have time to say goodbye. Cecily reached in her pocket, took out a couple of pills and threw them down her throat, and then she dropped her head back slowly.

****

Carl Jr. burst into Trudy's room, switched on the light, and jumped into bed with her. Rolling over, Trudy asked, "What's wrong, Darling?"

"I'm scared, Mommy," he said pulling the covers over his head.

"There's nothing to be afraid of, Sweetie," she said sitting up, putting on her bedroom slippers. She looked back at her child, pulled the covers off his head, and he was pretending to be already asleep. She smiled, got up, and walked downstairs. Trudy walked into the kitchen, opened the refrigerator, and took out a half-eaten cherry cheesecake pie. She placed it on the table, grabbed a folk out of the drawer, then sat at the table and began eating from the pan. She moaned with pleasure. She never knew she could get so much satisfaction from food. *Men!* Who needs them? Then she thought of Maurice and wondered why he never touched her. Is she *that* undesirable? What was his story? Maybe she needs to hire a private detective to check him out.

****

Lillian was having one of her common nightmares about an evil Spencer coming back to get her, then suddenly she jumped up in bed in a cold sweat.

She shook her head and looked at Alton lying on the other side of the king-sized bed, undisturbed. She rose from the bed slowly, pulled on a housecoat and walked out.

Lillian strolled into her huge kitchen and took a bottle of vodka from the cabinet. She opened it and took a big gulp, right from the bottle. It was so strong; she had to regain her composure again before taking another gulp. Then she stood there and drifted into the past:

*   *"All rise. The Honorable Judge Halstead presiding."*

"You may be seated," the judge said then looked at the jury. "Mr. Foreman, has the jury reached a verdict?"

"Yes, Sir, Your Honor," the man stood and said. "Will the defendant please rise." Lillian's lawyer took her by the elbow and helped her to stand on her wobbly legs. She exhaled deeply as the judge looked at the verdict, then past it back to the foremen. Then Lillian turned and focused on Alton, Trudy, and Cecily sitting all apart from each other in the courtroom. She could sense the nervousness and tension they all felt, but she knew that if she was going to jail, she deserved it, because she had taken a life, and she had no right to do that. "Mr. Foreman, on case number 569, the state of California verses Mrs. Lillian Renee Martin-Carter for first degree murder of Mr. Carl Daniel Spencer, what say ye, the jury?"

"Your Honor, we the jury finds Mrs. Lillian Carter not guilty, by reason of temporary insanity," the man said, and Lillian dropped in her seat, crying and laughing at the same time. Then she jumped back up and hugged

*her lawyer tight.   *

Lillian heard footsteps, which brought her back to the present, so she threw the bottle back in the cabinet and took out a glass. As Alton walked in Lillian was pouring herself a glass of water from the refrigerator. "Are you all right?" he asked her.

"I'm fine. Just thirsty," she said, taking a sip of water.

"It's five o'clock in the morning. Are you *sure* you're all right?"

"Yes, I'm sure. Don't hound me tonight, Alton!"   she snapped then walked out quickly. Alton picked up the glass Lillian placed on the counter and sniffed. To his surprise there was no alcohol smell. He had been concerned about her, and she acted as if he were there to harm her. He wondered what had happened to his beautiful, intelligent wife. He stood there and drifted into the past:

*   *"Mr. Carter, thank you so much for agreeing to participate in this seminar today," a medium build man with eyeglasses on said to Alton. "I have arranged for you to have a tour guide today because you will be flip-flopping in and out of classes all day, until the seminar begins, which is at three o'clock."*

"It's my pleasure to be here with you today, Professor Mills. I'm sorry my father couldn't come today, but I guess I can handle it."

"You're do just fine, Mr. Carter," he said, as Lillian entered through the door. "Here is your tour guide now."

"Wow, how did I get so lucky?" Alton smiled big, as she walked to them.

"Mr. Carter, this is Lillian Martin. She will be your tour guide today, and from your response, I don't think you have a problem with that."

Laughing, Alton said, "I most certainly do not."

"Lillian, this is Mr. Alton Carter from Carter Construction Company."

"Hello, Mr. Carter," she smiled sweetly.

"Hello, Miss Martin."

"Well, you kids have fun," Professor Mills said, walking away smiling.

"So, Mr. Carter, I know you can't be the CEO of such a large and prestigious company."

"And, why not, Miss Martin?"

"Because you're so young. You must be still in college."

"Well, you're absolutely right, Miss Martin. I....ugh...may I call you Lillian?"

"Sure."

"And, it's Alton. All right?"

"All right, <u>Alton</u>."

"Well, as I was saying, I graduated last year from NYU, and I'll be starting graduate school in the fall. My father is the man behind the name of the business," he said. "And, you are a....?"

"Junior."

"Well, Lillian, you are a very beautiful young lady," he said, and she smiled.

****

Alton and Lillian sat, kissing wildly, on a huge couch, in a very big, beautifully decorated mansion. He pulled her blouse up, unfastened her bra, and began fondling her breasts. Suddenly Lillian jumped up, knocking him on the floor and pulled down her blouse. "I'm sorry, Alton. I can't do this."

"Why, Baby?" he said crawling to her on his knees. "I love you."

"And I love you, too, but I can't. Not right now."

"Well, when?"

"I don't know. I've been saving myself for marriage."

"We <u>will</u> get married one day, but I need you <u>now</u>, Baby."

"I'm sorry. I can't," she said jumping up. "Please take me home." He blew hard in frustration, trying to calm down, then he jumped up and ran after her.

"Wait, Baby, wait," he said grabbing her arm. "You don't have to leave right now. I promise, hands off."

"But I don't want to stop you from seeing someone else, Alton. I know you can have your pick of women."

"There's only <u>one</u> woman that I want, and I'm looking at her," he said, then took her face in his hand and planted a soft kiss on her lips. "I love you, Lillian."

"Why, Alton. Why do you love <u>me</u>?"

"What'd you mean?"

"Look at this house. You have everything. I'm a poor girl who grew up with only my mother, who worked night and day to make ends meet. If I didn't work hard in school to get a four-year scholarship, I wouldn't be in college, because I wouldn't be able to afford it. Why do you love <u>me</u>?"

"Because you're <u>you</u>," he said softly. "Lillian, I knew from the first moment that I saw you that you would be my wife someday."

"Could you ever be faithful to <u>one</u> woman, Alton?"

"Of course, I could."

"I mean <u>really</u> faithful, because before you even decide to ask me to marry you, please make sure you can truly say yes to that question. If would kill me if I saved myself for my husband all these years, and he cheated on me. I would rather stay singer than to have <u>that</u> to go through. So, please, don't say you want to marry me some day unless you <u>truly</u> understand what I'm saying to you."

"I understand, Lillian. And I'll make damn sure that I can answer that question yes before I ask you," he said then smiled. "I love you."

"And I love you, with <u>all</u> my heart."   *

Alton came out of the past and closed his eyes tight to keep from crying. Was it *his* fault that Lillian has become what she is? He never meant to hurt his beautiful wife, but he knew he had. He had hurt her bad. He had hurt her bad enough to *kill*. Was it *his* fault?! He had to admit, it probably was. He cared a lot for Cecily, but if he was making his wife crazy, he *had* to let Cecily go for good this time. He knew it would hurt her because he, too, would miss her, but it had to be done, because he didn't know how much more of this his wife could take. When Lillian killed Spencer, she was really trying to kill Cecily, and Lord knows what she would've done to *him* if he was nearby at the time. God help him if she ever cracked again...and *Cecily.*

Chapter 12

"Wanda, get up!" Lillian yelled, stumbling.

"What is it, Mom?" Wanda mumbled, turning over in bed.

"Get up or you're be late for school."

"Mom, there's no school. It's *Saturday*."

"Oh, I'm sorry, Sweetheart," Lillian said, as she stumbled out and closed the door. She walked downstairs where Alton sat watching the television.

"Good morning," Alton said, but she didn't reply. She just dropped down in the recliner. "Gracie said breakfast would be ready in about fifteen minutes."

"What're *you* doing home?!" she snapped. "I thought you'll be making a house call to your favorite doctor by now."

"What's with you, Lillian?!" Alton snapped. "Can't we have one peaceful day at home?! Do you have to ruin *all* my time at home?!"

"I'm tired of you playing me for a fool, Alton! Everybody knows you're fucking Cecily! You should see the stares I get from people feeling sorry for me!"

"That's all in your mind."

"The hell it is?!" she yelled as Alton focused back on the television.

"Again, Boston Airlines Flight 747 from California to New York has crashed," the news anchor announced. "Football great Barry Jett, his wife, Valerie, and Football hall of famer William Benton and his wife Laura were aboard this flight. It is uncertain at this time as to either the cause of the crash or the number of passengers aboard, but it is certain that there were no survivals. I repeat, *no* survivals!"

****

"Cecily," Alton called softly as he entered her dark bedroom. He focused on Cecily lying in a heap on the bed, sobbing softly. He rushed to her, sat on the bed, and pulled her up gently.

"Alton, did you hear?" she squeezed out in between tears, looking into Alton's eyes with her red, puffed up, sad ones.

"Yes. I heard," he said softly, pulling her in his arms, letting her cry out her sorrows.

****

"What?!"

"Yeah, Girl. Barry is dead," Lillian said to Trudy over the telephone.

"Cecily must be crushed. They almost got married once."

"That's not all. He was with her just last night."

"Get outta here!"

"Yes. Valerie called me and told me how Barry drooled over Cecily at dinner. Then she said he disappeared for hours. So, she found out where Cecily lived, and she rode by there. Sure enough, Barry's rented car was there. She said she didn't go to the door, because she didn't want to make a scene, but she was seriously thinking about divorcing him."

"You lying!"

"It's true," Lillian continued. "And, now they're *dead*. Just like that."

"Then I know Cecily is freaking out."

"Should we go over there, Tru?"

"*What*?! I thought she was fucking your husband."

"Yes, but she might need us, especially if she's freaking out. I know Alton is there, but it's nothing like having your home girls in times of trouble." Lillian explained. "Should we go?"

****

When Cecily opened her weak eyes after she had fallen asleep in Alton's arms, she looked up and saw Alton sitting in a chair, with his head thrown back, asleep also. As she got up, Alton awoke also. "It seems you're always rescuing me out of bad situations," she said sitting on the edge on the bed.

Rising, he asked, "Are you all right, Baby?"

"Yes," she replied scratching her head.

Looking at his watch, Alton said, "I guess I'd better get going. I didn't tell Lillian where I was off to." He yawned, putting on his shoes. "Do you want me to take Keisha for a few days?"

"Would you, please?"

"Sure. She's asleep now, but I'm pick her up later," he said then planted a kiss on her forehead while they heard the doorbell rang. "Call me if you need me." She nodded, and he started out the door.

"Alton!" she called, and he turned. "Thanks."

"You bet," he said then walked out.

Cecily stood up, walked into the bathroom, and opened the medicine chest. She took out a bottle of pills, dropped two down her throat, then let her head drop forward until she heard Mae call, "Dr. Wade, you have guests." Before she could ask who, Mae was gone.

Cecily was halfway down the stairs, when she focused on Lillian and Trudy standing at the bottom of the staircase, and she stopped abruptly. "Lillian? Trudy?"

"Hi, Cecily," Lillian spoke.

"Hiya, Kid," added Trudy.

"We're sorry about Barry," Lillian continued.

Still in a daze, not believing her friends were actually here, Cecily managed to squeeze out, "Thanks."

"Cecily, it's time to settle our differences," Lillian said again.

"Yes," added Trudy. "I know Spencer's death wasn't your fault. I'm sorry for blaming you."

"And I know you weren't *totally* at fault for sleeping with my husband. If he wanted to cheat, if it weren't you, it would've been *someone*. I'm sorry for the way I reacted."

"You guys, I don't know what to say," Cecily finally said. "Trudy, I should be apologizing to *you*, not you apologizing to *me*. I had Spencer figured out all wrong. I hated that man for so long, for *nothing*. I never understood why he put me on the streets until that night. And all those years, I thought Spencer killed Cotton. I let my hatred get in the way of *your* happiness, and I'm sorry." She then turned to Lillian after Trudy gave her a nod of forgiveness. Cecily took a deep breath, and then walked down the rest of the stairs. "What do I say to you? I've loved you like a sister ever since we were kids. I don't know how I could've ever betrayed you of all people. Just to say I'm sorry doesn't seem to be enough. I took our friendship and stuck a knife in it until it was drained of every ounce of honesty, loyalty, and trust." Tears were rolling down her face as well as Lillian's and Trudy's. The only defense I have is that I fell in love with Alton long before I knew he was your husband. God in heaven knows that if I had any idea Alton was your husband at that time; I would've *never* gotten involved with him. But I didn't know, and I couldn't turn off my feelings once I knew. Then to make matters worse, I got angry at *you* for being angry with *me*, and you had a perfect right to be angry with me. *I* was the one who slept with your husband and betrayed *your* trust. I was so wrong, Lil, and I admit that. *I was wrong.* But I'm asking you to *please* forgive me." Lillian and Cecily fell in each other's arms, and they embraced lovingly. "I'm so sorry, Lil," Cecily added in tears, as Trudy joined the embrace. "Please forgive me."

"I forgive you, Cis," Lillian said in tears also. "I forgive you."

Chapter 13

Cecily lay, sunbathing on a big beautiful beach, with a two-piece, red bikini on and a pair of dark sunglasses covering her eyes. A big straw hat caressed her head as a volleyball came crushing down on it. "I'm sorry," a smiling man said.

"It's okay," she said, smiling and throwing it back to him.

"What's a beautiful lady like you doing sunning on the beach of Honolulu all by herself?"

"Vacationing."

"Would you like to join us? We could use another person."

"Why not," Cecily said jumping up.

"Craig Brooks," he introduced extending a hand to her.

Shaking his hand, she said, "Cecily Wade." Cecily couldn't help but to admire this extremely gorgeous man with his dark, suntanned olive skin and his dark wavy, black hair. Dimples on each side of his face just melted her heart while she wondered what nationality he was. He didn't have an accent, and Brooks is a very common American name, but she knew he had to be mixed with something. Her guess was Italian. She could play her hunch later. One thing she did know for *sure*. No matter what he was he was one *gorgeous* white man.

****

Cecily played volleyball for hours with Craig and the rest of the people on the sandy beach. It felt good to laugh again. She didn't think she could ever laugh again.   The double funeral of Barry and Valerie, and the devastation of all who loved them, was more than Cecily cared to think about. But the hardest thing for her to swallow was looking into the eyes of two children who had just become parentless, trying to be brave, and apparently dying inside. Her heart went out to Barry's kids, Mark, who was the splitting image of Barry, and Tammy, who resembled Barry only a little. She didn't think she could've gotten through it if Alton and Lillian weren't there, but they flew back right after the funeral to take the children off Trudy's hands. And, she decided to take a vacation, so she ended up in Hawaii.

****

Craig walked Cecily back to her hotel room, and they stood at her door as she said, "I really enjoyed the volleyball today. Thank-you for inviting me."

"Thank you for accepting. I enjoyed having you as well."

"Are you on vacation, too?"

"Oh, no. This is my home. It has been for the past four years."

"How'd you like living in a place where there're so many tourists?"

"It has its ups and downs."

"What about your family?"

"What about them? I'm not married. My mother passed away several years ago, and my father and brothers live on the mainland," he explained. "May I see you tomorrow, Cecily?"

"Craig, if you don't mind my getting personal, but how old are you?"

"Age ain't nothing but a number, Baby," he joked.

"I don't like robbing cradles."

"I assure you, I'm *no* baby," he said sarcastically, and they both laughed. "You have a beautiful laugh."

"Thanks. But you still haven't told me how old you are."

"Is it really that important, Cecily?" he asked, and she nodded. "Twenty-six. Am I old enough?"

"For what?"

"Your time."

"Craig, I'm nine years older than you. With all these pretty, *young* ladies on the beach, why me?"

"Why *not* you? I haven't seen *anyone* on this beach more beautiful or more charming than you."

"Thank you again."

"Now, may I see you tomorrow, pretty lady?"

Nodding she said, smiling, "Sure. Why not?"

"Until tomorrow," he said, then planted a soft, feather kiss on her forehead and left.

Cecily walked into the hotel room and closed the door. She couldn't stop thinking about this incredibly handsome man who flattered her so very much by wanting to spend time with her. She walked into the bathroom and turned on the shower. She pulled off her clothes slowly as she thought of Craig's soft kiss on her forehead, making her warm inside. This man may be young, but he was definitely a charmer, and she loved it. Neither age nor race seemed to make a difference to him. She smiled as she thought how much she was going to enjoy herself in Hawaii. Just as the water began to massage her body the telephone began to ring. "Damn!" Cecily spat reaching for a towel. She jumped out the shower and headed for the telephone, wrapping the towel around her wet body. "Hello?"

"Cecily, Craig"

"What's up, Craig?"

"I just wanted to say goodnight and pleasant dreams."

"That's sweet, Craig, but I'm dripping wet here. I had to get out the shower to answer the phone."

"Umm, that sounds delicious. May I come over and dry you off?"

"What?!"

Laughing he said, "I'm kidding. Be cool," He sobered. "Anyway, I'll see you tomorrow."

"I'll be waiting," she smiled as she hung up the telephone. Then she picked it up again and dialed.

"Hello? Carter's residence."

"Gracie, this is Cecily Wade. How are you?"

"Fine, Dr. Wade. How are you?"

"Just great," Cecily smiled thinking of Craig. "Gracie, is Keisha around?"

"Yes, ma'am. Hold on. I'll get her for you."

"Thank you, Gracie," Cecily said then waited.

"Mommy!" Keisha exploded into the receiver.

"Hi, Darling. How's my girl?"

"When're you coming home?"

"In a few days, Baby. Mommy misses you so much."

"What're you doing, Mommy?"

"Just relaxing, Sweetie."

"Daddy took me to the zoo yesterday. I fed the elephants."

"You did? That's great, Sweetheart."

"Mommy, can I come there with you?"

"Not this time, Sweetie, but I promise that you and I will visit here very soon. Okay?"

"Mommy, I wanna come *now*."

"Honey, you can't right now."

"Why not?"

"Keisha, please be a big girl for Mommy. I'll see you soon. All right?" Cecily explained, but the child didn't answer. "All right, Baby?"

With a sad face, she said softly, "All right, Mommy."

"I love you," Cecily said smiling, but the child didn't respond. "Don't you love me?" The child still didn't answer. "Keisha, please, don't be like that. Mommy will see you soon. I promise. Don't make Mommy feel bad. I need this rest. Please."

"I love you, too, Mommy," she finally said softly.

"That's my girl," Cecily smiled. "I'll call you again tomorrow. okay?"

"Okay."

"Let me speak to Aunt Lillian."

"She's sleeping."

"Oh, okay. What about Daddy?"

"He's not here."

"Who's there with you?"

"Wanda is playing with me."

"All right, Sweetie. Tell Wanda I said hello."

"Okay, Mommy."

"Keep sweet. I love you. Bye, Honey."

"Bye, Mommy."

When Cecily hung up the telephone, she wiped a tear from her face. She wanted to see Keisha so badly, but she desperately needed this time alone to sort out a lot of things. She knew it had to be over between Alton and her. Lillian had forgiven her, and she couldn't take the chance of losing her best friends again. Nobody was worth that, even *Alton*. She and Keisha have never been apart, and it was hard on both of them. But she would make it up to Keisha as soon as she returned. She loved that little girl so much. She didn't know if it was because Keisha was *hers* or because she was *Alton's*. All she knew was that she really loved her. She didn't know it was possible to love someone this much. Suddenly Cecily focused on a bottle of pills on the table. She wanted to take one. She needed to relax after talking to Keisha, but she had promised herself that she wouldn't take any more pills. After all, she *wasn't* an addict. It wasn't like she *needed* them.   She tried to get her mind off the pills, but her eyes wouldn't let her. When she witnessed the trembling in her hands, she thought that maybe *one* last time wouldn't hurt. She seized the pill bottle, opened it quickly, and gulped one down her throat, then another one. Then Cecily felt a chill and remembered she had to finish her shower.

Cecily rushed back, jumped in the shower and let the water satisfy her body while the pills satisfied her mind. A knock on the door brought her into focus.   "Damn! I'm never going to finish my shower!" she spat, grabbing a bathrobe. She tied it as she rushed to the door. Cecily yanked the door open. A tall man was standing there smiling, and her breath momentarily left her body as she squeezed out, "*Rocky*."

****

Lillian was outstretched on the couch as Wanda entered slowly and focused on her mother. Wanda took a deep breath, for she knew it would be a battle to awaken her mother to take her to dance class. If her mother was drunk again, she wondered if she should even bother her about taking her to dance class. She thought about the big recital coming up, and her lead in a routine, so she decided she *had* to be there. Then, after this recital, she would quit dance class until her mother got well. Wanda went to Lillian and shoved her gently, calling, "Mom, wake up." Lillian groaned and went back to sleep. Wanda shook her again. "Mom, it's four o'clock. I have to go to dance class. Are you going to take me?" Lillian opened her eyes slowly.

"What time is it?" she asked yawning.

"Four o'clock."

"Honey, Mommy doesn't feel well. Couldn't you skip today?"

"I missed *last* week," Wanda sarcastically replied. "We have a recital coming up, and...."

"Okay! Okay!" Lillian snapped, struggling to get up.

"Are you drunk again?"

"*No*! I'm *not* drunk!" retaliated Lillian, trying to balance her feet on the floor. "And, you better watch your tone with me, young lady!" Wanda turned to walk out. "Where's Keisha?"

"In the car," replied Wanda not looking back.

****

As Lillian drove Wanda and Keisha to dance class, Wanda's eyes were wide open, as her mother swerved in and out of lanes, dominating the narrow road. Motorists sounded their horns in frustration at the woman, forcing some of them on the curb. "Mom, are you all right?" Wanda asked cautiously.

"Yes. I'm fine!" Lillian snapped.

"Mom, you're driving on the line," Wanda warned, as Keisha, in the back seat, unbuckled her seat belt to sit up and look.

"Are *you* driving or I, Missy?!" Lillian snapped again. "You're getting very grown lately!"

"Keisha, put your seat belt back on!" Wanda yelled.

"Don't yell at her!" insisted Lillian as she attempted to pass a truck around a curve. The approaching car was coming just as quickly as Lillian, and she had to run off the road to avoid hitting it, but she lost control of the car and could not avoid a tree. Wanda and Keisha screamed as loud as their little vocal cords could manage, as they saw themselves plummeting into a tree that they *knew* wouldn't move.

****

Trudy sat watching television devouring a piece of chocolate cake as Carl entered. "Mommy, can we go to the park?" he asked sitting beside his mother on the couch.

"Mommy doesn't feel like it, Sweetheart," she said. "I know what, let's go and get a pizza, okay?"

"Oh boy!!" he exploded jumping up as the doorbell rang.

"Go and wash your face," she said wobbling to the door, as he ran upstairs.

When Trudy opened the door, she lost her breath, as she stood eye-to-eye with Ramon, her past Latin lover. "Ramon! What're you doing here?" she snapped.

****

Cecily opened her eyes slowly and focused on Rocky's smiling face sitting on the couch where she laid, and she jumped back. "It's me, Cecily," he said, trying to reassure her that she wasn't looking at a ghost. "I'm not *dead*." She stared into his brown eyes momentarily, until she mustered up enough courage to reach up and touch his face softly.

"Rocky?" she squeezed out. "You're *alive*."

"Yes. I am. Thanks to you."

"But I thought I killed you."

"No, you didn't. You *saved* my life."

"I don't understand," Cecily said, sitting up to face him. "I checked your pulse and you were dead."

"No, I wasn't."

"Oh, my God!" she said covering her mouth, then suddenly, she grabbed him in her arms, and they embraced long and happily, as tears flowed down her face. When she finally let him go, she looked at him and noticed that his head was shaved clean. "You're bald," she smiled.

"Yes," he chuckled. "I was losing my hair anyway, so I decided, what the hell, so I told my barber to shave it all off."

"It becomes you."

"Thank you," he smiled. "You're still as beautiful as I remember, just blossomed a little."

"Thank you."

"You saved my life, Cecily." he spoke sincerely. "I have you to thank for the breath I breathe today."

"But I didn't save your life, Rocky. I thought you were dead, so I left. I'm a doctor. I was supposed to have stayed until the ambulance arrived. If it were not for that person who found you, you would've died."

"Cecily, I was a walking dead man anyway. Clarence walked out on me, because I wouldn't give up the drugs. He later died of a heart attack, and I think I am somewhat to blame. Clarence spent his whole life trying to make me do right. That must've been so hard on his heart all those years. My life really went downhill after Clarence's death. After you put that knife in me, and I laid on my back for months, I had an opportunity to review my life. For the first time I realized how much I must've hurt you, and I felt very ashamed. Here you were a very young girl coming to me to do the right thing by you, just so you could raise our child, and I was too selfish to help. Right then and there I decided to change. I checked myself into a drug rehab the same day I was released from the hospital, and I'm proud to say, I haven't used drugs since, and that's been over five years."

"That's great, Rocky. Who found you?"

"I don't know. The hospital received an anonymous call."

"Spencer's photographer," Cecily squeezed out under her breath.

"Excuse me?"

"Oh, nothing," she replied shaking it off. She knew that if she told him about her idea that Spencer's photographer called the ambulance, she would have to tell him everything, and she wasn't up for that right now. "You sure are a sight for sore eyes. Why didn't I see anything about this in the newspapers?"

"We had to pay handsomely to keep it out the papers. I told them I didn't know the person who did it, and they just assumed it was a robbery. But anyway, it was my idea to print a story saying I was abroad."

"So, Rocky, tell me about your life after entertaining?"

"Well, there's not much to tell. I'm married to a terrific lady. As a matter of fact, you and Nicole, my wife, could go for sisters."

"You're kidding!"

"No, I'm not. She's also a doctor, and we love living here in Hawaii."

"I would love to meet her."

"Great! What about dinner tomorrow night?"

"Are you sure?"

"Yes, I'm sure. Nicole loves company."

"Well, okay, if you're sure it's all right."

Growing serious, Rocky asked softly, "Have you seen our child since the adoption?"

"She's dead, Rocky."

"What?!"

"She got pregnant and had a botched-up abortion. There were complications, and she died."

"It's all my fault. If I hadn't..."

"It's too late to start laying blame, Rocky. I'm just lucky I have another child."

"Yes, I know. I believe her name is Keisha."

With widen eyes, Cecily said, "Wow! How did you know?"

"My wife gets the papers from the mainland, and you're very famous."

"I'm impressed."

"You've earned it," he said standing. "Well, I've better get on my way."

As Cecily walked him to the door, she asked, "Is your wife a native Hawaiian?"

"No. As a matter of fact, she's from the east. She was born with one kidney, and I guess her parents didn't want to deal with it, so they put her up for adoption."

"That's terrible."

"Yes, but she turned out just fine anyway," he stated proudly, opening the door. "I just can't get over how much you and Nicole look alike."

"They say everyone has a double."

"Yes, but I would've never believed it if I hadn't seen it for myself," he added smiling. "I'll come by tomorrow around six for you." She nodded, and he planted a soft kiss on her forehead. "It's so good to see you again, Cecily." She watched as he walked away, and she thought how things change. She was once madly in love with this man, and now, he was just another man. He looked so great now. Muscular and strong like he did when she was a teenager. She took a deep breath. But one thing never changed about her, she still seems to always choose forbidden men. Men that couldn't be hers unconditionally. She closed the door and took another deep breath.

"Rocky is alive. Thank you, God," she said, then walked to the couch and dropped down. Spencer had lied to her again. Then her mind fell on her little girl. "Keisha, you would love Hawaii. I think I'll surprise you with a trip." she smiled big, thinking of how happy Keisha would be. She picked Keisha's picture off the table and hugged it tightly. "I miss you, Sweetheart. But I'm going to change that." Cecily picked up the receiver and dialed.

"Carter's residence."

"Hi, Gracie. This is Cecily Wade."

"Hi, Dr. Wade."

"Gracie, is Keisha there?"

"No Ma'am. She went with Mrs. Carter to take Wanda to dance class."

"Oh, okay. Listen, Gracie, would you tell Alton to call me when he gets in. I'm going to make arrangements for Keisha to come here with me."

"In Hawaii?!"

"Yes. I miss her so much."

"Oh, she'll like that, Dr. Wade."

"I think she will, too. So, as soon as Alton gets in, ask him to call me, all right, Gracie?"

"Yes, Ma'am."

"Thanks, Gracie. Talk to you later." As Cecily hung up the telephone, she focused on her trembling hands. She reached in the drawer of the table and pulled out a bottle of pills.

"What in the hell is wrong with me?! I *know* I can quit this shit! My body just doesn't want to cooperate," she said to herself, trying to resist. Her hands trembled more and more. "Once more wouldn't hurt." She dropped two pills in her mouth and swallowed hard, then she dropped her head back and hugged Keisha's picture tighter. "I can't wait to see you, Baby."

****

Alton nervously burst into the hospital and rushed to the desk. "I'm Alton Carter. My wife and daughters were brought here. They were in a car accident. How are they?!"

"Mr. Carter, they're in surgery. The doctor will talk to you as soon as possible. Please try to stay calm," the receptionist said.

"May I go in there?"

"That's not a good idea," she said coming from around the desk. She led him to a chair and guided him to sit. "Can I get you a cup of coffee?" She thought, *Damn, he's fine. Why are the fine ones always married or gay?*

"No, thank you," he said, and then looked in the petite woman's face, then at her nametag. "You're very kind, Janice." She smiled sweetly as Isaac and Cindy rushed in.

"Alton," Isaac said. "I just heard it on the news. How are they?"

"I don't know anything yet," Alton said standing. "Oh, God, what if..."

"Don't even think it, Alton!" insisted Cindy as she pulled him in her arms.

"I'll see what I can find out," Janice said walking away, and Isaac nodded.

"Isaac, how in the hell am I going to tell Cecily this," Alton said looking in Isaac's face. "If anything happens to Keisha, it will kill Cecily. It would just *kill* her!"

****

"*Trudy*?!" exploded Ramon, in his deep, Spanish accent, looking at her huge body with extreme surprise.

"What'd you want, Ramon?" she snapped as he entered.

"What in the hell happened to you?"

"What'd you mean?"

"You know damn well what I mean! Where is that gorgeous body?! You look like the Goodyear blimp!"

"Did you come all the way here to insult me, or did you have something more constructive in mind?"

"How in God's name did you let yourself get like this, Trudy? You were so beautiful."

"Well, I never felt fucking beautiful, Ramon! And if you don't like what you see, you can get the hell out!"

"Don't worry, Baby, I'm going," he said walking to the door. "And to think I left my wife for *you*!"

"Who in the hell asked you to?!"

"I spent years in therapy so I could get myself together for you, and you turn into the Pillsbury dough girl! I'm very disappointed in you, Trudy! I thought you had more pride in yourself then to let your body get this way!"

He opened the door, and then looked back at her with a frown and added, "You look disgusting."

"Get the hell out of my house, you fucking conceded, cocksucking bastard! Who in the hell do you think you are?! And, who in the hell told you I'd want a no-good, two-timing son-of-a-bitch like you anyway?! You disgusting piece of shit!" He shook his head then walked out, and Trudy ran to the door and slammed it behind him. Trudy focused on a mirror on the wall, and a tear fell down her face. She grabbed off her shoe and threw it at the mirror as she fell to the floor crying hysterically. She had to admit to herself, as rude as Ramon was, the bastard was right. She did look pathetic. She crumpled down in a heap on the floor, unable to stop the wail of tears from flowing.

Chapter 14

The sound of the doorbell awakened Cecily, and she struggled to position her feet on the floor, but they weren't cooperating. Finally, she focused on a bottle of pills on her nightstand. She reached for them as the doorbell sounded again. She dropped two pills in her mouth and swallowed. Then she dropped back on the bed to feel the effect of the pills. When she heard the doorbell a third time, she sprung up, threw on a housecoat and dashed for the door.

When Cecily opened the door, she became face to face with a smiling Craig. "I hope I'm not too early?" he asked cautiously.

"Early?"

"You forgot."

"About what?"

"About our plans to spend the day together."

"Oh. That." she said yawning. "Come in." As she stepped aside to let him in, he noticed that she stumbled.

"Are you all right?"

Closing the door, she said, "Sure. I'm just sleepy."

"I could come back later."

"Don't be silly. How about some breakfast?"

"That'd be great. I haven't had a home cooked meal in a long time."

"Make yourself at home while I shower and change," she said passing him. He couldn't help but to notice this gorgeous woman swaying pass him.

He shook his head quickly to avoid his thoughts of ravaging this beautiful creature. He proceeded to the stereo and turned on some soft music. Craig sat on the couch and began rotating his head to the beat of the music. Suddenly he heard a loud crash and a scream from Cecily's bedroom. He jumped up and rushed into the bedroom and found Cecily sitting on the floor with her leg curled under her, stark naked.

"What happened?" he asked picking her up.

"I tripped."

"Are you all right?" he asked sitting her on the bed.

Nodding, she said, "Yes. Just a little bruised ego." She chuckled and added, "I feel so stupid."

"Don't. It could happen to anyone," he said as their eyes locked, and she noticed that he was admiring her body. "You're so beautiful." Their lips met softly. Then their passion became more intense and seductive, and they grabbed for each other hungrily. He began pulling off his clothes, but Cecily stopped abruptly.

"I'm sorry," she said. "I'm just coming out of a bad situation. I'm not ready for another one right now."

Nodding, he said, "I understand." He stood, pulled his shirt back on, and started for the door. He turned around and added, "Hurry up. We have a big day ahead of us." She nodded with a smile for she knew he truly understood, as he smiled also, leaving her bedroom.

****

"Mr. Carter, your wife and older child are stable, but the little one isn't doing very well," the doctor said to Alton as Isaac and Cindy stood by his side. "We're doing all we can."

"Spare no expense, Doctor. Call in specialists from anywhere in the world. Whomever you need. I want her to have the very best."

"I understand," the doctor said. "Have you contacted Cecily yet?"

"No. Not yet."

"I think she needs to be here," replied the doctor, and Alton nodded. "I'll keep you informed."

Suddenly a voice boomed over the loudspeaker, "Dr. Brubaker, you're needed in emergency. Stat! Code red!"

"Excuse me," the doctor said turning and rushing away.

"What is it, Doctor?" Alton called.

"I'll let you know," the doctor called back, exiting behind the doors.

"Oh my God!" Alton said dropping in a chair. "I've got to call Cecily."

****

Rocky opened the door of his house and escorted Cecily and Craig in. "Darling, we're here!" he called, closing the door.

"I'll be right there, Honey," a lady's voice called back.

"Make yourselves at home, please," Rocky said guiding them into the den. "Name your poison."

"Scotch and soda," Craig said.

"Cecily?"

"I'll just take a glass of soda."

"Wow! I love a woman who lives dangerously!" Rocky joked, and they all burst into laughter. But the laughter soon seized when Rocky's wife entered the room, and Cecily locked her attention on the woman and thought she was dreaming. It was as if she was looking in a mirror.

"Incredible!" Craig gasped.

"I told you she looks like you." Rocky added to Cecily.

"You weren't kidding," Cecily replied.

 Smiling, Nicole said, "There's an explanation for it. No, I'm not a clone of you, Cecily."

"Then *what*?"

"We're *sisters*."

"What?!" Cecily's breath ran out.

And Nicole added, "Twins."

****

Trudy tearfully ran in Alton's arms in tears and hugged him tight. "I just heard," she squeezed out. "How are you?"

"Holding up," he sighed deeply.

"What did the doctor say?"

"Lillian and Wanda will be fine. It's Keisha they're worried about, "

Alton tried to explain, then stopped suddenly when he saw the doctor again. He ran to the doctor asking,   "What is it, Doctor. How is my little girl?!"

****

"Twins?!" Cecily gasped.

"Yes."

"But I was told..."

"That you were an only child," Nicole finished. "Well, in essence, you were, because I was given up for adoption."

"What?!"

"Cecily, you do know that our mother got pregnant from a black man?"

"Yes, but..."

"So, her parents tried desperately to raise you as a *white* girl, but you knew the truth because your skin was too dark. Right?"

"Yes. So, they had to tell me the truth."

"If you fellows don't mind, I would like to talk to Cecily alone."

"Sure," Rocky said then zoomed in on Craig. "There's a great little place down the street where we can shoot some pool."

"I'm right behind you, Man."

When the men left, Nicole handed Cecily a glass of tea then sat on the couch beside her. "Cecily, what I'm about to tell you might shock you, but these are facts. I've done my research," Nicole began, and Cecily nodded slowly. "Our mother was born with a silver spoon in her mouth. I know you know this, because so were you. Her parents tried to keep her away from *certain* people, mainly, people of color. But, the more they tried, the more determined she was to live her own life, but she chose wrong. She took up with a low-life black man who got her hooked-on drugs, and she had no one to turn to, because her parents had turned their backs on her. So, she started trading sex for money, to buy drugs."

"Our mother was a *prostitute*?"

"Yes, you can say that," Nicole said, then paused. "The man skipped out on her, then she learned she was pregnant. She swallowed her pride and went to her parents, who admitted her to a hospital for drug treatment and for prenatal care. When we were born, they found that her drug use affected only one child...*me*. I was born with one kidney. Her parents didn't want to deal with that, so they put me up for adoption and legally adopted *you*. Our mother was devastated so she took one final dose of drugs to end her life."

"She committed suicide?"

"Yes."

Standing, Cecily said, "This is all so incredible."

"Mind boggling, right?"

"Yes. It sounds like something on the soap operas."

"Yes, but it isn't. Our mother died a very unhappy lady."

"And she was so young."

"Very."

Focusing back on her sister, Cecily said, "My God, what your life must've been like."

"It was rough going from one foster home to the next, but when I was ten, I got lucky and was adopted by some great people. They're both gone now, but they saw me graduate from college and medical school. My father was a doctor himself."

"You must've loved them very much."

"I did."

"I had a similar situation myself. I'll tell you all about it someday."

"I can't wait to hear," Nicole said as the telephone rang. She picked it up quickly. "Hello?" Pause. "Yes, she's right here." Looking at Cecily. "It's for you."

"I left your number with my answering service. I hope you don't mind."

"Of course not," Nicole answered smiling. "It's someone name Alton Carter."

****

"Where am I?"

"You're in the hospital, Mrs. Carter," a nurse said to Lillian as she rang for the doctor. "Mrs. Carter is awake now."

"Hospital?"

"You've been in an accident."

"Accident?" Lillian said as the doctor entered.

"Hi, Mrs. Carter. How do you feel?" he asked.

"Like I've been hit by a Mack truck. What's going on?" she asked squinting her eyes and licking her dry lips.

"How much do you remember?"

"Nothing! I don't remember *anything*," she insisted. "Could you get me something to drink, please?"

"Sure," the nurse said.

"We're going to take good care of you, Mrs. Carter. Don't worry." the doctor said, and then walked out.

The nurse handed Lillian a glass of water, and she took a sip. "Don't you have something stronger?" Lillian asked.

"Like what?"

"Vodka."

Chuckling, the nurse said, "Not around here, I'm afraid."

"Please, get me some," Lillian begged sitting up. "I'll pay you whatever you want."

"You don't need that right now, Mrs. Carter. You just concentrate on getting well."

"Don't tell me what I need!" yelled Lillian throwing the glass of water to the door, shattering it in several pieces.

****

"What's taking so damn long?!" Cecily exploded to the lady behind the desk at the airport.

"Bad weather," answered the lady politely.

"Don't you understand that my little girl needs me, damn it?!" Cecily yelled, and Craig pulled her in his arms.

"Take it easy, Cecily. There's nothing she can do."

"She needs me, Craig. My baby needs me," Cecily wept in his arms. "Oh, God, she needs me."

****

"Did you get in touch with Cecily?"

"Yes. Her plane will be in this morning. Why? What's wrong?" Alton asked the doctor.

"I'm afraid she's not doing very well. We're trying everything, but she simply isn't responding," explained the doctor.

"Oh, my God," Alton said, and Trudy placed her arms around his waist.

"Alton, there's nothing you can do here," the doctor continued. "You've been here for two days. Why don't you go home and get some rest? I'll call you if there's any change."

"I just can't leave right now. Not until Cecily arrives," Alton insisted. "Doctor, may I see Wanda?"

"Of course. You may also see your wife, but I must warn you, Lillian doesn't remember anything."

****

"How much longer will it be before we land, Craig?"

"Take it easy, Cecily. We're almost there."

"Thank you for coming with me. I don't know if I could've made it alone," she said with tears in her eyes.

"I'm just glad I was available," he said pulling her in his arms, as the *fasten your seat belt* sign appeared.

"Please secure your trays in an upright position as we prepare to land," the flight attendant began.

****

Alton sat by Wanda's bed holding her hand as she slept. "Oh, my God, what have I done to you, my precious little girl? I knew your mother had a drinking problem, and I did nothing to stop her. This is just as much *my* fault as it is *hers*." He paused, blinking hard to fight back the tears. "I'm so sorry, my beautiful little angel." He stood, planted a soft kiss on her bruised forehead, then sat again. "I promise you, Baby, that I will always be here for you, for as long as you need me. I promise you that."

"Alton," the doctor said poking his head in the door. "I need to see you. It's Keisha."

****

"Where are you going, young lady?"

"To Jenny's house."

"Not today, you're not."

"Why not, Ma?"

"Angela, I don't feel like an argument today," Cindy stressed to her daughter. "I have to get back to the hospital with Isaac."

"Why?" the girl sarcastically asked in her tight mini-skirt, big, imitation gold earrings, tight sweater, high heeled shoes, and orange streaks mixed in with her blonde hair, sticking up on her head like a peacock.

"What'd you mean, why? Cecily is my boss, and her little girl is very sick."

"I don't understand it, Ma. Isaac was married to your boss. You get pregnant from him, and now you all in the woman's face like family."

"I don't like your tone, young lady, and I like your insinuations even *less*."

"We don't fit in with them, Ma. Don't you get it? Isaac isn't happy here."

"You don't know what you're talking about, Angela! So just stay out of it! And he's *Daddy* to you, not *Isaac*!"

"Yeah, right," she sarcastically replied again. "It's just a matter of time before he takes off, Ma, and you all in his face at the hospital. The man don't want us!" Cindy's hand flew back and landed on her daughter's face.

"I'm going back to the hospital, and you stay your little smart-ass home!"

****

Alton, Isaac, and Trudy stood in the waiting room, in hysterical sobs as Cecily exploded in the hospital, followed by Craig. She ran to them, asking, "How is she?" Alton turned to her, wiping his tears and locked eyes with her.

"Cecily..." his choked voice squeezed out.

"What is it?! How is my baby?!" Cecily yelled growing hysterical at his demeanor.

"She didn't make it," he squeezed out again.

"No," Cecily said softly, shaking her head. "Noooooo!" She screamed this time, jerking away and running down the hall to the emergency room. "Where's my baby?!" She demanded to the nurses. "Where in the hell is my baby?!" Alton finally caught up with her and grabbed her arm.

"Cecily..." he started, but she broke away. He fought to catch her again as she searched frantically for her child. The doctors tried to help Alton control the hysterical woman, but they couldn't. Finally, the doctor had to give her a shot to sedate her, and she collapsed in Alton's arms.

Chapter 15

Cecily, in a black dress, sat in Keisha's room, rocking, with Keisha's pillow in her lap, staring into space. Although the door was closed, she could hear people in the rest of the house, but she tuned them out. An image of her little girl's coffin being lowered into the ground, while others stood by, appeared in her memory because it had only happened minutes before. She didn't want to see anyone. She knew a large part of herself was buried with her daughter, and she really didn't care if she lived through the night or not. Tears still burned her red, puffed up eyes as they trickled down her sad face slowly. She could see Keisha's beautiful, laughing face, so full of life. Then her thoughts took her further in the past, and Cotton was beating her with a pillow as they laughed together. Then Barry. Sweet, sweet Barry. She could see his beautiful eyes as he kissed her lips softly. Then Maria, the child that never knew her. Everybody she had ever cared for left her one way or the other. Why was God punishing her? Would he continue to cause her pain, for the rest of her life? She wasn't such a bad person. But God continues to punish her over and over and over again. "Are you going to continue to punish me, God," she spoke softly. "If so, take me now. I just can't bear any more pain. I just can't. Please, take me *now*." Cecily cried hysterically as she rose a little and fell in a heap on the floor just as Alton rushed into the room, picked her up, and cradled her in his arms. As she held up and looked in his face, she noticed that he also had tears in his eyes, but she squeezed out anyway, "I want to die."

"No, Cecily. No," he replied, pulling her back in his arms.

"My whole world has tumbled down, and I don't know how to put it back together again."

"Take it one day at a time, Baby. One day at a time."

"I have nobody."

"You have *me*."

"No, I don't. Lillian and Wanda have you. I have *nobody*," she said, and then broke away from him. "Why, Alton? I just don't understand. I would've gladly gone in my baby's place, because I don't want to live without her anyway. Why?" She wept uncontrollably, and Alton could see the pain she suffered, and he felt so helpless, because he knew there was nothing he could do to ease her broken heart.

"I don't know, Sweetheart. I don't know. I wish I did," he finally said. "But, please, remember, you will always have me. And you have all of your friends."

"My *friend* killed my baby."

"It was an accident, Cecily."

"My baby is *still dead*," she insisted. "I have suffered the consequences for loving you. I have paid dearly. I have nothing else to give. Oh, God! I have *nothing* else to give!" She cried hysterically as Nicole entered the room slowly. She rushed to Cecily and pulled her in her arms.

"I don't know what to say, Cecily," Nicole squeezed out in between tears. "I'm just glad I could be here with you right now. I will be here as long as you need me, and maybe time and God will ease your pain."

"*God*!" she exploded. "God *hates* me."

"No, Cecily. That couldn't be further from the truth. The one thing you can always count on is God's love and mercy," Nicole explained. "God has a plan for everything that happens. It's not always for us to understand, but it will become clear to you, in time. *God's* time. Not *our* time." She paused and looked Cecily in her face. "God loves you, Cecily, and he loves your little girl. He was just ready for her to come home, *now*. God loves you." Trudy walked in, and Cecily stared at her, then she went to Cecily, pulled her sobbing friend in her arms, and hugged her lovingly.

****

"Let me out of here!" Lillian yelled, banging on the door of the empty room that she occupied. Suddenly the door flew open and a nurse in blue printed scrubs entered.

"Mrs. Carter, please control yourself. You'll disturb the other patients."

"I don't give a damn about the other patients!" Lillian raged on. "I want to get out of here! You can't keep me here against my will!"

"If you don't calm down, I'll have to restrain you again."

"I want to see my husband. He has no right to keep me here, that two-timing, son-of-a-bitch!"

"Your husband has *nothing* to do with this. The *judge* sent you here."

"I'm not an alcoholic!"

"You killed a little girl, and almost killed your own daughter and yourself."

"That was an accident," she said softly with tears in her eyes.

"I know it was, and so does the judge. That's why you're in *here*, to get the help you need and not in some *prison*," the lady said, and then Lillian dropped on the bed, curled up in the fetal position and cried hysterically.

Chapter 16

Cecily walked into her house slowly and dropped her medical bag on the floor. As she closed the door, she couldn't help thinking how quiet it was, and *that* was driving her crazy. Keisha was always so full of life when Cecily came home. She dropped in a chair and stared into space. She was alone for the first time, since Keisha's death, and it was more than she could handle. She had to *make* Nicole, Rocky and Craig go home. Although she hated to see them leave, she knew she had to stand on her own two feet sooner or later. She just had to have something to help her to cope with the emptiness. She picked up her medical bag slowly and opened it. She took out a small bottle of liquid and a syringe. Next, she removed a little rubber hose from the bag, and tied it around her arm. Then she filled the syringe with the liquid and injected it into her veins. Then she removed the rubber hose, folded her arm, dropped the syringe on the floor, and let her head fall back. She knew this wasn't good for her. She should know better. After all, she *is* a doctor. But the pills weren't doing it for her anymore. She needed something stronger. Besides, she wasn't an addict or anything like that. She could quit anytime she wanted to. She just needed something to help her through these hard times, and then she would give up the stuff *cold turkey*. She *would*!

****

"Angela!" Cindy called walking in the house.

"In here, Mom."

Walking into the den where Angela sat watching the television and eating popcorn, Cindy asked, "Where's Isaac, Sweetie?"

"I don't know."

"Isn't he home from work yet?"

"No," Angela nonchalantly replied, still focusing on the television set. "What's for dinner?"

"I don't know!" Cindy snapped growing a little aggravated at the child's attitude. "You're getting old enough to start dinner when I'm working late, Missy!"

"What did *I* do?!"

"Did Isaac call?"

"No, Ma!" Angela snarled growing a little annoyed by her mother's persistent interest in Isaac. "Why don't you call his *wife*?" Cindy's eyes locked with her daughter's, and Angela realized she shouldn't have said that, so she quickly looked away.

"You're getting too grown for your own good, Girlfriend," Cindy said, then walked out quickly. She went into the kitchen and started noisily taking out pots for dinner. Then she stopped suddenly and stared into space. "Where are you, Isaac?"

****

Cecily opened the door, and Alton was standing there. "Come in," she said softly.

"How are you?" he asked closing the door.

"Fine. Thanks," she replied as he followed her into the kitchen. "Trying to fix myself some dinner. Would you like to join me?"

"All right," he said, starting to help her.

"How is Wanda?"

"Fine. She misses her mother."

"I bet she does."

He turned her around by the shoulders to face him and asked softly, "How are you *really*?"

"How am I *supposed* to be, Alton? I don't know. Why don't *you* tell *me*," she sarcastically replied.

"Where is this coming from?"

"I'm just sick and tired of trying to be brave."

"You don't have to be brave with me, Cecily," he said, then pulled her in his arms gently, and planted a soft, feather kiss on her lips. "I love you, Cecily."

"What?"

"I love you."

"As long as I've loved you, and as much as we've been together, this is the first time you've ever said those words to me."

"Well, I'm saying them now. I don't know what I'd do without you. I need you."

"Oh, Alton, I've waited so long to hear you say this to me," she said as they ended in a long, passionate kiss. "I love you so much." They kissed savagely now, and he swept her up in his arms and carried her upstairs to the bedroom. Their lovemaking knew no boundaries, until they brought each other to the point of uncompromising joy. He then pulled her in his arms, and they drifted off to sleep together.

****

Wanda tossed and turned in her sleep. She could see their car plowing into that tree, and she woke up screaming. Gracie ran in her room, turned on the light and cuddled Wanda in her arms. "It's all right, Darling."

"I had a bad dream," Wanda squeezed out.

"It's okay now."

Holding off the lady, Wanda asked, "Where's my Daddy?"

"He said he was going to check on Dr. Wade."

Looking at eleven-fifteen pm on her clock, Wanda said, "I'm going to call him."

"All right, Sweetie. I'll get you some warm milk," Gracie said walking out.

****

"Hello?"

"Aunt Cecily?"

"Yes," Cecily said releasing herself from Alton's arms and sitting up in bed, as she turned on the bedside lamp.

"This is Wanda. Is my daddy there?" Wanda asked. "He's not answering his cell phone."

"Yes, Wanda, he's here. Hold on, Sweetie," Cecily said handing the phone to Alton.

"Wanda, are you all right?" Alton asked.

"Daddy, when are you coming home? I can't sleep. I'm having bad dreams."

"I'll be right there, Sweetheart," Alton said as the doorbell rang.

"Who can that be?" Cecily pondered, as Alton hung up the phone.

"We slept through dinner," Alton smiled, and they kissed.

"Is Wanda all right?" she asked pulling on a housecoat.

"Bad dreams. You want me to get the door, Baby?"

"No. I'll get it. You go ahead and take your shower," she said, and they kissed again, then she left.

When Cecily opened the door, her mouth flew open as she acknowledged, "Isaac!"

****

Cindy sat up in bed, watching television. Every time she heard a car, she would jump up and look out the window. This wasn't like Isaac to stay out without calling. Was he unhappy like Angela said? She loved him so much she didn't want to think such a thing. She knew she could make him happy if he would just give her the chance. *Where can he be? Where?*

****

Lillian was lying on the small bed, trembling so hard, the whole bed was shaking, for she needed a drink so bad. Perspiration popped out her entire body so drastically, her nightgown was completely soaked, but she laid there, staring blankly into space, in the dark room, as she drifted into the past:

*   *"Baby, what'd you mean, we can't get married tomorrow?" Alton asked Lillian in his office.*

Waving a letter in her hand she said, "Alton, one of my best friends won't be there! I got this letter from somebody named Spencer saying she's in a mental hospital. I've got to go and see her!" Tears were rolling down her face.

"Calm down, Sweetheart," he said, pulling her in his arms.

Breaking away from him she insisted, "Alton, please, postpone our wedding. Cecily <u>needs</u> me!"

Taking a deep breath, he said, "Lillian, think, Baby. Everything is all set. I have friends and family that have come from all over the world to be at our wedding, Baby. The wedding is only <u>one</u> day. Then you can go and *see your friend. I'll postpone the honeymoon, but please, <u>not</u> the wedding, Baby?"*

"Would you do that for me?"

"I'll do <u>anything</u> for you, Baby, but I want you to be my wife <u>tomorrow</u>, like we planned."

"Okay," she finally agreed, and then he grabbed her and hugged her tight. "And, I can leave as soon as the wedding is over?"

"Not <u>right</u> after, I hope," he smiled seductively. "I would like to spend our wedding night together tomorrow night. Then first thing Sunday morning, you can be on that plane. I promise. All right, Baby?"

"All right."

*Grabbing her in a big cuddly hug, he said, "That's my girl." He kissed her lips softly. "I've waited a long time for you, Lillian Martin. I never thought I could wait this long for <u>any</u> woman. That's why I <u>know</u> I love you." They both laughed.   ***

A nurse burst in Lillian's room, bringing her back to the present. "Bob!" she yelled hysterically, looking at Lillian.

"What is it, Peggy?" a man said at the door.

"Get Dr. Asala on the phone. Stat!" she said grabbing an unresponsive Lillian up.

"What is it?"

"She's going into shock! She could *die*!"

****

"Hi, Cecily. Can we talk?" Isaac said entering, and she closed the door.

"This isn't a good time, Isaac," she replied, not wanting Isaac to see Alton there.

"I've been worried about you, Cecily," he said again. "I've been riding around all night, trying to muster up enough courage to come here."

"I'm fine, Isaac. What's wrong?"

He walked to her slowly and took her face in his hands, and then he planted a soft kiss on her lips. "I love you, Cecily. I will always love you," he said softly.

"Isaac, I..."

"You don't have to say anything. I know you don't love me, but I do know you care for me." He took a deep breath. "We had a good marriage. We respect each other. I want that again.   We can have that again, Cecily. My life has been so empty without you." He kissed her lips again. "What'd you say, Baby? Can we start over?" Before she could answer, she saw his attention shift towards the staircase, and she knew Alton was on his way down, so Cecily closed her eyes to avoid Isaac's hurt ones. "I'm sorry. I didn't know you had company."

"Isaac, hello," Alton said, and Isaac nodded his greetings to Alton as he stepped away from Cecily.

"Take care," Isaac said weakly to Cecily then rushed out quickly.

"What's up?" Alton asked her.

Taking a deep breath, Cecily said, "I feel so sorry for him. I should've never allowed him to fall in love with me, knowing I couldn't return his love." A tear fell down her face. "I feel so responsible."

"You're not responsible for Isaac's happiness, Baby. He's a grown man."

"But, he's hurting, and it's because of *me*," she said, and he pulled her in his arms. "It just isn't fair."

"Who said life was fair?" Alton said, as he focused on a syringe on the floor then released her. He picked it up and asked, "What the hell is *this*?"

****

Isaac sat in a bar gulping down drinks as if they were pure water, instead of martinis, as he drifted into the past:

*   *"Excuse me, Ma'am, I'm here to see Dr. Allen. Is he here?" Isaac asked in blue jeans, T-shirt, sneakers, and a baseball cap, holding a pad in his hand.*

Swirling around to face him in a five by seven office, wearing blue jeans, T-shirt, sneakers, and a ponytail, Cecily said, "You've found <u>him</u>."

"You...?" his breath ran out as he focused on the most beautiful woman he had ever seen in his life.

Smiling, she joked, "Are you disappointed?"

"No, Ma'am!" he smiled also. "But, I ain't never seen no doctor that looked like <u>you</u>. If I had, I think I would get sick more often."

"Thank-you, Mr. ... agh."

"Wade. Isaac Wade," he said removing his cap and extending his hand.

Shaking his hand, Cecily said, "Now, I'm impressed. The boss himself is coming to sketch out a job."

"I sketch out all my jobs."

"That's great," she said. "Now let me tell you what we want."

"All right."

"We want a huge office building with the capability of accommodating about ten doctors, with separate facilities for each Doctor's patients and staff. Do you think you can handle that?"

"Yes, Ma'am. How soon do you need the blueprints?"

"Yesterday," she smiled.

Chuckling, he said, "How about next week?"

"Perfect," she smiled. "Is there anything else you need to know?"

"Yeah. Will you have dinner with me tonight?"

****

Isaac rolled off Cecily, fighting to catch his breath, and she snuggled up close to him, with her head in his chest. Their lovemaking was so gentle, but yet so satisfying. He had never known a woman that could captivate him in and out of bed as much as Cecily did. He ran his fingers through her soft hair gently and said very softly, "I love you, Cecily." She jerked up and stared at him.

"What?"

"I love you. I've never felt about anybody this way."

"I love you, too, Isaac."

"You do?"

"Yes, I do," she smiled, and then they kissed softly.

Looking deeply into her eyes, he asked softly, "Will you marry me?"

"What...?"

"I know we haven't known each other long, but I love you. Will you be my wife?"

"Isaac, there's a lot that you don't know about me. My past. I need..."

Placing his finger on her lips, he said, "Cecily, the past is the past. Everybody has one. All I need to know is if you'll marry me."

"Yes!" she exploded jumping on him. "Yes! Yes! Yes!"

"I love you."

"I love you," she said as they kissed hard.   *

A man came and sat beside Isaac, bringing him back to the present. "Aren't you having one too many?" he smiled.

"What's it to you?" snapped Isaac.

"I'm just concerned."

"Why in the hell should you be concerned about me?! You don't even know me!" Isaac snapped again, stumbling to get his footing but fell back on the barstool.

"Take it easy," the man said helping Isaac down. "I hope you aren't driving home."

"Home. Huh! I don't have a home."

"Everybody has a home," the man replied, and Isaac looked in his face for the first time.   The man was tall, with jet-black curly hair, which accented his pecan-tanned skin and hazel eyes. "By the way, I'm Maurice."

"You're a tall drink of water," Isaac snapped, trying to stand up again. He started out the door, staggering with every step. Isaac took out his keys and when he reached his car, he noticed that the man was still trailing him.

"You're in no shape to drive, Man."

"Get the hell out of my way," Isaac ordered, taking a wild swing at Maurice, but missing dramatically. As he hit the ground, he passed out cold.

"Umm, you're a fine hunk," Maurice said looking down at Isaac. "I'm getting tired of that fat ass Trudy Miles. Let me help you to my hotel room. We can have a good time together." He licked his lips. "A *real* good time!"

****

Lillian opened her eyes and a tall Caribbean man stood there in a doctor's smock and scrubs, looking at her chart. She looked around and noticed that she was in a hospital and not the rehabilitation center. The doctor looked at her and noticed she was awake. "How do you feel, Lillian?" he asked her in his deep Caribbean accent, as he walked close to her. "Lillian?" He sat in a chair next to her bed. "How do you feel?"

"Leave me alone," she nonchalantly replied.

"I'm afraid I can't do that, Lillian," he smiled. "I'm not going to let you die, so you can give up on *that* idea. I will *not* let you die!"

Tears ran down her face as she squeezed out, "God made a mistake. He should have taken me instead of that little girl, and then Cecily would have my whole family like she wants so badly and will *get* eventually. I should've died instead of that sweet little girl. I should've died. Why didn't you let me die? Why didn't you let me die?!" She cried hysterically, and he pulled her in his arms and held her tight.

"God doesn't make mistakes, Lillian. You don't *deserve* to die. It was an *accident*. You are a *very* sick woman."

****

"Where did you get that?"

"Right here on the floor," Alton replied. "What's it doing here, Cecily?"

Taking it out his hand, Cecily chuckled, "I'm a doctor, silly. Of course, I have syringes," She dropped it in the wastebasket. Alton grabbed her arm and pushed up her sleeve. His breath momentarily left his body when he witnessed the needle tracks on Cecily's arm.

"Oh, no," he finally squeezed out dropping her arms.

"Alton, it's not what you think."

"Then why don't you tell me what it is, Cecily!" he said growing upset. "Tell me what the hell is going on with you and tell me *now*!"

****

Isaac awakened to a warm sensation on his groins. He held up a little and saw a mass of black curls, so he thought it was Cecily. Soon he exploded to an ultimate high, satisfying his inner feelings, and for the first time, Isaac opened his eyes and focused on the person that had just made his world rock, and to his surprised it wasn't Cecily at all. It was the tall man at the bar. Isaac couldn't believe his eyes. He blinked several times to wake up, because surely, he was dreaming. "Was it good, Baby," Maurice was saying as he rose on the bed, coming towards Isaac, totally nude. Then, Isaac focused on his own nude body, and he knew he was *not* dreaming, as the man moved closer to him as if he was going to kiss Isaac. Suddenly Isaac jumped up, knocking Maurice aside, and he was on his feet now.

"What in the hell are you doing?!" Isaac fumed.

"It'll be good. I promise you," Maurice said coming to Isaac.

"You better back off, faggot!" Isaac raged, grabbing his clothes. "I ought to break every fucking bone in your faggot body."

"I can make you forget the bitch. I can make you forget *all* the bitches!"

"And, I can break your goddamn neck!" Isaac raged on, pulling on his clothes. "What in the hell did you do to me?!"

"I didn't do anything to you that you didn't want," Maurice insisted, and Isaac focused on this man standing there, bragging about what he had done to him, and his rage got the better of him, and he charged into Maurice like a wild beast.

****

"Alton, I just couldn't cope anymore. I have loved you for so very long. It was very frustrating for me to be so near to you, but yet so far away."

"That's no excuse, Cecily. Drugs will kill you. You know that better than anyone."

"I just couldn't cope with losing everybody that I loved."

"How long have you been putting that junk in your veins?"

"Just since Keisha's death!" she said with tears rolling down her face. "She meant everything to me. She was the one thing that I had that belonged to *you* also, that nobody could take away, but *Lillian* did, didn't she? Keisha was the one thing that kept me sane, and when she was gone, I had *nothing*." He stared in her eyes momentarily, and then he pulled her in his arms.

"Oh, my God. What have I done to you?"

"I love you so much."

"And, I love you," he said then planted a kiss on her lips. "We have to get you some help."

"I don't need that. I can quit on my own."

"No, you can't, Cecily."

"Knowing that you love me, Alton, I can do *anything*. As long as I know you're with me."

"I'm with you, Baby. As soon as Lillian is well, I'm asking her for a divorce. Then we can be together. Okay?" he said, and she nodded slowly.

"I really hate to leave you, Baby, but I need to check on Wanda." She nodded again. "No more drugs, Cecily!"

****

"Isaac?"

"Yes, it's me."

"I've been worried sick," Cindy said getting out of bed and meeting him at the door as he entered the bedroom. "Where have you been?"

"Driving most of the night, then the rest of the night getting drunk."

"Is something wrong, Sweetheart?"

"Just business. It'll be all right," he said, as she noticed the bruises on his face.

"You've been in a fight?"

"There was a problem at the bar. I'm all right."

"My God, Isaac! You could've been hurt!"

"I'm fine. Please quit smothering me like a mother hen!" he snapped, but felt sorry immediately, because her expression showed him that he had hurt her feelings. She headed for the bed, but he grabbed her arm gently. "I'm sorry. It's just that it's been a rough day. Please forgive me." He pulled her in his arms and hugged her tightly. He glued his eyelids shut, trying to forget about the ordeal he had been through with Maurice. He swore that if he ever, in life, laid eyes on that faggot again, he would finish what he started and *kill* the bastard.

Chapter 17

"Cecily, Trudy."

"Hi, Trudy."

"Listen, Girl, I'm having a small dinner party tonight with just my close friends. Can you come?"

"What's the occasion?"

"I have a new friend. He's moving in with me, and I want Y'all to meet him."

"You go girl," Cecily smiled.

"Can you come?"

"Sure. I'll be there. What time?"

"Around six."

"Great! Who else is coming?"

"Alton and Wanda, and Isaac, Cindy, and Angela. That's all. Very small."

"See you then."

"Great," Trudy said hanging up and looking up at Maurice, who had just walked in the room.

"Hi, Baby," he said, planting a kiss on her lips.

"Hi, Sweetheart," she said smiling, and then noticed the bruises on his face. "What happened to you?"

****

"Good morning, Sweetheart," Alton said, as he entered the breakfast nook, where Wanda and Gracie were having breakfast, and planted a kiss on Wanda's forehead. Wanda didn't answer, and what's more, Alton noticed that she looked very unpleased. "Good morning, Gracie."

"Good morning, Mr. Carter. I'll get your breakfast."

"Just coffee, Gracie. Thanks."

"Yes, sir," the lady said exiting into the kitchen.

"I'm sorry, Sweetheart. I just couldn't get away," he apologized, but she still didn't respond. "Wanda, you're supposed to be big enough to accept a person's apology."

"Daddy, I waited up all night for you," she said. "The hospital called looking for you. Something about Mommy, but they wouldn't tell me anything."

"They did?" he asked, and she nodded. "Did they call back?"

"No."

"I'll stop by there on my way to work, Sweetheart," he said, but she did not respond again. Wanda, Honey, I said I was sorry."

"Were you with Aunt Cecily?"

"What?" he asked with widen eyes as Gracie reentered with his coffee, then she took her plate in the kitchen. "Thanks." Alton told her as she left, and she nodded.

"Daddy, I'm not stupid. Keisha was my sister. That makes her *your* child. Are you having an affair with Aunt Cecily? And is that the reason she and Mommy aren't friends anymore? I can remember when I was a little girl, they were very good friends. Please, tell me the truth, Daddy. Are you going to leave us to live with Aunt Cecily like my friend Deshawn's dad did them?"

"No!" he insisted. "I will always be here for you." He took a deep breath and realized that his little girl wasn't so little anymore. He had been dreading this moment ever since Keisha was born, but *how* will he answer her questions. She *does* have a right to know, but how do you tell your little girl something like *this*? *How*?

****

"You look beautiful today, Lillian," Doctor Asala said in his deep Caribbean accent, as Lillian sat in front of his desk, hair combed, make-up on, and a blue, silk dress, but she didn't respond. "How do you feel?" She still didn't answer. "Your husband wants to bring Wanda to see you."

He got her attention now, as she blurted out. "No!"

"You don't want to see your daughter?" he asked with outstretched, dark brown eyes, in conjunction with his dark, ebony skin.

"I almost *killed* her. What in the hell would I *say* to her?"

"Tell her how you feel. That's a start."

"You don't know how I feel."

"I think I do," he said sitting up on his seat. "You feel like the whole world is against you. You feel trapped in here. You hate your husband and despise the judge for having the audacity to put you in here. You're not an alcoholic! How dare *them*!"

"I am," she nonchalantly said.

"What?"

"I *am* an alcoholic. I killed an innocent little girl. I almost killed my own child and I *truly* wanted to die last night. If I weren't an alcoholic, I could've never done such a thing. That's the *second* person I killed. I need to be punished," she squeezed out behind tears. "I don't know how I could ever face my friends again. I took someone so dear from *both* of them. I *am* an alcoholic, Dr. Asala!" She cried hysterically, and the doctor walked from around his desk, pulled her up, and held her tight in his arms.

"Welcome back to the real world, Lillian. You should be going home soon. You've made quite a breakthrough. Congratulations!" He walked to the door, then added, "Oh, Lillian, you have a visitor."

"I don't want to see..." Lillian started, but stopped abruptly when she focused on Pastor Graham standing at the door.

"Hello, Lillian," he said softly.

****

"Honey, you got a phone call last night from a man named James."

"James?!" Maurice repeated, trying desperately to hide the anguish in his voice.

"Yes. He said for you to call him. He said you're representing him in a lawsuit."

"Yes. The firm handed me his case."

"Well, don't forget to call him back."

"I won't," he said then planted a kiss on Trudy's forehead. "See you later."

"Don't forget about our dinner party tonight."

"I won't. I'll be home early. I'm in court today, but that will be over by the afternoon."

"All right."

"What're you going to do today?" he asked as if he didn't know. He knew whatever it was the refrigerator would be nearby.

"I have a million things to do, to get ready for tonight."

"Well, don't work yourself too hard," he said, thinking, *As if she would. She'll probably work the poor maid to death while she sits on her fat ass.*

"I won't," she said then blew a kiss at him, and he smiled and left. As he left, he wondered why he put himself through this shit, then he found the answer. The *money*. The fat ass bitch was loaded, and his funds were fast approaching bankruptcy. He just couldn't resist those tight ass young boys, and they'd take him to the cleaners every time. His lifestyle was getting too expensive. Hotel rooms every night. Dinner. Booze. Etc. Oh, well, it's a tough life, but somebody has to live it. After all, this woman has all the qualities he loves. Low self-esteem because of her weight, and plenty of money. You can't beat those qualities. And, he didn't have to fuck her too often, because half the time, she's too full from eating so damn much, and the other half she's too tired from being so damn fat. One thing's for sure, he didn't ever want to see that dumb mutherfucker he'd had last night. He thought the son-of-bitch broke his jaw.   Usually when they're as drunk as that man was last night, there're pretty easy to get, but not him. The sick bastard! Probably drowning his sorrows over some damn bitch. But he had to admit. The man was fine. What a waste! But moving on was the name of the game. And what in the hell did James mean, calling him at home. That was one son-of-bitch he'd hated he fucked. Fuck 'em one time and they think they own you. Somehow, he had to get rid of that pest. One way or the *other*!

****

"Wanda, I love you very much," Alton said, trying to find the words to comfort his daughter.

"What about Mommy? Do you still love her?"

"I will always love your mother. I married her for better *and* for worse. I guess we're just going through the worse right now."

"And, what about Aunt Cecily? Do you love her, too?"

Taking a deep breath, he said softly, "Yes, I do." Then he added quickly. "But not in the same way as I love you and your mother. I care for Cecily very much, but I'm committed to you and your mother, until *death* do us part." For the first time Wanda smiled, and he stood and planted a kiss on her forehead. "I've got to go, Sweetheart."

"Daddy, Aunt Trudy invited us to dinner tonight."

"She did?"

"Yeah, so don't be late."

"What time is dinner."

"Six."

"I'll be here," he said, but don't forget we're going to see Mommy today."

"I can hardly wait," Wanda said smiling big.

"See you, Princess," he said, planting another kiss on her forehead, then starting out the door, but he turned and added. "I love you."

"I love you, too, Daddy," she smiled big as he left, then she added to herself. "You can't have my daddy, Aunt Cecily!"

****

"Pastor Graham, I don't want you to see me like this," Lillian said sitting down. "I'm so ashamed."

Taking a seat in the chair, he said, "Lillian, there's nothing to be ashamed of."

"I'm an alcoholic. I killed an innocent little girl. And, I don't have anything to be ashamed of?! I let everyone down, you, the children, the church, my little girl, and most importantly, God," she said with tears running down her face.

Pastor Graham went to Lillian and sat in the chair beside her and said very softly, "Lillian, what's important now is that you also let *yourself* down. Don't worry about God, he will love you no matter what you do, and he will forgive you. Now, what you need to do is start forgiving *yourself*."

"How can I do that? I killed a little girl and almost killed my own child. How do I forgive myself for that?" she asked crying hard now.

"It's going to take time, patience, and a belief in God. You've already accepted responsibility for your actions, so your work is halfway over. Trust God, Lillian. He won't let you down."

"It should've been *me*," she cried. "It should've been *me*. Why did God have to take that *sweet* little girl? It should've been *me*."

"God was not ready for you yet, Lillian," he said pulling her in his arms. "But he *was* ready for little Keisha."

****

"Cis, hi," Trudy greeted as the two women touched cheeks. "You look beautiful."

"So, do you," Cecily replied, smiling also in her pink chiffon dress that ballooned at the tail, with a trail of sequins spread throughout. Her hair was placed in a bun with ringlet of curls surrounding her face. She looked like a little princess going to a ball.

"Hi, Alton," Trudy continued. "I'm glad you could come." Although Trudy's makeup was dazzling and her hair was stunning with her braids wrapped together in a neat French roll, that royal blue dress covered her huge body like an elephant under a tent. It was a loose-fitting dress from top to bottom.

"Hi, Trudy. You look stunning," Alton replied in his black tuxedo.

"Wanda!" Trudy exploded, grabbing the child in her arms and squeezing her tight. Wanda was very conservative in her lace, cream-colored dress and ribbons pinning up her hair. Angela spotted Wanda and thought she looked like a geek in that church girl Easter dress, and not in a stylish black, leather miniskirt and white silk blouse like she wore. Wanda focused on Angela's spiked hair, sticking on top of her head and wondered what horror movie she exited from.

"Hi, Aunt Trudy," Wanda greeted.

"Angela is here," Trudy said, and then called, "Angela!"

"I'm here," replied the girl shuffling over, dragging her feet.

"You and Wanda can go in the game room and play on the computer with Carl," Trudy suggested, and the girls left as Maurice walked in.

"Dr. Wade, it's a pleasure to meet you," he said. "I've heard so much about you." He kissed the back of her hand as he thought, *Now, this is a beautiful woman. If <u>any</u> woman could make me go straight, this woman could.*

"Thank you," Cecily smiled.

"Cecily, Alton, I would like for you to meet Maurice Campbell. Maurice, this is Cecily Wade and Alton Carter," Trudy introduced, smiling big, holding on to Maurice's arm as if they were a very happy couple, which is exactly what *she* thought.

"I'm happy to meet you, Maurice," Cecily said.

"Same here, Man," added Alton, and they shook hands.

"Are we the last to arrive?" Cecily asked.

"No. I picked Angela up early to help me, so we're still waiting on Cindy..." Trudy said, but the doorbell silenced her. "Here they are."

When Trudy opened the door, She, Cindy, Alton, and Cecily extended greetings, then, Trudy introduced Cindy to Maurice. "Everyone, name your poison," Maurice stated as the door opened again, and Cindy took Isaac's hand, as he froze solid in his tracks when he locked eyes with Maurice.

****

"You mean you did it before?!"

"Haven't *you*?!" Angela asked Wanda.

"No! My mother would *kill* me!"

"Did what?" Carl Jr. asked.

"Nothing. Play with your Nintendo," added Angela giggling. "My boyfriend's sixteen."

"And he goes with *you*?! You're only ten, like *me*," Wanda tried to whisper.

"So!"

"What if you get pregnant?"

"My boyfriend knows what he's doing."

"My mother said girls should wait until they get married."

"Ask her if *she* waited," Angela joked, and they burst into laughter.

Sobering, Wanda said, "But, seriously, I think she did."

"Hey, when is your mother coming home?"

"Next week."

"How long has she been gone?"

"Six months," Wanda said. "And, she wouldn't let me come to see her the entire time she was there."

"You lucky girl. I wish I could get rid of my mama for six months," Angela said laughing, and Wanda laughed with her.

****

"Isaac, can we talk?"

"About what?"

"About what happened," Maurice said walking out on the balcony with Isaac.

"There's nothing to talk about."

"I want to clear the air. Look, Man. I'm sorry, okay? We're both adults here. Can't we just let bygones be bygones?"

"And what about Trudy?"

"What about her?"

"I care about her. Why are you playing these games with her? Obviously, she doesn't know what you are."

"What I am is a caring person. Trudy enjoys me, and I enjoy her. No more. No less."

"You are a *sick* son-of-a-bitch! Trudy needs to know about you."

"What I do in my spare time is nobody's business but mine."

"Trudy deserves better than you!" Isaac insisted, growing angry, but trying to keep his voice low.

"I am good to Trudy, and that's more than she'll get from anyone else!" Maurice retaliated. "And if you tell her about me, you'll only be hurting her for no good reason, other than to ease your own conscience and to punish me for what happened between *us*!"

"You are *disgusting*!" Isaac said between clenched teeth, observing that Maurice was standing near the edge of the balcony.

****

"Are you sleeping with Lillian's husband, Cis?" Trudy wanted to know, and Cecily turned her back to her friend. "Are you?"

"Yes," Cecily said weakly, and Trudy dropped her head.

"Oh, Cis."

Turning back to face Trudy, Cecily insisted, "Tru, please understand. I love Alton. I really love him."

"*Lillian* loves him, too, Cis. Remember *her*? His *wife*! *Our* best friend!"

With tears running down her face, Cecily said, "I don't know what to do, Tru. I love Alton so much."

"Well, you've better think of something, Kid. Lil will be coming home next week."

"*Next* week?"

"Yes. Didn't Alton tell you?"

"No, he didn't."

"Cis, there're a billion men out there. Many of which who would jump at the chance to be with a beautiful, intelligent woman like you. Why *him*? Why your *best* friend's husband?"

"Tru, you don't understand. All you see is he's Lil's husband. You don't know the past Alton and I have shared. I was a hooker, and he treated me like royalty. To just say I'm in love with him is a drastic understatement. He never looked down on me. He's seen me at my weakest point, and he still looked at me with love and respect. Alton is a part of my very soul," she stopped and wiped her tears, then blew hard and added, "as I said, you don't understand."

"Cis, I understand what you're talking about, but it's *insane*! To put *any* human person on a pedestal that high is absolutely insane! You are setting yourself up to be hurt. What will you do when Lillian comes home, and Alton has to go back to just sneaking around with you? You will never have a future together."

"Alton's going to ask Lillian for a divorce."

"What?!" Trudy exploded, and Cecily nodded. "And, *you* can live with that?"

"Of course, I can," she chuckled. "Lillian is a grown woman. She'll bounce back."

"Cecily, you're dreaming. Wake up, Girl, before it's too late."

"Trudy, why are you trying to hurt me? Why can't you just be happy for me?"

"Because you can't see reality. Alton is spending time with you out of hurt and obligation. Lillian is responsible for your and his child dying. He's angry with her right now, so he's turning all his attentions to you, because you both share a common hurt. But, make no mistake about it, Alton *loves* Lillian! He will *never* leave her."

"You don't know what you're talking about, Trudy," Cecily chuckled.

"Yes, I do. I've been there, done that! Names may change, but situations never do."

"Well, we'll see next week, won't we?" Cecily said, then walked away.

****

"Aren't you ready to see your daughter yet, Lillian?" Dr. Asala asked, sitting in a chair as Lillian lay on her bed in her small room.

"No. Not really."

"But you're going home next week. What will you do then?"

"I'll cross that bridge when I get to it."

"If you could see the look on her face every time I tell her she can't see you, it would break your heart. You can't undo the past, but you can work through it."

"Am I truly ready to go home?"

"Yes, you *truly* are."

"What if I have an urge to drink again? May I call you?"

"You will be assigned a support group. You *must* attend those meetings, or you'll end up right back here. Do you understand, Lillian?" he asked, and she nodded. "But I think you'll do just fine. Your husband seems to support you well."

"Husband, huh! Doctor, I may not have a husband anymore."

"What're you talking about?"

"Things are *not* always what they seem to be."

"What'd you mean?"

"I would bet you any amount of money that there hasn't been too many nights that Alton hasn't slept with my *best* friend, Cecily."

"Ah, you're letting your imagination run away with you."

"Dr. Asala, I waited twenty-one years to have a man in my life. I was a virgin when I married Alton. I have never known any other man sexually. And, what does he do, he runs around with a *prostitute*," she laughed. "Isn't that hilarious? So, what did I do it for? Why was it worth it? Saving myself all those years for my husband? Can you tell me that?"

"Lillian, your husband isn't perfect. He's human. He will make mistakes. It's commendable that you got married still a virgin. Not many people can say that, but you did it, and you should be proud, no matter what your husband does."

"So, you don't have an answer."

"I'm afraid not."

"Thanks for listening anyway."

He smiled sweetly at her as he stood. "Well, pretty lady, I must take my leave."

Standing also, she asked, "Do you have to go right now?"

"I'm afraid so. I'll see you tomorrow."

"Thank you for being so nice to me," she said walking to him.

"It's my job."

"No. Not all of it," she said softly. "And I appreciate it." Lillian stood on her tiptoes and extended a kiss to him, and he bent down to accept it. Their lips touched lightly.

"Goodnight, Lillian," he said softly.

"Good-night, Elijah."

****

"Hello, Boys."

Isaac turned around and looked in Cecily's face, then he turned back around and stared into space. "Hi, Dr. Wade," Maurice said.

"Agh, none of that. It's *Cecily*," she smiled.

"Cecily it is," Maurice replied. "Well, if you'd excuse me." She nodded, but Isaac didn't turn around to face either of them. Cecily walked to him slowly as Maurice exited back into the house.

"Isaac, about last night."

Turning around he said, "Forget, Cecily. You have whom you want. I'm just sorry I came by. Please forgive me."

"Isaac, I care a great deal for you. Those years that we were married were some of the best years of my life."

"Don't patronize me, Cecily. Please, don't."

"I'm not. I'm telling you the truth," she said then took a deep breath. "You're a great guy. I wish I could love you the way you do me, but..." she paused, looking for a way to emphasize this delicately, because she didn't want to hurt him any more than he was already hurting. "I will always have a special place in my heart for you. *Always*." A single tear fell from her eye, and he wiped it with his finger. Then he kissed her on her lips softly.

"If it's one thing I learned last night, it's that I've got to let go of the past before it kills me. That's what I'm doing. I'm letting go. What we had is in the past, and that's where it will stay. Don't worry about me. I'm fine. If you ever need me," he continued. "You know where to find me."

"You, too," she squeezed out, and he grabbed her in his arms and hugged her tight, just as Cindy walked to the door, but she didn't let them know she was there, as she turned and strolled back into the house.

Chapter 18

A beautiful, healthy Lillian, with her black, curly hair outlining her thin face, walked slowly into her big, beautiful house, in a deep pink Hauser dress with a belt pulled snugly around her tiny waist, followed by Alton with a small suitcase in his hand. She took a deep breath as she looked around the luxurious house in amazement. It had seemed like years instead of months since she'd been in her living room. Wanda strolled in slowly, and she and her mother locked eyes. Wanda's long white shirt covered her tiny waist, where a belt surrounded her blue jeans. "Wanda," Lillian said softly.

"Hi, Mom," Wanda replied weakly.

"You've grown two inches in the short time I was away," added Lillian as tears burned her eyes. She and Wanda took a deep breath, and then they simultaneously ran into each other's arms. "Oh, my baby. I missed you." Lillian cried as she held her daughter tight, while Wanda wept also.

Alton tipped out quietly and went into the den, but not unnoticed by Lillian. He closed the door and picked up the telephone and dialed. "Dr. Wade's office," Cindy said on the other end.

"Hi, Cindy. It's Alton."

"Hi, Alton. How are you?"

"Fine. Thanks. Is Cecily available?"

"Hold on. I'll get her."

"Thanks, Cindy."

"Sure thing, Alton," she said then buzzed Cecily.

"Yes, Cindy," Cecily responded as she sat at her desk, motioning with a wave for a couple to come in and have a seat in front of her desk, and they did.

"Cecily, Alton's on line two."

"Thanks, Cindy," Cecily said, then looked at the couple. "Excuse me, please." They nodded. "Hello."

"Hi, Baby."

"I'm in a conference right now. May I call you back."

"I just want to tell you that I need a rain check for tonight. I just brought Lillian home, and I think I need to be here tonight. I hope you understand, Baby."

"Will you discuss with her what we talked about?"

"I can't ask her for a divorce tonight, Baby. This is her *first* night home in six months."

"Why put it off?"

"I'll come by early tomorrow. We'll talk then. I love you."

"Me, too."

"Bye."

"Bye."

Lillian, in the bedroom, replaced the telephone receiver in its cradle also. "You want him, Cecily?" She said to herself. "Well, it'll be over my dead body! I won't let you have my husband, *Friend*!"

****

Trudy wobbled into a big fancy office building and to a receptionist. "Hi," she said smiling big.

"Hello," the lady replied with a turned-up nose, obviously repulsed by Trudy's size, and wondering how women let themselves go like that. "May I help you?"

"Yes. I'm here to see Maurice."

"Who should I say is calling?"

Sarcastically, Trudy replied, "You may tell him Miss Trudy Miles is *calling*!"

"*You're* Miss Miles?!" the lady stressed. "I thought..." She stopped suddenly.

"I don't think Maurice pays you to *think*, Dearie!" Trudy snapped. "I'll see myself in. Thanks for your *kindness*!" As Trudy walked away, she thought that that slut has got to go. She'll talk to Maurice about her. She wondered if he was sleeping with this conceded, rude, bitch.

When Trudy opened the door, her purse fell to the floor as her mouth flew open when she focused on a scene that took her totally by surprise. There was Maurice, her handsome live-in lover, with his pants dropped down around his ankles, servicing a man from the rear, who was bent down over Maurice's beautiful oak desk. She had heard of things like this, but she, never in her wildest dreams, could have imagined such a thing. It made her sick to her stomach, and she actually felt herself gag for breath.

Although Maurice froze, he did not change his position. His eyes locked with Trudy's, and the man's face turned a bright red. Trudy closed her eyes momentarily, hoping that this was all a bad dream, but when she opened her eyes again, the horrible scene was still there; so she knew she had to be wide awake.

****

Cecily stood with a surgical mask on her face, and a surgical bonnet on her head, as she looked down at the little boy lying on the operating table, fast asleep. Her hand trembled a little as she received the scalpel from the nurse. "Are you all right, Dr. Wade?" the nurse asked. Cecily nodded and looked at the child again, and perspiration began popping out of her face. As the scalpel in her hand approached the child, it shook violently, and she froze as she thought, *This is not happening to me. I haven't used drugs in a long time. This can't be happening to me. I'm not an addict.* She looked at the doctor standing nearby to assist her.

"Take over, please, Don," she said then dropped the scalpel in the pan and ran out, leaving a stunned surgical team.

Cecily entered the surgical scrub room and bent down over the sink. Perspiration popped from her forehead when she took off the mask and cap. She turned on the water and splashed it on her face hard. Her hands trembled uncontrollably, so she stuck them in her pockets, but that didn't stop them. "Oh, God, no!" She squeezed out as she melted to the floor, covering her ears with her hands as if she was hearing loud noises, and in fact, she was. The loud noises of her body, begging for drugs. Then suddenly she began to scratch her head vigorously. Then her legs. Then her arms. She was scratching like a wild animal, beckoning to be tamed, until she felt the tinge of blood stinging her arms, so she jumped up and ran out.

Cecily entered the medical supply room, where she searched frantically for a bottle of pills, whimpering like a little lost puppy. Finally, she spotted what she was looking for. She yanked the bottle of pills from the shelf, opened it, and threw one in her mouth. She felt nothing, so she dropped another one in her mouth. She continued to throw pills into her mouth, until she noticed that the bottle was completely empty. Cecily's legs became weak, so she melted to the floor and sat like a little child afraid of the world. Her eyes closed slowly. All of a sudden, her head jerked up, bulking uncontrollably as she clutched her stomach. Sharp pains exploded through her fragile body. She struggled to locate her feet so she could stand, but her body wasn't cooperating. She even tried to crawl to the door, but her body was numb, and she couldn't feel her legs at all. Tears flowed down her frightened face because she knew death was near, and there was no one to help her. She even tried to scream, but her voice was nowhere to be found. Cecily's weak body collapsed on the floor, and she could see the door, but she could not reach it. A drastic chill overtook her body, and she shook violently. Her eyes began to close on her, and she could do nothing. She was dying and she knew it, but there was nothing she could do. Finally, she was drained of her state of consciousness, and her body surrendered to darkness.

****

"Hi, Wanda," a young boy said running up to a fast-walking Wanda, carrying her schoolbooks in her arms.

"Hi, Juan," Wanda nonchalantly replied, without breaking her stride.

"I'm glad you're back in school."

"So am I."

"How're you doing?"

"Okay, I guess."

"Would you like me to walk you home?"

Chuckling, Wanda replied, "I live across town."

"I know," he said laughing.

"My dad's coming," Wanda said as she stopped, seeing Alton's gray Rolls Royce pull up. "There he is. See you, Juan." She ran and jumped in the car. "Hi, Daddy."

"Hi, Baby," he said looking at a sad faced Juan standing by watching Wanda leave. "Who's that?"

"That geek?"

"Yeah. That *geek*," Alton smiled.

"Juan."

"What makes him a geek?" Alton asked pulling off.

"He makes straight A's."

"And what's wrong with that?"

"Oh, Daddy, you don't understand."

"I understand this, and that's by the time you start looking for a husband, you're be looking for a geek like Juan," he said while she frowned like he was crazy, as his cell phone rang, and he picked it up. "Alton Carter."

"Alton, this is Cindy."

"Hi, Cindy. What's up?"

"Alton, Cecily is in the hospital. I thought maybe you'd like to know."

"Hospital?!" he exploded. "What's wrong?"

"I don't know. They won't tell me anything," Cindy replied. "Johnston Memorial."

"All right, Cindy. I'm on the way."

"Please call me as soon as you know anything."

"You bet," he said then hung up.

"Who's in the hospital, Daddy?"

"Cecily."

"What's wrong with her?"

"I don't know, Sweetheart," he said then took a deep breath. Wanda could see the worried look on her father's face, and she knew he really did love this woman, whom she once loved enough to call Aunt, but now carried such a hatred for, because Aunt Cecily was taking her daddy away.

****

"I just came to get my things," Maurice said, standing in Trudy's bedroom door, dressed in a three-piece, dark-blue suit, and Trudy thought he'd never looked more handsome, and wondered why had God played such a terrible trick on such a gorgeous man. She put her cookies down on the nightstand and turned the television volume down, as she watched him pack the few things he had brought to her house. He momentarily focused on the huge lady who sat on the satin sheets, and he felt sorry for her. He had remembered seeing her on the cover of *Fashion and Glamour Magazine*. She was one beautiful and classy lady. It seemed like such a long time ago now. "I'm sorry if I hurt you," he added weakly.

"Save it, Freak!" she snapped.

"I'm not a freak," he nonchalantly replied.

"What in the hell do you call it?!" she yelled, jumping off the bed to confront him. "When I think of the times I left you here with my son, it makes me want to throw up!"

"I would *never* do anything to that child!" he insisted growing angry. "I'm gay, not crazy!"

"I don't know what in the hell you're capable of! Until today, I didn't think you were capable of fucking another man, either!"

"Why do people immediately think gay people will molest children? There are more heterosexual pedophiles than homosexual's!"

"Why in the hell did you lead me on, Maurice?!"

"Bad choice! I tried to change, but I just couldn't."

"But why *me*?"

"Why *not* you? You are a woman with very low self-esteem because of your weight."

"And to think, I let you *touch* me."

"You should *thank* me."

She grew very angry now and yelled, "Get the hell out of my house!"

He walked to the door with his bag in his hand, stopped and turned to face Trudy, then added, "I don't like myself for deceiving you, Trudy, but it's who I am, and I'm not going to hide it anymore. I didn't ask to be this way, but I am, and I'm going to live my life for the first time. *Live* it, not *hide* it! I suggest you do the same." Her eyebrows raised, and he knew she didn't understand. "Your weight. You used to be so beautiful. Take off the weight, Trudy. You're a beautiful person, inside. You could put that beauty on the outside again. Start *living*, Trudy. I sure am."

"Don't tell me what to do!" Trudy snapped. "Now get the hell out of my house!" He glared at her one final time, and then he exited quickly. Trudy dropped on the bed in tears.

****

Alton walked in the hospital room slowly and sat in a chair beside Cecily's bed. Cecily opened her eyes slowly and spotted his worried face. "Hi," he said with a smile. "How are you?"

"Alton, I'm sorry," she said weakly as tears began to roll down her face.

"Shhh," he said taking her hand. "I'm sorry I wasn't there for you."

"I really thought I could handle this myself, but I lost it. I don't ever remember being so scared in my whole life. I just lost it."

"Well, we'll find it together," he replied giving her hand a soft kiss.

"I love you so much."

"And, I love you," he said then grew serious. "And you're getting help for this thing before it's too late."

****

"Cindy, I'm moving out."

"What?!" Cindy exploded, jumping off the couch and following Isaac to their bedroom.

"I'm going to pack."

"Is it something I did, Isaac?" she asked frantically.

"No. You're wonderful! It's *me*."

"What about you?"

"I can't do this anymore. I can't continue to live my life unhappily anymore."

With tears rolling down her face she begged, "Isaac, tell me what you want me to do, and I'll do it. Please, Baby, don't leave me. I love you so much."

"But *I* don't love *you*, Cindy. It's unfair to you, and to me. You are a beautiful, intelligent young lady. You deserve more than I can give right now. You need to find someone who will gladly return your love," he explained then resumed his packing.

Grabbing his arm, she shouted, "I don't want anyone else!" She dropped on the bed, crying hysterically. "It's Cecily, isn't it? You still love her!"

Looking at the heartbroken woman he said softly, "It's no one. I am just not happy. I can't deny my feelings for Cecily, but she's not the reason I'm leaving. It's true, when I married Cecily, I thought it would be forever, but she didn't see it that way." He paused. "I care about you, but it's not love. I'm sorry to hurt you. Believe me, I *know* how you feel. I've been there. It's terrible to love someone so deeply and not have your love returned. For the first time in my life, I really and truly understand why Cecily couldn't stay married to me. She was pregnant with another man's child, and I still wanted her, but *she* chose to end our marriage, not *me*. I thought I would die, but I survived, and so will *you*." He paused again and took a deep breath, then bent down on his knees to comfort her. "I will always care for you deeply. You bore my only child. I will always be grateful to you for that, but that's not love. Not the kind of love *you* deserve. I must gain my self-respect back," he said remembering the night with Maurice. "In more ways than one." He planted a kiss on her hand, stood up, and walked to the door. "I'll keep in touch." He walked out quickly, and Cindy dropped to the floor, crying hysterically. She suffered an emptiness that she believed only she had experienced, at losing someone whom she loved with all her heart.

Chapter 19

Cecily opened the door, and Wanda was standing there, smiling. "Wanda!" Cecily smiled. "Who brought you here?"

"Uber," she said entering the house.

Closing the door, Cecily said, "It's good to see you." She gave the child a big hug. "Come on in. Have a seat."

"I wanted to see if you were all right. Daddy told me you were in the hospital."

"That's very sweet of you," Cecily said as they sat on the couch. "I'm doing much better."

"Good," Wanda said smiling. "Aunt Cecily, I miss Keisha."

"So do I, Sweetheart," Cecily said with a fading smile, remembering Keisha's smiling face. "So do I." Soon Cecily broke the silence, saying, "I'll get us some ice cream." Wanda nodded. When Cecily was out the room, Wanda drifted in the past:

* *Wanda picked up the telephone at the same time that Alton did, and she heard him say, "Hello?" She almost hung up until she heard Cecily's voice.*

"Can you talk?"

"Yes. What's up?"

"What time will you be over tonight?"

"Around six."

"Okay, that's fine. I have to work late, but I'll be home by then."

"Are you sure, because we can do it another night."

"Don't be silly. I'll be waiting."

"Put on that black teddy I love so much."

"You naughty boy," she laughed.

"Bye."

*"Bye." she said then hung up.   ***

"I hope you like chocolate chip," Cecily said bringing Wanda back to the present.

"My favorite."

"Good!" Cecily replied as they began eating. "How is your mother, Wanda?"

"All right. Why don't you come over to see her?"

"Your mother and I aren't on good terms these days."

"Why?" Wanda wanted to know. "When I was little you were best friends."

"It's a long story, Wanda."

"Do you blame her for Keisha's death?"

"No. Not anymore. She was very sick then."

"Then why don't you make up? I know she would like that."

"Maybe we will. Very soon," Cecily said as she looked at five fifteen P.M. on the clock and wondered how long Wanda would stay. Wanda mustn't see Alton come. Her attention to the time did not go unnoticed by her young visitor.

"Aunt Cecily, do you love my daddy?"

With widen eyes, Cecily exploded, "What?!"

"I know my daddy's coming over here. I overheard you on the phone."

Jumping to her feet, Cecily insisted, "Wanda, you shouldn't eavesdrop!"

"It was a mistake," Wanda said sadly. "But, do you love my daddy? And, are you planning to take him away from mommy and me?"

****

"I have to go out for a while," Alton announced to Lillian as she lay on the bed in a housecoat.

"Alton, is our marriage over?"

"What?"

"Is our marriage over?" she repeated. "Has Cecily totally replaced me?"

"What're you talking about?" he chuckled.

"I know I'm responsible for the death of your child. And, I'm very sorry about that, but I can't change it," she explained.

"You should've gotten help a long time ago, Lillian!" he yelled.

"Don't you think I know that now, Alton?!" she yelled back. "I was *sick*! *Sick*! Don't you understand that?!"

"But that doesn't bring my baby back, Lillian!"

"I know, but *we're* still here. And, I need to know if it's impossible for you to forgive me or *not*. I'm tired of living like this. I *need* to know," she cried. "Do you still love me?"

****

Trudy put a big spoonful of ice cream in her mouth, and then stood to put on a housecoat, but she froze when she caught sight of her huge body standing there, in a bra and panties, in the full-length mirror on her door. She noticed the folds in her balloon belly, which drooped down, over her cellulite thunder thighs. Her behind stuck out as far in the back as her stomach in the front. She knew she looked like a round beach ball, and she could see the look on Maurice's secretary's smug face when she looked at her. Then she could see Maurice's face when he said she should thank him for his attentions. Next, she focused on a framed picture of her on the wall, in a bikini when she was on the cover of a magazine. She was once very beautiful. She had it all, and she could have it again. She *will* have it again! Trudy began to put the ice cream on the nightstand when she knocked her purse on the floor. She struggled to bend down to pick up the contents that were on the floor when she noticed a card. It was Pastor Graham's card that he had given her years ago. She was tired of trying to do everything herself and failing. Maybe she had better give God a try.

****

Isaac moved back in his house next door to Lillian and Alton. He insisted on Cecily keeping the house when they divorced, but she didn't want it, so he kept it out of some kind of sentimental reason. because he had shared a life with the woman he loved there. He never thought he could ever live in the house again without Cecily, and especially because it was next door to the man whom she loved, but now, here he is, moving back in and loving it. Life is funny. It took someone like Maurice to get *his* life back on track, so that he would have the courage to go on without Cecily and moved back in his house. He had to admit that he still loved her very much, and his heart felt as if it had broken into a thousand pieces, but at least *now*, he's *willing* to move on.

Isaac began putting his clothes in the closet when he focused on a golden Angel pin on the lapel of his suit. He drifted into the past:

* *"What's this?"*

"Open it," Cecily said handing him a small box. He took it and opened it, then looked at her. "It's an Angel. To protect you when I'm not with you."

"That's so sweet," he said softly. "I love you, Baby. Thank you."

"I love you, too," she said as he grabbed her up and kissed her hard. *

Isaac came back to the present, took the Angel pin off, and started to put it in the coat pocket when he felt something in the pocket. He reached inside and pulled out a card. It was Pastor Graham's business card that he received at Lillian and Alton's house at dinner. He smiled and closed it up in his hand.

****

"Wanda, I don't know what to say," Cecily stood there stunned. She didn't even know Wanda knew what love was. "Your daddy will always be special to me, just like you and your mommy. I could never hurt you and your mommy, if I can help it."

"But, do you love my daddy?"

Cecily sat beside Wanda, and took the child's hand in hers, then took a deep breath and said, "Sweetheart, I can't lie to you. I care for your daddy very much." She saw a single tear roll down Wanda's face, and she felt as if her heart actually broke in two, and tears filled her eyes also. "Don't you worry your pretty little head. Aunt Cecily would *never* take your daddy from you. That's a promise." She pulled the child in her arms, hugged her tight as he thought, *Oh, God, please help me to mend fences with my best friend again.*

****

"Do you still love me?" Lillian asked again, and he walked to her, pulled her off the bed, and held her hands in his.

"I've loved you from the first moment that I laid eyes on you, and I've loved you ever since. How could I ever stop loving you?" he said softly, then kissed her lips gently.

"I thought I lost you. You haven't touched me since I've been home."

"It's not because I didn't want to. I didn't know if you were ready."

"I'm ready," she said, and they kissed hard. "Oh yes, I'm ready!" He pulled her housecoat off her shoulders, and she let it drop to the floor, and he admired his wife's beautiful, brown body in her short nightgown.

"Lillian, you are so beautiful," he said breathlessly, then they grabbed each other savagely, but their lovemaking was very gentle. They melted into each other's world of passion together, then he pulled her in his arms so tight, as if she would run away, but she wasn't going *anywhere*. She had her husband back, and it felt good.

"I love you, Alton," she cooed.

"And, I love you, Lillian. More than you'll ever know," he replied softly then planted a kiss on her forehead.

Chapter 20

Pastor Graham preached a sermon entitled *Working It Out*, and Trudy sat there thinking it applied to her, while Isaac sat thinking it was just what he needed. Then Lillian sang a beautiful rendition of *Amazing Grace* as she focused on her husband and daughter sitting, smiling at her. She thought how good it felt to be back on track again, and back in church. When the service was over, Lillian ran to Trudy and hugged her. She looked around for Isaac, but she didn't see him. Trudy walked out of that church feeling better than she had felt in a long time. "Trudy," she heard a voice say.

Looking up, she said, "Isaac. How are you?"

"I'm great," he said, and he *really* meant it. He hadn't felt this good in a long, long time. Pastor Graham had said just what Isaac needed to hear. He was definitely working it out and going on with his life, *without* Cecily.

"Lillian said she thought she saw you."

"Lillian has a golden voice. She should've gone pro a long time ago."

"Lillian, *pro*! She would laugh," Trudy said laughing herself.

"What're you doing for dinner, Trudy?"

"I guess I'll have something at home."

"I know this great little Italian restaurant around the corner. I would be honored if you'd join me."

"Are you serious? You want *me* to have dinner with *you*?"

"Yes. Why are you so surprised?"

"Isaac, I haven't been asked out to dinner by a man in so long, I forgot how it feels."

"Men are crazy in this town. Trudy, just because you've put on a little weight doesn't take away your beauty or your charm," he said. "Well, what'd you say?"

"Sure."

"Where's Carl?"

"He's with his best friend next door."

"Okay, I guess it's just you and me."

Chapter 21

Wanda ran into the house yelling, "Mommy! Mommy!" She dropped her schoolbooks on the table, and ran into the kitchen, then froze when she focused on Louis, coming from under the sink.

"She ain't here," he said exposing yellow, cigarette-stained teeth.

"Where is she?"

"I don't know," he said staring at her small frame, in her blue jeans. "She don't report to me."

"Is my daddy here?"

"No," he said again. "And I don't know where *he* is, either," he added sarcastically.

"Okay," she accepted, turning to leave because she didn't like the way he was looking at her.

Following her, he asked, "What're you doing home so early from school?'

"A water line burst at the school," she said, feeling very uncomfortable because she could feel him undressing her with his eyes. "I have some homework." She grabbed her books and ran upstairs.

When Wanda reached her room, she closed and locked her door, then blew hard. Louis frightened her. She wished her mother wouldn't leave him in the house alone, but Lillian didn't know she would be home early. She picked up the telephone and dialed.

"Hello?" Trudy said on the other end, biting on a celery stalk.

"Aunt Trudy, is my mother there?" Wanda asked. "She's not answering her cell phone."

"Not yet, Wanda. She said she had to run a few errands, but she's on her way."

"We got out of school early today because of a water line bursting. Could you ask her to call me when she gets there?"

"You're home?"

"Yes. Natasha's mom brought me."

"I sure will, Wanda."

"Thanks," Wanda said then they hung up.

Wanda started on her homework. This new math was getting the best of her. She got up, opened the door and went to the bathroom. She was so tired of this homework, she forgot all about Louis being in the house. She walked back in her room yawning big. The door closed behind her, and she whirled around to come eye-to-eye with a dirty-haired, sweaty-swelling Louis. "Get out of my room!" Wanda demanded, trying to appear brave, so he wouldn't hear her heart pounding.

"I will," he said walking to her, exposing those yellow teeth again. "*After*!"

****

"Cecily, Alton's here to see you," Cindy said through the intercom.

"Send him in, Cindy," Cecily said, standing. She opened the door and let him in.

"Hi," he said, closing the door.

"Hi."

"We need to talk."

"Yes, we do," she said. "Sit down." They both sat on the couch.

"Cecily, this is hard for me because I care about you so much."

"I'll make it easier. I'm leaving town."

"What?"

"I'm going to Hawaii to stay with my sister. We can practice together."

"You sound like it's for good."

"I haven't decided yet."

"Why, Cecily? Why are you leaving?"

"Because I love Lillian and Wanda. I don't want to hurt them anymore than I already have. This thing with you could never work because I would always feel guilty. Lillian is my best friend, and I've done her wrong. I just hope she can find it in her heart to forgive me."

"I'm just as much to blame as you are."

"No, you're not. You don't understand the bond Lillian and I shared. We were like sisters. I should've been strong enough to resist my feelings for you, but I wasn't. And, I'm still not. That's why I *have* to leave," she explained as tears rolled down her face. "I will always love you, but I can't hurt Lillian and Wanda anymore. Wanda is my Goddaughter, and it kills me to think how our affair has hurt her."

"I do love you, Cecily, but I love Lillian, too, and I'm committed to her, *and* Wanda."

"I know," she replied, then kissed the palm of his hand. "Your compassion. That's what I fell in love with. Don't ever lose it." They stood, and he took her face in his hand and planted a soft kiss on her lips, then he walked out quickly.

****

Cecily knew it was her time to stand as all eyes fell on her, but her knees were weak, and she didn't know if she could do it. The man standing in the front gave her a nod with the most incredible smile, and she found the courage to stand. She cleared her throat then said very softly, "Hi, I'm Cecily."

"Hi, Cecily," the crowd responded.

Cecily took a deep breath then added, "I'm an addict."

****

"You said she was home?" Lillian asked Trudy, holding the telephone in her hands.

"Yes."

"I wonder why she didn't call me on my cell phone," Lillian said.

"She said she tried but you didn't answer."

"Oh, that's right. My battery died." Lillian remembered. "Huh, that's strange. She's not answering the phone."

"Where's Gracie?"

"She's off today," Lillian answered. "I wonder why Wanda's not answering the phone."

****

The telephone rang and rang and rang. There was a trail of Wanda's torn, bloody clothes lying on the floor in her room. Beside them laid Wanda's crumpled, nude, body, bruised and bloody, curled up on the floor, unconscious. Louis was nowhere to be found. The telephone continued to ring and ring and ring.

Part Three

Five Years Later

February

Chapter 22

"Will the defendant please rise," the Judge spoke. "In case #1367, the people verses Alton Carter for the murder of Louis Williams, Mr. Foreman, what say ye?"

"We, the jury finds the defendant, Alton Carter, guilty of murder in the first degree."

"Noooooooooo!!" a voice yelled above all the disturbance, capturing everyone's attention. The woman stepped forward and peeled off her dark sunglasses, and her big Jean Pereo hat to reveal a mane of silky, black curly hair which appeared to be unruly, but expressed beauty.

"Cecily!" Lillian muttered to herself.

"Alton did not kill that man. He couldn't have. He was with me when that man was murdered," she stated, and Alton received a venom stare from his lawyer as the courtroom burst into excitement.

"What's all this about, Alton?" his lawyer wanted to know, and he just dropped his head.

"Who are you, Ma'am?" the judge asked, wrapping for silence.

"I'm Dr. Cecily Allen."

"And what makes you think you can come into my courtroom with this outburst after the jury's verdict? If this is true, you should've come forth a long time ago."

"There were extenuating circumstances, Your Honor, if I may be heard."

"Mr. Carter's lawyer may appeal. I see no reason to delay these proceedings any further," the Judge said, and Alton's lawyer rose quickly.

"Your Honor, I beg the court to please set aside the verdict on the bases of this new evidence," she demanded.

"What *new* evidence?!" the Assistant District Attorney chuckled on his feet now. "We have a hysterical woman coming in at the last minute to save her lover, no doubt."

"Your Honor, you owe it to this man to at least hear this woman out!"

"Your Honor, you *owe* this man nothing. He has been tried and convicted for a murder. The only thing left to do now is to sentence him!"

"That's enough you two," the judge ordered. "I'm calling a thirty-minute recess to meet with both counselors, Mr. Carter, and Dr. Allen in my chambers. After which, I will decide if the verdict will be set aside or not. Court in recess." He rapped his gabble.

****

"Hi, Wanda," a tall teenage boy walked up to her saying.

Pushing her shoulder-length braids out her face, Wanda replied, "Hi, Juan." She continued to walk briskly in her blue jeans and sneakers, while carrying her books across the school campus.

"Would you like to see a movie tonight?" he asked towering over her, smiling big with his boyish good looks.

"I don't think so, Juan," she said as she heard a car horn blow. Wanda looked behind the wheel of a 1974 red Chevy convertible and spotted Angela.

"Whose car?!" Wanda exploded.

"Marc's!" Angela replied, smiling big behind her dark sunglasses, and spiked, mouse-downed purple hair.

"He let you drive his car by *yourself*?!" exploded Wanda again. "You don't have a driver's license!"

"He knows!" Angela said popping gun. "Get in!"

"Hi, Angela," Juan said shyly.

With a slight frown, Angela snarled, "Hi, Juan." Then with a sarcastic smirk she added, "Blowing up any more chemistry labs?"

Laughing he said, "Where did you hear that?"

"Wouldn't you like to know," Angela added as Wanda leaped into the car.

"Juan, I'll..." Wanda started, but Angela spun off before she could finish. "Slow down, fool!"

"Say, what're you doing with that nerd, Juan?" Angela asked, turning up the volume on the radio to the top of its mechanical strength.

"He won't leave me alone."

"Just tell him to fuck off!"

"I can't do that. He's so nice."

"Nice?! You don't need nice! You need excitement!" Angela continued. "Like my Marc!"

"Where're you going?"

"To pick up Marc."

"Where is he?"

"At work."

"In the warehouse?" Wanda asked, and Angela nodded. "I thought he said never to come to the warehouse?"

"He said not to come *in*!" Angela exploded in laughter. "He has a cranky boss. Maybe his boss needs to get laid or something!" She burst into laughter again as she sped around a curve on two wheels.

"Will you slow your ass down!" Wanda screamed.

"Ooooo, I'm gonna tell your mommy you cursed," Angela joked in a little girl's voice then laughed.

"She would do some cursing herself if she knew I was riding in a car with *you*!" Wanda said laughing also.

"Why?"

"Because you don't have a license, Fool!"

"Oh, that. A mere technicality," Angela replied, and they laughed again.

Growing serious, Wanda pondered, "I wonder how my dad made out in court today."

"He'll get off, Kid. After what that creep did to you, he deserved to die."

"But my dad didn't kill him."

"That's why he'll get off. Anyone can see your dad ain't no murderer," Angela said spinning around a curve, almost crashing into another car. The person in the car sounded his horn in anger. "Fuck you, Creep!" she yelled, practically standing up in the convertible, sticking up her middle finger to the man.

Pulling her friend down, Wanda yelled, "Sit your butt down before you get us both killed!"

"I've got to be there in two minutes when Marc get off work."

"You're going to get us killed!"

"Shut the fuck up! I know what I'm doing!" Angela yelled at Wanda.

"No, you don't!" Wanda retaliated, yelling also. "Now, you either slow this car down or stop and let me out of here!"

"All right! All right!" Angela gave in, slowing down and turning into a driveway. "We're here, Babe." She smiled.

"You're impossible," Wanda smiled also, shaking her head.

"I scared the hell out of you, didn't I?!" Angela asked laughing, and Wanda couldn't help but to laugh also. She didn't know why she hung with Angela. The girl was obviously a lunatic. But Angela was her best friend, and she was *fun* to be with.

"Let's go," Angela said jumping out the car.

"Go where?"

"To the moon," she sarcastically replied. "Inside, silly."

Following Angela reluctantly, Wanda said, "I thought Marc said no one was allowed inside."

"He has to know I'm here," Angela insisted, running up to the building in her blue sneakers and skin-tight, acid-washed blue jeans. Wanda took a deep breath and ran behind her friend, against her will, but she didn't want Angela to leave her. Something about this place gave her the creeps.

When the girls entered the warehouse, they heard a man's voice scream, "Please don't!"

"What the hell was that?" Angela whispered.

"Let's get out of here," Wanda suggested in a whisper also, but Angela proceeded towards the sound of the terrified voice anyway.

"Where the hell is my money, Antonio?" a gruff voice demanded, in an Italian, godfather-type sound.

"I'll get it back, Boss. I swear!" the weaken man's voice replied.

Angela and Wanda peeked from behind some large cartons and witnessed a scene that caught them totally off guard. A man was scraped to a chair with all sorts of gadgets attached to his body. They didn't know the nature of what was going on, but they did know, by the occasional screams heard from the man, that he was being tortured.

"My God!" Wanda whispered, covering her mouth with her hand.

"Marc," Angela said, looking at a young teenager standing among the other suits.

"Angela, let's get out of here," Wanda whispered again.

"Okay," Angela finally agreed, turning around and tripping over Wanda, who was standing right behind her.

"What was that?" one of the suits asked.

"I don't know, Boss," another suit responded.

"Check it out," the boss replied, and they witnessed the two suits pulling out guns.

"Run, Wanda!" Angela yelled. "Run!"

****

"Dr. Allen, why didn't you come forward sooner?" Alton's pretty, pecan tanned attorney asked Cecily, who was now sitting on the witness stand.

"I live in Hawaii. I didn't know Alton was accused of murder."

"You mean, after you and Mr. Carter had an affair, you didn't hear from him again?"

"We didn't have an affair, Miss Burns," Cecily insisted. "We just talked. That's all."

"Yes. You talked," the lady lawyer replied sarcastically with a chuckle. "So how did you find out about the trial?"

"Oddly enough, a tourist," she replied. "A woman came into my clinic to renew her medication, and she had a newspaper with her. She was having a conversation with another patient about the trial, and I overheard them. I was mortified to learn that Alton was accused of murder. I've been trying to get here ever since. I just arrived here on the mainland, and I came straight here." She paused. "Alton didn't kill that man. He was with me that entire weekend."

"In Hawaii?"

"Yes. In Hawaii."

"Thank you, Doctor," the attorney replied then focused on the Assistant District Attorney. "Your witness, Counselor." He sat staring at Cecily with his calculating glaring eyes, with his chin propped on his fist.

Turning his attention to the judge, the Assistant District Attorney said, "Your Honor, this has been an interesting turn of events. I need time to prepare my cross examination. May I reserve my rights to cross examine this witness at a later date?"

"Very well. I agree that it is getting late," the judge said. "Court will recess now and resume at ten o'clock in the morning." He rapped his gabble.

Turning to Alton, his attorney said coldly, "We have to talk, Mr. Carter."

"I know," he replied weakly.

"My office. One hour!" she demanded then proceeded to walk off.

"It won't stick, Counselor," the six feet, two inches, good looking, brown-headed, brown-eyed, clean faced Assistant District Attorney said to the lady lawyer.

"Wanna bet?" she sarcastically replied, as he walked with her.

"Correct me if I'm wrong, but I smell a love triangle," he smiled with his perfect teeth. "And, that spells *cover-up*."

"You never give up, do you, Counselor?" she chuckled as she walked away from him.

****

"You went to Hawaii to see Cecily?" Lillian asked Alton.

"Yes," Alton said weakly.

"I can't believe you. After all we've been through, you would go to *Hawaii* to see her!"

Reaching out to her he said, "Baby, please don't..."

Pulling away from his touch, she snapped, "Don't touch me, you son-of-a-bitch!" She slapped his face hard then quickly walked away.

"Ouch!" Cecily said walking to Alton.

"You didn't have to come."

"And let you spend the rest of your life in jail for something you didn't do?"

"That wouldn't have happened. My lawyer would've appealed."

"On what grounds? Her client's stupidity?" she smirked sarcastically, and then took a deep breath. "You should've called me, Alton."

"I didn't want to lose you *and* my family."

"Is that important now that you're on trial for your life?"

"Yes. It's *always* important."

Taking a deep breath, Cecily replied, "I don't think you'll lose your family, Alton. I have faith in you."

"Is that why you lied, Dr. Allen? Because you have faith in me?" he smiled. "You know we did *more* than just *talk* that weekend."

"Yes, but *they* don't, and there's no reason to rehash all those memories and get everybody all upset and hurt again. The point is, you *were* in Hawaii."

"Yes, I was," he smiled, remembering their time together. "You look great."

"Thank-you."

"But, there's something different about you. I can't put my finger on it."

"That's right, you *can't*, so get your mind out the gutter," she laughed, and he burst into laughter also.

****

Alton walked into an office labeled, *Tandra Burns, Attorney at Law*. Sitting at her desk, the lady looked over her wire framed eyeglasses and said, "Sit, please." He planted himself in a chair in front of her desk. She finished what she was writing, took off her eyeglasses, and leered at Alton. "Let's hear it."

Taking a deep breath, he said, "I did go to Hawaii to see Cecily?"

"The *same* weekend Louis was murdered?" she asked, and he nodded. "Damn it, Alton!" she exploded, jumping up. "You had the perfect alibi and didn't use it!" She raged on. "I can't believe you would rather go to jail than to come forth about a lover! The D. A. is going to make mincemeat out of her testimony now! This looks like a woman desperately trying to save her lover, and believe me, he *will* use it!"

"You don't have to yell, Tandra. I hear you just fine!"

Apparently, you haven't heard *anything* I've said from the very beginning. I can't defend you if you're not honest with me! The jury found you *guilty* because you withheld vital information! Why in heaven's name didn't you tell me about the doctor?"

"Because at one time Cecily and I were lovers. It's common knowledge. We even had a child together, but she was killed in a car wreck with Lillian. Cecily and Lillian had been friends for years until Lillian found out about Cecily and me. We didn't plan to fall in love. It just happened," he explained so sincerely that even Tandra felt sorry for him.

She took a deep breath then asked calmly now, "You didn't answer my question. Why didn't you tell me?"

"Because I was afraid of losing my family."

"Why?! You said you love another woman anyway?"

"I love my wife, too."

"So, you're in love with *both* of them?"

"I don't know. I guess so," he said then walked to the window.

"You're not only in love with two women, but you want to *have* both of them as well? Is that correct?"

"No, not really."

"Then what, Alton?! I don't understand why you'd rather go to jail then to tell your wife the truth about you and this other woman!"

"There's nothing to tell. I went to Hawaii that Friday evening to ask Cecily to come home. Since I wasn't carrying divorce papers, she wanted nothing to do with me. I stayed all day Saturday and flew back that Sunday morning."

"And Louis was killed that Saturday night when you were with Cecily," she stated matter-of-factly.

Nodding slowly, Alton replied, "Lillian warned me that if I ever got involved with Cecily again, she would take Wanda and leave me. I hurt Lillian very badly with Cecily. I just couldn't risk losing my family."

"But you would go all the way to Hawaii to see another woman."

"It was stupid, I know. I just didn't want to lose Cecily either."

Taking a deep breath, Tandra said, "I guess you wouldn't still have your airline receipt for your ticket?" He shook his head.

"I didn't want Lillian to find it," he replied. "She thought I was on a business trip in Chicago."

"Come on," she said heading for the door.

"Where're we going?"

"Maybe someone will remember you."

Following her out the door, he asked, "From where?"

"The airport."

"That was almost *five* years ago!"

"Airlines keep records," she replied. "Come on, lover boy, we've got a plane to catch!"

****

Tandra dragged into her huge, elaborate penthouse apartment, kicking off her shoes. She dropped her briefcase and walked into the rose and white decorated bedroom slowly. "You're keeping late hours, Counselor," a soft, masculine, familiar voice said from the bed in the dark room.

"Worried?" she teased smiling as she sat on the edge of the bed. The man turned around and turned on the bedside lamp to reveal the face of her courtroom adversary, Charles Lewis, the Assistant District Attorney himself. They kissed sweetly. "How long have you been here?"

"Long enough to know that lawyers don't confer with clients until two o'clock in the morning," he sarcastically replied as she pulled her blouse off.

"You're jealous?" she chuckled, removing her skirt.

"Alton Carter has quite a reputation with the ladies. You should know that," he replied. "*Should* I be jealous?"

"What do you think?" she smiled cuddling up in his strong, muscular arms and ending with a long passionate kiss. "I love you, Charles, and *only* you. I don't give a damn about Alton's reputation. And besides, I don't think he's a big playboy like everyone says." They kissed again as he unfastened her bra.

"Well, I know of one lady in particular that's the apple of his eye, and she's *not* his wife."

"Well, that has *nothing* to do with *me*."

"Then why won't you marry me," he asked between kisses, and she stopped abruptly.

"You sure can change a subject, Counselor," she said getting up.

"And you sure can *evade* an *answer*, Counselor."

"Let's just concentrate on this trial, and when it's over, we'll talk about it, just like we said. Okay?"

"The trial *is* over."

"Oh no!" she chuckled. "Not by a long shot!"

"Face it, Tandra. You lost. Your client is guilty as hell. His so-called alibi is nothing more than a ploy by a desperate woman to save her man."

"That's where you're wrong," she said walking towards the bathroom.

"But you're entitled to your own opinion, Counselor. After all, how could you justify sending an innocent man to prison, if you didn't *believe* in what you're saying? Anyway, no shop talk tonight, okay?"

"Your client is guilty," he stated seriously.

"Drop it, Counselor. I'm going to take a shower."

"What makes this man so damn appealing to women?"

"He's not appealing to *me*. I just happen to think he's innocent, and I don't want to discuss it any further," she stated then smiled as she let her pink, lace panties drop to the floor. "Would you like to join me, or do you want to continue this no-win conversation about Alton Carter?"

Licking his bottom lip slowly, with a seductive smile, he said, "Alton who?" Then he leaped out of bed.

****

Wanda jumped up in bed in a cold sweat. She sat up to catch her breath and drifted into the past:

*   *"Well, Girls, have you decided to join my little family?" the Italian Boss asked, standing over Wanda and Angela with his short, stalky body as they sat in two chairs.*

"Yes, we have," Angela's trembling voice replied, as she and Wanda focused on the chair where that poor man was just tortured to death, then hauled away like a piece of garbage.

"Marc, you have nice friends," the man said smiling, patting Marc on the shoulder. "My family calls me 'Papa Roma', girls. Welcome aboard." He motioned for the girls to stand, and they did. He planted a kiss on each of their forehead. "We need some young blood in the family." Then he turned his attention to Marc. "Bring the girls to our meeting tomorrow." Marc nodded as Papa Roma's focus fell on the other two men. "Let's go. I'm <u>dead</u> tired." Papa Roma sarcastically said with a yawn then started out the door followed by the two men.   *

Wanda came back to the present, with tears rolling down her face. She buried her head in her pillow and cried hysterically, trying not to wake her parents. She didn't know what she was going to do. She had never been involved in anything like *this* before. What in heaven's name was she going to do?!

Chapter 23

"Dr. Allen," Charles Lewis said walking to Cecily, who sat on the witness stand. "Tell the court your relationship with the defendant, Alton Carter."

"Alton and I are friends."

"Come on, Doctor! You're *more* than just friends, aren't you?!"

"Objection, Your Honor," Tandra jumped up yelling. "The question has been asked and answered."

"Objection sustained," the judge ruled.

"Dr. Allen, are you and the defendant lovers?" Charles went on.

"Objection, Your Honor," Tandra was on her feet again.

"Your Honor, the emotional ties this witness has with the defendant has a direct bearing on her credibility to testify on his behave!" Charles retaliated.

"I'll allow it, but watch it, Mr. Lewis," the Judge spoke. "The witness may answer the question."

"No. We are not lovers," Cecily answered.

"Then why did he allegedly go to Hawaii to see you?" Charles wanted to know.

"Objection, Your Honor!" Tandra interrupted. "The reason Mr. Carter went to Hawaii to see Dr. Allen has no bearing on this case. The fact is that he *did* go!"

"*If* Mr. Carter went to Hawaii, Your Honor," Charles stood his ground with the persistent defense attorney. "It has not been established as to *when* he went!"

"Asking *why* is much different from asking *when*, Mr. Lewis!" Tandra sarcastically defended her position.

The judge rapped to silence the two feuding attorneys, then he demanded, "Counselors, approach the bench at *once!*" Tandra and Charles stepped briskly to the judge's bench. "I will not have such outbursts in my courtroom! If this happens again, I will hold you *both* in contempt."

"Please accept my apologies, Your Honor," Tandra spoke softly.

"And, Mine, too, Your Honor," added Charles.

"Accepted," the judge calmed down. "Just make sure it doesn't happen again!" He took a deep breath. "Now, Mr. Lewis, where is this line of questioning leading?"

"Your Honor, I plan to show that this lady is not a credible witness because of her relationship with the defendant."

"She is a respected doctor, Your Honor," chuckled Tandra.

"That doesn't make her credible when it comes to love, Counselor," Charles said, and his eyes locked with Tandra's.

Blowing hard, the judge said, "Miss Burns?"

"My objection still stands, Your Honor," she spoke softly.

"So noted, but I'll allow it for now, and my warning still stands, Mr. Lewis."

"Yes, Sir, Your Honor," Charles said, as he and Tandra strolled back to their places.

"Miss Burns' objections are so noted, but I will overrule them at this time," the judge said for the record. "You may continue, Mr. Lewis."

"Thank you, Your Honor," Charles acknowledged then walked back to Cecily. "Dr. Allen, why did Mr. Carter allegedly come to Hawaii to see you?"

"To talk to me."

"About what?"

"He wanted me to come back here."

"Why?"

"He said he..." she paused as she looked in Alton's sad face, then she added softly, "he said he missed me."

"Correct me if I'm wrong, Doctor, but isn't Mr. Carter a married man?" he sarcastically asked.

"Yes."

"Was he planning to leave his wife?"

"No."

"I see," he said then walked to his desk. "Dr. Allen, about ten years ago, didn't you give birth to a child fathered by Mr. Carter?"

"Yes."

"And you still say you're not having an affair with him, Dr. Allen?"

"Yes, I do, Mr. Lewis," Cecily insisted, growing angry. "What Alton and I once had is over. It has been for a long time now."

"But he went all the way to Hawaii to tell you he *missed you*," he sarcastically replied. "It doesn't sound *over* to me, Doctor."

"Objections...!" Tandra started.

"Withdrawn!" Charles cut her off, and then he focused back on Cecily. "So, Dr. Allen, do you expect the court to believe that you now have no feelings for a man who *fathered* your child?"

"I didn't say that," she stood her ground. "I said we aren't lovers anymore."

"But you still care for him?"

"Of course, I care for him."

"What about love? Do you still *love* Alton Carter, Dr. Allen?"

Standing, Tandra said with a slight chuckle, "Your Honor, pardon my ignorance, if it's just *me*, but I fail to see where this is going. The witness has stated over and over her relationship with the defendant. The counselor is beating a dead horse to *death*."

"Mr. Lewis, I have to agree with Miss Burns," the judge spoke. "I can't see where this is going either."

"I'll get right to the point, Your Honor," Charles spoke.

"All right," the judge said. "A little bit more."

"Thank you, Your Honor," Charles said then focused back on Cecily. "Dr. Allen, isn't it true that you used to be Dr. Wade?"

"Yes."

"What happened that your name changed?"

"I was divorced and went back to my maiden name."

"Dr. Allen, isn't it true that you gave up your husband, your best friend, and your home, all for the love of this man, Alton Carter?!"

"No!" Cecily yelled.

"Think back, Dr. Allen. When you became pregnant with Mr. Carter's child, you didn't communicate with Lillian Carter, your *best* friend since childhood, anymore. And your affair with Mr. Carter didn't stop!" He raged now. "You lost your husband, your best friend, everything! You would do *anything* for this man, wouldn't you, Dr. Allen?! *Anything*! Even perjure yourself to help him, by furnishing an alibi that just doesn't exist!"

"Objection, Your Honor!" Tandra yelled on her feet, now.

"No further questions," Charles yelled as he sat, leaving the courtroom in a state of turmoil as the judge rapped for silence.

****

Cecily walked out the courtroom and came face to face with Alton and Lillian. She took a deep breath then proceeded over to them slowly. "Hi, Guys," she spoke sweetly.

A reluctant Lillian replied softly, "Cecily."

"Hi, Cecily," Alton added.

"Lillian, I know I'm the last person in the world that you want to see, but can we please have some time to talk?"

"What could we possibly have to talk about, Cecily?" Lillian wanted to know. "Compare notes on how you can steal my husband, *Girlfriend*?"

"Lillian, please," Alton said trying to contain his wife's temper.

"Please *what*?!" she retaliated.

"Lillian, I know what you must think, but I swear to you, what Alton and I once had is *over*.   All I want to do now is see if there's any way we can mend *our* friendship," Cecily explained, but Lillian didn't reply. "Please, Lillian. All I'm asking for is a few minutes of your time."

"All right," Lillian finally agreed.

Smiling, Cecily replied, "Great! How about dinner tonight at The Diamond?" Lillian nodded. "Seven o'clock?"

"Fine."

****

Tandra stormed into her penthouse where Charles sat on the couch, eating a sandwich in a terry towel bathrobe and wet hair. "Cute, Counselor!" she snapped.

"Thank you," he sarcastically replied. "I'm glad you enjoyed it."

"What the hell was that in court today?!"

"Don't you know, Counselor? It's called getting the truth out to win a case. *You* should know that. You do it so well." She blew hard. "Let's face it, Baby. In the courtroom, you're just another pretty face, and I'll try to bury you."

"Do you honestly think he's guilty?" she wanted to know. "Or are you just looking for a win, at *any* cost?"

"I think he's guilty as hell, and twelve men and women agreed with me" he insisted. "Don't get me wrong. I think the slime ball deserved what he got, after what he did to that child, but your client didn't have the right to make that call. It should've been handled in a court of law."

"Save the politics, Counselor. Is winning all you care about? I can't *believe* you could *possibly* think he's guilty after the doctor's testimony."

"The *doctor* is a woman in *love*, trying to save her man....at *any* cost!"

"I don't think so."

"Well, that's why you're paid the big bucks, because you *think* so well," he chuckled. "When you agreed to take this case, we both agreed we wouldn't bring our work home, to keep it from interfering with our relationship. I would like to keep it that way."

"Just one more question. Why do you *hate* him so much?"

"Why do you *like* him so much?"

"He's my client. That's *all*!"

"Are you sure?"

"What kind of question is that?! Of course, I'm sure," she defended. "You never answered."

"I'm not crazy about your client because he uses women for his own personal little playthings."

"Says *who*?"

"Says *you*! You said he was with another woman when this murder took place. The doctor said he was trying to convince her how much he missed her, and at the same time, he had a beautiful, intelligent wife and a sweet little victimized girl at home. Why did he need the doctor?'

"So, you're afraid he'll use his charm on *me*?" she asked smiling shyly.

"*Will* he?" he wasn't smiling.

"You can't be *serious*?" she blurted out. "You *are*, aren't you?"

"Tandra, some guys make it a game to see how many women they can reel in, and I think your client is one of those men."

"And I'm supposed to be so gullible, I'll fall for him."

"I didn't say that. If I thought you were *that* gullible, I wouldn't love you so much."

"Well, that's good to know."

"Enough about your client," he said, pulling her in his arms. "I hope he knows you're taken."   He kissed her lips hard, and she kissed back. He swooped her up in his arms and started towards the bedroom when the telephone rang. "We're off duty!" Charles yelled at the telephone, and Tandra laughed, jumping down. "Where're you going?"

"It might be important, Baby."

He took her hand and placed it under his robe, and said, "So is this."

"I'll keep it brief," she said, picking up the telephone anyway. "Hello?" She paused, as Charles proceeded on into the bedroom.

"Hurry," he called back, and she smiled.

"What?!" Tandra exploded into the receiver. "Are you there now?" She paused. "Stay there. I'm on the way!" She hung up and grabbed her keys, as Charles entered.

"Where're you going?" he demanded.

"I won't be long, Darling," she said, then planted a quick kiss on his lips, and was out the door before he could protest any further.

****

"Marc, what is this meeting about?" Wanda asked, sitting in the back seat of the car, while Marc drove, and Angela sat on the passenger's side.

"I guess Papa Roma wants to introduce you to everyone and tell you your duties," Marc explained.

"Like selling drugs?" Angela asked carefully.

"You don't *sell* them. They're already sold. All you do is deliver and pick up."

"I don't want to *deliver* or *pick up* drugs!" exploded Wanda.

"Angela, if you'd only listened to me when I said not to come in the warehouse. Now, I not only have myself to worry about, but you two as well."

"How did you get involved with these people, Marc?" Angela wanted to know.

"I was tricked into it, trying to do a favor for a friend. I don't know how to get out. Anyone who has ever tried, ended up dead."

"Why don't you go to the police?" Wanda asked.

"Yeah! Right!" Marc sarcastically answered with a chuckle. "Papa Roma has people *everywhere. Even* the police."

"I'm scared to death, Marc," shared Angela.

"And, if you aren't careful, that's exactly what you'll be...*dead*!"

"You're scaring me, Marc," added Wanda

"You should be scare. Papa Roma is not a man to mess with. You saw what happened at the warehouse," Marc explained, turning his car in the driveway of a big luxurious mansion, with armed guards, dogs, elaborate security systems and more, to inspect every visitor before they entered into the gate. "Remember, be careful. These people are dangerous. This is no *damn* movie. They have *real* guns that shoot *real* bullets!"

****

"Would you ladies like a cocktail while you wait on your dinner?" the waiter asked.

"White wine," replied Cecily.

"Ginger ale," Lillian added.

"Very well," the waiter said taking their menus and walking away.

"So, Cecily, are you here to stay?"

"Oh, no. I have a wonderful life in Hawaii. My sister and I have formed a wonderful partnership. Sometimes we stay up until two or three o'clock in the morning just talking. We try to learn everything about one another. After all, we lost thirty-five years. It's great having a sister. And every night while I'm here, before I go to bed, I have to call her. If I don't, she will call me."

"It sounds like you two are very close."

"We are, and I love it."

"What about Rocky? How is he?"

"Oh, Lil, I thought you knew. Rocky died about a year ago."

"No, I didn't know. I'm sorry," Lillian said. "What about that man that came here with you? Are you still seeing him?"

"Craig," Cecily said smiling. "Yeah. He's terrific!"

"Any wedding plans?"

"No, not yet," Cecily said still smiling, basking in enthusiasm. "You look great, Lil."

"Compared to *what*, Cecily?" Lillian sarcastically asked. "You never once came to the hospital to see me. Instead, you were too busy trying to *steal* my husband!"

Taking a deep breath, Cecily said, "I deserved that, Lil." The waiter returned with their drinks.

"Would you care for anything else?" he asked, and they both shook their heads. "Your dinner should be ready soon?"

"Thank you," Lillian replied.

"I'll check back in a few minutes," he said then left.

"Lil, during the time when you were in the hospital, I was sick also," Cecily said, and she drew Lillian's attention now. "That's right. I was addicted to amphetamines and barbiturates. Then it progressed to heroin." Lillian's eyes really widen. "That's right. I'm an addict. Me. Cecily Allen. All my life I've heard how beautiful Cecily is, how smart Cecily is, and how brave Cecily is. But, it's funny; I didn't feel like *that* Cecily. As a matter of fact, I felt just the opposite. My self-esteem was very low. I didn't think anyone could love me. I was in bad shape."

"I'm sorry, Cecily, but it's hard for me to feel sorry for you," Lillian said. "You had *everything*. You even grew up with a *nanny*, for heaven's sake."

"Yes, I had *material* things, but that was nothing compared to what I really needed," Cecily said wiping a tear from her face. "I grew up a black girl in a white home. I never felt loved. I never felt like I belonged. The one thing I really wanted and needed was *love*, and my grandparents couldn't give that to me. They could never get over the fact that their precious little white girl fucked a black man and gave birth to a black child. The only people that I really felt loved me, for *me,* when I was growing up were you, Trudy, and Cotton. You all accepted me for *me*, unconditionally. And, I'm still hurting for the way that I hurt you, Lil. Sure, I fell in love with Alton long before I knew he was your husband, but when I found out, he should've been off limits to me, and he wasn't, and I'll always be sorry for that." Her tears were falling heavily now, and she had to pause to regain her composure. Lillian, too, had to wipe her own tears. "Going to Hawaii was the best thing I ever did. It gave me a chance to share some time with a sister I never knew I had and to go into treatment for my addictions of drugs *and* Alton." As Cecily paused, a shadow covered them. They both looked up at the same time into the face of a thin, 110 pound, beautiful Trudy, dressed in a white Karen Monet jumpsuit, accessorize by gold and diamonds, with her honey blonde hair pulled back in a single cornrow braid extending to the middle of her back.

"Trudy?" Cecily asked slowly, not believing her eyes. "You're *beautiful.*" Cecily jumped to her feet, and they embraced lovingly, then Trudy sat.

"You're beautiful, yourself, Girlfriend," Trudy said smiling big as the waiter returned with Cecily's and Lillian's dinner.

"What may I get for you, Miss Miles?" he asked.

"Your freshest garden salad, Pierre," Trudy responded. "And a glass of unsweetened iced tea."

"Yes, Ma'am," he said then walked off again.

"I'm sorry I'm late. I had to reshoot a commercial," explained Trudy.

"A *commercial*?!" Cecily exploded. "So, you're modeling again."

"Little stuff. Nothing major. I'm too old for anything major," Trudy said bursting into laughter.

"That's still good, Girl. Good luck," Cecily laughed.

"Cecily, I appreciate what you said," Lillian said. "I pray that we can finally be friends again. I want that."

"Lil, for as long as I live, you never have to worry about me going after your husband again. That's a promise. I love you too much to let that happen again."

"Thank you, Cecily," Lillian smiled. "You know, I can't put my finger on it, but there's something different about you, and I like it."

"I see it, too," added Trudy.

"Alton said the same thing. I guess it's called growing up," smiled Cecily.

"Thank God for change," Lillian said.

Growing serious, Cecily said, "We've come a long way, Ladies. Five years ago, I was a drug addict, Lillian was an alcoholic, and Trudy was..."

"I know what I was thankyouverymuch," Trudy interrupted laughing.

"But here we are," Cecily continued. "Here we are, still able to share a dinner and a laugh. I thank God for that."

"Amen," Lillian added.

"Amen," echoed Trudy, and they toasted their glasses together.

****

"We have two new ones added to our little family," Papa Roma spoke to a room full of men in dark suits and a few women. "Stand up. Girls." Angela and Wanda stood slowly, and the room filled with applause. An extremely handsome, Italian man, with wavy, jet-black hair, wearing a Martinez dark blue suit walked in and whispered something to Papa Roma.

"That's Tim. Papa Roma's oldest son," Marc whispered to Wanda and Angela.

"He looks like a lawyer instead of a mobster," Angela said.

"He *is* a lawyer," replied Marc. "And, a damn good one. He gets everyone out of legal hassles, if possible. If not, well...you know."

"Timmy has just informed me that the D. A. insists on going ahead with Rick's trial. He wants my boy to rot in that stinking jail. Well, that's one D. A. that must be taken care of," Papa Roma spoke. "We'll deal with you, Mr. Charles Lewis."

Chapter 24

"Your Honor, in light of new evidence I would like to call another witness to the stand," Tandra spoke, emphasizing her shapely form in a deep green Paula Hinson suit with pearl buttons, and her hair swept up in a bun.

"Objection, Your Honor!" Charles was on his feet also, in a dazzling, Jos A Banks double-breasted, navy-blue suit. "We know nothing about another witness!"

"Your Honor, may we approach the bench, please?" she suggested, and the Judge nodded, waving them forward. "Your Honor, this is not a new witness. He was on the list of character witnesses for my client, but he became ill. Now he is able and ready to testify."

"Who is this witness?!" Charles wanted to know.

"Mr. Harry Williams, the deceased's father."

"And he *wants* to testify *on behalf of* your client?" the judge asked.

"Yes, Your Honor, he does."

"Your Honor, this is a desperate attempt by the defense to grasp at straws in order to free her client," Charles chuckled.

"Your Honor, you allowed Mr. Lewis some leave way in the examination of Dr. Allen, my client's alibi. Please, give to me the same opportunity now," defended Tandra.

The judge took a deep breath then concluded, "I'll allow it."

"Thank you, Your Honor."

"Your Honor, I would like it put on the record that I strongly object to this witness," added Charles.

"So noted," the judge said. "However, Miss Burns, let me remind you that I don't like my time wasted, so if this is a delay tactic, don't even *think* about it!"

"Yes, Sir, Your Honor," Tandra said, as she and Charles proceeded back to their seats.

"Objection is overruled, but so noted," the judge addressed the court. "You may call your witness, Miss Burns."

Standing again, Tandra said, "Your Honor, the defense calls Mr. Harry Williams to the stand." A short, gray, red-faced man entered and took the witness stand. He was sworn in, and then Tandra approached him. "Mr. Williams, please tell the court the relationship between the defendant and yourself."

"Mr. Carter is my boss," the man spoke softly.

"How long have you been employed with Carter Construction Company?"

"Thirty-five years," the man said again, clearing his nervous throat. "Before Mr. Carter took over the business, I worked for his father."

"Mr. Williams, tell the court your relationship with the deceased."

"Louis was my son," he said, and the judge had to rap several times to regain order in the courtroom.

"Mr. Williams, how did your son get the job as handyman in the Carter's household?"

"Louis was always a lazy boy. He didn't even finish high school. But, one thing about that boy, he was always good with his hands. He could fix *anything*. So, one day Mr. Carter said he had to call a plumber for a clogged drain. I told him he could save some money by letting Louis do it, so he did, and Louis became the handyman around their house," Mr. Williams explained with a slight smile, remembering Louis.

"Mr. Williams, do you believe Alton Carter killed your son?"

"Objection, Your Honor!" Charles stood. "Speculation!"

"It's *his* opinion," Tandra stressed.

"Objection overruled," the Judge stated.

"Mr. Williams, do you think Alton Carter killed your son?"

"No, Ma'am, I don't," the man replied, and the courtroom burst into loads of conversation again. The judge had to rap several times again to silence it.

When the courtroom was quiet again, Tandra continued, "Why don't you believe Mr. Carter killed Louis, Mr. Williams?"

"Well, I took Mr. Carter to the airport to go to Hawaii that Friday night before Louis was killed," he said, and the courtroom filled with noise again.

"Go on, Mr. Williams," Tandra said.

"I helped Mr. Carter pack his things from the office before he left, and his gun was locked up in his desk, like it always was. I saw it that night, and he didn't take it with him, and *everybody* knows Mr. Carter has a gun in his office at work."

"Mr. Williams, why didn't you come forward earlier?"

"I was out of town on an extended leave of absence for my health, and to be with my daughter. She is sick. I don't read too good, so I don't read the newspaper."

"When did your daughter become ill?"

"The night Louis died."

"And, when did *you* get sick?"

"The same night."

"So, you didn't know Mr. Carter needed your help all those years?"

"No. Like I said, I don't read too good."

"What about the television?"

"My daughter ain't allowed to have a TV, so I learned to do without one," he said, and Tandra noticed a strange look on the man's face when he talked about his daughter, so she felt he was just weak from his illness.

"Thank you, Mr. Williams. No further questions," she announced, and then sat.

Charles stood slowly then asked, "Mr. Williams, you think a lot of Mr. Carter, don't you?"

"Yeah. He's good people."

"Didn't you think it was a little strange that Mr. Carter would leave town, and his wife wasn't there to bid him a farewell?"

"It ain't my job to question the boss. I just thought she was busy or something."

"You like your boss very much, don't you, Mr. Williams?"

"Yeah. I do. As I said, he's good people."

"What about your job? Do you love it as well?"

"Yeah."

"And you wouldn't want to jeopardize your job? Would you Mr. Williams?"

"I don't understand."

"Well, let me make it perfectly clear to you," Charles said then ended in a yell. "You would do *anything* to protect your boss, even *lie* for him? Wouldn't you, Mr. Williams?"

"Objection, Your Honor!" Tandra yelled amongst the noise.

"I withdraw the question!" Charles said walking to his seat. "No further questions!"

"Your Honor, may I redirect, please?" Tandra wanted to know.

"Very well."

Tandra walked slowly to the witness stand, looking at the nervous man wring his sweaty hands. It came to her. The feeling that she had about this man was now clear to her, and she had to gamble. What the hell? Her client was going to jail anyway if she was wrong. Then she took a deep breath, exhaled slowly and played her hunch, "*You* killed your son, didn't you, Mr. Williams?"

****

Wanda walked in the park with a manila envelope. She zoomed in on a man sitting on a bench, reading a newspaper. She strolled slowly to him and sat beside him. She was so nervous; her palms were sweating like crazy.

"The grass is lovely this time of year, isn't it?" she said cautiously, barely able to get it out. He folded the newspaper and looked at her.

"Lovely indeed," he replied with a smile as he stood, handing her a small white envelope, and she handed him the manila envelope. She took a deep breath as he walked away. She dropped the white envelope in her purse quickly then stood to leave.

"Hold it right there, Little Missy," a deep gruff voice demanded, and Wanda turned around and looked right in the face of a tall, red-faced policeman. "You're under arrest!" he added, slapping handcuffs on the frightened child's tiny wrists.

****

Angela walked into a dimly lit, oily, dirty mechanical garage, looked on a piece of paper, then yelled, "Big Blue!" There was no answer, and she was about to leave when a big, burly, greasy, dirty man stepped from behind a car, with a wrench in his hand.

"Who're you?!" he barked.

"Papa Roma sent me."

"You kinda young, ain't cha?" he said undressing her with his eyes.

"You Big Blue?" she asked with trembling lips. She didn't like the way this big man was looking at her. He had to be at least seven feet tall and three hundred pounds.

"Yeah. I'm Blue. What cha got for me?" She extended the manila envelope to him. He took it, opened it, and stuck a dirty finger in it. White powder was attached to his finger, and he licked it off. "Ummm, that's good stuff. This all he sent?!" She nodded slowly. Then he went to a drawer and pulled out a white envelope and extended it to her. As she reached for it, he grabbed her tiny hand and pulled her close to him. "Wanna have some fun, little girl?" he said smiling, exposing dirty, cigarette stained, rotten teeth.

"I have to get back," she blurted out, trying to stay calm, but felt her heart pounding so fast, she thought it would explode.

"Not just yet!" he insisted, ripping off her blouse with one stroke as she screamed to the top of her young lungs.

****

"What're you talking about?" chuckled Mr. Williams.

"How old is your daughter, Mr. Williams?" Tandra asked, as Charles sat on the edge of his seat. He wanted to object, but he was curious as to what she was up to.

"Lisa is eight," he smiled thinking of her.

"You said earlier that she was sick? Correct?" she asked, and he nodded. "Is she in a hospital?"

"Yeah."

"Mr. Williams, isn't it true that Little Lisa is in a *Mental* Hospital?" she asked, and he nodded again. Tandra noticed a tear rolling down his face, and her heart went out to this man, but she had to continue, because she had a job to do.

"Mr. Williams, please answer yes or no so it can be recorded," the judge advised.

"Yes, Sir," Mr. Williams said weakly.

"How long has she been there?"

"Five years."

"The same year that your son was shot with Mr. Carter's gun?"

"Yes."

"Mr. Williams, what did you do after you dropped Mr. Carter off at the airport?"

"I went to a bar for a little while, then I went home."

"Was anyone there?" she asked, but he didn't answer, so she repeated. "Was anyone there when you got home, Mr. Williams?"

"Yeah."

"Who?"

"Louis and Lisa."

"What were they doing?"

The man began jumping in his seat as he yelled, "Louis, get your filthy hands off your sister!" In his mind, he was seeing that terrible night as if he was living it all over again. The courtroom became so silent, you could have heard a pin drop. "Louis, you animal!" the man raged on. Mr. Williams drifted into the past as he relived that horrible night, right in the courtroom:

*   *Mr. Williams ran to his little girl, who laid on the floor with bloodstained*

clothes while her little blue dress lay thrown over her waist and her panties rested on one of her ankles. The child was motionless, as Louis pulled his pants up and ran out. The distraught man cradled the little girl in his arms, crying hysterically.

After a long moment, Mr. Williams caught a hold of his emotions and cleaned the child up as he talked to her, telling her she would be all right, and to be strong, but he received no response from the child. The little girl was as if she was already dead. The only life left in her frail little body was her shallow breathing. Mr. Williams saw that she wasn't going to snap out of it, so he called the ambulance. He told them that she was attacked, but he didn't tell them by whom. He said he didn't see her attacker.

After the ambulance took her away, Mr. Williams started packing up some things to take to the hospital when he focused on a family picture with himself, Louis, smiling Lisa, and their late mother. He thought of his precious wife and the promise he'd made to her on her dying bed; that he would always take care of their little baby girl. Then he placed the little baby girl in her arms. She gave the baby one final kiss, then she closed her eyes forever. Tears burned his eyes as he torn down the picture, ripped Louis's face out of it and tore it to shreds. Mr. Williams was like a madman now as he stormed out of the house. He knew Alton was out of town, so he went to Alton's office and retrieved his gun, then he left.

When he returned Mr. Williams found Louis in the back yard of the house chopping wood. He pointed the gun at his son's back and opened fire. *

Mr. Williams came back to the present weeping hysterically. "That animal destroyed my baby," he cried. "She was so full of life. So smart. So beautiful. So happy. She was the splitting image of her mother. She was so full of life. He took it all from her." He fought to regain composure, then he focused on Alton and squeezed out, "Mr. Carter, please forgive me. I didn't think they'd send a rich man like you to jail. Please forgive me." Alton returned a smile to the hysterical man, with a slight nod of the head.

As the man continued to babble on incoherently, Tandra wiped away a tear from her own cheek, looked at the judge, and said, "Your Honor, in light of this new evidence I move that all charges against my client be dropped."

"The people concur, Your Honor," added Charles.

"Very well," the judge spoke. "All charges against Mr. Alton Carter for the murder of Louis Williams is hereby dismissed. Mr. Carter, the court apologizes for any hardship this may have caused you." Alton nodded. "Court adjourned," the Judge announced then signaled for a policeman to take Mr. Williams.

Alton grabbed Tandra and hugged her tight as Lillian, Cecily, and Trudy ran to them. "You did it!" Alton blurted out in laughter. "Thank-you so much!"

"You've welcomed," Tandra said laughing also.

"Is this nightmare *really* over?" Alton asked.

"It *really* is," Tandra smiled, as Alton grabbed Lillian in a big hug.

"It's over, Baby," he said then planted a kiss on her lips.

"Yes, it is," Lillian smiled also.

"Congratulations, Alton," Trudy said receiving her hug from him.

"Thank you, Trudy.

"Ditto," added Cecily receiving her embrace from him.

"Thank you so much," he whispered in her ear.

"Tandra, we've got to celebrate. Come to dinner tonight." Lillian announced.

"That would be nice," Tandra accepted. "Thank you for asking."

"Bring a date," Lillian added. "Sevenish."

"I'll be there," Tandra called as Alton, Cecily, Lillian, and Trudy exited, while Charles walked over to her.

"Congratulations, Counselor," he said smiling.

"Thankyouverymuch."

"How did you know the old man killed his son?"

"Well I remember Alton telling me that the girl was in a mental institution, and she wasn't born that way. He said something had happened to the girl that her father would never talk about," Tandra explained as they walked out the courtroom. "I checked and found that Louis was killed on the same day the girl was institutionalized. Well, knowing what kind of person Louis was, and the look on Mr. Williams' face when I asked him about his daughter, confirmed my suspicions, so I took the gamble. I had nothing to lose. Alton was going to jail anyway, after you tore down Dr. Allen's testimony."

"My father said it couldn't be done," he said smiling.

"What?"

"To find beauty and brains together," he said then laughed. "When are you going to meet my folks anyway. You keep putting it off."

"Well, first thing's first. I would like for you to accompany me to dinner tonight at the Carters, for our victory celebration."

Chuckling he said, "I don't think I'll be a welcomed guest in that household."

"They're intelligent people. They know you were only doing your job and nothing personal."

"Well, I think it's a little personal when you try to put someone in prison for the rest of his life," he still laughed. "Especially for something he didn't do."

"Think about it, will you, Baby?"

"All right, I'll think about it, but I can't promise," he said, as they reached their cars. "Damn, I left my keys. I'll see you later, Baby."

"I can wait for you."

"No. I don't want you waiting in this garage all alone. I'll see you later."

"All right," she said, and they kissed quickly. "I'll sit in the car and lock my doors." He smiled at her, as he left.

Charles ran back to the empty, dark courtroom, and to the table where he sat. He picked up his keys, turned to leave, but froze when he witness a silhouette of a man, dressed in a trench coat and hat, standing at the door. "Mr. Lewis?" the man called.

"Yes."

"I have a message for you," the man said then paused. "From a disgruntled family."   Suddenly Charles heard what sounded like firecrackers to him, but soon realized they were bullets, and he felt a burning sensation in his chest just before he dropped to the floor and rested in his own blood, unconscious.

****

"Please, don't take me to jail!" Wanda pleaded in the back seat of the police car as the man who arrested her, drove in the front seat. "I wasn't doing anything wrong!" Tears rolled down her worried face heavily.

"Selling drugs is a crime, young lady," he snapped.

"I wasn't selling drugs!" she insisted, wiping her tears in frustration.

"That's what it looked like to me."

"You can't do this," she squeezed out. "You have no proof."

"I don't need proof," he smiled. "Look, Little Lady, why don't you cooperate?"

"I'm trying to."

"I'll be honest with you, Kid. I'm not after you. I know you're working for someone. Who is he?" the policeman said matter-of-factly.

"I don't know what you're talking about," her trembling lips replied, remembering the warning Papa Roma had given to Angela and her about accidents could happen to their families if they told anyone.

"You know damn well what I'm talking about. I know you're working for someone. Who is he?" he demanded.

Remembering Marc's warning also that Papa Roma has policemen on his payroll, Wanda stood her ground, and squeezed out weakly, "I'm not working for anyone. I wasn't selling drugs."

"Have it your way, Kid," he said then hit the accelerator harder, and Wanda's heart dropped as she dropped her head in despair, allowing the tears to flow uncontrollably.

****

Angela laid on the floor, naked, bruised, experiencing pain she had never experienced before in her whole life. She could only move her head. She glanced around and spotted the big brut pulling up his pants. She lay on the floor, motionless, in excruciating pain. She couldn't believe what had just happened. The man had treated her like garbage, as he thrust himself in her over and over again, forcing her legs open above her head with his strong hands. Then he came, and she wanted to die right then and there, but at least, he was finished, she *thought*. But the animal flipped her small, already bruised, body over quickly, like a sack of potatoes and sodomized her virgin rectum, and she prayed to God to take her right then and there, for she had never known pain like *that* before. She felt as if he were ripping her insides out with every painful thrust, and she couldn't do anything to stop him. The more she screamed, the more he seemed to enjoy it, so she just suffered in silence, and hoped that the torture would soon be over. When she finally felt him tremble, she knew he was having his second orgasm, and she begged God to be merciful, and stop this inhumane treatment of her body, and finally God heard her. She must have passed out briefly, because the next thing she felt was her clothes falling on her back, and hearing his gruff voice say, "That was nice, Baby. We'll try it again soon!" Then he burst into laughter and walked out, leaving her there, lying on the cold, dirty, hard floor, in immense, unbearable pain.

Angela tried to get up, but she was too weak to move. She fell back to the floor, crying hysterically for the first time. She was sure that the maniac had damaged her for life. He showed no mercy, as he rammed it in her like some common whore on the streets. She hated this man like she'd never hated anyone before in her whole life. And, if she does nothing else in her entire life, she would get the bastard! He would never get away with treating her like that! With God as her witness, the animal would pay for what he had done to her!

****

The courtroom was in a state of turmoil as doctors rushed in to attend the wounded Assistant District Attorney. Cecily rushed back into the courtroom also and witnessed a hysterical Tandra screaming wildly, trying to get to Charles as the EMS Staff tried to keep her away. Cecily grabbed Tandra and pulled her in her arms to comfort her. "Who could've done just a thing?" Tandra cried.

"Shhh," Cecily said cradling the weeping attorney in her arms.

"He's *dead*," Tandra cried. "Oh, my God, he's *dead*!"

"No!" insisted Cecily. "He isn't dead." Tandra jumped towards Charles' blood-soiled body, being carried out on a stretcher and took his hand, as she walked alongside the moving stretcher.

"Charles, I love you," she squeezed out softly as flashbulbs exploded in her face, while the reporters asked question after question, all of which went unnoticed by Tandra. The only thought that clogged her mind was that of her wounded lover.

"I'm sorry, Miss. You can't go in the ambulance," a doctor said to Tandra.

"I'm his fiancée," she replied weakly.

"It's all right, Jerry," another man said. "We don't have time to argue." Tandra and Cecily both hopped into the ambulance, and it sped away, blasting sirens.

****

It seemed like hours to Tandra that Charles was in the emergency room, as she and Cecily waited in the waiting room to hear something about his condition. As Cecily cradled the weeping woman in her arms, she couldn't help but to wonder whom this young, intelligent lawyer really was. She seemed so familiar to Cecily. She couldn't have been one of Spencer's girls. She's too young. Suddenly the two women heard a strong, masculine voice say, "I'm Judge Lewis. Where the hell is my son?!"

Tandra jumped to her feet, wiping her tears, and headed towards the voice. Cecily followed her. "Judge and Mrs. Lewis," Tandra spoke softly, trying to hold her composure. "I'm Tandra Burns."

"Are you with the D.A.'s office?" the man asked behind his silky gray hair and expensive dark blue suit.

"No, Sir. I..."

"Do you know anything about our son?" the lady spoke in her soft, soprano voice, dazzling in a sky-blue silk dress, and her salt-and-pepper hair cut short on her head.

"No, Ma'am. He's still in surgery."

"Here comes a doctor," Cecily added, and the group ran to the approaching doctor.

"I'm Judge Lewis. How is my son, Doctor?"

"Hi, Judge Lewis. I'm Dr. Curry. We managed to get two bullets out. But, there's a third one that's hard to reach," the doctor spoke then sighed deeply. "I must be honest with you. The bullet appears to be dangerously close to the spine. We won't know the extent of the damage until we go in."

"Then, do it," the father insisted.

"There are risks," Dr. Curry spoke again. "There's a chance that he could be paralyzed."

"Oh, my God!" it was the mother's turn, and her husband pulled her in his arms.

"Charles may not walk again?" Tandra said as her breath ran out, and

Cecily threw her arm around the young woman to hold her up.

"Do what you have to do, Doctor," Judge Lewis insisted again. "His life is the most important thing right now."

"I'll get the papers ready for your signature," Dr. Curry replied then walked away.

"Charles, I feel faint," Mrs. Lewis said weakly.

"I'll take you somewhere to rest, Dear," Judge Lewis responded as he held his wife up, and they walked out slowly.

"Charles may not walk again," Tandra said in a trancelike state. "Oh, God, what will that do to him?" Cecily helped her to a seat and sat beside her.

"You love him very much, don't you?"

"More than anything in this whole world," she said as tears rolled down her face again.

"You should've told his parents."

"I just couldn't. Not now, anyway, but I will," Tandra said then looked in Cecily's face. "You've been so kind. Thank you." As Cecily sat eye to eye with this sad young lady a shock of recognition hit her like a ton of bricks. Cecily knew why this woman looked so familiar to her. But that can't be. No. *Never*!

****

"Get out, Kid!"

"What?"

"You heard me! Get out!"

Wanda sat staring at the policeman, as he held the car door open for her to get out, in the same park that he had arrested her. "I'm free to *go*?" she asked cautiously with widen eyes.

"Get out!" he said again, and she obeyed. He removed the handcuffs, leaped back in the car and drove off. Wanda was so relieved and so happy, she dropped to the ground and cried like a newborn baby.

****

"Papa Roma, Sergeant Bundy's here," a lady said through an intercom in Papa Roma's office.

"Send him in," the stout man said, getting up. He walked to the door then jerked it open quickly. "Did she talk?"

"Not a word," the policeman, who had just let Wanda out his car, said as he entered Papa Roma's office. "I must've driven her twenty miles, and the little lady didn't say a word."

"Good," Papa Roma said smiling big. "Real good!" He walked back to his desk. "I *had* to know if I could trust my little new canaries. Keep your ears opened, Luke, and let me know if either of my little songbirds start singing."

"Will do, Boss."

"Cause, if they do, I'll have to end their singing career..." Papa Roma said smiling big. *"permanently*!"

Chapter 25

"Hi, Lillian," Cecily said on her cell phone, standing by the vending machines in the hospital. "Is Alton there?"

"Yes. What's up?"

"It's Tandra Burns, his lawyer. She needs a friend right now."

"What's going on, Cecily?"

"Charles Lewis has been shot."

"Yes. We heard about it on the television," Lillian said. "What does that have to do with Tandra?"

"They're lovers."

"What?!" Lillian exploded. "Are you *serious*?!"

"Very."

"Alton!" Lillian called. "Pick up the phone. It's Cecily."

"Yes," he said into the telephone receiver in the kitchen. "What's up, Cecily?"

"Alton, did you know Tandra and Charles Lewis were lovers?" Lillian blurted out.

"No," he said. "He was shot today, wasn't he?"

"Yes," answered Cecily. "Tandra's a wreck. I've done all I can, but she doesn't know me. She needs a friend right now."

"We'll be right there, Cecily," Alton said hanging up.

****

Cecily walked back to Tandra, who was lying on the couch in the waiting room lounge, asleep. Cecily stood at the door, staring at the cute, ebony woman. "No. She can't be," Cecily said to herself, as she drifted into the past:

*   *Cecily and Nicole sat shelling beans. "This is a first for me," Cecily said laughing. "I'm a city girl."*

"It's not so bad to be a country girl," Nicole said laughing also.

"Cotton took me to a farm once. A very long time ago. She was from the south."

"How was it?"

"I enjoyed it, until Spencer showed up."

"I thought you liked Spencer when Cotton was alive."

"I did. I just didn't like the way Cotton would change when he came around," Cecily said. "That's one man I really didn't understand, Nicole. He let me think he killed Cotton all those years, and I hated him for it."

"Maybe he wanted to spare you the pain of Cotton's suicide."

"Spencer never wanted to spare pain on anybody in his whole life," chuckled Cecily. "He wanted me to be afraid of him, so I would be too scared to leave him!" She paused. "It's more to it than that."

"So, what was Spencer doing on the farm?"

"Who knows," Cecily sarcastically replied. "Cotton told me one time that she and Spencer were once lovers. I always felt it was something

special between those two, but Cotton never talked about it. Like a bond of some sort. I used to think it was because she was afraid of him, but I don't think she was." She paused. "I guess whatever it was, it was buried with the two of them." *

"Cecily," Tandra said waking up, bringing Cecily back to the present.

Walking to her, Cecily said, "I'm here. Feeling better?"

"Yes," Tandra said yawning. "What time is it?"

"Nine thirty."

"In the *morning*?!"

"Yes."

"I can't believe I slept that long!"

"I have a confession to make. I slipped a sedative in your coffee. You needed to rest."

"Thanks, Cecily," she said standing and stretching. "I don't know what I would've done without you. You've been great to me. It's as if we've been knowing each other all our lives."

"Yes, it is."

"I wonder what's taking so long."

"These things take time, Tandra."

"I..." Tandra stopped suddenly when she saw Dr. Curry and rushed to him. "How is he, Doctor?"

"He's in recovery," Dr. Curry said. "The surgery went well, but we won't know his status until he wakes up."

"May I see him?' was Tandra's question.

"I'll let you know when he's in a room," the doctor said, then patted her shoulder. "Go home and get some rest. It'll be quite a while before he's ready for visitors."

"I'll wait," she said, and the doctor nodded with a smile then walked away.

"Sit down, Tandra," suggested Cecily, and she obeyed. "Why don't you go home and get some rest?"

"I want to be here when he wakes up."

"That could be quite a while."

"I know but I still want to wait."

"Do you have family here, Tandra?"

"No. My family is in Ohio."

"So, how did you get *all* the way out here in California?"

"I received a scholarship from UCLA."

"I'm impressed," Cecily said smiling. "Do you have family in New York?"

"New York?!" exploded Tandra. "I don't think so. Why?"

"You remind me of someone there."

"You know, it's funny you should mention New York. I was born there."

"Yeah?"

"I was adopted, and my family moved to Chicago."

"I'm from New York. Do you know who your biological parents are? I might know them."

"I doubt it," she chuckled.

"Why?"

"About a year ago I found out who my parents were. She was a hooker and he was her pimp. His named was Carl Spencer."

"*Spencer* is your father?!"

"Yes. Did you know him?"

"Yes, I did."

"It's a small world," she said. "Was he a nice person?"

"We'll talk about it someday."

"I'll like that."

"Maybe that's why you look so familiar," Cecily said. "What was your mother's name?"

"Well, she was hard to find."

"Why?"

"They're both dead now."

"I see."

"No, I don't think you do," she smiled. "Let me explain." She paused. "He was easy to find because everyone called him Spencer, but my mother was hard to find, because her name was Christina Baker, but everyone who knew her called her Cotton."

****

"Did she fight much?"

"No. I had that little filly before she knew what hit her," Big Blue smiled to Papa Roma as he told his story.

"Good."

"When will I get another chance at that little mama?" Big Blue grinned wide, with his yellow-stained, bucked teeth.

"Soon, my man. *Very* soon," Papa Roma replied. "I want that little lady ready to make me some *real* money."

"Oh, she'll be *ready*, Boss," Big Blue smiled. "You can count on that!"

"Yes, Sir," Papa Roma said thinking aloud. "The clients will flip over that little young, hot blonde. She's going to make me a bundle." He and Big Blue caught each other's eyes and simultaneously burst into laughter.

****

"*Cotton*?" Cecily exploded as her breath ran out. "You're Cotton's daughter. Of course. You're the splitting image of her, but I would've never guessed."

"Did you know her?"

"Yes, I knew her *very* well," Cecily smiled. "Everything I am today; I owe it to Cotton."

"Tell me about her," Tandra said but stopped when she saw the doctor, Alton, and Lillian headed her way, and she jumped to her feet.

"You may see him now. He's in room 111," the doctor announced.

"How is he?" Tandra wanted to know.

"He's stable, but as I said before, we won't know anything until he wakes up."

"Thank you, Doctor," she said, and he nodded then left.

"Tandra, I'm so sorry," Alton spoke, pulling her in his arms.

"Thank you."

"If there's anything we can do, please don't hesitate to ask," added Lillian.

"You're very kind," she replied. "I'm going to see Charles now. I'll keep you posted." She looked at Cecily. "Thank you for everything." They touched cheeks. "We'll talk later." Cecily nodded, then Tandra hurried away.

"She's a nice girl," Alton said. "I had no idea she and Lewis were lovers. The way they battled it out in court, who would've thought?"

"Cecily, it was nice of you to stay with her," Lillian observed. "After all, you don't really know Tandra."

"I know her better than you think." Cecily responded.

"Excuse me," was Lillian's response.

"She's Cotton's daughter," answered Cecily.

"What?!" Alton exploded.

"And *Spencer's*," added Cecily.

****

Tandra sat beside Charles' bed, holding his hand, as he lay, unconscious, with several tubes extending from his body to various machines. "Darling, I'm trying to be strong for you," she sobbed. "It's very hard." His parents walked in the room, unnoticed by Tandra. "I love you so very much. Please, get well soon. I can't go on without you. I need you." She burst into tears, dropping her head on his bed as Mr. and Mrs. Lewis' eyes locked momentarily. Then, Mrs. Lewis walked over to the bed, and Tandra held up to face the woman.

"You're the woman in Charles' life?" Mrs. Lewis asked, and Tandra nodded slowly. "He never told us about you."

"I know. That was *my* decision. Not *his*."

"Why?" Mrs. Lewis wanted to know, and Tandra couldn't answer, so Mrs. Lewis speculated, "Because you're *black*?"

"That's part of it," she answered, sniffing.

"If my son loves you, you must be a very special lady," she said, then smiled sweetly. Mrs. Lewis held out her hand to Tandra, and Tandra stood, then the two women embraced lovingly.

****

"I know how you feel, Angela," Wanda said as the two girls cried, sitting on Wanda's bed.

"He was so big!" Angela sobbed. "It was awful! He was an animal!"

"Remembering her own crisis with violence, Wanda replied very weakly, "I know."

"What're we going to do?" Angela cried. "We can't let that man do this to us! I have a feeling everything that happened to us yesterday, Papa Roma is responsible!"

"I know that's right," Wanda agreed. "But, what can we do? If we tell anyone, we're putting their life in danger also."

"Let's see what Marc thinks."

"I think we should leave Marc out of this, Angela. We don't know how loyal he is to Papa Roma."

"But I trust Marc."

"Do you trust him with your *life*?" Wanda demanded. "Cause, if you're wrong about him, it is your *life* you're gambling on, and *mine*!"

Chapter 26

Isaac's eyes stretched as the news reporter announced, "AIDS has an incubation period of ten to twenty years. Anyone could be in danger." Isaac could see Maurice's face after he had gone down on him, and he closed his eyes momentarily. Then he sat up in bed, wiped his sweat with a handkerchief and coughed. The announcer continued, "Some symptoms are cold sweats, dry coughs, and stomach pains." Isaac's face turned as white as a sheep as Trudy entered with a bowl of hot soup.

"How're you doing, Sweetheart?" she asked, sitting on the bed, placing the soup on the nightstand.

"I'm not hungry, Baby," he said weakly.

"You need to eat something, Sweetie. You have to keep up your strength," she said planting a kiss on his lips. She sat back and pulled him in her arms as her attention focused on the television set. "It's a good thing I found out about Maurice! Those are the ones who carry that disease, you know."

"I know," he said then asked cautiously, "Where is Maurice now?"

"In hell!" she spat. "He died two years ago." Upon hearing *that* news Isaac strangled on his own saliva, coughing violently. "Are you all right, Darling?" Trudy asked, patting him on the back. Then she pulled him in her arms and cradled him like a baby as his cough quieted. "I can't tell you how relieved I was to be tested negative." She planted a kiss on his forehead.

"You got tested?"

"Of course, I did. I *lived* with Maurice!"

"I love you, Trudy," he said weakly. "I never thought I could love anyone else after Cecily but thank God I was wrong."

"I love you, too, Baby. I thought I wouldn't love anyone else after Carl. Who knew that we would end up together?" she said then kissed his forehead again. "Life is funny."

"Yes, it is," he said, then thinking to himself, *I would die if I gave Trudy anything like AIDS. God, please be merciful. I have finally found a woman who loves me the way that I love her. Please, don't punish her for loving me. I can accept my own destiny, but please, God, not <u>her</u>. She doesn't deserve this. Please*! She began rocking Isaac in her arms and humming a soft melody to him, and he wiped a tear from his eye before she noticed.

****

"Tandra?" Charles squeezed out, and Tandra jumped to her feet, as his parents ran behind her to his bed.

"I'm here, Darling," she said squeezing his hand, laughing and crying at the same time. "Oh, it's so good to hear you, baby."

"I love you, Counselor," he squeezed out again.

"And, I love you," she smiled then planted a kiss on his lips.

"How'd you feel, Son?" his father asked.

"Dad?"

"Yes, Son." His father answered.

"Where am I?" Charles wanted to know.

"You're in the hospital," his mother added, taking his other hand.

"Hospital?" Charles was confused.

"I'll get the doctor," Tandra said exiting.

"Do you remember anything, Son?" his father wanted to know.

"About what?" Charles asked then frowned from pain.

"You had an accident," Mr. Lewis replied.

"I don't remember," Charles said as the doctor entered.

"How do you feel, Mr. Lewis," Dr. Curry asked Charles.

"Thirsty."

Smiling, the doctor asked, "What do you remember about the accident?"

"I don't remember an accident," Charles spoke more coherently.

Looking at the worried trio, the doctor said, "I need to examine him. Would you mind stepping out for a moment, please? It won't take long."

"Sure," Mrs. Lewis said as a nurse entered.

"We'll be right outside the door, Honey," Tandra said, and Charles nodded as they walked out.

Two men were standing outside of Charles' door when Mr. and Mrs. Lewis and Tandra walked out. "Hello," the short, curly-headed man said. "I'm Detective Hinson. I'm sorry about Mr. Lewis."

"Thank you," Mr. Lewis replied.

"We will be investigating this case," the other man spoke. "We will do everything in our power to make sure the perpetrator is brought to justice."

"I'm sorry. I didn't catch your name," Tandra announced.

"I'm sorry, Ma'am. My apologies," the tall man spoke. "I'm Sergeant Bundy. Luke Bundy."

****

"Have a seat, Isaac."

"Thank-you, Cecily," Isaac said as he and Cecily sat on the couch in her hotel suite.

"Would you like a drink?" she asked, and he shook his head. "What's wrong, Isaac?"

Blowing hard, he said, "Cecily, I think I'm in trouble."

"What kind of trouble?"

Standing, he walked to the window, and Cecily followed him. "This is very hard for me," he finally said.

"Isaac, take your time and tell me what's wrong? I've never seen you like this."

He turned to face her. "Do you remember that night, a long time ago, when I came to see you to ask you to give me another chance, but Alton was there?"

"Yes, but..."

"Let me finish, please."

"Go on."

"I was devastated that night, Cecily. I felt lower than I've ever felt in my life. I went to a bar and got drunk," he said then paused. "The next thing I knew a man was..."

"What, Isaac?"

"He had his mouth..."

"He was having oral sex with you?" she continued, and he nodded. "Oh, my God."

"Well, that sobered me up very quickly, but I lost it, and beat the shit out of him then left."

"Isaac, I'm so sorry. I feel like this is all my fault."

"No! It isn't. I was weak. I loved you so much. I didn't want to lose you. But that night made me realized that I had better get a hold of my feelings and accept the fact that you just didn't want me anymore," he explained, and tears rolled down Cecily's face. "It took going into therapy to get over you. But, I'm fine now, and I've managed to do something I thought I could never do, and that's fall in love again." He paused. "I love Trudy so very much, Cecily. I *really* do."

"Hey, you don't have to convince me. I believe you. Trudy's a great girl," she smiled. "And, I know Trudy feels the same way about you. I couldn't be happier for both of you. So, what's the problem? You seem to be doing fine."

"The man that took me to that hotel was..." he paused. "I'm having symptoms of...AIDS!"

"*What?*" her breath momentarily deserted her body.

"That's right. I need to be tested. Will you...?"

"Oh, my God, Isaac. I'm so sorry," she said, pulling him in her arms.

"I'm so sorry." Her heart went out to Isaac, but suddenly, Cecily's mind revealed a thought so frightening; she could barely squeeze out, *"Trudy!"*

****

"I told you. I don't remember!" insisted Charles, lying in the hospital bed.

"So, you don't remember who shot you?" Detective Hinson asked. "You were shot at very close range."

"The last thing I remember is going back for my keys."

"Mr. Lewis, do you know of anyone who would want to kill you?" Sergeant Bundy added.

Chuckling, Charles said, "I'm the Assistant D.A., Sergeant. I put people in *jail*. Take a number."

"He really needs his rest, Gentlemen," the doctor spoke. "If he starts to remember I'll call you right away."

"Thanks, Doc," Detective Hinson said.

"We'll be right outside this door, in case you need us," added Sergeant Bundy, then the two men exited.

"I sent your parents and Miss Burns home to freshen up," the doctor said. "But they'll be right back, so rest before they get here."

"Hey, Doc, lets me ask you something," Charles said softly. "Why in the hell can't I feel my legs?"

****

"You have something for me, Little Lady?" Big Blue barked as he smiled at Angela, walking towards her in the dimly lit garage.

"Yes," she said extending an envelope towards him. As he handed her the money, he grabbed her hand exactly as he had done before, and threw her down on the cold concrete floor, ripping off her clothes. Then he began zipping down his pants, looking down at her smiling.   Angela did not fight because his hits were painful, but she knew he would never do this to her again. Suddenly he dropped down hard on her, and tried to pry her legs open, as she scrounged the floor for her purse. Soon Angela seized a switch blade from her purse, and yelled,   "You'll never hurt me again, you Bastard!"

****

A shaking Wanda strolled slowly into a dirty, filthy, garage, calling, "Is anyone here?" There was no answer. Suddenly she heard steps approaching, and her heart pounded so hard she thought the intruder would hear it. Nerves got the best of her, and she began to run. The steps quickened behind her, and she ran faster and faster, until, suddenly, she dropped behind a big bail. She wondered if Papa Roma had sent someone to kill her, or rape her, like he had done to Angela. Her heart pounded faster and faster. She had never been so scared in her entire life. She was going to *die*! But, why?

She hadn't told anyone anything about Papa Roma! "Oh, God, please let this be a bad dream and wake me up," she prayed in a whisper, as she closed her eyes so tight, they hurt. Suddenly from the rear, a hand landed on her shoulder, and she exploded into a roar of wild, hysterical screams.

****

"Cecily."

"Hi, Tandra, may I come in?"

Stepping aside, Tandra said, "This certainly is a surprise. How did you know I was home?"

"I called the hospital, and they said you were gone. I hope you don't mind my dropping by?"

"Of course not," Tandra said. "Please, have a seat." They both sat. "I came home to freshen up."

"Is Charles awake?"

"Yes."

"What about his paralyses?"

"He didn't say anything about it, so he must be all right."

"That's great," Cecily smiled, then grew serious. "Tandra, I guess you're wondering why I'm here. I just had to talk to you. I won't take up a lot of time. I know you want to get back to the hospital."

"Yes, I do."

"I just wanted to drop by for a few minutes and talk to you about your parents."

"Yes, I've been wanting to talk to you, also."

"Tandra, your mother was a wonderful lady. When I was fifteen, I ran away from home.   Cotton rescued me from the streets and brought me to live with her."

"What?" Tandra couldn't believe it.

"That's right. Your mother raised me. She meant the world to me. We became very close, and I truly loved her like a mother. Spencer was her pimp, and she kept me away from him while she was living, but when she died, I got involved with Spencer anyway, and pretty soon, he had me on the streets as well. I loathed that man. I thought he had killed Cotton, but I was wrong. I didn't know the truth until Spencer's death. He deliberately hid the truth from me all that time."

"You were a...?"

"That's right."

"But, you're a *doctor*. How?!"

"*Cotton* is how. She had provided for my education before she died. When Cotton died, I was getting ready to graduate from college and had just been excepted to medical school," She paused to wipe her tears. "I lived with Spencer for three years. He took care of me. I was his lady. Then one day he forced me to go on the streets. I didn't understand why at the time because I thought he loved me. When I finished medical school, I booked and never looked back, until one day Spencer showed up in my office and forced me to supply drugs for him, or he would let my past out of the bag.

Lillian, Trudy, and I devised a plan to stop Spencer, but the plan backfired. Trudy fell in love with him, and Spencer ended up dead."

"Oh, this is all too complicated for me to comprehend right now."

"I know it is. It's a lot to absorb all at once," Cecily continued. "But the bottom line is that you had a *wonderful* mother. I never knew what the bond was between Cotton and Spencer, until I met you, but I knew there *was* a bond. Spencer was an okay type of guy, too, but I didn't know it until after he was dead. Talk to your adopted parents. I'll be willing to bet you, that if Cotton knew where you were, she did things for you, even if they were anonymous. She was a wonderful woman." Cecily reached in her pocket and pulled out two pictures; one of Cotton and one of Spencer and handed them to Tandra. Tears flowed down Tandra's face as she looked at the pictures. "I'm sure you can understand why she gave you up. She wanted more for you than what she could give you. She would be very proud of you, Tandra."

"If she was as wonderful as you say, I wish I could've known her...and *him*."

"Me, too," Cecily said. "How old are you, Tandra?"

"Twenty-five."

"Cotton gave birth to you just before I came. No wonder she took me in so quickly. I guess I was the daughter she gave away."

"You sound like you loved her very much."

"More than words could ever say, Tandra," Cecily replied with a far-away look in her eyes as she wiped her tears. "More than words could ever say."

****

"The bullet scraped your spine, Mr. Lewis," the doctor explained. "You will experience some paralyzes."

"For how long?" Charles wanted to know.

"It's hard to say what the extent of the damage is. You might have a speedy recovery with physical therapy," the doctor explained. "Or you might not recover from this for a long time. It's hard to say."

"Come straight with me, Doctor," Charles probed. "Am I paralyzed for life?"

"I can't tell you that for sure, Mr. Lewis."

"Is there a *possibility* that I'm paralyzed for life?"

It hit Charles like a steel plate when the doctor took a deep breath and answered, "Yes. That *is* a possibility."

****

"That's it?" Isaac asked Cecily as he rolled down his sleeve.

"That's it. Just a little blood is all it takes."

"When will I know?"

"In about four days."

"*That* long?!"

"Be patient, Isaac. You want the *right* results, don't you? It'll be all right."

"What're my chances?"

"I don't know, Sweetheart."

"Guess!"

"You didn't have anal sex?"

"*No!*"

"Oral sex isn't as great a risk as anal sex, unless there were lacerations in his mouth," Cecily explained. "Just don't freak out, Isaac. I'll call you as soon as I know."

"Thank you, Cecily," he said sadly, and she pulled him in her arms.

"Are you going to tell Trudy?"

Pulling away, he insisted, "No! And don't *you!*"

"Of course not, but how're you going to keep from having sex with your wife for four days without telling her *something*?"

"I'll think of something."

Taking a deep breath, Cecily said, "Let's just pray, Isaac. That's all we can do. For your sake and *Trudy's.*"

****

"What's wrong, Darling?" Tandra asked Charles. "You're so quiet. Are you in pain?"

"You *know*, don't you?"

"Know what, Sweetheart?"

"That I'm paralyzed."

"You are?!" she exploded.

"You didn't know?"

"The doctor said there might be a possibility, but you never said anything, so I didn't know for sure. Besides it's only temporary."

"It might be permanent."

"I don't think so."

"Tandra, you're living in denial. We have to consider the possibility that I may never walk again, for the *rest* of my life," he insisted. "Or worst, what if I can never make love to you again."

"Charles, you're overreacting," she chuckled. "Even if that were true, I don't love you because of *sex*. And besides, we *do* know other ways to make love."

"It's not a joke, Tandra."

"Who's joking?!"

Taking a deep breath, he said, I want you to leave... and never come back."

"What?" she chuckled again.

"You heard me, Tandra."

"You can't be serious."

"I'm *very* serious."

"What in the hell is wrong with you, Charles?"

"I'm *paralyzed*! Damn it!" he yelled so loud, she jumped, and then he calmed down. "I can't put you through this, taking care of an invalid for the rest of your life."

"Charles, I love you. I want to be here for you," she said as tears rolled down her face, and his mother entered, unnoticed. "Please, don't push me away."

"Tandra, I don't think you understand. I may never walk again."

"Then, we'll deal with it, *together*. Please, Baby, don't do this to *us*."

"Tandra, you don't understand. It would kill me to have you so close and not being able to hold you, to make love to you."

"How do you know you won't be able to make love to me, Charles?"

"Damn it, Tandra, I can't feel anything below my hips. How in the hell would I be able to make love to you?"

"Charles, making love isn't just *sex*. I thought our relationship was built on more than that."

"I love you too much to be a burden on you."

"Will you quit talking crazy!" she insisted. "What if it were *me*? Would you turn your back on *me*?" He didn't answer. "Would you?!"

"Of course not. I love you."

"Then don't ask me to turn my back on you. I love you."

"I can't handle it, Tandra. Please understand!" he insisted. "Get the hell out and don't ever come back!"

"You're so wrong, Charles," she said jumping up. "You're so unfair!" She ran out crying hysterically, and Mrs. Lewis ran after her.

"Tandra!" she called, and Tandra stopped, so Mrs. Lewis walked to her.

"I'm so sorry, Dear. I'll talk to him."

"There's no talking to him. He's so proud and so stubborn," she wept uncontrollably.

"Give him time. It's a shock for him."

"I'll give him *all* the time he needs. I love him. I can't stand the thought of being without him." She paused. "Please, excuse me, Mrs. Lewis." She ran off in wails of tears.

Mrs. Lewis walked back in Charles' hospital room. "Hello, Mother," Charles said weakly.

Mrs. Lewis charged to his bed, looked Charles squarely in the face, and demanded, "What in the hell was *that*, Charles?!"

****

"What the hell matter with you?" a voice said, and Wanda turned around and looked in Angela's face.

"Angela!" Wanda breathed a sigh of relief. "You almost scared me to death."

"Sorry."

"Why didn't you say something? Didn't you hear me call you?"

"I was trying to see who was following you."

"So, there *was* someone following me?"

"Yes," Angela replied blowing a bubble with her gum. "Who the hell are you meeting in this rat hole?"

"A man named Birdie."

"Well, Birdie's not flying in, so let's get the hell outta here."

"What're you doing here?"

"Oh, *me*? I just killed a man."

Chapter 27

"Go ahead, Lil. I'll wait for Wanda," Cecily said as Lillian pulled on a jacket to her double-breasted, navy-blue suit.

"Are you sure?"

"Sure, I haven't had time to talk to Wanda in a long time. I'm looking forward to it."

"Thanks, Cis. I don't know how Wanda left her keys here. It *had* to be when Gracie is off, and I have to go back to the office."

"It's okay. I'll stay and let her in," Cecily said watching Lillian pick up a leather briefcase. "Lillian, the *Executive*! How do you like working after all those years of leisure?"

"Girl, I love it," Lillian smiled heading for the door. "Lyle, my Boss, is fantastic!"

"I hear ya, Girl," Cecily smiled with her.

"If Alton calls you can tell him to bring his butt home so you can leave."

"I don't mind staying. Go!"

****

Isaac lay in bed looking at the television when Trudy entered with a pink negligee on and stood at the door. "Hiya, Big Boy," she cooed, and his body responded immediately, but he knew this couldn't happen tonight. It had been three days now since he took those tests, so Cecily should have the news for him tomorrow.

"Hi," he said, wondering how in the world could he stop her tonight. And how could he stop *himself.* She is so beautiful and so sexy; he would get excited just *thinking* about her during the day at work. Trudy strolled over to the bed in the most seductive sway he had ever seen in his life, and slid her smooth, soft body right on top of his lean, strong, masculine frame. *Oh, God, give me strength,* he prayed silently. How could he stand not touching his beautiful wife tonight? More importantly, what excuse could he make up tonight? He had managed to work late one night, pretended to be sick the next night, and played with Carl on the play station the following night until Trudy was asleep. But, what tonight? He didn't have a clue, as she slid her tongue down his throat. He knew she was not going to be denied tonight, especially after she sent Carl off to Tandra's, in hopes that they would come to know each other as siblings. She was bathing his chest with tender kisses, as she slid down his smooth body, unbuttoning his pajama shirt with gentle stokes of her soft, slender fingers.

"Trudy, Baby..." he started to protest, but she was not surrendering to any disturbances, as she eased her fingers around his lips, then into his mouth, and he toyed with them with his tongue. He knew he had to stop her, but how? Just as it was about to get out of control, his prayers were answered, and the ringing of the telephone seized her intentions.

"Damn!" she snapped. "Who in the hell could that be?" She paused. "Maybe they'll go away."

Then he had to appeal to her maternal instincts and said, "You don't think it's Carl, do you?"

"He's with Tandra."

"Maybe you better get it, Sweetheart. Anything can happen."

"I guess so," she said, then jumped up and snatched the cordless phone up. "Hello?"

"Mom," Carl whispered on the other end. "I'm ready to come home."

"What's wrong, Sweetheart?"

"I'll tell you about it when I get there. All she does is cries. Please come and get me *now*."

"All right, Darling. I'm on my way," she said then hung up. "It's Carl. He wants to come home."

"What's wrong?" Isaac asked sitting up.

"I don't know. He sounded upset. He said something about Tandra's crying."

Getting up with her he said, "I'll come with you," Then he said a silent, *Thank-you, God.*

****

Cecily lay asleep on the couch when Alton walked in. He stopped when he saw her and admired her beauty. The years had been kind to her. Suddenly Cecily jumped, and their eyes locked. "How long have you been standing there?" she asked sitting up feeling a little embarrassed.

"Not long," he smiled. "You look like an Angel sleeping."

"Now, Alton Carter, how do *you* know how an *Angel* looks?"

Laughing, he asked, "What're you doing here?"

"I was waiting for Wanda. She doesn't have her house key. I guess I fell asleep," she said yawning, then standing to stretch.

Looking at his watch, he asked, "Wanda isn't home yet?"

"Not yet."

"I'm afraid we're going to have to give that young lady a curfew," he said. "And, Lillian is out, also?"

"Yes. She had to go back to work."

"She's working quite late these days."

"Mr. Carter, do I hear a hint of jealousy in your voice?" Cecily joked, and he smiled with her. "Well, I guess I'll be on my way since you're here."

"I'm afraid I won't be here long. I came home to get some papers and to see if Lillian wanted to accompany me to a late dinner meeting."

"Yeah, I know about your *late* dinner meetings," she sarcastically said smiling.

"Dr. Wade…excuse me…*Allen*, whatever are you implying?" he chuckled. "I have been totally faithful to my wife for a *very* long time. And you know better than *anyone* when *that* was."

"Are you saying I was the last person who had *dealings* with you besides your wife?"

"I'm saying you're the *only* person I've ever cheated on Lillian with," he said, then lifted her head with his finger and grew very serious. "I never found another *Cecily*." Cecily had been around Alton long enough to know trouble when she saw it, so she quickly pulled away from his touch.

"I'm flattered."

"You *should* be," he said with a smile; then strolled to her and planted a feather kiss on her lips so softly she barely felt it. "You're still very beautiful, Dr. Allen."

"And, you're still so damn sexy and irresistible," she replied very throaty. Then she quickly cleared her throat to regain her composure and added very businesslike, "You have a meeting to attend, Mr. Carter."

"Thank you, Dr. Allen," he said backing away. He gave her one final glance and grabbed some papers off the mantle before making a quick exit. Cecily dropped in the chair and took a deep breath.

Soon Cecily came back to earth, stood, and walked into the spacious, black-tiled kitchen. She opened the refrigerator and poured a glass of milk when she heard the front door open. Then she remembered, she forgot to lock the door behind Alton, but she knew it had to be Wanda. Cecily closed the refrigerator, placed the glass of milk on the counter, and tiptoed behind the door. She was going to scare the life out of Wanda when the child opened the door. She giggled at the thought as she covered her mouth. Soon she heard Wanda call, "Mom!" Then she heard Wanda say, "I guess she isn't home." And she knew Angela had to be with Wanda. Disappointment sobered Cecily as she realized Wanda wasn't coming in the kitchen. She was about to enter the room with the girls when she heard Wanda say, "Angela, what're we going to do? I can't sell *drugs*!"

****

An ebony Haitian man sat on a king-sized, brass bed, in an extremely lavishly decorated bedroom, with silk blue sheets pulled up to his waist, exposing his jet-black, muscular bare chest, covered with thick, black, brassy hair. He watched the long silky legs of a woman as she entered from the bathroom, wearing only the skin she bore when she entered the world. He smiled as she slid onto his strong, masculine body, and they ended in a long passionate kiss. "You are so beautiful, Lillian," he said in his deep, accented voice, then he caressed her neck with his big, thick, full, soft, ebony lips. "I love you so much."

"I love you, too, Lyle," Lillian cooed as he covered her body with his.

Their lovemaking was so passionate, Lillian became lost in the ecstasy, and when it was over, he pulled her in his arms and said, "I really and truly love you, Lillian." He kissed her forehead, and she snuggled up even closer to him. It felt so good to be loved unconditionally, and then he added weakly, "I don't like this sneaking around."

"Well, what else can we do?" she chuckled.

"You can *marry* me."

"*What*?!" she exploded.

"You don't love Alton anymore, and I know you love me," he stated. "Divorce him and marry me."

****

Cecily had heard enough. What in God's name had Wanda and Angela gotten themselves into.   She swung the door open forcefully, and the girls froze in their tracks. "I've gotta go," Angela blurted out, zipping for the door, as Wanda jumped up to follow.

"Freeze!" demanded Cecily and the girls stopped abruptly. "Sit down, Girls." They reluctantly obeyed, and Cecily sat in a chair across from them. "What in the hell is going on here?"

"What'd you mean, Aunt Cecily?" Wanda chuckled.

"You know *exactly* what I mean."

"Aunt Cecily, please don't make us tell you. You will be in danger."

"I've been in danger before!" Cecily insisted. "*Talk!*"

"Papa Roma is making us work for him," Angela spoke.

"Papa Roma?!" Cecily's breath ran out. She had heard of this gangster.

"We saw them kill a man, and now we must work for him or *else*," It was Wanda's turn.

Cecily stood, shaking her head and walking to the window. Suddenly she turned around swiftly and said, "Let me get this straight. Are you telling me that you two girls are mixed up in *organized crime*?! The *mob*?!" They nodded slowly, and Cecily took a deep breath. "I don't believe it. Papa Roma is one of the most notorious mobsters in the west, and you are working for *him*?!" They nodded again. "You're *kids*! What in the hell are you *doing* for him?"

"Pick-ups and deliveries," Wanda said.

"*Drugs*?!" Cecily asked, and Wanda nodded.

"And he's trying to break me in to be a prostitute," added Angela with tears burning her eyes.

"What?!" Cecily couldn't believe her ears.

"He had Mr. Lewis, the D. A., shot," added Wanda.

"Oh my God!" Cecily exploded, thinking of Tandra.

"I almost killed a man," Angela said. "I thought he was dead when I stabbed him, but he wasn't. Papa Roma said he would take care of it." Tears rolled down Angela's face. "He *raped* me."

"You poor girls," Cecily said with tears in her own eyes now. "Don't worry. We won't let him get away with this. I promise you that. Papa Roma will be *stopped*!"

Chapter 28

Lillian walked into a restaurant and focused on Alton, waving to her, so she walked over to him, and he pulled out her chair, and then planted a kiss on her cheek. "Hi, Darling," he said smiling as she sat.

"Have you been waiting long?"

"Yes," he joked taking his own seat again. "But, as beautiful as you look, it was worth the wait."

Ignoring his compliment, she asked, "Did you order?"

"Just this martini. I was waiting for you," he replied, still admiring her beauty with a big smile plastered on his handsome face.

"What?" she chuckled, feeling a little uncomfortable.

"I can't get over how gorgeous you look."

Sighing deeply, she asked, "Who is *she*, Alton?"

"What?"

"Who is your latest bimbo? *Cecily* again?"

"No!" he snapped. "Do I need a reason to take an interest in my wife?"

"Oh, don't play the wounded with me, Alton Carter!" she insisted, trying to keep her voice at an even tone. "I know you! Remember?! It took me a long time, but I finally know the *real* you! You haven't asked me out to lunch in years, so why *now*?"

"Why *not* now?" he defended.

"If memory serves me right, every time you asked me out was because you were having an affair."

"Regardless of what you may think, Lillian. I *don't* fool around."

Sarcastically laughing, she retaliated, "Oh *no*?! What about the child you fathered by my so-called *best* friend?!"

"That was a long time ago," he said softly. "But you'll *never* put it in the *past*, will you?"

"You're so right, I won't!" she spat. "Oh, and what about the time when you were supposedly murdering Derrick Williams, but you were making house calls to the *good* doctor in *Hawaii*!" She took a deep breath to regain composure because her tone was rising, due to her anger, regardless of how she tried to restrain herself. "You're never hurt me again, Alton Carter. *Never*!" As she and Alton locked eyes, he knew that a few lunches and a lifetime of faithfulness would *never* make up for the hurt he had caused his wife, so where do they go from here?

"Lillian, hello."

Looking up in the man's smiling face, a smile then brightened Lillian's face from the sour one she had just moments ago shared with her husband, as she said, "Lyle, I thought you were eating *in* today."

"At the last-minute Mr. Peabody called to say he was leaving town, and we had to move our meeting up."

"Do you need *me*?"

"No. Enjoy your lunch. I'll handle it," he said then focused on Alton. "You must be Alton." He extended a hand. "It's good to finally meet you."

"Alton, this is Lyle Desir, my boss," Lillian spoke.

Shaking his hand, Alton replied, "Nice to meet you." The Waiter waved to Lyle as an elderly man entered.

"Mr. Peabody is here. Enjoy your lunch. I'll see you later at the office, Lillian. Alton, it was nice meeting you."

"Likewise," replied Alton. As the man walked away, Alton couldn't help but to notice the lasting smile on his wife's face. "Is *he* the reason I could never hurt you again, Lillian?"

****

"Are you sure?"

"*Very* sure," Cecily replied on the telephone.

"Would you have to do it again?"

"No. It's been a long time since the incident with Maurice, so there won't be any need to repeat the tests. It would've shown up by now. You are definitely *negative*. No HIV. No AIDS,"

"Oh, thank-you, God!" Isaac prayed and laughed at the same time. "And, thank you, Cecily."

"You're welcome," Cecily smiled. "I'm very happy for you, Isaac."

"Thanks, Baby," he said, not being able to stop smiling. "Talk to you later." When he hung up, he jumped up and down praising the Lord for his good health, as Trudy entered.

"What's going on?" she asked.

"Hi, Baby," he said grabbing her and kissing her hard. "Life is good."

Pulling away, she said, "Isaac, we need to talk."

"No, we don't," he replied, kicking the door closed with his foot. "Not anymore." He pulled her blouse off over her head and dropped it on the floor, as he bathed her face and neck with soft, wet kisses.

"I was afraid you didn't love me anymore," she cooed, surrendering herself to her husband.

"If you ever have *any* doubts about *anything* concerning me, *never*, *ever* have any doubts about my love for you."

"But you've been so distance lately. I thought..."

"I'm sorry, Baby, but that's over now," he said positioning her on the bed. "*Over!*"

"I love you so much."

"And I love you. Words can't express just how much," he said, as he took his wife tenderly, in his own way, like he had wanted to do for days now, then they melted into each other's arms, slipping into dreamland together. But before Isaac closed his eyes, he had to whisper one last, "Thank you, God."

****

Tandra sat on the couch in her living room, hugging Charles' picture close to her bosom as tears escaped from her redden, swollen eyes. His big beautiful smile invaded her thoughts as Whitney Houston's *Saving All My Love for You*, softly filled the atmosphere. Her thoughts traveled back in time to when they shared their lives together: laughing, jogging, pillow fights, kissing, cuddling, watching television, and even disagreeing, but he would grab her arm, sweep her up, lay her on the bed, and they would make warm, passionate love together. "Charles," she squeezed out weakly in between tears, dropping to the couch in a lying position. The ringing of the doorbell went unnoticed by her as she wept uncontrollably now. Soon Cecily entered the room quietly and witnessed the hysterical suffering of the estranged woman.

"Oh, Tandra, no!" Cecily said as she sat on the couch and pulled the woman in her arms. "Honey, you've got to pull yourself together."

"He doesn't want to see me," she sobbed. "He doesn't want to see me."

"Of course, he *wants* to see you, Honey. Just give him time."

"I want to be there for him, but he won't let me."

"Tandra, the man is going through a difficult time. He loves you just as much as he always has. Just give him time to sort things out. You simply have to understand."

Pulling away from Cecily's embrace, she said, "He says he can't look at me without thinking about the good times we've shared. And he realizes that we can never be as close as we were before, so he doesn't want to see me. What he doesn't understand, Cecily, is that sex isn't important to me if it's not with *him*. I will wait as long as it takes. I love him." She fell back on Cecily, still in tears.

Cecily pulled her up by the shoulders, "Tandra, listen to me. You and Charles love each other. If you can't go on without him, tell him so. Let him know that you're *not* leaving him, no matter *what*."

"But we're not married. I have no rights."

"You're in love, and both of you are single. That's all the *rights* you need."

****

"He made it, Boss."

"Damn!" Papa Roma spat. "Get Luke on the damn phone!" The man dialed the number as Papa Roma walked to the window.

Pointing the receiver in Papa Roma's direction, the man said, "Here he is, Boss."

Grabbing the receiver, Papa Roma snapped, "Luke, what the hell's going on with that D. A.?"

"He's paralyzed, Boss," Luke whispered from a desk in a busy police station. "He won't be going to no *court* no time soon. Mack and I are protecting him." He laughed softly.

"Who the hell is Mack?"

"Detective Hinson."

"Is he on the payroll?"

"No, Boss."

"Maybe he *should* be. I want that D. A. *dead*!"

"I'll check it out."

"Yeah, you *do* that. I don't want Ricky rotting in that stinking jail!"

"Boss, I'm telling you, we don't have to worry about Lewis right now.

He won't even see his girlfriend. He's a wreck."

"I don't give a fuck about..." Papa Roma stopped abruptly. "Who's his girl?"

"Some hotshot lawyer name Tandra Burns."

"Burns. Where have I heard that name before?" Papa Roma went into thought. "Keep in touch, Luke," He hung up. Suddenly Papa Roma snapped his finger. "Burns. She was the lawyer that slaughtered Lewis in some murder case recently!" He paused. "She defended some hotshot named Carter."

"Yeah, so what, Boss?"

Papa Roma exploded, "Moe, we're home free!"

"I don't get you, Boss."

"The kid we just took in. Wanda. She's Carter's daughter!"

"We knew that, Boss."

"But we didn't know about the lawyer. Carter has to be chummy with his lawyer, and his lawyer is Charles Lewis' girl."

"And?"

"And people like them are always having dinner parties."

"I don't follow you, Boss."

"Wanda Carter. She has contact with *Lewis*!"

"So?"

"So, she's the *one* to do the *hit*!"

****

Tandra opened Charles' hospital room door slowly, and his parents were watching television with him. "Hello," she said softly.

"Hi," Mrs. Lewis smiled, and her husband nodded his greetings.

"What're you doing here?" Charles asked quietly.

"Can't I still be concerned about how you're doing?" she asked walking over to his bed.

"We'll be back soon, Son," Mrs. Lewis said, and then she and her husband left quickly.

"Well, how are you?"

"I'm paralyzed. How *should* I be?"

"You certainly don't have to be so nasty. Besides, that doesn't answer my question. How are you?"

"Terrible. Does that answer it?"

"Charles, don't do this."

"Don't do what?"

"Don't take it out on the world because you can't walk right now."

"Right *now*?! This may be permanent."

"Yes. *May* be," she took a deep breath. "But, if it *is* permanent, then you'll deal with it."

"How? I've never been paralyzed before."

"One day at a time. The most important thing you've failed to realize is that the person who shot you meant to *kill* you, and *that* person is still out there. So, be grateful you're still *alive*," she explained. "I know *I* am." She paused. "So, count your blessings and don't push me away, because I'm not going *anywhere*. My place is with you, and that's *exactly* where I'll be. You can like it or not."

"I don't want to be a burden on you."

"You've *always* been a *burden* on me." she said smiling.

"I'm serious."

"I'm serious, too," she chuckled. "But, that's one of the reasons I love you so much. And I wouldn't have it any other way," She paused and sighed deeply. "Now, we really don't need two apartments. I'll move in with you."

"Do you know what you're getting yourself into?"

"Yes."

"It's going to be tough with an invalid husband."

"Is that a proposal, Counselor?"

"Since I can't get rid of you, you might as well marry me."

"Yes, I will!" she burst out then fell on him, kissing him all over his face. They laughed together.

"I love you, Baby."

"And, I love you," she said. "Nothing will ever come between us again." They ended in a long, sultry kiss.

Chapter 29

A tall, slim Caucasian man with horn-rimmed eyeglasses, freckled face, and donkey ears, surrounded by short, red, straight hair, walked into an office labeled, *Federal Bureau of Investigations* on the door. He sat behind a cluttered desk, picked up the telephone, and said in a very southern drawl, "Ray Jones here."

"Hiya, Country Boy. It's Sissy."

"Who?"

"Sissy. Spencer's girl."

"Sissy," he said leaning back in his chair. "Hi, Beautiful. How are you?"

"Fine. Just fine."

"Ummmmmm, I *bet* you are," he cooed.

"All right, Country Boy, get your mind out the gutter," she said laughing, and he laughed with her.

"What can I do for you, Sissy?"

"Ray, I need a big favor."

"I'm the man to see."

"I'm living in California now."

"Wow, you're a long way from New York, Baby. What's up?"

"And, I'm a long way from *Sissy*, too," she said. "It's *Cecily* now."

"I heard that."

"Ray, this is really big. I wouldn't trust it to anyone but you, because I *trust* you."

"What's wrong, Sis...Cecily?"

"I need you in California."

"*California*?!" he blurted out.

"You won't regret it, Ray."

"But, California's out of my jurisdiction."

"*Every* place is your jurisdiction."

"That's not what I mean. I mean we have people out *there* to handle jobs *there*."

"I want *you*, Ray. As I said, I don't know who I can trust here. I *know* I can trust you."

"Give me some idea what this is about, Baby."

"How would you like to bring down one of the biggest, most powerful crime families in California?"

****

Tim, Papa Romalotti's eldest son, burst into his father's office, yelling, "Papa, you can't be serious! What's this I hear about you're considering a *kid* doing the hit on Lewis?!"

"Timmy, she can get to him. You know he's being guarded around the clock. And, who would ever suspect a *kid*?" Papa Roma explained, walking to Tim, whose tall, slender, bronzed frame towered over his father's.

"But, it's *absurd*!" Tim continued. "You *know* she'll freak out."

"It doesn't matter."

"What?! Now, you've lost me."

"All I want the girl to do is to get the D. A. where *we* can handle it. She will think she's doing the hit, but when they're all together," Papa Roma announced, looking his son squarely in the eyes, then added solemnly, "We'll just blow up the world goddamn house!"

****

** She strolled in the big room wearing a black lace bra and black fishnet stockings that were held securely on her upper thighs by black lace girdle straps. She stood tall on six-inch black, stiletto heels, as she strolled over to the bed where he lay staring at her approaching, swaying hips. "Hi, I'm Sissy," she purred. "You must be Ray."*

"Yes," he said swallowing a large lump in his throat. She stood very close to him to let him get a good look at her gorgeous body and he did, every <u>inch</u> of her. "You're so beautiful," he finally said, finding his voice.

"Oh, you're <u>southern</u>," she smiled. "What's a nice country boy like you doing in a great big ole place like New York City?"

"Just lucky, I guess," he said as he touched her smoothed thigh softly.

"You like what you see, Country Boy?" she smiled, and he nodded like a hungry little puppy, anxiously anticipating a meal in view. "Why don't you show me how much." She didn't have to say anymore before he attacked her hungrily, but gently. She gently pulled away from his grasp and sat on the bed, then removed his pants. He was still trying to lap at her

*like a hungry little puppy. When his pants hit the floor, her eyes widen for she realized the myths about white men were just that, <u>myths</u>. Whoever said white men didn't have much to offer a girl should see this country boy's stock. He most definitely had <u>plenty</u> to offer. He smiled at her because he knew what she was thinking, and he could see the embarrassment in her eyes as she shyly smiled back. He was surprised and angry with himself for exploding so quickly. This beautiful woman was one in a million. But the next time, he was proud of himself, for he lasted long enough to even satisfy <u>her</u>, but he was right behind her with another explosion of his own. That was the start of a long and continuous relationship.   *

"Ray!" a big, black, muscular man called, bringing Ray back to the present.

"Yeah. What is it, Bill?"

"A woman in your past?" the tall man teased. "You were smiling like she was a goddess."

Ignoring the man's jest, Ray asked, "What's up, Man?"

"Maybe Noreen better go with you on this *so-called* business trip," Bill continued to joke.

"My wife knows she's the *only* girl for me," Ray smiled. "When I married her, I gave up everything. And I do mean *everything*!" Ray chuckled, thinking of the beautiful Sissy, and then he shook his head, sobered, and asked, "What's up?"

"I have your flight booked to LA."

"Good. For when?"

"In the morning."

"Bill, I want you to drop everything and join me as soon as possible in LA."

"What's this about, Ray?'

"I don't know all the details, but if I'm right, we'll going to bring down one of the most notorious crime families in the west."

****

"Where've you been?"

"I had to work late," Lillian replied removing her coat as Alton sat up in bed watching her.

"You've been working late a *lot* lately," he snapped.

"We've been working on a big account," she defended, letting her dress drop to the floor.

"And, it takes to one-thirty in the morning?" he sarcastically added.

"*Yes*," she retaliated. Alton rolled out of bed and went to his wife and held her shoulders in his hands.

"Where the hell have you been, Lillian?!" he demanded.

"At the *office*," she insisted wiggling out of his hold and sitting in front of her vanity dresser.

"No, you weren't. I called," he said, and she froze momentarily.

"Nobody is at the switchboard after hours," she rebounded quickly.

"Yes, someone was there," he said. "And she said that you had been gone for hours."

Lillian stood and burst into laughter. "I don't believe this. You're *jealous*!"

"It's not funny, Lillian."

"Oh, yes, it is."

"Where's your cell phone?"

"The battery died."

Alton took a deep breath then charged, "You're fucking him, aren't you?"

"Who?" she was smug, and he hated it.

"You know *who*. Your *boss*. That goddamn, nappy-headed Haitian bastard!"

"What's it to you if I *am*?" she snapped. "You're afraid you can't take care of home *and* your women anymore? It never bothered you before!" His hand flew up and the back of it handed on her face, knocking her to the floor. "Go ahead and hit me again, Alton!" she raged. "If it makes you feel like a *real* man! Hit me!" His fist stopped in midair as he closed his eyes tightly to regain his composure, then he quickly rushed out the room. "You can't hurt me anymore, Alton Carter!" Lillian continued to yell. "*You can't hurt me anymore*!" She burst into laughter.

****

Trudy sat up in bed watching the television, while Isaac slept with his head resting in her lap. She stared at him with a loving smile as she ran her hands through his soft blonde hair, while she drifted into the past:

*   *Trudy opened the door in a warm-up suit, and Isaac was standing there. "Trudy, you look great," he said smiling big. How much is it, now?"*

"Only twenty pounds, but it's a start," she smiled. "Come in, Isaac. You always make me feel so good."

"Well, you're doing great."

"Would you like something to drink?"

"What're you having?"

"Unsweetened tea."

"Ugh," he frowned, and she laughed.

"You may have sugar in yours. Carl can't drink it like this, either," she laughed, as he followed her into the kitchen.

"Where is Carl today?"

"With Hakim," she laughed. "They're inseparable."

"It's good to have a buddy."

"Speaking of buddies. Have you heard from Cecily lately?"

"No. We don't communicate much after the divorce."

"Do you still think about her a lot?"

"Hardly ever."

"Oh, come on," she laughed.

"Trudy, I'm serious. Cecily is a thing of the past now. I'm enjoying

working with you and the young people in the church now. I don't have time to think about Cecily. And, before I knew it, she was out of my heart. I don't know when it happened, but it did, and I thank God for it."

"Well, hallelujah," she smiled as they sat at the kitchen island.

"I just hope I'm not in your hair too much."

"No. Carl and I enjoy having you around. Carl needs a man in his life."

"That's good to hear."

"Well, is there anybody special in your life, Isaac?"

"No, not really. I'm just taking it slow," he said. "Which brings me to the reason I came."

"Oh, there's a motive for this visit," she laughed, as she punched his arm.

"A little one," he laughed with her.

"Let's hear it."

"Let me start by saying, if you can't do it, I'll understand."

"Um, this must be serious."

Laughing, he said, "Stop that. It's just that my company has a dinner party every year for Christmas, and I find myself without an escort this year. Will you, Miss Miles, do me the honors of accompanying me to the party this year?"

"You want <u>me</u> to go to the party with <u>you</u>, for your company?!"

"Yes. Will you?"

"Isaac, I'm flattered. I haven't been asked out to <u>any</u> thing in so long, I forgot how it feels."

"I told you, the men in this town are crazy," he smiled. "Well..."

"Are you sure?"

"Trudy, what is this? Twenty questions. I want you to go with me to the party. What don't you understand?"

"Why?"

"I told you why."

"Isaac, I know any number of women would jump at the chance to go anywhere with a handsome, charming man like you, skinny girls. Why me?"

"Why not you. Trudy, you're a very beautiful lady, at any size," he said. "Beauty is on the inside. And, you are very beautiful, inside and out. Now, will you go?"

"Sure."

"Great."

"When is it?"

"Friday night."

"This Friday night?!" she exploded.

"Yes. Is that a problem?"

"Well, you sure don't give a girl a lot of notice."

"Friends can do that," he smiled, and she punched his arm again.

****

When Trudy stepped into the party with Isaac, she felt so special. She was dazzling in a blue, sequined, straight dress, which complimented her full figure. She had had it specially made at a boutique, and when Isaac saw her, he raved about how beautiful she looked. Her braids were redone to perfection, as they encircled her head like a goddess, with a few hanging down around her pretty, round face. She felt like the Belle of the Ball. Then the unthinkable happened. While she was in the restroom, she overheard two women talking about her.

"Who is she, Dorita?" the young, thin, blonde woman asked.

"She used to be a big fashion model," the older woman replied.

"What did she model, elephant tents? All this time I've waited for Isaac to noticed me, and he shows up with the Goodyear blimp," the woman laughed.

Smiling, Dorita said, "Carla, that's terrible. Trudy Miles is a nice person."

"Yeah, but she's got <u>my</u> man!"

"He's not <u>your</u> man, or anyone else's. He single. And, not only that, I think they're just friends. Miss Miles was Isaac's ex-wife's friend."

"Well, maybe he brought her here out of a sense of charity," Carla said bursting into laughter.

"You're too much," Dorita said, shoving her. "Let me get back to my husband, Girl, before he sends the S.W.A.T. team after me."

When Dorita left, Carla sat at the vanity mirror to freshen up her lipstick. When Trudy stepped out of the stall, you could've knocked Carla down with a feather, when she locked eyes with Trudy. Carla just closed her eyes tight, as Trudy silently washed her hands then left.

****

Trudy sat, riding a stationary bicycle when the doorbell rang. She jumped off, grabbed a towel, wrapped it around her neck and went to the door. "Isaac," she said when she opened the door. "What're you doing here in the middle of the day?"

Coming in, he said, "Trudy, I just found out what happened at the party. I'm so sorry."

"Who told you?"

"That doesn't matter, but Carla had no right to talk about you like that."

"She was only stating her opinion, Isaac," she said walking away. "You can't blame her for that."

"Yes, I can. That was cruel and vicious. I can't use anyone in my company who gossips like that."

"What did you do, Isaac?"

"I gave her a month off with no pay, so she can think about what she says from now on."

"Isaac, it's okay, <u>really</u>."

"No, it isn't, Trudy," he said turning her around by her shoulders. "You've made tremendous progress. I don't want you to feel less than anybody just because you're a little heavier than them. You are still a very beautiful woman." A tear fell down her face, and he pulled her in his arms. "I'm sorry, Trudy." He held her head up with his finger, wiped her tears,

and then planted a kiss on her lips. "You're very special to me, Trudy. Why do you think I spend so much time over here?" Her eyes widen. "I'm falling in love with you."

"Isaac."

"It's okay if you don't feel the same way, but I just had to tell you. I love you, Trudy."

"I love you, too, Isaac."

"What?"

"I've waited so long to hear you say that, but I didn't think you would ever love me with all those beautiful women you see every day at the office."

*"You are the most beautiful woman I've ever seen," he said, and they kissed hard then. They made beautiful, passionate love, right on the kitchen floor.   ***

Isaac turned over, bringing Trudy back to the present. "Aren't you asleep yet?" he asked, as she slid down in bed.

Seeing her wiping her tears, he said, "What's wrong, Baby?"

"Nothing. Everything is just *perfect*."

"Then, why are you crying?"

"I'm just so happy to have you," she said, and then he kissed her lips softly.

"I love you."

"And I love you. You're the only person who ever loved me unconditionally. You made me feel beautiful at *any* size, and I love you for that."

"You *are* beautiful, Trudy, and I do love you with all my heart," he said, and they kissed again, as they held each other tight.

Chapter 30

"Hiya, Country Boy."

"Cecily," he said smiling, speechless at her beauty, and then he grabbed her and hugged her tight. When he finally let go, he just stared at her. Soon he found his voice again, and added, "You're still as beautiful as I remember." He led her in his hotel room. "Please, come in."

"It's good to see you again, Ray," she smiled also.

"Me, too, Baby. Me, too," he hugged her again, then planted a soft kiss on her lips, and she kissed him back.

"Can I get you something to drink?"

"No, I'm fine," she said, as he helped her out of her coat.

"Sit down," he said hanging her coat on the coat rack, and then he joined her on the couch. He took a deep breath then added, "I just can't get over how good you look."

"Thank you, Ray."

"What're you doing now?"

"I'm a doctor."

"What?!"

"That's right. When I worked for Spencer I was in medical school?"

"Wow. I never knew."

"No one did," she said. "And *you*? How have you been? Are you married yet?"

"Yes. With three kids."

Smiling, she said, "That's great, Ray. Do you have pictures?"

Taking out his cell phone, he said, "I sure do." He started naming his family. "This is Noreen, my wife."

"She's very pretty."

"Thank you."

"And, this is Ray, Jr. He's ten. Houston is seven, and little Carol is five."

"They're gorgeous, Ray."

"Thank you, Cecily," he smiled, putting his pictures away. "And what about *you*? Are you married and are there any kids?"

"I'm divorced."

"I'm sorry."

"Oh, don't be. It was my fault," She paused in her thoughts. "And, I had two daughters, both are dead now."

"Oh, I'm sorry, Honey."

Sniffing to keep her tears in, Cecily said, "But I'm coping." He handed her a handkerchief and she blew hard. "Thank you, Ray." She seized her emotions again then added, "Now, let's get down to business."

"Yes. What is this about taking down a big crime family?"

Taking a deep breath, she said, "How would you like to take down the Romalotti Family?"

****

"Carl, turn your music down," Isaac said, poking his head in the boy's door, barely able to hear himself think because of the loud rap music. Carl turned over on his bed and did not respond. "Carl, did you hear me?" The boy still did not respond, so Isaac entered the space decorated room and turned the music down himself, and Carl jumped up with the kinky hair sticking up in the top and the sides bald.

"You can't turn my music down!" he shouted.

"I most certainly can. I ask..."

"You can't tell me to do *nothing*. You ain't my father."

"I'm the *only* father you've got!" Isaac retaliated, as Trudy entered.

"What's going on in here?" she wanted to know.

"He's messing with my music, Mom!"

"I asked him to turn it down, and he refused," Isaac defended his position.

"Why can't you two get alone?" Trudy insisted.

"That honkey ain't my father!" Carl yelled to his mother, and she slapped him across the face.

"I will not have that disrespect from you, young man. Now, you apologize to Isaac this instant!" Trudy demanded.

"Sorry," Carl mumbled softly.

"Now, when Isaac asks you to do something, I want you to obey. Do you hear me?!"

"Yeah, I hear you," Carl sarcastically said. "How many other men do I have to *obey*, Mom, before you decide on keeping one?!"

"What?!" Trudy was stunned that her child would talk to her like this.

"I don't have a daddy. I don't even have a *Mama*. You're taking up for that white dude over me." The child's anger forced him to rage. "And, *he* sure ain't my daddy, *whoever* my daddy is." He dropped on his bed in tears, and Trudy and Isaac's eyes locked. Trudy had no idea her son was being tormented about not knowing his father. Was it finally time to tell him about Spencer?

****

Alton buttoned his coat as he walked out of his office and into his secretary's office. "Patty, I'm leaving for lunch," he said to the lady that was busy typing.

"Sure, Mr. Carter," she said, and then he started out. Patty quickly picked up an envelope on her desk and called, "Oh, Mr. Carter, this just arrived for you. A man brought it in."

Taking the envelope from her, he said, "Thanks, Patty."

When Alton got to his red Corvette, he fastened his seat belts then opened the envelope. His eyes widen when he read:

If you want to know where your wife spends her late-night hours, check out the Martian Hotel. I suggest you go now, for an awakening experience.

Alton looked for something else on the envelope to tell him who had sent this note, but he saw nothing. He threw the note down on the soft, black leather seat and sped away quickly. He felt it was a prank note, but by the way Lillian was acting lately, he *had* to be sure.

****

"That's crazy!"

"Ray, hear me out," Cecily begged walking towards him.

"The Romalotti Family is one of the most powerful crime families in California!"

"I know that," she insisted. "But I can do it!"

"Cecily, Baby, that's suicide. I can't let you do it," he insisted taking a deep breath. "That's a job for the police and the FBI!"

"You haven't managed to get Papa Roma yet," she sarcastically replied. "If you help me, Ray, we can get him *together*!"

"I will help the *police*!"

"We can't go to the police. I told you, two little girls' lives depend on it. We don't know who we can trust. You know how that goes."

"Cecily, *everyone* on the police force is *not* on the mob's payroll."

"Yes, but we don't know who *is* and who *isn't*. I can't take that chance!" she insisted.   "That's why I called *you*." He blew hard, and she knew she was getting through to him. "I'm going to do this, Ray. *With* or *without* you, and you can't stop me."

He blew hard again and said, "I must be outta my cotton-picking mind. What's your plan, pretty lady? And it had better be good, cause *I* ain't suicidal!"

****

"I love you, Lillian," Lyle said as he held her in his arms, while they stood in the bedroom suite of the Martian Hotel, fully dressed.

"I love you, too, Baby," she said as their lips touched softly.

"Then why don't you marry me?"

"It's not that simple, Lyle" she insisted walking away. "I have Wanda to consider. She worships her father."

"And, what about *you*?" he said taking a deep breath. "Don't you have obligations to *yourself*? Don't you love me as much as I love you?"

"You know I do, but..."

"No buts, Lillian. I don't like sneaking around with you. I want everyone to know that you're mine and *only* mine. I can't even take you to my house, in fear of my ex-wife finding out and going to your husband, and I *know* she will. The woman will do *anything* to hurt me."

"Why does she hate you so much?"

"Because she didn't get anything in the divorce. She slept with half the men in California, but yet, she thinks *I* owe *her* something. I thank God every day that we didn't have children together." He placed his arms around her tiny waist. "I love you, pretty lady." Their lips entwined lovingly as a knock pounded on the door. Taking a deep breath, Lyle asked, "Who is it?"

Their eyes locked, and Lillian's heart seemed to drop when the voice said, "Alton Carter!"

Chapter 31

The heads of all the males turned as Cecily's six-inch hills tapped as she strolled in a big lavishly decorated office building, wrapped in an off-white mink coat with her hair in an upsweep bun on the top of her head, encircled with a row of shiny diamonds. Two tiny diamond earrings kissed her lightly made-up, bronzed face. She glided to the secretary's desk in the center of the room, lowered her mink coat off her shoulders, and removed it slowly. All the men's mouths dropped opened when they focused on a split so high in the back of her dress, it exposed long, silky, bronzed legs and thighs. They felt that if they looked long enough, they would be able to see further up that split because it left little to the imagination. Then they all focused on another bright spot on this beautiful creature. Her low-cut dress held her breasts with pride, as they stood straight up, like saluting soldiers, exposing just enough of her lovely, perfectly rounded features to fill their hearts with newfound excitement. The imaginations of the men were working overtime, as the small number of women in the office frowned and wondered why God had been so good to this *one* little slut. Clearing her throat, the secretary glared from behind rounded, thick eyeglasses and asked, "May I help you?"

"Yes," Cecily said speaking very stern and proud. "I'm here to see Mr. Timothy Romalotti."

"Do you have an appointment?"

"No, I don't," she replied. "But I'm sure he'll be more than happy to see me." The men all agreed silently.

"What is the nature of this business?"

"I'm sorry. I can't say," Cecily smiled sweetly. "Is he in?"

"Yes, he is, but he doesn't see *anyone* without an appointment."

Cecily was becoming annoyed at this woman. The nerve of her to work for mobsters and act as if she were holier than God almighty himself, and Cecily replied very sarcastically, "Why don't you *ask* him."

"I'm sorry, Miss ugh..."

"Sissy."

"Miss, ugh...Sissy, I'm sorry, but you *must* make an appointment," the lady insisted as the door to her Boss's office opened, and a tall, dark, extremely handsome Tim stepped out, in a Taylor-made dark blue suit, and focused on Cecily. His heart melted as he stared at her with his beautiful hazel eyes, totally in contrast with his dark Italian skin and jet-black hair. Cecily knew, without a doubt, that this *had* to be the most gorgeous white man she had ever seen in her life. His smile exposed beautiful, pearly-white, perfect teeth, as he walked in her direction.

"Hello," he said in a strong California accent. "I'm Timothy Romalotti. Are you here to see me?" He thought, *Please say yes.*

Finding her voice that had vanished at the sight of this gorgeous man, Cecily replied weakly, "Yes, I am, but I'm having problems, because I don't have an appointment. I'm Sissy." They shook hands.

With a slight smile, he said, "I'm sorry to inconvenience you, but my secretaries are very efficient." He pointed in the direction of his office and added, "Please, this way." As he followed her, he thought to himself that he hadn't seen a woman this beautiful and exotic in his entire life, and he had *seen* a lot of beautiful women. "Please, have a seat," he spoke again, pointing to a chair. Instead of sitting behind his huge oak desk, he sat in a chair in front of Cecily. When she crossed her beautiful, silky legs he knew it would be very difficult to concentrate on business with those legs staring him in the face. "Would you care for something to drink?"

"No, thank you," she said then added. "You have a beautiful office."

"Thank you, and if I may be so blunt, you are a *very* beautiful woman."

"Thank you."

"I can't recognize your heritage. Italian or Latino?"

"American," she smiled.

"American?"

"I am the product of mixing Irish American with African American."

"I see," he chuckled. "That's interesting. Well, you are *very* beautiful."

"Thank you again, but I didn't come here to talk about my heritage."

"Right. What can I do for you, Sissy?"

"You don't know me, but we had a mutual acquaintance," she said, and he raised an eyebrow to hear more. "Do you remember Carl Spencer?"

"Spencer from New York?"

"Yes."

"Yes...uh...he died, didn't he?"

"Yes, he did."

"What was your connection to Spencer?"

"We were partners," she replied. "At first I worked *for* him, then later we worked *together*."

"You mean you..."

"Yes," she finished for him. "I was Spencer's lady, then I was his meal ticket." He couldn't imagine why such a beautiful woman would have to sell her body. Surely there were loads of men that would've taken care of her, absolutely free, just for the opportunity of waking up beside such a classy woman every day to bask in her beauty. He wished it had been *him*. He thought, *Spencer must have been a fool.*

"How involved were you with Spencer?"

"*Very* involved. He told me everything."

"We were unaware that Spencer had a *partner*."

"Because I was a *silent* partner. I know how to keep my mouth *shut*!"

"So, you want to continue his business, but you need our help."

"Yes. I think we can help each other."

"I think we can at that," he said smiling, focusing on her breasts. Cecily couldn't help but to thank God that Ray had known about Spencer's involvement with this family. She only knew a little of Spencer's dealing with this family, but Ray knew *everything*, but he just couldn't prove *anything*. Everything was going as planned. And when they checked her out, Ray had arranged a cover for her. He stood and helped her up by the hand and squeezed gently. "Together, pretty lady, we shall get everything that's coming to us."

"Yes, Tim, we shall get *everything* that's coming to us!"

Part Four

Eight Months Later

October

Chapter 32

"Can I get you something, Honey?" Tandra asked Charles as he sat in a wheelchair looking at the television, while she lay on the couch.

"No. Thank you," he nonchalantly replied.

"Need a pillow?"

"No."

"What about something to drink?"

"Tandra, please, stop it!"

"Stop what?"

"Stop treating me like an *invalid*!"

"I don't mean to. I just want you to be comfortable."

"*Some* things I can do for myself," he insisted, and she went to him and sat on his lap.

"I'm sorry, Baby. I don't mean to get on your nerves," she planted a kiss on his forehead.

"You're not getting on my nerves," he said, and they kissed. "I just wonder if it was such a good idea for you to have moved in here with me."

"Of course, it was a good idea," she said softly. "I love you." This time they kissed harder, and she moved her kisses to his ear and then his neck, and then he abruptly stopped her.

"Don't do that!"

"Don't do what?"

"Don't tease me when you know I can't finish it!"

"I don't mean to tease you. I just want *romance*, not *sex*."

"You don't understand, Tandra," he insisted. "Please, get up!"

Standing, she said, "You're right, I don't understand! We can have a very meaningful relationship without *sex*, but you'd rather feel sorry for yourself, remembering the things we *used* to do, instead of building on the things that we still *can* do."

"I can't make love to you anymore!"

"Of course, you can. We might can't have sex anymore, but we sure as hell can *make love!*" she insisted. Suddenly she took control of her emotions again and bent down to him. "I love you, Charles. You don't seem to understand just how deeply I love you. I don't expect you to give me anything that you can't give, but *affection* is one thing that you *could* give me if you *really* wanted to."

Staring deeply into her sad eyes, he said, "I knew this was a mistake. I want you to leave, so you won't have to play nurse maid to me any longer." He turned and rolled away in his wheelchair, and Tandra dropped her head.

****

"Hi, Baby," Tim said planting a kiss on Cecily's lips then entered her rented penthouse.

"Hi," she said smiling, running her hands through her unruly mass of curls on her head, wearing a big nightshirt of his.

Taking off his tie, he chuckled, "Hey, that looks better on *you* than *me*."

"It's comfortable," she laughed. "Are you hungry?" she asked helping him out of his suit coat.

"No. Beverly had some kind of shit at the house I ate."

"Does she know about us?"

"Who?"

"Beverly, your *wife!*"

"She doesn't know *who* you are, but she would have to be pretty dumb not to know I have someone, especially when I don't come home for days sometimes."

"I thought you usually tell her you're on business trips or something."

"Yes, I do, but she's no dummy."

"Why do you think she stays?"

"Because she has no other choice. That's why! When I married her, it was for *keeps*! Papa wouldn't have it any other way."

"Why not?"

"Hell, you know the kind of business we're in. She might go running to the cops. She knows a lot," he explained then threw her down on the couch as she laughed, and attacked her with wild, wet kisses. "Enough about my wife. She's no problem for us."

"I love you, Tim," Cecily said between kisses, and their eyes locked.

"I love you, too, Baby. Sometimes I wish we could have a normal life, just *you* and *me*."

"Do you really, Tim?"

"Really," he said softly, and they ended in a long passionate kiss, as he rolled on top of her and pulled off her shirt. Cecily could not believe that he brought her to satisfaction so quickly. Tim was a real pro. She wondered how many other affairs his wife had been forced to endure.

"I love you more than words can say, Sissy," he finally said, running his fingers through her curly, soft hair.

"And I love you, Baby. My only regret is that I can never be your wife."

"Do you really *want* to?"

"Don't tease me, Tim" she chuckled. "You said you couldn't get a divorce."

"There are *other* ways of getting rid of a wife, My Darling," he smiled.

"Stop it," she laughed. "Stop teasing."

"You just say the word and Beverly won't be a problem any longer," he said again, and she knew he was *serious*, so an overwhelming feeling of fear attacked her. He had just reminded her that he *wasn't* just this sweet, attractive man that had become her lover. But he was a whole lot more. A *whole* lot more. She was doing the same thing that Trudy had done with Spencer, and she couldn't let that happen. She realized then that she had to stay focused on what her purpose was. Although this well-groomed, attractive man captivated her, he still was who he was; a thug, a murderer, and only God knows what else. "Well, how bad do you want to marry me?" he wanted to know.

"Not *that* bad," she chuckled. He grabbed her and kissed her hard.

"Hey, I was kidding," he said laughing. "What kind of person do you think I am? What's up, Baby?"

"How's Ricky?" Cecily asked changing the subject, because she didn't want him to sense how frightened she was.

"He's hanging in there," he said. "We've got to get that D. A., though. If he has his way, my brother will never see daylight again. Papa has a plan that just might work. I'll tell you about it when we put it together."

Cecily didn't want to hear this, so she changed the subject again, "Tim, I heard that you have another brother. Where is he?"

"I don't know. Marco left when he was eighteen. He was ashamed of the family and wanted nothing to do with us."

"I'm sorry," she said, seeing the hurt in his eyes.

"Well, that's life," he said. "Oh, by the way, we have a shipment coming in on Friday. Papa wants you there."

"That's great," she said, thinking *This is finally it*. This was what she had been working on for so long, and it's finally here, and she didn't know how she felt about it.... or about *Tim*.

"Papa really likes you. He said you're smart and beautiful. Qualities hard to find in a woman, *together*. So, he wants to teach you *everything*. You know, Papa might just allow a divorce after all."

"Don't count on it," she chuckled. "Who else is coming?"

"Everybody, Baby. Everybody who's anybody in the business will be there. This shipment is coming in from South America. Good stuff! This will be a great opportunity for you to meet all our connections. Are you ready?" he explained very proudly, as he lit a cigarette.

"I hope so," she said smiling, as she thought, *This is it! Am I ready?!*

God, help me! Am I ready?!

****

Alton opened his eyes and focused on his beautiful wife, lying beside him on her back, still asleep. He couldn't help but to wonder where have all the years gone. There have been a lot of ups and downs, but never have they been as far apart as they are right now. She has finally gotten sick and tired of his relationship with Cecily, with good reason. He didn't know if he could bounce back and forgive as much as his wife had forgiven him. He had flaunted Cecily in her face one too many times. Has someone else finally picked up the pieces and stolen his lovely wife's heart? He wasn't ready to give up on his marriage yet. He bent over and planted a kiss on her soft lips, and she moved a little, then he planted a more forceful kiss on her lips, and she opened her eyes slowly. "Good morning," he smiled.

Yawning, she asked, "What time is it?"

"Time for you to be my wife again," he said softly then kissed her again. His emotions took control, and he began to slip her nightgown off her shoulders, and she resisted a little. "Please, don't push me away today, Baby." Although her heart wasn't in it, she felt it was her wifely duty to give in to him this one time. He had waited a long time, and since Cecily was gone, to heaven knows where, she knew he wasn't getting his comfort from her best friend right now. They made love tenderly. It meant a great deal to Alton, to be close to his wife again, but unfortunately, the feelings were not mutual. She knew it, and *he* knew it. When they were finished, he politely thanked her, kissed her forehead, and then went to take a shower.

Lillian rolled over on her side, stared into space, and drifted into the past:

*   *There Lillian was, standing in a hotel room with another man, while her husband stood at the door. "What're we going to do?" Lillian whispered to Lyle.*

"Let's tell him the truth," he whispered back.

"No!" she blurted out, trying to stay calm. "Not yet, please, Lyle. Not yet!" As perspiration adorned her forehead, he could see how afraid she was, so he grabbed her hand.

"Come on," he said as another knock came to the door.

"Where?"

"In the shower," he said to her then yelled, "Just a moment!" She grabbed her purse and coat and followed Lyle. He stripped, jumped in the shower, wet himself, and then wrapped a towel around his wet body. He pulled the shower curtains back halfway and said, "Here, squat right behind this curtain."

"He'll see me."

"No, he won't. I'm leaving the door open to the bathroom, so he can see right in here. Just don't move a muscle," he explained then rushed to the door, dripping wet. "What is it?!" Lyle demanded, yanking the door open.

"Is my wife here?"

"Your wife?! Lillian?!"

"No. Tinker Bell," he sarcastically replied.

"What would Lillian be doing <u>here</u>?" Lyle said as Alton searched the hotel with his eyes. "I'm living here right now while my apartment is being painted. I'm just getting back from out of town. Lillian <u>should</u> be at the office."

Feeling very embraced, Alton said, "Look, I'm sorry, Man. I got this note saying she was here. Pardon me." He left quickly, and Lillian dropped to the floor, releasing her breath, when she heard him leave.   *

"I'll be home early tonight, Baby," Alton said bringing Lillian back to the present. He was fully dressed, in a black, double-breasted suit. "What about you?"

"Yes, I should be home early. I don't think we have a late appointment scheduled."

"Maybe we can do something together with Wanda, like take in a movie or something. We haven't done anything together in a long time," he said, and she nodded.

"Sounds good," she tried to smile, but her heart just wasn't in it.

"I'll see you," he said, bending down and kissing her softly, and to his surprise, she returned the affection, which made him feel warm inside, then he left.

"Oh, God, help me," Lillian said softly. "I can't go on like this. This isn't *me*. Something must be done.... *now*."

Chapter 33

Cecily and Tim walked, arm in arm, down the street as two bodyguards trailed them. "It's a beautiful night, Darling," she said smiling. "Thank you for taking this stroll with me."

"I haven't done this in a long time," he chuckled. "But, then, you *do* bring out the *best* in me."

"Ahh, that's sweet," she cooed, and their lips met briefly. "Oh, look, Baby, an ice cream truck." She pulled his arm gently. "My treat." He obeyed, laughing hard. He couldn't believe the energy this beautiful woman possessed. "I'll have a Nestle Crunch ice cream bar," she told the man, with the big straw hat and unruly beard.

"I'll try one, too," Tim added reaching for his wallet.

"No, Baby," she protested. "I told you, it's my treat."

"Okay," Tim laughed. "A woman after my own heart."

"You betcha," she laughed also, reaching into her coat pocket and handing the man a bill. "Keep the change." Cecily and Tim continued their stroll.

The man in the ice cream truck, held up to straighten his money. He noticed there was writing on the bill that Cecily had given to him, and he put it under the other bills. When Cecily and Tim were well out of sight, Ray, Cecily's FBI friend, removed the big, straw hat and closed his ice cream shop, *forever*.

****

Tandra began to get out of bed when Charles placed his hand on her arm and said very softly, "I'm sorry, Sweetie." She turned to face him. "I've been terrible to you, and you've been so understanding. I love you so much."

"You're not going to run me away, Charles. I'm here to stay," she smiled then held down, and they kissed. Charles rolled over on her with his arms as his strength, and their passion soared.

"I love you, Counselor," he whispered in her ear.

"And, I love you," she said back as she rolled over on him. To her surprise she discovered that he was *very* capable of making love to her. She tried to help him but found that he needed *no* help at all. Their blissful reunion was filled with passion, but above all, *love.* When it was over, she collapsed on his body as he made small, tender circles on her back with his fingers. Soon she found the strength to hold up, and they smiled at each other as their lips joined in unison, then she proceeded to roll off him, but he stopped her.

"Not yet" he whispered. "I want to feel your warm, soft body next to mine." And she held back down to receive his tender loving care.

****

"Hello, Wanda," Papa Roma spoke as the child sat in his office with Tim and Moe present.

"Hi, Papa Roma," she squeezed out of frightened, trembling lips. These people really scared her.

"You and Angela are doing such a wonderful job for us."

"Thank you."

"Well, child, I want you to do something else for me," he announced, and she raised an eyebrow. "That D. A. we've been trying to eliminate. I hear your father knows his girlfriend. In fact, we hear that she's your father's lawyer. Is it true what we hear?"

"Yes, Papa Roma, but I didn't say anything. I..." she blurted out.

"I know. I know," he said talking quickly to regain control of the conversation. "You have been doing a fine job."

"I don't understand why I'm here."

"We want you to ask your family to have a little dinner party and invite Charles Lewis and his girlfriend."

"You do?"

"Wanda, we don't mean to scare you, " Tim spoke up. "Just calm down and listen." She nodded slowly. "What Papa is saying is that he wants you to have Mr. Lewis and Miss Burns over to your house for a little social gathering. You can do that, can't you, Wanda?"

"Why?"

"We have a job for you to do," added Tim.

"We want Angela there, too," Papa Roma spoke. "She can help you with the D. A."

"Help me?" Wanda asked. "Help me to do what with Mr. Lewis?"

Papa Roma looked at the other two men connivingly, and then he looked back at Wanda and announced, "I want you to *kill* the son-of-a-bitch!"

****

Ray walked in a small, dilapidated room, pulled off his disguise, sat under a fluorescent lamp, and read from the bill that Cecily had handed to him, *Ray, 9:00 p.m. Desert Mountain. East side. Friday. The big showdown. This is it, Country Boy. Don't leave me hanging.* He folded the bill, placed it in his pocket, and then grabbed his cell phone.

****

"Get the phone, Baby," Bill said to his wife, as the ringing telephone awaken them from a sound sleep. She picked it up quickly then handed it to him.

"You know it's for you *this* time of night."

He grabbed the phone then snapped, "Hello?"

"Bill. Ray."

"Ray!" Bill exploded sitting up in bed. "Man, what's going on there. I've been waiting to hear from you."

"Bill, this is it," Ray said. "We are about to land a big fish, and I don't want any mistakes. How soon can you get here?"

"I'm already there, Man."

"Listen carefully. This is what I want you to do."

****

Cecily walked in Papa Roma's office, and Tim met her at the door with a kiss. "Hi, Baby," he said.

"Hi," she said focusing on Wanda sitting in a chair, twisting her hands nervously.

"Sissy, it's always nice to see you," Papa Roma said as they touched cheeks.

"Thank you, Papa. My pleasure," Cecily smiled. Then indicating Wanda, she added, "What's up?" Wanda looked so strange to Cecily; she wondered what in the hell had these bastards done to the frightened child.

"Sissy, Wanda's going to do the hit on Lewis," Papa Roma announced.

Swallowing hard, Cecily blurted out, "What?! She's a *kid*!"

"Yeah," Papa Roma smiled. "Ain't it great. They can't do *nothing* to a kid!" Suddenly the door flew open, and two men threw Angela and Marc in the office.

"Here he is, Boss," one man announced.

"What's going on, Papa Roma?" Marc wanted to know.

"Marc, I treated you like my son."

"Yes, Sir," the nervous boy replied.

"How could you betray me?"

"I never..."

"Don't bother denying it, Marc. We have proof." Papa Roma barked.

"I was going to pay you back every cent, Papa Roma. I swear," Marc begged as sweat exploded from his forehead.

"I'm very disappointed in you, Marc," Papa Roma said then nodded to the man standing at the door. All of a sudden the man whipped out a gun, and although the girls didn't hear much of a sound, they witnessed Marc's limp body falling to the floor with a blood gushing hole in the back of his head, while Angela and Wanda screamed in agonizing horror.

****

"Hi, Sport. How about a game of basketball," Isaac asked, poking his head in Carl's door.

"Who am I playing? You and who *else*?" Carl joked getting up.

"Oh, it's like *that*, huh?" Isaac laughed. "I guess I gotta teach you a thing or two about basketball."

"Hey, I don't see Michael Jordan on your team," Carl laughed also, as he threw Isaac the ball on their way out, almost hitting Trudy.

"Hey," she exploded.

"Sorry, Mom," Carl said. "I gotta teach this old man how to give the kid some respect."

"We'll see about that," Isaac continued to laugh, throwing the ball back to Carl. As they walked out the door, Trudy smiled, for it did her heart good to see them getting alone, finally.

****

Lillian walked slowly into the back of the church. It had been a long time since she was last here, and it felt strange to her, but so *good*. Pastor Graham and his wife have been so good to her through her ordeal. Pastor Graham walked out his office and froze when he saw her. Then he smiled, and she ran into his arms. "Thank-you," she whispered in his ear as he cradled her close in his arms. "Thank you."

****

Wanda was still trembling when she walked in her bedroom. She could still see the image of Marc's bloody body lying on the floor, and Papa Roma saying, "Take out the garbage," as if Marc's life was meaningless. She hated that man. She hated him so much she could die. Then she thought of how he handed her a small vial and said, "This is lethal poison. It can't be traced. Just slip it in Lewis's coffee, and *that* will be the end of that bothersome D. A." As tears flowed down her face, she thought of how much she hated that fat man! Wanda walked slowly into her adjoining bathroom and poured a glass of water from the sink. Then she walked back into the bedroom and opened the vial that Papa Roma had given to her. Her hands were shaking so violently, she could barely open it, but she knew she could no longer live like this.   Aunt Cecily would explain it to her parents, and maybe they will forgive her. Just as she aimed the liquid in the vial towards the water, her cell phone began to ring, halting her actions. She stared at the cell phone for a while before picking it up.

With trembling lips, her shaky voice squeezed out, "Hello?"

"Wanda," Cecily said on the other end. At the sound of her Cecily's voice, Wanda broke into hysterics.

"Aunt Cecily, I'm so scared," she wept uncontrollably.

"Shhhhh, Darling," Cecily tried to comfort her. "Wanda, listen to me, Honey. This nightmare will *all* be over soon. I promise you."

"They killed Marc, Aunt Cecily. They just shot him in cold blood."

"I know, Sweetheart," Cecily consoled. "But, Wanda, you have to trust me. This mess will *all* be over *very* soon. Hang in there, Sweetie. Promise me, Wanda. Promise me you'll hang in there."

"I promise," she finally squeezed out.

"I love you, Baby. Try to get some sleep," Cecily added. "Bye." She hung up her cell phone, standing outside in front of her building. Moe stepped from behind the shadows and watched her as she ran inside. He couldn't help but to wonder *whom* she was talking to, and *why* was she using her cell phone *outside*. Maybe he'd better do another check on Miss Sissy Allen. A more *extensive* check.

****

Cecily took off her coat and slid in the bed beside Tim. He turned around, yawned and said, "You're just coming to bed, Baby?"

"Yes," she said, thinking of the pitiful little girls. "Tim, I have something to tell you."

"What is it, Baby," he asked sitting up in bed.

"I wasn't going to tell you this, but I slipped downstairs and called Wanda and Angela," she confessed. "I just can't keep anything from you. Forgive me?"

"Honey, I don't understand. Why didn't you want to tell me?"

"I thought you would think it was silly for me to worry about the girls, and you'd say I'm treating them like babies. The fact of the matter is that those girls have never seen anyone killed before, especially a *friend*. I knew they would be upset, and they were."

"You see; that's why I love you so. You're so caring," he smiled then planted a kiss on her lips. "Were you able to calm them down?"

"I think so."

"I told Papa it was a mistake to ask that girl to do the hit. Both of them are still too new at this."

"You can't talk him out of it."

"No. His mind is made up."

"What if they can't go through with it?"

"It doesn't matter."

"Why?"

"Didn't I tell you? We just want all of them together. Once that happens, we're going to blow up the house anyway."

"*What*?!" Cecily exploded as her breath seem to leave her body. "You going to *blow* up the house?!"

"Yes. It's no big deal. We've done it before," he chuckled. Cecily panted for air as she thought of Wanda, Angela, and all her friends in that house. He mistook her breathlessness as desire and pulled her on top of his lean, smooth, body. For the first time since Cecily had been involved with the mob, she felt really frightened. She knew she had to get to Wanda and tell her, no matter what, not to schedule that dinner...but *how*? She was so heavily in thought; she did not feel him enter her. She knew they watched her every move. She had seen Moe outside just now. That's why she decided to tell Tim about the calls she made. She had to think of something. "I love you, Baby," he cooed. Cecily looked in his gentle face, and she couldn't comprehend how such an intelligent, handsome, charming man could be involved in something so cruel and vicious. She hated this man dearly. "Oh, Baby! Baby!" he chanted bringing his pleasure to a climatic end. Oh, how she *hated* this bastard. And, she would make sure he would pay. He would pay *dearly*. "That was great, Baby," He replied bringing her down on him and cuddling her close. "I love you," he said kissing her forehead. She *loathed* the bastard.

Chapter 34

Wanda stopped halfway down the stairway, focused on her trembling hands, and took a deep breath. She jerked her hands in the pockets of her blue jeans and stared into space as she saw an image of Marc's bloody body hitting the floor. She covered her mouth as her lips trembled. "Wanda, come on!" Lillian called from downstairs, causing the child to sober. She proceeded down the stairs slowly and entered the breakfast nook where her parents sat.

"Good morning," Wanda squeezed out of trembling lips.

"Good morning," replied Alton, putting the newspaper down and focusing on his daughter. "Are you all right, Kitten?"

"I feel sick, Daddy," she said weakly as a tear trickled down her cheek. Lillian jumped up and felt Wanda's forehead.

"You don't have a fever," she said. "But maybe you've better miss school today, and I'll call the doctor."

"Don't cry, Sweetie," Alton said. "You'll feel better."

"Do you want to go back to bed, Sweetheart?" Lillian asked, and Wanda nodded. "You're excused."

"Thank you," Wanda said getting up quickly and walking out.

"I wonder what's going on with her," Alton said.

"The principal called. Her grades are dropping."

"What?! When?!"

"He called yesterday."

"Maybe we've better get to the bottom of this. She and Angela have been staying out a lot lately," replied Alton. "I wish you'll spend more time with her, instead of that damn office."

"I have a life, too, Alton!" Lillian retaliated between clenched teeth. "I gave her fifteen years while you whored with your women in the streets! It's *your* time, now!" She stormed out before he could respond.

****

Cindy entered Angela's dark room and focused on the child lying in bed. "Angela?" she called, turning on the light. When Angela turned around her red, swollen eyes were soaked with tears from crying all night. "Honey, what's wrong?"

"I don't feel well, Mom. May I stay home from school today?"

"Honey, what is it?"

Sniffing, she said, "My stomach hurts."

"I'll call Dr. Michaels."

"I don't need a doctor. I think it was something I ate."

"I've better call in to work. I can't leave you here like this," Cindy said leaving. "I'll be right back, Sweetheart." When she left, Angela turned over. She could still see Marc's bloody body lying on the floor, and she cried hysterically. She really loved him. She could see his smiling face, his perfectly straight teeth, and his beautiful soft hair. She will miss him so much. Those bastards killed him. She hoped Cecily was right when she told her it would all be over soon, and those bastards would pay. She could hardly wait.

****

"She's no spy!" Tim shouted to his father and Moe.

"Boy, you better think with your brains instead of your balls," Moe snapped. "I saw her outside on her cell phone when you were inside."

Chuckling, Tim said, "Because she wanted to check on Wanda and Angela and was afraid that I wouldn't understand." He paused. "But she told me anyway because she can't keep anything from me." He looked at Papa Roma. "Papa, I'm sorry, but I agree with Sissy. I don't think you should let kids do a so-called hit. They might freak."

"Some of our *best* hits have been with kids," Papa Roma insisted.

"But these girls are *too* new to the business," Tim responded.

"That's another story," Papa Roma said looking at Moe. "Tell him the rest."

"I did some checking on your girlfriend," Moe continued.

"Checking?" Tim's breath ran out. "What in the hell are you talking about? We've already checked her out!"

"We saw what the Feds *wanted* us to see," added Papa Roma.

"She's not a Federal agent," Tim insisted.

"No, she isn't," Moe said. "She's a *doctor*. Dr. Cecily Allen Wade."

****

"Honey, are you picking up Angela today?" Trudy asked over breakfast.

"No. Cindy said Angela isn't feeling well. I'll wait until the weekend." Isaac said. "Hey, have you heard anything from Cecily?"

"No. Why?"

"I was going to get her to look at Angela, but no one seems to know where she is."

"You seem worried."

"No. Just concerned. It's rather strange for Cecily to disappear without a trace."

"Cecily is *full* of surprises. You know that."

"Yes. I guess so," he chuckled.

"Maybe she's gone back to Hawaii. She said she wasn't here to stay."

"She did?"

"Yes. That's what she told Lillian. And, anyway, Cecily is *one* woman that can take care of herself," she said, then looked at Carl, who was moving his food from side to side but not eating. "What's wrong, Honey?"

"May I be excused, please?"

"You haven't finished your breakfast," she observed.

"I'm not hungry."

"Not *hungry*?!" Trudy exploded in laugher. "You *gots* to be sick!" She laughed, but Carl didn't find it amusing.

"May I be excused?" he asked again.

"Sure, Honey," Trudy said, and he jumped up and started out. "Get your books ready for school."

"What wrong with him?" Isaac asked.

"Some of the kids at school teased him for having a *white* daddy."

"Kids!"

"Yes. They don't know it hurts him. They're just playing."

"Want to let's take him to a movie tonight then out to eat."

"Oh, that's great, Honey," Trudy smiled. "Hey, I was thinking, let's have a dinner party this weekend. We haven't done that in a long time, and I think we *all* need to relax and to get to know each other."

"That's a good idea, Baby."

"Just a few people. Lillian and her family, Angela, Tandra, and Charles," Trudy said. "And, Cecily, too, if anyone can find her." Then she sarcastically added, "Since you're so *interested* in her where-a-bouts."

"Oh, where did *he* come from?" Isaac laughed.

"Who?"

"That old green-eyed monster? Now you just put him right back where you found him. I'm just concern about Cecily because she's a human being. Nothing more and nothing less."

Laughing, Trudy said, "I'm just kidding you, Baby." He reached over the table and kissed her lips.

"Honey, do you think it's a good idea to put Alton and Charles Lewis in the same room? The man *did* try to send Alton to jail."

"He was only doing his job," Trudy said. "I'm sure Alton understands that. You'll see. It'll be a *blast*!"

****

"What in the hell are you talking about, Moe?!" Tim demanded.

"I did some checking on your lady friend," Moe continued. "She *did* work for Spencer at one time, but it's common knowledge that she and Spencer hated each other. He wouldn't have told her *nothing* about the business. Anyway, she skipped out on Spencer to become a doctor. A very *good* one. In a small place near L.A. called Poka. It wasn't hard to find out about her when I had a picture, because apparently, she's known all over the world. Recently, she lived in Hawaii with a sister and practiced there. The only reason she came back is to testify in a trial. She got three close friends. They've been friends since childhood. The three of them were there when Spencer got iced. *One* of them killed him. Spencer left everything he had to the other one. She's a hotshot fashion model named Trudy Miles-Wade." He caught Tim's attention. "No relation to the doctor. She married the doctor's ex. The doctor went back to her maiden name after the divorce. That's why she's an Allen now. Get this, our little Angela is this Wade guy's daughter, and he and the doctor are still good friends. We checked her messages, and he left a couple."

"I can't believe this," Tim said.

"It gets better," Papa Roma said then nodded to Moe.

"The other friend's name is Lillian Carter," Moe paused. "Wanda's mother. Cecily is Wanda's *Godmother*."

"*What*?!" Tim exploded.

"Wanda calls her *Aunt* Cecily," Moe continued. "The trial she testified in was Wanda's old man's murder trial."

"We believe," Papa Roma continued, "that Dr. Allen is working with the Feds." Tim dropped in a chair and buried his head in his hands.

"What's makes you think she's working with the Feds? They're not accustomed to using civilians."

"That much we're guessing on," Moe spoke. "Only the Feds could've covered for her when we checked her out the first time."

"And, this is a smart woman," Papa Roma added. "I don't think she'd be foolish enough to tangle with us solo. She *has* to have back up. And, remember, this *is* personal. These people are her friends. We believe the doctor is the only person the girls confided in. We haven't found out who in the Federal office is helping her. We have a man watching the situation."

Closing his eyes tight, Tim squeezed out, "I love her."

"I know, Son," Papa Roma said sadly. Then he placed his hand on his son's shoulder and said in a weak voice, "It's all right, Son. We'll get the cunt! We're going to make her wish she never heard of the name *Romalotti*!"

****

"Want to talk?" Trudy stood at the door of her son's room. He turned over on his back and wiped his tears. Trudy sat on his bed. "I wish I could wipe your pain away, Sweetheart, but I can't."

"The kids say my daddy was a hood."

Sighing deeply, Trudy said, "Carl, your father was *many* things." Carl sat up in bed, as Isaac entered at the door. "He was strong. He was smart. He was loving. A lot of people didn't understand him, because he was so complex." She paused to wipe a tear from her own face. "Your father wasn't a nice man at times and *that* caused his death."

"I heard that Aunt Lillian killed him."

"It was an accident, but yes, that's true. Regardless of what your father was, he was *still* your father, and you must cherish his memory."

"What *memories*, Mom? I don't have *any*. I didn't *know* him."

Picking up Spencer's picture from Carl's nightstand, Trudy insisted, "Yes, you do. You have the many long hours I sat up with you, telling you stories about your father. You have very good memories!" She paused. "And, don't you let *anyone* take them away from you!"

"Carl," Isaac said, walking to the bed also. "I may not be the same color as you and your mom, but I love you and your Mom very, very much. I would be more than happy to be your dad, if you'll let me, Son. And, if anyone picks on you, you just ask them, if their daddy is as good to them as I am to you, and I bet they'll say no. You see, Carl, people come in all different colors, sizes, and shapes. We must learn to live with *everyone*. And, if we can't, mankind is doomed. We have a good time together. Don't let *anyone* make you feel ashamed of that." He extended his hand to the boy, and Carl took it. Then Isaac grabbed him up, and they embraced lovingly. Tears flowed down Trudy's face as the telephone began to ring.

Picking up the receiver in Carl's room, Trudy sniffed and said, "Hello?"

"Trudy?" Lillian said on the other end.

"Hi, Lil," Trudy replied. "Hold on a minute."

"Let's go to school. Okay?" Isaac suggested to Carl, and he jumped up, kissed his mother and ran out.

"Thank you, Baby," Trudy told her husband, and they kissed softly.

"See you later," he said then left.

"I'm back, Lil. What's up?"

"I hadn't heard from you in a while. I was wondering how you were."

"I'm great, Lil. Just great," Trudy beamed. "Oh, by the way, I was going to call you. I'm planning a small dinner party Friday night. Can you come?"

"I'll check with Alton, but I'm sure it's all right. Wanda's a little under the weather, though."

"What's wrong?"

"I don't know. She probably just ate something. She's been acting so strange lately. I can't put my finger on it."

"Teenagers go through different stages."

"I guess so," Lillian said, as Lyle entered the office. "I'll see you Friday, Tru."

"Okay," she said, and they hung up.

Lillian walked around the desk and into Lyle's arms, and they ended in a long passionate kiss. "Ummm, I've been wanting to do *that* all day," he cooed. "Who is the new girl?"

"She's a temp," she said, closing the door as the new secretary looked on. Then the secretary picked up the telephone receiver and dialed.

"Good morning," she said into the phone. "May I speak to Alton Carter, please?"

****

"Hi, Honey," Cecily greeted Tim at the door with a big kiss.

"Hi," he said looking in her eyes.

"What's wrong?" she asked looking in his stern eyes and sensing trouble.

"What could be wrong?" he attempted a smile, walking away.

"Is the meeting all set up?" she asked, sitting on the chair next to him.

"Yes," he said. "Is there any coffee, Baby?"

"Yes," she answered getting up. "I'll get you some." Cecily went into the kitchen and leaned against the counter. She knew something was going *very* wrong. She couldn't put her finger on it. Could he know about her? No, he *couldn't*! She and Ray had planned everything so well. She must find out if he knew something. She proceeded to fix the coffee.

Tim sat on the chair, deep in thought. He couldn't believe that this beautiful woman could have enough brains to outsmart *him*. But, then, she *is* a doctor. She had to have some intelligence. How dare she *use* him like that! How dare her! He took out a vial; like the one that Papa Roma had given to Wanda with the poison in it. He would make her *pay*. He would make the lying bitch *pay* for using him!

****

Tandra opened the door and called out to Detective Hinson and Sergeant Bundy, who were sitting outside the door of the apartment," Would you like some coffee?"

"That's very kind of you, Miss Burns. Thank you," replied Luke as they entered the apartment. They sat at the table, and she put the coffee pot and some cups on the table for them, as the telephone rang.

"Hello," Tandra said into the receiver, while the men helped themselves. "Oh, Hi, Trudy." She paused. "That's very nice of you to invite us. Friday night at seven. I'll check with Charles, but I'm sure we can make it." She paused again. Luke's ears were wide open as Tandra picked up a pad and pencil. "1819 Harmon Meadow Terrace. Got it." She paused. "The doctor is with him now." Pause. "Okay. Thanks again. Bye." She looked at the men and said, "Make yourselves at home. I'll be right back." They nodded then stood up briefly as she left.

Luke sketched the address, day and time in his memory, until he could write it down. He smiled connivingly as he thought to himself, *This is it.*

****

Cecily was rushed to the hospital on a gurney while Tim walked alongside her as she complained of stomach pains. When they took her in a room, Tim had to leave while they worked on her. He searched Cecily's cell phone and found the telephone number for Carter residence and dialed.

"Carter residence," the maid said on the other end.

"May I speak to Mrs. Carter please," he said.

"I'm sorry, but Mrs. Carter is at the office."

"Do you have the number there?"

"What is this in reference to, please?"

"Her friend, Dr. Cecily Allen."

"The number is 555-3123."

"Thank you very much," he said, then hung up and dialed again.

****

Lillian and Lyle were lying on the couch in her office, kissing very passionately as he unbuttoned her blouse when the secretary buzzed. "You make me so bad," Lillian cooed.

"Yes, but you're *my* bad girl," he said then helped her up. She went to answer the buzz.

"Yes, Lois."

"Mrs. Carter, there's a gentleman on line one. He wouldn't give his name, but he says it's about Dr. Cecily Allen."

"Cecily?!" she exploded.

"I'll see you later," Lyle said exiting.

Nodding to Lyle, she asked the secretary, "What line, Lois?"

"Two."

"Thank you," she said sitting at her desk, then pushed the button. "Hello. Lillian Carter."

"Mrs. Carter, you don't know me. I'm a friend of Cecily's. I just thought you'd like to know that she's in the hospital," Tim said.

"*Hospital*?! Cecily?!"

"Yes. She was just brought in."

"What's wrong with her?"

"They don't know yet," he said. "She's in Brunson General." Before Lillian could ask any more questions, he hung up. Tim looked at the vial still in his pocket. In a way, he was relieved Cecily had gotten sick before he had had an opportunity to put it in her coffee.

****

"Hi, Ma'am," a man stood at Trudy's door smiling in a uniform. "I'm with Telco Security Company. You use our alarm system in your home. I'm checking all systems today because we've received complaints."

"I'm not having any problems."

"That's great, and we don't want you to start having problems. That's why I'm checking all the systems," he said handing her a card. "You may call the company and verify this service call, Ma'am."

"That won't be necessary," she said looking at the truck parked in front of her door with Telco Security Company on it. "Come in."

****

Tandra walked into the bedroom, and the doctor was putting his equipment up. "Finished?" she asked.

"Yes. That's it for now," he said. "Charles, I discussed your case with a surgeon, and he told me some news I think you and Tandra need to hear."

"What is it, Jacques?" Tandra wanted to know.

"He said he thinks he can help Charles."

"What?!" Tandra exploded.

"You mean help me to *walk* again?" Charles asked.

"He looked at your x-rays, and he thinks he might be able to repair the damage. He said he's had lots of successes with this kind of procedure."

"That's great!" exploded Tandra.

"But, of course, there are risks," the doctor continued.

"What kind of risks?" Charles asked.

The doctor took a deep breath, then announced, "You could *die*."

****

"Hello, do you have a Cecily Allen there?" Lillian asked in the telephone receiver.

"Hold on, please," the lady said. "No Ma'am. We don't."

"You don't?!" Lillian asked, and then another thought came to her. "What about Sissy Allen?"

"Yes, we do. Hold on, please."

"Hello?" Cecily weakly said into the receiver.

"Cecily?"

"Lillian?" Cecily exploded. "How did you know I was here?"

"A man called me," Lillian said. "Are you all right? And where have you been all these months? I thought you went back to Hawaii!"

"Lillian, I'll explain everything later."

"What's wrong with you?"

"My appendix ruptured. I had to have an emergency appendectomy," Cecily replied hearing the door open. "Gotta go, Lil. Please, don't tell anyone where I am. I promise, I'll explain everything later." The telephone went dead to Lillian's ears.

"Cecily!" she called. "An *appendectomy*?!" She replaced the receiver in its cradle and stared into space. "Appendectomy?" She squeezed out again. "You've already had an appendectomy, Cecily. What is going on with you?! And *why* can't you tell me?"

****

"How'd you feel?" Tim asked Cecily entering her room.

"Not too good," she replied, receiving a kiss from him.

"Who were you talking to?"

"What?"

"Weren't you just putting the telephone down?"

"Oh, that was the wrong number!"

"The doctor said you can go home tomorrow."

"Great!" she said smiling as the doctor entered.

"Hello, Miss Allen," he said.

"Hi, Doctor. I hear I can go home tomorrow."

"You sure can," he smiled. "Normally, we wouldn't have kept you *this* long, but we wanted to make sure the baby was all right."

"*Baby*!" Cecily and Tim both exploded simultaneously.

"I thought you knew," the doctor said.

"Are you sure?" Cecily was crushed. "I'm forty years old."

"And *pregnant*," added the doctor smiling. "About ten weeks."

****

Papa Roma opened his office door, and the man who entered Trudy's house from the Telco Security Company walked in. "Is it all set?" Papa Roma wanted to know.

"Boss, I planted enough explosives in that house to reach China."

Patting the man on the back, Papa Roma replied, "Good work! *Real* good work!"

Chapter 35

"It's good to be home," Cecily said entering the penthouse apartment, followed by Tim, carrying her bags.

"It's good to have you back."

"What do you think about the baby?'

"I think it's great. I've always wanted kids."

"Why didn't you and Beverly ever have any?"

"Right after we were married, Beverly found out about the business, and she fell down a flight of stairs," he explained. "It ruined her for life."

"That's horrible."

"It wasn't a mistake," he said again. "She did it on purpose."

"Why?"

"Because she was pregnant. She didn't want to bring her baby into the family business," he said then looked in her eyes. "How do you feel about it?"

"I don't know. I just know I couldn't *kill* my baby for *any* reason."

"God, you're beautiful," he squeezed out, then proceeded to gently pull her closed to him, squeezing her so tight, she thought she would die. Then it occurred to her that that's exactly why he did it, because she *was* going to die. He must've been the man who called Lil. Somehow, they had found out about her. She must warn Wanda and Angela, for she didn't know how much these bastards knew.

****

Wanda stared at the vial for a long time as the telephone rang. She jerked it up at the same time as her father. "Hello?" she said. Alton was about to hang up until he recognized Cecily's voice.

"Wanda, I don't have much time," she whispered. "Don't schedule that dinner party. It's a trap. They will blow up the house!"

"Aunt Cecily, we're having..." Wanda started, but the phone went dead to her ears. "*Aunt Cecily*!!" she screamed, as Alton dropped the phone and dashed to Wanda's room.

****

"So, it is true," Tim said standing behind Cecily, and she swirled around, dropping the telephone. "I was hoping they were wrong about you, Sissy, or should I say, Dr. Allen?!"

"Tim," Cecily said standing up from the bed and walking to him. "They are *children*. I don't care what happens to me, but Wanda and Angela are *babies*. Please, don't harm them."

"I love you so much, and you made a fool of me."

"No, I didn't. I do love you, Tim. More than words could say," she said as tears burned her eyes.

"You will pay for betraying me, Dr. Allen," he announced, holding his hand up slowly with a gun extended at the end.

****

Alton exploded into Wanda's room, and she was lying unconscious on the floor. He picked up the empty vial near her hand. "Oh, God, no!" he exploded as Lillian tore into the room. "Call the ambulance!" he demanded, cradling Wanda in his arms.

"What's going on?" Lillian asked.

"Call the fucking ambulance!!"

Chapter 36

"Why are we stopping here?" Cecily asked Tim, as he pulled up on a hill, in his black Jaguar, with a view of Isaac and Trudy's estate.

"A friend of *yours*, Dr. Allen?" he sarcastically asked.

"Why are we here?"

"Shut up, Bitch!" he yelled as she noticed Tandra and Charles at the gate and going in.

"What is going on?"

"You're a smart lady. Haven't you figured it out yet?" he smiled. "The party is hosted by the *present* Mrs. Wade instead of Mrs. Carter."

"What?" her breath ran out. "You're going to blow up Trudy's house?" He didn't answer, but his smile told her all she wanted to know. "Oh, my God. No, Tim, please!" she begged. "Please stop this insanity! Please God! Please!"

Looking at his watch, Tim counted, "Five, four, three, two, one." As he said blastoff, they witness a sight that Cecily knew she would remember for the rest of her life. She covered her ears as she dropped to the ground, crying hysterically as her friend's house blew up in flames, with all of them trapped inside.

****

"Is everybody all right?" Ray asked as he, Alton, Bill, and Isaac helped the others out of the huge swimming pool as they dripped of water also. "I'm sorry we couldn't save your house, Mrs. Wade, but we didn't have time to find all the explosives." Trudy nodded, hugging Carl tight. Ray then turned to his walkie-talkie. "Yeah. Go ahead."

"A car is headed east on Canyon Run. It just left where you are," the voice said in the walkie-talkie.

"Right!" Ray said then looked at Bill. "Let's go!"

****

"Where are we going?" Cecily asked Tim, still in tears.

"You don't think we're holding our little meeting in the *same* place, do you?"

"Oh, my God," she breathed, remembering the note she had given to Ray, telling him where the meeting place would be. She knew she was a dead woman. It was just a matter of time.

****

"Are you all right, Darling?" Alton asked Lillian.

"Yes," she said as Trudy walked to them.

"We owe you so much, Alton," Trudy said. "If you hadn't overheard Wanda talking to Cecily, and then questioned Angela, we..."

"Don't even *think* about it," Alton said. "We're all safe now."

"I can't believe those bastards would kill all of you just to get me," Charles raged. "They *will* pay!"

"Alton, I want to go to the hospital to see Wanda," Lillian said.

"We will, Baby. Let's go home and change first."

"Has anyone seen Angela?" Isaac asked.

"She was here before the explosion," answered Carl.

"Where can she be?" Trudy added.

"And, where is Sergeant Bundy?" added Detective Hinson, coming from around the other side of the house with other police officers.

****

"Here she is, Boss," Sergeant Bundy said shoving Angela hard towards Papa Roma, in a big, dark, open field, as a number of people stood around with guns, waiting for the shipment and their guests.

"Yes, our little insurance," Papa Roma smiled. "What happened at the house?"

"I grabbed her before it blew and took off."

"Good," Papa Roma said as a car approached. "Here comes Timmy."

Tim stopped the car, grabbed Cecily out, and pushed her towards his father. She and Angela ran in each other's arms. "Where is Wanda?" Cecily whispered to her.

"She's in the hospital. She took the poison," Angela cried.

"Oh, my God. Is she all right?"

"I don't know," she replied still crying hysterically. "They all blew up, Aunt Cecily! They all blew up!" Cecily pulled the girl in her arms. "I'm so scared."

"Shhh," Cecily tried to comfort the weeping girl. Suddenly her attention fell on Tim, and she spat, "You said you loved me! Please, if you do, let her go! You have *me*, and... our *baby*."

"*Baby*?!" Papa Roma exploded, locking eyes with his son. "Is this true?" Tim nodded slowly. "What're you going to do, Son?" Just then three helicopter choppers flew overhead, and two men jumped off each of the choppers with guns. Then neatly wrapped and tied bails came rolling off the choppers, and Papa Roma's crew gathered them up and threw them on huge trucks. "Our shipment!" Papa Roma announced, running towards the excitement, followed by Tim, as Sergeant Bundy held Cecily and Angela at gunpoint. Cecily looked across the wide, opened field, and in the dark moonlit area, she thought she spotted someone standing there over the hills, and she knew it *had* to be Ray. And, if she was wrong, it didn't matter. She and Angela would die anyway.

Cecily bent down to Angela and whispered, "When I tell you to run, you head straight for those hills as fast as you can. No matter what, don't you stop and don't look back!"

"What about *you*?"

"I'm fine," she said placing the child behind her.

Once the choppers had landed, another circle of choppers suddenly appeared overhead, with a message, "This is the police. You are all under arrest. Put your weapons down! You are completely surrounded!" Suddenly it was like World War III as weapons blasted in the dark air. Cecily shoved Angela and attacked Sergeant Bundy.

"Run, Angela, Run!" Cecily shouted, and the child took off like a flash. Ray ran to Angela and pulled her to safety, as Sergeant Bundy's gun went off. Tim focused on Cecily's body dropping to the ground.

"No!" he yelled, jumping up and running to her. When he reached her, he crippled over receiving a stinging bullet in his chest and fell to his death on top of Cecily's bloody body. Papa Roma and Moe headed for the chopper with two other men. They reached it, jumped in, and started up. Bullets attached the chopper so severely, it surrendered under the pressure, and came crashing down to the ground in a flaming mass. At witnessing the demise of their leader, Papa Roma's people began throwing down their weapons. The war had finally ended, and Angela ran as fast as she could to Cecily.

Angela dropped on the ground, and lifted Cecily's head in her lap. Cecily opened her eyes slowly. "Hang in there, Aunt Cecily. You'll be all right." Angela said wiping her tears.

"Is it over?" Cecily squeezed out as Ray and Bill approached.

"Yes. Thanks to you," answered Ray.

"Tim?" Cecily asked, and Ray looked to her feet, then she held up a little and saw his crumpled, bloody body at her feet.

"He was coming for *you*," Ray said.

"Thanks, Country Boy," Cecily said as she coughed and drew her last breath.

"*No!!!* Aunt Cecily, *No!!!*" Angela roared into hysterics, as Ray closed his eyes tight to hold back his own tears.

Ray focused on all the dead bodies that surrounded him, and thought, *What a waste. When will it all be over? When will the drug pushers stop and say enough? When in the hell will it ever end?* Bill came and stood at Ray's side as if he could read his friend's thoughts. They looked at the bloody mess together as the sound of ambulances raced towards the horrible scene, and they knew there would be a lot of unhappy families tonight. *God help them*!

Part Five

Fourteen Months Later

Christmas Eve

Chapter 37

A little five year old girl, with Shirley Temple blonde curls hanging on her shoulders, strolled down the aisle of the huge Cathedral-style church, in a white, lace, floor-length dress, dropping rose petals, as she approached the happy, smiling groom, his best man, the preacher, and the maid of honor. The little girl took her place beside the other people in the wedding party, standing, awaiting the bride. Then the music changed to symbolize the bride's arrival, and the congregation of people stood to welcome her. She strolled down the aisle, arm in arm with her tall handsome father, with a beautiful, trembling smile glued to her happy face, while she walked, with a long train on her gown trailing behind her, to her future, who was standing, awaiting his lovely bride, dressed in white lace, pearls, and sequins. When she finally reached the happy groom, they smiled especially to each other, as he whispered softly, "You look beautiful."

The preacher began the ceremony. "Charles, will you take this woman as your lawfully wedded wife?"

"I will," the handsome Charles stood happy and proud.

"Tandra, will you take this man as your lawfully wedded husband?"

"I will," Tandra answered strong and happy. As the preacher continued with the ceremony, Lillian and Lyle sat hand in hand, with Lyle admiring their own wedding rings. She and Lyle smiled at each other, remembering their own private ceremony. Lillian felt a little sad that Wanda wasn't there, but she knew she would see Wanda later. Trudy smiled big at her son, standing in the wedding party, watching his sister marry the man of her dreams. Isaac took Trudy's hand, for he felt her pride at seeing her handsome son so poised. Alton sat alone, watching his ex-wife in the company of another man, trying to be happy for the wedded couple, while he felt so unhappy, because the woman he loved was now gone, and it's ironic she died trying to help *his* daughter. "What God has joined together, let no man put asunder," the preacher continued. Then Lillian stood and sang the *Our Father's Prayer*. There were few dry eyes in the church as Lillian sang from her heart and for the happy couple, but especially for the Lord. When she finished, Tandra and Charles smiled very sweetly at her as Charles wiped his bride's tears from her face, then Lillian took her seat again beside her new husband. The Preacher announced, "By the powers vested in me by God and the state of California, I now pronounce that Charles and Tandra are husband and wife. Charles, you may kiss your bride." When Charles took a hold of his new wife, it was as if he was kissing her for the very first time. As she received this kiss from the man that she loved unconditionally, it was as if time had frozen, and they were the only two people that existed in this world. They marched out with gaiety as the audience shared in their happiness. Before leaving out the door, Tandra presented Charles' mother with a single red rose, and he did likewise for her mother.

****

Lillian and Lyle walked into a dark room of a hospital with wrapped gifts in their hands. Lillian walked to the windows and pulled the curtain open to let the sunshine in. Then she walked to the bed where Wanda lay on her back, staring into space. Lillian sat in a chair beside the bed. "Hi, Darling," she said rubbing the child's hair. "Lyle's here with me. Mommy brought you some Christmas gifts." Wanda lay motionless and unresponsive, but Lillian proceeded to open the gifts and showing them to the comatose child anyway.

"Did the doctor say if she's making progress?" Lyle asked.

"It's hard to tell, but I *know* she is," Lillian said. "She'll pull out of this one day. They can't see any brain damage, so it's all psychological. When I think about what she went through, my heart goes out to my baby."

****

Alton opened the door of his apartment. Just as he was about to go in, a voice behind him asked, "Are you Alton Carter?"

He turned around and looked in a man's face and said, "Yes, I am."

"I have a special delivery for you, Sir."

"All right."

"Sign here please," the man said, indicating where. Alton signed, and the man handed him an envelope. Alton gave the man a bill. "Thank you, Sir." Then the man left.

Alton closed the door and walked to the sofa. He kicked off his shoes and dropped on the sofa. He dropped his head back and closed his eyes. He could see Cecily's smiling face. He still couldn't believe she was gone. He remembered the good times they once shared. Then he could see them lowering her body in the ground. All her friends were there, including her sister from Hawaii and her friend, Craig Brooks. He couldn't help but to wonder if Cecily had had an affair with this young man. It made him jealous at the thought. After all, why would a man come all the way from Hawaii to her funeral if they hadn't had something together? Alton wiped a tear. Then Lillian cried as she sang a beautiful solo of "May the Work I've Done, Speak for Me". Then, as if he wasn't hurting enough, Lillian stood in front of him in their living room, right after the funeral and proudly an-announced that she didn't love him anymore and wanted a divorce, because she was in love with her boss, Lyle Desir. He agreed without hesitation because he wasn't sure if he loved her anymore either. Life goes on. He had to admit that Cecily meant a great deal to him. All she ever wanted was to be loved. He did actually *love* her, but it's too late now. He wished he had been better to her. She had loved him unconditionally, and he let her go. He really did miss her. All his philandering days with Cecily ended like this: *alone*. He now had no one. He took a deep breath then focused on the envelope. "What in the hell is this?!"

Chapter 38

"How is Wanda?" Trudy asked Lillian as they sat on Lillian's sun porch, drinking iced tea.

"The same," Lillian replied. "How is Angela?"

"Isaac has her in therapy, but with what those girls went through, it's going to take time." replied Trudy. "Have you seen Alton lately?"

"No, not since Tandra and Charles' wedding."

"Are you finally happy, Lil?"

"Yes, Trudy. Lyle makes me *very* happy. Now if Wanda would get better, my life would be perfect."

"I'm glad you and Lyle are married. You don't have to worry about his crazy ex-wife anymore," Trudy said. "I still can't believe she sent Alton notes to try to catch you and Lyle."

"Well, she did," Lillian said. "And, she also planted her cousin in the office as our secretary to report to Alton our every move, but Alton just ignored it all but that *one* time. She's in the hospital now."

"For what? A broken heart?" Trudy laughed.

Laughing also, Lillian said, "No, silly. An appendectomy." Lillian suddenly stopped and exhibit a faraway look in her eyes.

"What's wrong?"

"An appendectomy..." she trailed off.

"What is it?"

"Trudy, do you remember my telling you that Cecily was in the hospital just before she died?" Lillian asked, walking to the window.

"Yes, so what?"

"Think, Trudy. Don't you remember when we were in Old Lady Jones' class?"

"Yes. Seventh grade."

"Cecily was out of school a whole week."

"So?"

"She was in the hospital," Lillian paused. "An appendectomy."

"You must be mistaken. You only have *one* appendix!"

Swirling around and sitting near Trudy, Lillian insisted, "She isn't dead, Trudy. The little witch pulled it off."

"Pulled *what* off?" Trudy was confused.

"She finally got the man she has always loved... *Alton.*"

"Lillian, you're deranged. We saw them bury Cecily. Remember?"

"No, we didn't."

"Yes, we *did!*" insisted Trudy. "We stood right there."

"We didn't see them bury *Cecily*, Trudy."

"What're you talking about?"

"Think, Trudy. Don't you remember how different Cecily was when she came back from Hawaii? She didn't run after Alton anymore, and she wanted all of us to be friends again. I even commented at the restaurant about how she had changed." She paused. "They must've switched placed."

"Who? What're you talking about?" Trudy wanted to know. "If we didn't see them bury Cecily, then who *was* it?"

Lillian took a deep breath then replied, "*Nicole*! Cecily's twin sister."

Chapter 39

Alton strolled along a beach with two drinks in his hand. He reached his destination and handed a drink to another person. "Are you happy, Baby," he asked.

"Very," Cecily replied receiving a kiss from him. "I still can't stop thinking about all the things that happened to Wanda and Angela, and *especially* Nicole. What was she *thinking* to get involved like that? Maybe it wasn't a good idea for us to change places. She was only supposed to go back and help *you*. I knew I was your alibi when that man was killed, but you didn't want to lose Lillian. And, I knew I would've had to say we slept together, so Nicole knew she could say you and she didn't sleep together and tell the truth. But instead, she must've found out about Wanda and Angela and decided to stay."

He pulled her up swiftly and caught her in his arms. "It might be selfish, but I'm glad it wasn't you who died. It was the happiest moment in my life when I received that special delivery letter from your secretary telling me that you were alive." Alton explained then kissed her lips.

"I never told Barbara to do that, but I'm sure glad she did."

"I knew there was something different about you, but I just couldn't put my finger on it."

Laughing, Cecily said, "When Nicole called me, she was sure you were suspicious, but she was careful about not spending too much time with you."

"You are so beautiful," he said, and they entwined closely with a kiss, as a small person separated them. They both focused down on the child then burst into laughter.

"Altonia!" Cecily exploded, bending down to the little four-year-old girl, who resembled her dead daughter, Keisha. "What is it, young lady?"

Pushing her long curly hair out her face, the child exploded, "Mommy, it's time to go to the Hula Hoop Contest!"

Knelling down to the little girl with Cecily, Alton asked, "Are you going to hula hoop?"

"No, Daddy!" she exploded. "*Mommy* is!" She burst into laughter.

Straightening up the child's small bikini top, Cecily added, "Go ahead, Darling. Daddy and I are right behind you."

"Yeepee!" the little girl yelled, skipping ahead of them, singing to herself.

"Not so fast!" Cecily called to Altonia as she and Alton stood, watching their daughter.

"I wish I had known about her from the start," Alton said smiling.

"I just couldn't come between you and Lillian again. That night when you came to Hawaii, and we made love, I knew that very moment that I was pregnant. I was glad when Nicole agreed to testify for you at the trial. I don't think I could've let you go if I saw you one more time," Cecily explained. Their eyes locked as they held each other around the waists.

"That's all behind us now," Alton said then planted a kiss on her lips. "God has given me another chance with a family. I'm not blowing it *this* time. That's a promise."

"I love you, Alton Carter."

"And, I love you, Cecily Carter," he said, and they ended in a long kiss.

"Ummm, Cecily Carter," she said smiling. "I like the sound of that. I've waited so long to have it."

"And, now, it's yours forever," he said softly, and they kissed again then started their pace behind their daughter, hand in hand. As they walked along the beach, Cecily's mind drifted in the past:

*   *Cecily sat in a chair with tears running down her face as she held Nicole's picture in her hand. "Okay, God, here I am. I've been running from you a long time, and nothing seems to go right for me. I've always heard that if I put my trust in you, you can make everything all right. Well, I'm tired of suffering. I've paid my dues. Please, take over my life, as broken down as it may be, and clean me up, and lead me in the way that you want me to go. Here I am. No more fighting with you. No more anger. Please help me to be what you want me to be. I'm tired. I'm so tired." She paused. "I know I've done wrong by my friend Lillian. I know I have to pay for hurting her so deeply. I'm asking you to please forgive me. Please forgive me and give me a life back. Please give me the strength to go on with my life," she cried hard as Altonia walked slowly in the room.*

"Mommy, are you sad?" the little girl asked, and Cecily picked her up in her arms and hugged her tight. Then all of a sudden, a feeling came over her that she had never experienced before, and Cecily witnessed a bright light that only she could see, and she knew God had forgiven her. Then the

doorbell rang.

"I'm fine, Sweetheart. Just fine," Cecily smiled, wiping her tears as she got up.

When Cecily opened the door, her breath ran out as she focused on Alton standing there, looking as handsome as he'd ever looked before, holding his divorce papers in front of his body for her to see. Simultaneously, they ran in each other's arms, laughing and crying at the same time. "I love you," he finally said. "I love you. I love you."

"Oh, thank-you, God. Thank-you, God," she chanted over and over.   *

"A penny for your thoughts," Alton said bringing Cecily back to the present.

She stopped, looked in his beautiful, brown eyes, and said, "Alton, I don't want to make the same mistakes all over again. I used to think Lillian was crazy for saying God this and God that, but now I truly understand her convictions. God is truly the *light* of the world. Real happiness comes *only* from Him, and not from another human being. From now on, I'm putting God first in everything I do."

"Amen to that."

"Let's go to church tonight," she said, and he grabbed her in his arms, and they hugged tightly.

Chapter 40

Perspiration popped from his bronzed, shiny muscles as he huffed and puffed, while he extended large barbells above his head. He then placed them down and walked to a desk and picked up a picture, in which Papa Roma sat strong and confident, smiling big. His hand brushed across the picture lovingly. "I'm sorry, father. I'm sorry I turned my back on you. I was weak, father. Please, forgive me." A tear dropped on the picture. He walked to a mirror and placed the picture on the dresser. "I'll go back, Father, and make your organization stronger than you've ever imagined it could be. I'll make you so proud." He paused as another tear fell. "I swear on your grave, Papa, that your death will be avenged." He looked up in the mirror, and Craig Brooks, Cecily's Hawaiian friend, wiped more tears from his face, as an imaged of everyone standing around Nicole's grave came to his mind. He looked back at his father's picture. "I swear, Papa, if I do nothing else for the rest of my life, *everyone* who is responsible for your death..." he paused and took a deep breath as he pounded his fist on the dresser, "...will suffer the *consequences*!"

THE END

Thank you for reading my book.

Please read my other books:
Sister Lucy
Sister Lucy II (Kip & Lucy)
Single Mom

Soon to be released: *Toni Talk*

Lurma Swinney